WHO AM I.

Also by J. J. Zerr

<u>The Jon and Teresa Zachery stories</u>:

Book One: The Ensign Locker
Book Two: Sundown Town Duty Station
Book Three: The Junior Officer Bunkroom
Book Four: A Ticket To Hell – On Other Men's Sins

<u>Other novels</u>:

Noble Deeds
The Happy Life of Preston Katt
Guerilla Bride
The Ghosts of Chateau du Chasse

<u>Short story collection</u>:

War Stories

WHO AM I.

a novel by

J. J. Zerr

Primix Publishing
11620 Wilshire Blvd
Suite 900, West Wilshire Center, Los Angeles, CA, 90025
www.primixpublishing.com
Phone: 1 (888) 585-7476

This is a work of fiction. The great majority of character names and place names are products of the author's imagination. The isolated exceptions are historically significant personages and places.

Published by Primix Publishing   04/22/2021

ISBN: 978-1-953397-92-8(sc)
ISBN: 978-1-953397-93-5(hc)
ISBN: 978-1-953397-94-2(e)

Library of Congress Control Number: 2021902005

For parents and teachers.

Please, God, bless everybody
with enough of each.

God bless editors and my Coffee and
Critique bubbas and bubbettes.

<u>The Walsh family</u>

Patrick (Pop)
Loraine (Mama)
Eddie
Lennie
Bobby
Ronnie
Laura

Eddie's uncles and aunts, Walsh side	Eddie's uncles and aunts, Schneidermeier side
<ul><li>Sylvester</li><li>John</li><li>Patrick (Pop)</li><li>Sister Constance</li><li>Sister Deborah</li><li>Molly</li></ul>	<ul><li>James</li><li>Homer and Fred (the ignorant louts)</li><li>Lucille (Sister Noreen)</li><li>Father Maury</li><li>Beatrice (married John Walsh)</li><li>Ed</li><li>Loraine (mama)</li><li>Ruth</li></ul>

1

A

I don't remember a lot of things from when I was five, but I remember three things.

The first one, I, Eddie Walsh, was special. Mama may have told me, but I don't remember her saying so. Just after my fifth birthday, I realized that when I pulled some mischief—stealing cookies, leaving the gate to the chicken pen open, or trying to lasso Mrs. Hemsath's poodle—my four-year-old brother Lennie got blamed for it.

Like with the poodle. Mama had given Lennie and me some clothesline for playing cowboy. Dolly the poodle was old and lay in the sun, mostly. So, I didn't have any trouble sneaking up on her and throwing my loop. The loop didn't go over the dog's head though; it smacked her in the face. Dolly yipped and lit out.

Lassoing a laying-down poodle wasn't much of a game, but one hot-footing it around the corner and between our houses, now we were talking actual cowboy stuff. The only thing missing was a horse, but that didn't matter. Not like running after Dolly and twirling the loop above my head, and picturing the rope cinching tight around the white poodle's neck, and me jerking her off her feet. I'd be a real cowboy.

From behind me, I heard Mrs. Hemsath holler, "You little Walsh devil, let my poor dog alone!"

Which changed the game. Now it was an Injun' ambush. I dropped the rope, tore past the chicken pen, through the garden, and hid in the trees along the creek. Mrs. Hemsath didn't even chase me. She wasn't a real Injun, and she was almost as old as Dolly.

I hid till my stomach grumbled. Walking back to the chicken house, I peeked around. The coast was clear. After crossing the yard, I pulled open the back screen door, and the spring made that *scroing* sound. Mama looked up from placing sandwiches on plates on the table.

"Find your brother. Both of you wash your hands and leave your shoes outside. I just mopped the floor."

I turned away to do as told.

"Don't let the screen door—"

Slam!

Mama said, "Ach!" She said that whenever I let the door slam. If Lennie did it, she said a lot more. "How many times do I have to tell you?

Don't slam the door. But do you listen? You do not. The next time you slam, you get a spanking. You hear? A spanking so you won't sit down for a week. Maybe then you remember."

Pretty much everybody knew I was the good Walsh boy. I heard the ladies talking when they quilted in the living room. "At least you got one good boy, Lorraine." That was Mrs. Woodworth talking to Mama. "Me. I got Davey and Danny. What mischief one doesn't think of, the other does."

When Lennie got spanked for something I did, it seemed fair. He was the bad boy and must have thought it was fair, too. He never said, "I didn't do it." He never said, "That rotten Eddie did it, and I always get blamed."

It was easy for Lennie to get blamed. We both had blond hair and wore identical clothes. Mama sewed our outfits from one pattern, and she left room for us to grow into. Most times, I folded my pants legs once, and Lennie folded his twice. Mrs. Hemsath thought we looked enough alike to be twins. To tell us apart, you had to count the folds in the pants cuffs.

Fetch my brother, she told me. I stood two feet away from the screen door and hollered, "Lenneeeeeeeeeeeeeeeeee!"

Mama said, "Ach!" again.

Double-cuffs came around the outhouse holding the red tractor. Pop had put in a sandbox for us to play in with our truck, farm toys, and a yellow bulldozer.

"Lunch," I said.

Lennie threw the Farmall in the direction of the sandbox and ran toward the house. We washed up in the basin on the bench. I used soap. Our shoes we left by the backdoor and went inside. When Lennie crawled up onto his chair, about a bucketful of sand ran out of his cuffs and onto the floor.

Mama screeched, "Lenneeeeeeee!"

As Mama drew a breath, we heard a knock at the front door. She wagged a finger in Lennie's face, stomped out of the kitchen and down the hallway, and opened the door.

I heard Mrs. Hemsath say, "Dolly," followed by some mumbles. "Your boy," came through loud and clear. As did Mama's, "I'm so sorry. That boy will be, too."

The door closed. Mama returned. Lennie stood by his chair in his underpants, his strap trousers in a heap atop a pile of sand. Mama sat and pulled Lennie across her lap. The *smack* of her hand on his almost bare butt sounded like it hurt. I'd never been spanked. If I did, I was sure I'd cry.

Lennie didn't cry. He never did. When Mama sent him to his room, he never said, "Yes, ma'am," or anything else either. He just walked sock-footed and barelegged to our bedroom, entered it, and closed the door softly. If I went in there, I knew I'd find him paging through a book, looking at the pictures. But I had my baloney sandwich to finish.

That's the first thing I remember from when I was five. I was the good Walsh boy.

B

Another thing I remember from that age happened in early fall. Grade school started, but I had to wait another year. My birthday came in August and I was only five. Simon Grossman also turned five that August, but he got to go to school.

Mr. Grossman owned the funeral parlor, the furniture store, the bank, and St. Ambrose Farm Implements. Everybody knew Simon's dad paid to add the steeple to the church.

I asked Mama why Simon got to go to school and I didn't.

"The Grossmans are rich. Rich people get to do things the rest of us can't," Mama said.

"Are we poor?"

"Ach! We're not poor. Don't ever say that."

I was glad I wasn't Lennie asking that question. I glanced at him sitting on the wide, low to the floor windowsill by the coal oil stove.

He was flipping through a picture book with cardboard pages.

I said, "So, what are we then?"

"There's rich and there's poor, and we're in between."

"Oh," I said as Mama tied the laces on Lennie's clodhoppers. She bought shoes with room for feet to grow.

Lennie and I played together that morning. We had to play together. Our house was the only people-house on our end of town. Except for the Hemsaths next door, and they didn't have kids. Only a poodle. From our place you had to pass the Hemsaths, the funeral parlor house, the drugstore, which looked like a house, the general store, and the volunteer fire building on our side of Main before you got to a people house. On the other side of the street, after the bank and other Grossman businesses, there was Oscar's tavern, Elginfritz's garage, and the American Legion post. After that, it was all people-houses to the other end of town.

Boys my age lived in some of those big houses down there. Besides the Grossman boy, one of Elginfritz's sons was my age. I asked Mama why I couldn't go to the other end of town to play with them. "Is it because that's the rich end of town and they don't want to play with an in-between?"

Mama wrung soapy water from a pair of

Pop's bib overalls and dunked it in the rinse tub and wrung it as dry as she could with her lips bared and teeth clenched. Sometimes she didn't answer my questions. I was thinking up a new one to ask.

"It's not that. You see, the older Elginfritz boys ride their bikes all over town. They play with the Kline kids from Second Street. The Klines aren't rich."

"They're in-betweens, too?"

"Yes. The reason you can't play with the Grossman and the Elginfritz boys is you are too little to be wandering around the streets by yourself. When you grow some more, Pop will get you a bike. Then you can play anywhere in town you want to. *Verstehe?*"

That was German. Mama's family talked it sometimes.

Someone knocked on the screen door. Mama dried her hands on her apron.

A big man stood there holding a cap and a bundled-up red bandana—like the one Mama tied on her head when she dusted furniture and cleaned house. He wore bib overalls, like Pop's, except this man's pants had one knee ripped open. He was bigger than Pop.

"Missus, you got some work needs doing?"

"Can you dig potatoes without chopping them in half?"

"I can't promise I won't chop one, Missus, but I can dig spuds."

"Fine. There's a shovel and a bushel basket in the shed next to the outhouse. Eddie will show you where the potatoes are. When you fill the basket, bring it to the house. I've got fried chicken left over from last night."

"Thankee kindly, Missus."

The man talked funny. I'd heard people call Mama Missus Walsh, but never just Missus.

As he dug—he called them taters—I asked him his name.

"Ezekiel, but folks call me Zeke. You can call me that."

"Mr. Zeke, are you poor?"

"Dirt poor. I ain't got two nickels to rub together, and I cain't find no work nowheres these days."

"Mama says I shouldn't say ain't and nothing that rhymes with it."

"My mama used to tell me that, too."

"Why don't you listen to her then?"

"She's dead and gone a good spell."

"So, when your mama and pop die, you can do what you want?"

"Eddie, you're a piece of work, ain't you now?"

Despite how funny he talked, I liked Mr. Zeke and helping him dig the taters. We filled the basket pretty quick. Then, just like Pop did, he took a pocketknife and scraped dirt off the shovel blade and returned it to the shed. He carried the basket to the house and dumped it out onto the grass. He primed the pump over the cistern with the can of water from the washstand and pumped a pail of water. After refilling the priming can, he and I set to cleaning the dirt off the potatoes, which could also be called spuds, but I liked that tater word.

Mama stuck her head out the back door and said, "I'll dish up your supper while you wash your hands." She nodded to the washstand set against the back of the house. He flung the old water out of the basin onto the grass and refilled it. The pump still held its prime.

Zeke used soap; then he dried with the old flower-sack towel.

Mama handed him a plate heaped with mashed potatoes and gravy and string beans and chicken. He sat on the back step and set to eating.

Mama said, "Now don't pester him with your questions."

"His name is Mr. Zeke."

"Don't pester Mr. Zeke."

"You got a good boy here, Missus."

The funniest thing happened to Mama's face. It was like her face was sort of dark, but what Mr. Zeke said turned on a switch, and she lit up.

Zeke wiped his plate shiny clean with bread

and ate that, too. The chicken bones were as clean as the plate. For dessert, Mama gave him the biggest slice of peach pie I'd ever seen her serve anyone. After he finished eating, Mama handed him a clean pair of pop's overalls and a clean work shirt and told him to change in the outhouse.

"Bring me your old things. My rag bag is getting low. And, Mr. Zeke, I'll pray you find work soon."

"Missus, thank you for your kindness. It was a fine supper. I ain't et off a plate in some time. And the clothes, thanks for that, too. Maybe they'll help me land a job. Funny, ain't it? The more you look like you need a job, the less likely somebody is gonna' give you one."

When he came out of the outhouse, I walked alongside Mr. Zeke and carried his rags to the back door, where he thanked Mama again. Then he hiked past the chickens and the garden toward Second Street and the railroad tracks beyond.

"Why'd you give him Pop's clothes? Is Pop going to be mad at you?"

"Mr. Zeke is poor. He's a good man, though. You can tell that by how he did the job with the potatoes. He washed them without me telling him to. Times are hard right now, and those of us who have been blessed are obliged to share with those less fortunate."

At the time, I understood this not at all.

Only later, in second grade, we had an hour of religion each day. On Mondays, Sister Everest covered the first reading from Mass on Sunday. Tuesday was catechism. Wednesday was the second reading from Sunday. Thursday: catechism again. I'm pretty sure it was a Gospel Friday when me and my classmates heard about giving stuff to the poor. Of course, I thought of Mr. Zeke, and I was sure Mama would go to heaven. During first grade though, I thought she was going to hell. But I'll tell that part later.

Because this was only the first part of the second thing. The second part of it, I have no idea if it happened the afternoon of the Zeke day, or a day or two later. Or maybe even weeks later. I do know it happened before Christmas.

So, here's the second part of the second thing I remember from when I was five.

Lennie and me were outside. We were throwing rocks at chickens but hadn't scored a hit. Getting a rock to sail through the chicken wire was hard enough, never mind getting one to go through the wire AND hit a clucker! Any rate, it was time for lunch. I didn't need a clock with the little hand and the big one pointing straight up to tell me. My stomach knew when it was time to eat better than any stupid clock.

So, we washed up. I used soap. And we left our shoes outside. Mama wasn't in the kitchen, but we could see her down the hall. She had the front door cracked open and peeked through the crack.

I walked down there to see what she was looking at. Lennie pushed past me and squeezed by Mama's leg and pulled the door open.

"Lennie!" Mama half screeched, half-whispered, half hissed. "The nigger'll see us!"

She eased the door shut. But not before I saw him, a black-skinned man on the sidewalk in front of the bank. He looked poor. Skinnier and shorter than Zeke. His clothes were even rattier. His hair was white. He walked funny, like one leg did more than half the walking. He sure looked poor.

Mama seemed afraid of him. Zeke was poor. He was young and strong, but Mama wasn't afraid of him. She helped him.

This man was old and crippled and needed help more than Zeke did, but Mama wanted to hide from him. If Mama wanted to hide from a man, it sure seemed like a good idea for me to hide too.

When I was five, I didn't know it was a sin to say the N-word. There was another N-word, Negro, and it was okay. But it wasn't *THE* N-word. Sister Mary Everest told all of us in first grade that saying *THE* N-word was a sin and anyone who said it would go to hell.

I raised my hand—

But that I'll tell later.

C

Now the third thing.
Christmas Eve.

Christmas Eve was the bestest day of the year. And, finally, it was here.

I only had to get through the morning and the afternoon and Mass in the evening. When we came back home after, we'd go into the front room. There'd be a big tree with lights and tinsel and ornaments and a star on top, and underneath; presents. I, the good Walsh kid, expected a lot of loot.

But the morning was loooooooong. And I can tell you how long it was.

After Mass on Thanksgiving, I walked out of the church with Simon, the Grossman kid.

"Do you know why we celebrate Thanksgiving?" he said.

I didn't.

"It's because Christmas and Santa Clause

are only a month away, and we go to church to thank God Almighty for that."

Simon, the five-year-old first-grader, knew some stuff. Because of him, I knew how long Christmas Eve morning was: a month. That morning was just as long as all the time between Thanksgiving and Christmas.

Finally, the looooooong morning got itself over.

Uncle Ed ate lunch with Lennie and me. He was home from the Army. As usual, when we had company, Mama didn't sit right away. She served all of us and kept Uncle's coffee cup full. I asked him why Mama liked him more than the other uncles Lennie and I had.

"When your mama and I were little," he said, "our two older brothers teased your mama mercilessly."

That sidetracked the conversation until we got that *mercilessly* worked out.

"Your uncle protected me when Homer and Fred teased me," Mama said. "Sometimes, they even beat him up for taking my side."

It was easy to see Mama liked Uncle Ed, and now it was easy to see why.

"I did stick up for her," Mama's brother said. "Grandma was sick, and Lucille went into the convent and became Sister Noreen. Beatrice married your uncle John. Your Mama did the cooking and cleaning and took care of baby

Ruth. Homer and Fred were bigger and older. It wasn't right for those two ignorant louts to pick on her in the first place, and sure wrong to pick on her when she kept the house running, starting before she was ten."

Homer and Fred were ignorant because they never went to school beyond the third grade, and louts meant bullies.

Then Uncle Ed said, "I stuck up for her like you should stick up for Lennie."

Which I didn't understand at all. Lennie was the bad boy. If someone picked on him, didn't he have it coming?

Uncle Ed thanked Mama for a fine meal and said he'd see us again at supper. He left to visit Grandma's grave in the church cemetery; then he planned to visit Grandpa, Aunt Ruth, and the ignorant louts at the farm.

When Mama washed dishes, I was her dish dryer. Lennie didn't dry. He always dropped and broke one. It earned him a one smack spanking, and, "Ach, I spend all my green stamps on new dishes."

Lennie sat on the wide, low-to-the-floor windowsill near the coal oil stove and paged through a book. After Mama stacked the plates in the cabinet, I put on my coat and went outside. Mama handed me the basin with the dirty dishwater in it. I was to carry the water carefully, so it wouldn't spill. If I spilled, it would freeze and make a dangerous slick spot on the brick walk to the outhouse. So, I carried it to the fence around the chicken pen. Carefully. We weren't supposed to bother the hens because that could make them stop laying eggs. I checked behind me to make sure Mama wasn't looking, then I flung the water at a couple of layers pecking lunch from the ground. The hens scooted away to avoid the dousing and returned to their pecking without so much as a disapproving cluck, which disappointed me some.

Christmas Eve morning was loooooong. The afternoon felt even longer.

As I headed back inside, four-year-old Lennie came out bound for the outhouse. When he was three, I had to go with him to make sure he wouldn't fall in.

With him gone, I got the windowsill.

After I'd complained about having to wait another year to go to school, Mama said I could go to school at home. She wasn't a nun, but she would be my teacher, anyway. I took my tablet and practiced writing A B Cs and 1 2 3s. Which I did for a whole minute. A B Cs and 1 2 3s made the time go slower.

So, I read the funny papers. I knew all the letters, but I couldn't read so good yet. So, I would spell a word inside one of those bubbles in the comics, and Mama would say what it was and what it meant. The only problem was, by the time I got to the last word in a sentence, I'd forgotten what the first word meant. Sometimes she ach-ed at me. This morning though, she hummed as she baked and went over the same sentence with me five times and was still humming.

Lennie came in from the outhouse and Mama let him stand on the stool to wash his hands in the zinc. The water in the basin on the washstand outside was frozen.

I think I was in second grade when I found out that the proper term was sink.

Anyway, Lennie looked at me occupying his spot. I smiled at him. Lennie didn't smile back. He just ambled to our room.

I finished the Lone Ranger comic. Dick Tracy was on the other side and I had to fold the paper. As I folded, I noticed the threads had started coming loose from the inseam of my jeans just below the fly.

Hmmm!

I stuck Booger Picker—

I should explain I learned to call it Booger Picker from Simon Grossman at the parish picnic last summer. The next day I told Mama. She aaaaached like never before and said saying Booger Picker was worse than saying ain't. "People will think we're no account poor trash."

"But Simon Grossman taught me that finger name."

"People know he's rich."

"Don't people know we're in between?"

"People know what we are by how we dress, how we act, and how we talk. That finger's name is Mr. Pointer. *Verstehe*?"

So anyway, I stuck Mr. Pointer into the hole in the inseam to see if he would fit. At first he didn't, but then he did. I looked up. Mama was baking and humming.

Dick Tracy had a five-panel strip that day. Mama helped me through the bubble in the first panel. I looked down at the finger-sized hole I made in my inseam. Mama was cooking and humming. I stuck Mr. Pointer in the hole and pulled gently. A couple more threads gave way. Mama was still busy. I could almost get two fingers in the hole, but not quite. I pulled.

Rip!

"Ach! Eddie. What are you doing?"

"There's a hole in my pants." I moved the paper aside and showed her.

"A little hole I can fix it in two minutes. Don't make it bigger."

The next panel had Dick Tracy talking on his two-way wrist TV. Always before Mama said she didn't have time to explain what a two-way wrist TV was. But this time she started explaining.

A TV was like a radio that showed movies. I looked at our radio atop the icebox. I couldn't figure out how anybody could show a movie on that thing.

As she spoke about getting a radio that shows movies into something the size of the watch Uncle Ed wore on his wrist, I couldn't understand any of it. But that hole I'd started in my inseam, that I understood. I reached my hand under the paper covering my lap and got two fingers in the hole. Mama talked, and I pulled very carefully so that when threads pulled apart, they didn't make noise.

Uncle Ed came back when the little hand on the wall clock pointed to three. He put a carton of ice cream in the icebox. When he turned around, he looked at me funny, walked over to my windowsill, and lifted the funny paper off my lap.

The way Mama screeched hurt my ears. My left pants leg inseam had gotten itself ripped apart from the crotch to my ankle, exposing my skinny white leg.

"Boy," Uncle Ed said, "you're in for it."

"Go put on another pair of pants," Mama said.

I headed for my room.

"If that had been Lennie, you'd have blistered his butt good."

Mama mumbled something.

Lennie sat on his bed with a book. He watched me change pants, and then he followed me back to the kitchen.

I climbed back onto my windowsill.

"You ain't even gonna' say you're sorry?" My uncle glared at me with his hands on his hips.

"Ach, Ed. Let him be. Those pants were getting old."

Uncle Ed shook his head. "Boy, not only did you do a real bad thing, you did it on Christmas Eve. And now, you won't even say you're sorry."

I glanced at Mama and hoped she'd save me. She just went back to fixing supper.

"You know when boys and girls are bad, they get sticks and coal in their stockings and no presents. If boys and girls are really, really bad, Santa's—and here he said that N word—comes with a sack. His name is Ruprecht. He puts the bad boy in the sack and carts him away to Bad Boy Land. There's no games, no fun there, and a spanking before breakfast, lunch, dinner, and bedtime. Every blessed day."

I didn't understand why Uncle Ed was mad at me. And I didn't understand why Ruprecht had never taken Lennie to Bad Boy Land. But he couldn't take me. I was special. I was the good Walsh boy.

Uncle got his coat. As he pulled it on, he said to Mama, "You got that boy spoiled rotten."

Then he left and didn't come back for supper, which I didn't notice, but Lennie did.

"Uncle had something to do," Mama said. "He'll be here tonight. After Santa comes while you're at church."

Me, I just wanted to get done with supper and get to church and get back home again. The endless day had finally gotten down to just those three *gets* to do.

During supper, Mama fussed at me to slow down and to chew my food. "People see you eat like that, what will they think?"

I wasn't hungry, only anxious for supper to be over, and I sure didn't care what people would think.

This was Christmas Eve. Santa was coming. I looked at Lennie, eating the way he always did. "Eat, Lennie," Mama would say, and he'd take a bite. She'd say it again later, and he'd take another bite. He wasn't helping get us through supper. Last year when I was four, I was as dumb as Lennie about Santa. He seemed to think Santa was no big deal, as interesting as the ham and potato salad on his plate.

Being five, I knew Santa was a very big deal, the biggest deal of the year, bigger even than a birthday. "Eat, Lennie," I said. He took another bite. I sighed and looked at the stupid clock. The hands must have got stuck.

During most of the year, we only ate supper

with Pop on Sundays. When he came home from work, Lennie and me were already in bed. When he did eat with us, he didn't say much. When we had company for supper, he never said anything at all. That Christmas Eve he spoke.

Pop said, "You and Lennie go to the outhouse."

"Use paper," Mama said.

I grabbed the flashlight.

"Wait for your brother," Mama said to me.

"When you finish, wait for him. Don't leave him there in the dark," Pop said. "Then get dressed for church."

"Wash your hands first," Mama said.

We did our business and washed our hands at the *zinc*. I used soap. Lennie didn't, but I wasn't about to say anything and slow things down even more.

Mama didn't come to church with us. Other times she did. Not on Christmas Eve, though.

The church was jam-packed. Pop shoved us into the second to last pew. People kept coming, and they had to stand along the side aisles. During sitting times. Lennie sat on Pop's lap. I was next to them. Sitting seemed to make time go slower, as if it weren't slow enough. I fidgeted.

Pop hissed, "You best hold it."

He thought I'd gone to the outhouse but didn't do my business. I did, only I was real anxious for church to be over, to get back home, and to open the door to the front room. In there I knew we'd find the Christmas tree, and Santa would have left a big batch of presents under it.

It took forever, but church ended. The drive back home took forever, but it ended, too. Pop stopped the car, and I tore out the rear door. I was almost to the house when the car door slammed, and I heard Pop say, "That's a good boy." To Lennie! But there was no time to worry about that.

Mama was in the kitchen.

I tore off my cap with tie-under-your-chin straps to the ear flaps. "Can we go in the front room now?"

"Wait for Pop and Lennie. Take your coat off."

More waiting.

Finally, I had my hand on the doorknob to the front room.

"Go ahead," Mama said.

I pushed in the door, and there it was. The tree stood in the corner and went from floor to ceiling. All covered with lights and tinsel and ornaments with a big star on top.

But wait. No presents. Not one. Nothing but the bare wood floor under the tree.

There were two doors into the front room off the hallway, one close to the kitchen, the other by the front door of the house. There was a knock at that door.

Then I heard, "Ho, Ho."

I ran and opened that door.

Santa stood there. He "Ho-Ho-ed" again. He was all in red and white and his beard covered his face so all I could see of it was eyes. He had a big red sack over his shoulder.

Toys!

Mama said, "Come in, Santa."

"I understand there's a good boy living in this house," he said.

Of course, there was a good boy living here. Everybody knew that.

Pop brought Santa a chair from the kitchen, and he sat and pulled a long box from his sack. It was wrapped in brightly colored paper. Santa checked the tag on the present. "Lennie," he said.

Lennie was the youngest. Even if he was the bad one, it was okay for him to be first. And if Lennie got such a big present, mine would be even bigger.

Lennie knelt on the floor and tore the paper off a fire truck. With a ladder you could crank up with a little wheel on the side. Whoa! A very cool present.

My turn, Santa.

He pulled a smaller present from the sack and read the tag.

"Lennie," he said.

This one was a baseball mitt.

I stood next to the tree. I felt like a party was

going on, and I was outside watching through a window.

Santa pulled a third present from the bottom of his sack.

"Lennie," he said once again. Then he folded his empty sack.

Now I felt cold. As cold as I felt last spring when Pop threw me in the creek, and I came up choking and coughing and flailing.

"Swim!" Pop hollered.

I turned so I could see him standing on the bank and flailed my way to him. He reached down and grabbed me and pulled me out. He slapped my back until I stopped coughing. I shivered something fierce.

"You okay?" he said.

I nodded, and he threw me in again.

Next to that Christmas tree, I felt that same cold and shivered. Something bad was going to happen, and it was going to be something I could not swim my way out of.

Bang, bang, bang rattled that other door to the front room. Uncle Ed went to answer it. I hadn't seen him come in.

Uncle pulled the door open and a big man, big as a lout, stepped into the room. He was dressed in black ratty clothes, and his black beard covered his face so all I could see were eyes. He had an empty black sack over his shoulder.

Ruprecht!

He looked right at me.

Pictures flashed through my head like I was looking at a Dick Tracy wrist TV.

I saw myself sitting on the windowsill and finding the little hole in my pants.

I saw Mama tell me to not make the hole bigger.

I saw my pants ripped from crotch to bottom.

I saw the black sack over Ruprecht's shoulder.

I screamed and tore out of the room, through the kitchen, outside and past the chicken house, through the garden, and into the brush along the creek. I hunkered down there and tried to make myself quiet, so Ruprecht wouldn't hear me. But it was hard being quiet. I'd peed my pants, and it was really cold out. The leaves on the ground were dry. I couldn't stop shivering and the leaves couldn't stop making noise.

There was ice on the creek, but it wasn't thick enough to walk on. "Stay off that ice," Pop said. And he'd said it in a way that made me want to stay off it, but if Ruprecht came for me, I was running across the ice.

I heard Uncle Ed call my name. He called several times. The last was from next to the chicken house. I clamped my jaw shut and clenched my muscles and made them not shiver. He went back into the house. I didn't trust him.

Pop came out and hollered. I didn't trust him either.

Finally, Mama came. "Ruprecht is gone. He won't come back. Come out, Eddie."

I came out. Mama wrapped her coat around me and took me back inside. Pop and Uncle Ed were there.

Mama told Pop to heat water to prime the cistern pump.

"Ed," Mama said, "Your namesake needs a bath, and you're going to give him one."

Uncle Ed heated two buckets of water on the stove and dumped them in the tub mama used to scrub clothes and her sons.

"I can give myself a bath," I said.

Uncle Ed looked at Mama.

"Give him a bath," she said.

He scrubbed my back, and I let him. The bathwater was nice and warm, and pretty soon I stopped shivering.

As Uncle Ed dried me off—which I could have done myself—I glanced around the room. Nobody was talking and everybody looked like they were mad at everybody else.

Lennie got three presents, and all I got was a bath for Christmas. It mattered a little bit, but Ruprecht was gone. That mattered a big bit.

That's the last thing I remember from being five. I'm pushing eighty now. That Christmas sure marked me, though. Branded my soul with an iron of ice. To this day, I fall asleep easier with a nightlight burning. No amount of education, nor reading a bazillion books on the legends of Santa, philosophy, world religions, and history, has been able to convince my mind and my soul that Ruprecht is not there, blended with the dark, just waiting to grab me and stick me in his sack and take me to Bad Boy Land.

The next year when I started school, I found out there were places even worse called Purgatory and Hell.

2

T he August I turned six, Mama let me run errands. One errand, actually. Go to Fenstermacher's drugstore. The drugstore sat on the corner of Elm and Main Streets. To get there, you only had to walk past Hemsath's house and the funeral parlor.

"You cannot, *cannot,* cross Elm or any other street. You cannot step onto Elm or any other street. *Verstehe?*"

"Sure, Mama."

She gave me a note for Mr. Fenstermacher. "Stay on the sidewalk. Do not step off the sidewalk."

"Yes, Mama."

Out the front door, past Hemsath's and the funeral house, and past the drugstore, I stopped with the toes of my shoes over the edge of the curb along Elm Street. *Scootching* my feet farther, and farther still, my feet got as far over the edge as possible without having to step into the street.

A car coming down Elm honked and scared me. The note fluttered out of my hand and landed on Elm Street.

Get the note.

Tires screeched as the car stopped a few feet from me.

The driver hollered out the window. "Get outta' the street, you stupid knucklehead."

I picked up the note and got outta' the street. The car pulled up next to me. The driver was not a man, but he wasn't a boy either, which made him an in-between. He told me I was a stupid knucklehead again and drove away.

Inside, after giving Mr. Fenstermacher the note, I noticed a girl and a boy, both the same age as that driver, sitting on stools at a counter. They were talking and laughing and sucking on straws coming out of tall glasses filled with what looked like chocolate milk with whipped cream on top. Looking at those two glasses set my mouth to watering. They sure looked like they held something a lot better than plain old chocolate milk. Maybe when I got to be in-between-age I could have one of those.

Back at home, Mama took the little bag from Mr. Fenstermacher and entered her bedroom. It was Pop's too.

Atop her dresser sat a little glass bowl with a glass lid. She lifted the lid.

"Mama, what's a knucklehead?"

Like a robin, she cocked her head to the side. Questions, she asked lots of them. Pretty soon I felt like a worm.

I explained about losing her note and that I had to step onto Elm Street to get it back.

"Ach!" she said. "Then what?"

"The car stopped, and the driver called me that name."

"Ach! Did I not walk with you one hundred times to Fenstermacher's? Did I not tell you to stay on the sidewalk one hundred times?"

I tried to figure out how big a hundred was and sort of knew how to get there. One to ten was easy. Next came the teens, which were hard at first but easy after three-teen. The bigger numbers weren't too hard. You only had to remember that two, three, four, and the rest of them got a new name ending in "-ty", and they had another number stuck onto the backend of them.

I was about at the point of working out a hundred when Mama sat on the bed, grabbed me by the arm, hauled me across her lap, and spanked me.

Me! The good kid! Laying on Lennie's place across Mama's lap and my behind taking Lennie's smacks from Mama's hard hand. It was over before I thought to cry. Eddie, the good kid just got spanked!

She set me back on the floor, and I rubbed my butt with both hands.

"Do not step off the sidewalk. Did I tell you that?"

"Yes, Mama, but I dropped the note."

"No buts! Not one! *Verstehe?*"

Well, of course I *versteh-ed,* but there were times when a rule got laid down, and a minute later, a very good reason to break that rule popped up. But I saw the look on her face, and said, "Yes, Mama."

Then she looked at the slip of paper from Mr. Fenstermacher and took money out of the little bowl and put it in the little bag. After folding the bag up, she stuck it in my pants pocket.

"Do not take that bag out of your pocket until you are standing in front of Mr. Fenstermacher. Then you take it out and hand it to him. *Verstehe?*"

The way she looked at me made my butt hurt, and I rubbed it some more and nodded.

Grabbing me by the arm again, she led me outside the front door and onto the sidewalk.

"Eddie, I want you to imagine I have drawn a chalk line right down the middle of the sidewalk."

Looking at the concrete, and trying hard, I could not see a line, but said, "Yes, Mama."

It seemed the best way to not feel like a worm again.

"Go on now. Take that bag to Mr. Fenstermacher. Do not take it out of your pocket until you are standing in front of him. And stay on that line!"

She pushed my shoulder, and I started walking with my head down, my hands out a bit for balance as I walked right on that line I couldn't see. Checking behind after twenty steps, Mama stood there and shooed me on with her hand. At forty steps, still watching. At eighty, Mama had gone inside.

I turned back around, determined to count to a hundred.

After a few steps, though, Dolly the poodle appeared in front of me, standing right on the line I couldn't see. The dumb dog looked up at me with her pink tongue hanging out and wagging her rear end. She only had a nubbin of a tail and probably couldn't tell if the little thing was wagging or not, so she wagged her whole butt.

"Move, you dumb dog."

"You're taking up the whole sidewalk, you little Walsh devil. Move out of the way." It was Mrs. Hemsath. I stood in front of the funeral parlor, and she hustled toward me in that step, step, move-the-cane way. She sure hustled slow but had a mighty mad look on her face.

"Move aside."

I didn't. I couldn't.

"Won't even get out of the way for a crippled old lady! Wait till I tell your mother, Lennie—"

Her mouth dropped open. "Eddie?"

She stood at the edge of the sidewalk, staring down at me and leaning on her cane. I reached down, moved Dolly aside, and resumed following my line.

Sure as shootin', Mrs. Hemsath would tell Mama. Was I in for another spanking? For doing exactly what Mama told me?

Five-year-old life was easier than a six-year-old life.

Rats!

I forgot where I'd been in counting steps. Something more than eighty-one but less than ninety-nine. *Start over.* This time no stupid poodle kept me from getting to one hundred.

Counting got me close to Fenstermacher's. I looked up and saw Simon Grossman with his in-between-age sister Darlene. They stood on the curb, at Elm Street, on the general store side.

"Look both ways," Big Sister said.

Simon did, and holding hands, the Grossman kids crossed Elm. After he stepped up on the curb, Simon jerked his hand free. Darlene rolled her eyes, then hurried to catch up to her brother who was pulling open the door to the drugstore.

I followed them in.

Darlene lifted her brother onto a stool. Simon pulled a dollar out of his pocket and laid it on the counter.

"Two chocolate malteds," he said to Mrs. Fenstermacher. "For me and my sister. It's my birthday."

I thought about telling him to say please.

"You have something for me, Eddie?" Mr. Fenstermacher said from behind.

I dug the folded-up paper bag out of my pocket and handed it to him.

He looked inside and said to tell Mama thanks.

My eyes wanted another look at Simon holding the tall glass below the counter and sucking on the straw.

Huh. Simon didn't have to wait till in-between age to get one.

When I got back, we ate lunch. Mama sent Lennie out to play and washed the dishes. I dried. When she started setting up the laundry tubs, I slipped down the hallway between the front room and the bedrooms and checked to make sure Mama wasn't watching. She wasn't.

I entered Mama's bedroom, lifted the lid off that little bowl, took out a bill, stuck it in my pocket, left by the front door, closed it real quiet, hustled back to Fenstermacher's, and climbed up onto a stool.

"A chocolate malted, please," I said to Mrs.

Fenstermacher. "It's my birthday—um, last week it was."

"That's a ten-dollar bill, Eddie. Where did you get this?"

"Um. From my Uncle Ed. I'm named after him."

She looked at me, like Mama did, like a Robin, but then she scooped ice cream, turned on a noisy machine, and made the shake. She slid the glass over the counter. Holding it as Simon had, I slurped on the straw and had to suck really hard, but what came out of that straw was the best thing I had ever tasted in my whole life. I sucked and sucked. The level in the glass went down and down until sucking made a gurgling sound. I licked off the straw and would have licked out the inside of the glass, too, but couldn't figure out how to do it. I sighed and placed the glass on the counter and slid off my stool.

"Don't forget your change," Mrs. Fenstermacher said. She came around the counter, folded some bills, handed them to me. I put them in a pocket. She held out coins. They went into the other front pocket.

Going back home, I skipped on that line I couldn't see and passed through the yard between our house and the Hemsath's and found Lennie in the sandbox. He was playing with his fire truck from last Christmas. I played with the yellow bulldozer.

Suddenly I heard, "Eddieeeeeee! You come here! Right! Now!"

Uh oh.

Lennie got a little smile on his face. I tried to remember if that was the first time he smiled.

"Eddieeee!"

I rounded the outhouse and saw Mama standing by the back door. Her face looked like Mrs. Hemsath's when I wouldn't get out of her way. I hustled.

When I got there, she grabbed me by the arm and jerked me inside, and slammed the door.

"You stole. That's a sin. A bad one."

She unbuttoned my pants straps and pulled them off. Sand fell out of the cuffs and coins rattled on the floor next to the sand. Then she pulled my underpants down and spanked me. This time I cried till snot ran out of my nose and into my mouth.

My first and second spankings on the same day. And the second one was bare-heinie. Years later, I came to appreciate that a bare-heinie spanking ranked just below capital punishment.

B

I didn't get any more spankings the rest of my birthday month. But every day, from breakfast to bedtime, Mama kept me right by her side. When she worked in the garden, when she gathered eggs, even doing the wash. She made me wring out the clothes. I gritted my teeth and wrung. Then she'd wring 'em and get a lot more water out.

As I worked beside her, and she redid my work, she talked to me.

"Ach," she said. "I taught you ABCs and 123s. I should have been teaching you about sin."

Avoiding sin wasn't too hard. There were only ten *Thou shalls* to remember. Eight of them were *Thou shall nots*. The others, *Thou shall* honor thy father and thy mother, and *Thou shall* keep holy the Sabbath.

Mama said Sabbath meant Sunday.

"Why can't I write Sunday, then?" which got me a look but not an "Ach!."

Each day, before supper, I sat on my windowsill and took the paper Mama handed me. It had ten *thou shalls* along the left side of the page. I had to put eight *nots* where they belonged, along with the sin to not do. And the two to do. A lot rode on me getting it right. Dessert.

School started. I thought Mama had rules. Sister Mary Everest had a lot more. She didn't spank. She whacked knuckles with a ruler. Boy knuckles, she whacked. Simon Grossman, the six-year-old second-grader, said Sister Everest thought all the girls were going to be nuns and that nuns, even nuns who weren't nuns yet, could not commit a sin.

One of the rules was *Silence!* If you wanted to speak, you had to raise your hand and get permission. That was the hardest rule. For boys and girls. The girls didn't get a whack. They got: "Priscilla!" followed by a snake hiss. Like the big black snake hissed at the four of us who cornered it against a tree at the parish picnic grounds and beat on it with sticks.

By Halloween, I had pretty much worked out the connection between rules and rulers. The Monday after collect-candy-in-a-sack day, a black-skinned man showed up at school. His name was Mr. Wilson, Sister said. He was our new janitor.

Without raising his hand, Jimmie Joe Meinerschlagen said, "I ain't never seed no nigger before."

"Jimmie Joe Meinerschlagen!" Sister screeched. Like Mama screeched, "Lennieeeeee." And lately, "Eddieeeee!"

Sister grabbed her ruler and hopped down off the thick cushion atop her chair, which she needed to see over the edge of her wide desk atop the platform at the front of the classroom.

"Come up here, Jimmie Joe!"

Jimmie Joe slid out of his desk and walked forward with his head hung low and his left hand raised.

Sister took his hand and said, "Ain't," and whacked his knuckles. "Never." Another whack. "Seed." Again, a whack. "No." At this whack, Jimmie Joe jerked his hand back.

Sister swept her eyes over all of us, all eleven first-graders and all eight second-graders.

"That was the most egregious display of the English language I have ever heard. If Sister Superior heard that, I … I don't know what she would have done."

I stuck my hand up.

"Not now, Eddie Walsh."

I was going to suggest Sister Superior might whack Sister Everest's knuckles for being a bad teacher for one thing, but I also wanted to know what that "gregious" word meant.

"Ain't never seed no," Sister said. "Louis, tell us the proper way to say these words. Just these, not the other word Jimmie Joe said."

She was talking to Large Louie, in his third year in first grade.

Large Louie stood up. He was large, all right. The second tallest kid in school and taller than the three teacher nuns. Housekeeper Nun was taller, and so was Eunice Fenstermacher, an eighth-grader.

Louie looked up at Sister, then back down at the floor again.

"Good ahead, Louis. Say it."

Louie raised his eyes and said, "I." He looked like he had a headache.

"Never." He shifted his weight from one foot to the other.

"Saw!" He sat back down with a grin all over his face.

"See," Sister said. "Even Louis knows how to speak properly. From this day forward, if anyone of you in either class ever desecrates—"

My hand shot up.

Sister's mouth and eyes hissed at me. I pulled my hand down.

"If anyone in this classroom ever speaks so improperly again, there will be no recess for a week for the entire first and second grades."

Sister took in a big breath and *phoo*·ed it out. She laid the ruler on her desk and stuck her hands up the opposite sleeves of her habit.

"Now, First and Second Graders, we must deal with that other word Jimmie Joe said. It is the N-word. You must never, ever say that word. It is an abomination."

My hand shot up.

Now Sister looked like she had a headache.

"Not now, Eddie." Followed by a hiss.

"The N-word is ugly, it is awful, it is a sin."

My hand shot up.

She put her hands on her hips. "Yesssss, Eddie."

"Does that mean it's a 'Thou shall not', like, 'Thou shall not say the N-word?'"

Sister frowned. A second later, she smiled at me. "Why, yes, Eddie. That's a very good way to put it."

She took her hands out of her sleeves. "Thou shalt not say the N-word. That word is not only ugly and awful and hurtful. It is a sin. Anyone who says that word will go to hell."

"My mama's going to hell," I said.

Uh, oh. I forgot to raise my hand.

Sister stood there at the edge of the platform with the blackboard behind her and the desk beside her. Her mouth hung open as she looked right at me. She closed her mouth and her eyes. It got real quiet in the room.

The church bell rang once. That meant it was a half-hour. It was funny. That bell sounded farther away than when I heard it from Main Street in town, a really long way away.

Finally, Sister opened her eyes, and then things started happening.

Housekeeper Nun came over from the convent and taught first and second grade. Sister Everest and Sister Superior took me to a room a lot smaller than a classroom. I had to go to second grade the rest of today, Sister Superior told me. She left and Sister Everest told me about sins and confession and commandments. And commandments were full of *Thou Shalts*, not *Thou Shalls*. Breaking any of the commandments, the *Thou Shalt Nots*, or the *Thou Shalls* was a sin. She told me next year when I turned seven, I will have attained the Age of Reason. Attained meant *got to*. Once a person attained the Age of Reason, sins counted.

Sister Superior stuck her head in the door just as I asked, "If you commit a sin when you're six, it doesn't count?"

Sister Superior had a headache, too. I could tell.

That day wound up being long, almost as long as Christmas Eve waiting for the time to go into the front room. But Sister taught me some stuff about sins and misbehaving, about confession, and how Sister was sure Mama had gone to confession and received absolution for saying the N-word, so she wasn't going to hell. Absolution meant forgiveness, but more than that. It also meant the confessed sin was wiped away, like the chalkboard when it was wiped down with a wet rag. Nothing but pure clean black left behind.

Finally, the final bell.

Sister closed her eyes, bowed her head, folded her hands, and whispered, "For the souls in Purgatory."

"Can I go home, Sister?"

"Please do."

The first week of school, Mama drove me there and picked me up after. Since then, I walked to and from with Eunice Fenstermacher.

When I met Eunice and we started home, she said, "I heard your mama's going to hell."

"No. She went to confession, so she doesn't have to go to hell."

As we walked, I told her about being in second grade all day.

We got to my house, I watched her continue through our backyard and along the creek levee to Second Street. Her house sat behind the drugstore.

I headed for the back door.

Some November days are cold, some cold and nasty, and some are warm. That was a warm one. The kitchen door was open.

Mama was crying.

"Now, Loraine, it's okay." Pop? Pop was home before dinner?

"It's not okay." More crying. "Everybody knows I'm going to hell. Eddie told them."

"Eddie didn't mean it. He's just a boy. He starts talking before he starts thinking."

"Everyone is laughing at me. Everyone! I can't go to the store. I can't go to church."

"Now, Loraine. It's not that bad, and it'll blow over.

"I'm in hell. Does hell blow over?"

Whoa.

Mama was in hell, and I put her there.

C

As third grade started, I wondered why I had to go to school any longer. It seemed to me I had learned all I needed to know. Sins, confession, reading, writing, and arithmetic, not speaking egregiously, I knew all that stuff. At noon recess, I discovered the point of continuing my education.

Baseball.

In third grade, we played baseball at recess. The younger kids played dodge ball. Baseball was like Christmas—without Ruprecht—five days a week.

At recess, two fifth graders, Ollie Weisendinger and Norb Siling, quickly picked sides from the third, fourth, fifth-grade boys. Me, and the rest of the *thirders*, got taken last. But that was okay. Baseball was so much fun, being last didn't matter. But by the time fall arrived, team captains selected me ahead of half the fourth graders. Then we switched to football, which disappointed me.

But then football turned out to be fun, too. And it didn't put an end to my new kind of Christmas.

In fourth grade, when I ran with the ball, nobody, not even a fifth-grader, could catch me. When I ran after the guy with the ball, I always caught him. And tackled him. And often made Ball-boy fumble, after which I'd scoop up the ball and run it the other way. I ran fast. I practiced running a lot. Lennie brought a lunch box to school all the time. I brought one if there was ice or snow. Other times I raced home for lunch, ate, and hurried back, and returned to school before the brought-their-lunchers finished eating. Noon recess was Christmas to me. I sort of needed it to be, since that year Simon Grossman told me was no Santa Claus. No Santa meant no Ruprecht, either, but knowing it did not stop me from needing a night light.

Also, when I started fourth grade, Large Louie moved to third, directly from first. Fifth-grader Esther Wiggins figured at the rate of completing two grades every six years, Large Louie would graduate from grade school at the age of thirty. One morning as we marched back to school after Mass, I heard Esther whisper that to another fifth-grader. We were supposed to be quiet. At Mass, we got fresh Jesus in our hearts, and we were supposed to be mindful of that. Sister didn't hear her, so Esther didn't get a hissing.

But I wondered if she had done the arithmetic right. That night I took a tablet and sat on the windowsill in the kitchen, and with the pencil in my teeth, tried to figure how to lay out the problem.

"Ach, Eddie. Don't chew the pencil. Nobody else wants to use it when it's all chewed up."

Chewing a pencil made it easier to figure things out, but Mama was watching.

It took Louie six years to advance two grades. Grade school was eight years long. *Oh!* Eight divided by two equal four. 4 x 6 = 24. All of us, except for the Grossman kid, were six when we started school. 24 + 6 = 30. Esther had figured it out without paper or chewing on a pencil. Well, she was a girl. She couldn't play baseball or football. At least she was good at something. Girls should try to be good at something, even if the something doesn't matter as much as base- or foot- ball.

Which I was good at. So was Jimmie Joe Meinerschlagen. Starting in fourth grade, Jimmie Joe and I picked the teams. At baseball, I always took Large Louie first. He couldn't hit. Ground balls went through his legs. Pop flies bounced off his forehead. But it made the game interesting. Otherwise, my team won all the time.

At football, I never picked Large Louie. What I liked to do was to get the ball and run right at him. I'd zig left. Louie stepped sideways to stay in front of me. I'd zag right. He moved that way, too. Then I'd zig left again, and Louie's feet would get tangled and he'd fall down. It would have been easy to avoid Louie, but I really liked to see him stumble all over himself. Funny as all get out. Even though Jimmie Joe and his team knew I was gonna' do that, and they lined up behind Louie, and as soon as he tumbled, they gang-tackled me. We'd wind up a pile of bodies all laughing hard enough to wet our pants. It was more fun than scoring a touchdown.

Jimmie Joe and I were walking home from school one afternoon, and we were talking about the recess football that day.

"Usually you only make Large Louie trip once," Jimmie Joe said. "Today you did it three times. It cost you the game."

"That third-grader Heiny Stiert got up from the pile the first time holding himself like he had to pee. I wanted to see if I could make him wet his pants. But he didn't."

"Don't you play to win?"

"Winning's easy. It's not as much fun as laughing at Large Louie or little Heiny."

A big paw grabbed my shoulder, spun me

around, and a bright white light exploded in my head. We'd been walking down the street next to the ditch. I wound up on my butt on the far side of the ditch with my feet in the muddy water.

Large Louie pointed at me and laughed. "That's funny. That's really funny." And he walked away.

My nose hurt. My lip hurt. When I felt them, they hurt more, and my hand came away bloody. And I couldn't close my mouth properly. One front tooth had been bent back, so it didn't fit over the lowers.

I thought about crying. I thought about running home to Mama, but Large Louie was ahead of me. I'd have to pass him, and he'd laugh at me again.

Jimmie Joe stuck out a hand to help me back across the ditch. I reached out to take it.

"Not that one," Jimmie Joe said. "It's full of blood and snot."

Once I was back up on the road, I started squish-squishing toward home. My friend walked alongside me. Neither of us said a word.

A few minutes ago, Louie was someone to laugh at. Now I was.

When I got home, Mama screeched, "Ach!" Then she grabbed me and hugged me. Fortunately, I thought to lift my chin over her shoulder or who knows what would have happened to my nose.

She grabbed my upper arms and pushed me back. "What happened? Did you get in a fight? Who did this?"

"Uh, it *wathn't* a fight. Large Louie hit me."

"Ach! That, that Goliath simpleton." Mama looked at me. "What's the matter with your mouth?"

I pulled up the half of my upper lip that wasn't swollen.

She ach·ed again, and said, "*Dentist* and doctor. I don't have that much egg money saved. Bank, dentist, doctor."

By the look on her face, it hurt to take money out of the bank. It hurt me more at both the dentist and the doctor than getting punched by Large Louie.

The dentist said, "I'm going to stick my thumb in your mouth and straighten out that tooth. If you bite me, I'll pull all your teeth out."

When Louie hit me, my head filled with white light, but it didn't hurt right away. When the dentist pulled my Bucky Beaver straight, my head filled with that same white light, but I felt it. Nothing ever hurt so badly. It made me sweat. But I didn't bite his thumb. It would have hurt my tooth to do that.

The doctor had to straighten my nose. More white light. More sweat and I wound up with my nostrils packed with gauze and this honking nose boot made of gauze, tape, and a couple of strips of metal to hold my nose in place. Driving home, I kept forgetting I couldn't breathe through my nose.

When we walked into the kitchen, Lennie and Pop sat at the table eating bacon, eggs, and fried potatoes. I couldn't smell the bacon.

Lennie looked at me. "Does it hurt?"

I nodded with very small head bobs.

"Are you all right?" Pop asked Mama.

Why did he ask her that? Large Louie didn't punch her.

Eating was the last thing I wanted to do. I went to bed. As I pulled the covers up, Pop came in. Maybe he was going to ask me if I was all right.

"You come home bleeding and beat up, you vex your mama. Do not vex your mama ever again."

The only time Pop ever fussed at me was at Christmas Eve Mass when Lennie and I fidgeted in the pew. This sure wasn't Christmas.

"Louie punched you because you laughed at him. Laughing at somebody bigger than you is plain stupid. Laughing at somebody smaller than you is as big a sin as there is."

Pop left and closed the door.

I was tired. Plumb tuckered. But sleep would not come. It wasn't even close by. What Pop said hurt the inside of me, just as bad as Louie hurt the outside.

It felt like I had just fallen asleep when Pop was rousting Lennie and me from bed. "Get dressed. Fast," he said. "Your mama's sick. I have to take her to the hospital."

Pop drove us to St. Charles, dumped Lennie and me with Uncle John and Aunt Beatrice, and hurried away.

It took until senior year of high school before I figured what happened because I'd vexed Mama.

D

On the first day of fifth grade, I walked into the 3rd, 4th, and 5th grades classroom with my ball bat on my shoulder and the strap of my glove over the barrel of the bat, and halfway through the door, I stopped dead in my tracks. Standing in the middle of the platform with the clean blackboard behind, the big desk beside her, and the windows beyond her looking out at the church and cemetery stood a nun like none I'd ever seen before. She smiled at me.

Her face was young. She looked downright pleased to see me. And she smiled at me.

"Well, come in and tell me your name please."

I stepped in. The door swung shut and knocked the bat out of my hand, and it clattered on the floor.

Little Heiny Stiert hollered, "You're out."

On the playground, if you swung at a pitch and the bat sailed out of your hands, it was an automatic out.

"Yeah," Jimmie Joe Meinerschlagen said, "It's five hours before recess and Eddie already made an out."

Which pretty much got the whole room laughing.

"Yeah," Large Louie said, "Five hours before recess and you made an out." He pointed at me. "That's funny."

Which made my nose remember when he broke it.

The door busted open behind me, hit me in the back, and sent me sprawling on the floor.

"What is the meaning of this wild behavior?"

The laughter stopped. I rolled over and quit breathing. Sister Superior stood in the open doorway, glaring at the new nun. I just had time to feel sorry for her when Sister Superior swung her mad-as-all-get-out eyes on me. She started into the room, stepped on my bat, and probably would have fallen if she hadn't had her hand on the doorknob.

It might have looked funny, except not with Sister Superior already mad. Even Large Louie kept his mouth zipped.

Sister kicked the bat out of her way. "So, Eddie Walsh, you caused this ruckus. No recess for a week."

This was worse than when I got my first spanking. Worse even than Ruprecht Christmas.

"Eddie Walsh, get up off the floor and gather

up your litter lest someone trip on it and break a leg. Sister Mary Daniels, in the hallway, now. As for the rest of you... you... heathens, we march over to church in seven minutes for Mass. Spend the time purging your souls of summer sin and mischief."

Sister Mary Daniels, the new nun, passed by me as I got to my feet. My bat and glove were close to Sister-mad-as-all-get-out. I didn't want to get close to her.

The new nun walked into the hallway. The old nun said, "I best not hear one more peep out of this room. Not. One. Peep." She shut the door. It didn't make a peep.

On tippy-toe, I gathered my litter. From next to the door, I could hear Sister Superior fussing at Sister Daniels in what was a shout and a whisper at the same time. Most of her words weren't clear. But, "Egregious behavior," "Sacrilege," "Heathen deviltry," "Discipline first, learning second." Those came through clear enough.

Still on tiptoe, I put my bat and glove in the cloakroom. Actually, it was a closet with hooks on the wall for coats and caps and shelves for lunch boxes and ball gloves. There were thirty of us kids. The thirty of us students wore coats when it was cold. There was one nun, and she wore a cloak over her habit. So it was a cloakroom.

When I passed Little Heiny, he asked me what I heard at the door.

I put my finger to my lips and hissed at him like I was a nun fussing at a girl.

I took my second last seat in the fifth-grade row—Linda Zigmund sat behind me. Our row was against the hall wall. The stupid third graders got the window row.

The door opened. Sister Mary Daniels walked in, stepped up onto the platform in front, and wrote on the chalkboard.

> It is not a sin to have fun.
> Necessarily.
> God wants us to be happy.
> Sister Superior wants us to be quiet.
> We shall endeavor to satisfy both.

Sister stepped aside so all of us could read what she wrote. I put up my hand to ask about that endeavor-word, but she put her finger to her lips and pointed, with the other hand, toward the door. Being quiet was something we all did together, third, fourth, and fifth graders, and Sister Daniels, too. It was something we were putting over on Sister Superior. Silence was fun.

Then she made the sign of the cross and said, "Father in heaven, we are about to enter Your holy house on earth, to be in Your presence. In the quiet of our hearts, we invite You in. Help us be attentive to Your holy presence. In Jesus's name, we pray."

Then Sister erased the blackboard and told Agnes Ashe to lead us to church.

Across from our room, kids from the sixth, seventh, and eighth grades filed into the hallway. Many of them whispered, some giggled. Sister Superior hissed incessantly at her rowdies. We, Sister Daniel's angels, marched with our heads bowed slightly, silent, steadily, with no shoving or pinching or pushing.

That day, I felt like I went to church for the first time in my life. I had been in church—I had no idea how many times. Maybe a thousand. Daily Mass during school. Every Sunday since I was baptized. Funerals and weddings on Saturday since I started serving in the third grade. While the other kids were at recess, I would figure out how many times I'd been to Mass. It seemed important because that day it seemed like, for the first time, church entered me as much as I entered the church.

I took my place in the fifth-grade row behind the third and fourth-grade rows on the right of the center aisle. Sister Superior's rowdies were behind us. Across the aisle, the first graders occupied the first two rows. Sister Everest had the next pew to herself with the second graders behind her. During Mass, she slid up and down the pew to chastise one of her pagans.

But all that commotion on the other side of the aisle didn't concern me. I mean, I noticed it, but it didn't concern me. I was sort of full of Sister Daniel's silence.

During recess, while the other kids played, I counted up the number of times I'd been to Mass. Near as I could figure, it was one thousand four hundred and twenty-five, counting that morning. Out of all those times, more than a hundred I had served up at the altar with the priest. Closer to God than those in the pews. But the first Mass of my fifth-grade year, that's when I became a Catholic. Not at baptism. At least that's how it seemed to me, not necessarily then, but sometime later it came to me.

Back to that morning. After Mass, we had an hour of religion class. Sister again wrote that sentence about it's not a sin to have fun, and she wrote "Necessarily" again.

Then she explained about necessarily.

We all knew cussing was a sin, she explained. Thou shalt not take the name of the Lord thy God in vain.

"But is it fun to cuss, to act grown up?" she said.

"Well hell yes, Sister." Little Heiny Stiert.

Big Louie laughed. I stared at Sister. She got this hurt, disappointed look on her face. I gritted my teeth. I was this close, this close to going to Heiny's desk in the row next to me and punching him in the snot locker.

Then Sister's smile came back and warmed the room. "See, boys and girls, Heiny thought it would be fun to say what he did, even though he knew it was a sin. Not a big one. A little one. But it was a sin, and he committed it even though he knew it was wrong to do so. Having fun is not a sin. Necessarily."

She went on to explain that many things would appear to be fun, but we should always remember that word, and take a moment and decide whether the fun was good fun, that would make not only us, but God happy as well, or was it the other kind.

Sister Daniels. The Happy Nun.

She was other nuns as well. One of them being Recess Nun. She played softball with the girls and baseball with the boys. A nun played baseball with the boys! And she played good. She pitched, so she didn't have to run too much in the field. She hit home runs so she didn't have to run too fast around the bases. Her team won most of the time, which made me happier than if my team won. I was never on her team. Otherwise, we'd have won all the games.

Turns out, she was also Good Teacher Nun.

My September and October report cards had grades all in the nineties. In the past, I'd gotten eighties and some seventies. Mama was pleased. She told Pop to tell me he was proud of me.

"I'm prouda' you, Eddie." He went back to reading his paper.

But in October, it got too cold for baseball, and so we prepared to switch to football. We played tackle. The field ran up a hill, but that wasn't the problem. It was a hill with grass, not asphalt, like the church parking lot where we played baseball. It wouldn't *necessarily* have been much fun playing tackle football on asphalt. Anyway, we thought since we played tackle, we'd seen the last of Sister Daniels on the playground until the spring.

But.

Was I surprised!

On the football field, just before the first kickoff, Sister Daniels showed up.

"I'm playing," she said.

"We play tackle," I said.

She held up two white strips of cloth and tucked them in the sash around her waist, one on either side. "Pull a flag, that's the same as tackling me."

"You want to run the ball?" *Crazy, right?*

Sister smiled ever so sweetly.

Jimmie Joe Meinerschlagen said, "She's on your team, Eddie."

"Wait," I said, But Jimmie Joe's team was already running to the kickoff position.

"Get set," I hollered. On my team, everybody but me was a blocker. I said to Sister, "If the ball comes to you, lateral it to me. You know what lateral means, Sister?"

She smiled ever so sweetly.

Jimmie Joe kicked the ball on a sort of low line drive, not the high-end-over-end he normally lofted to me to give his tacklers time to run down the field and get me before I worked up some speed. He kicked it to Sister. She'd insisted on being back behind the blockers with me to receive the ball. And Jimmie Joe booted that hard liner to Sister. Well, she caught the ball and just stood there staring at Jimmie Joe's team, all running and screaming toward us from the high end of our football field on the side of a hill.

"Lateral the ball to me, Sister," I hollered.

Instead of doing what I'd told her, which was so very obviously the right thing to do, she took off. And holy hell, could that nun run! Even I, Eddie Walsh, couldn't catch her.

So I stopped trying to catch her and just watched. She had the ball tucked in her left arm and straight-armed a couple of kids who were trying to get at her flags. Then she shifted the ball to her other side, straight-armed another would-be tackler, busted through the last of Jimmie Joe's team, sailed over the goal line, stopped and turned, and with a smile that stretched from one side of the helmet kind of thing nuns wore to the other, she said, "Touchdown."

We kicked off to Jimmie Joe's team. Our rules said you had to score a touchdown in four downs, or the other side took over the ball. They scored a touchdown, but it took all their downs.

They kicked off to us. This time, Jimmie Joe aimed his liner at me, just like Sister said he would. I caught the ball and started running close to the left side of the field. Jimmie Joe's horde of screaming tacklers bunched in front of me.

"Now, Eddie," Sister said.

I lateraled the ball to her, and she cut down the wide-open right side of the field, a streak, like a black ghost. With her habit down to the tops of her shoes, you couldn't see her legs, so it was like she floated, but she sure floated fast.

At the goal line, she turned, smiled again, and said, "Touchdown!"

That's when I noticed Sister Superior standing on the sidewalk by the edge of the school building. She had her hands tucked in the sleeves of her habit, and she looked mad. But she always looked mad, and we had to kickoff.

Jimmie Joe's team scored again, but it took all their downs. And It was close to the end of recess. I could tell, just like I could tell lunchtime, whether or not there was a clock around. This was going to be the game. If we scored before the bell, we'd win three touchdowns to two.

Before he kicked off, Jimmie Joe huddled his team, then they split apart and formed two rows of tacklers. Two-boy teams made up each row. I knew what he was doing. Sister could straight-arm one kid at a time. Jimmie Joe wasn't a dummy.

But then, I was pretty smart, too. Though it would have been a Deadly Sin of Pride to say so out loud. You could commit sins by words, thoughts, and deeds, but I was sure that didn't apply on the football field. Anyway, I didn't dwell on how smart I was.

Large Louie and Little Heiny anchored the right side of the first row with Little Heiny against the sideline.

I called time and huddled up my team, or it might have been Sister's, and I told them how we were going to score a touchdown. If the ball didn't come to Sister, I would get it to her, but then I'd streak down the field, through the first row of tacklers and take out one guy of a two-man tackler in the second row, and Sister could straight-arm the other one. In the meantime, I assigned two guys to take out the tackle-twosome next to Large Louie and Little Heiny. So Sister should head for the hole between Large Louie and the next guys, while I would do my job against the second row. Large

Louie couldn't move fast enough to stop Sister, the Black Streak. And klutz Louie would block Heiny against the sideline.

I could taste *Touchdown*. I could taste *VICTORY*.

Jimmie kicked a high-end-over-ender to the center of the field. Sister moved over and caught it.

It was eerily quiet. Jimmie Joe's guys weren't screaming like demented demons. A lot was riding on this. For them, a tie wasn't a loss. For us, a tie wasn't a win.

I tore down the field and was about to plow into Jimmie Joe and leave his sidekick for Sister to handle when Jimmie Joe's hand flew up to his mouth. I knew what he was trying to do. He was trying to Tom Sawyer me, fake me out. So I plowed into him going all out and laid him out flat. I rolled clear and looked behind me, expecting to see Black Streak zipping toward Touchdown City.

What I saw though, next to Large Louie, who had his mouth hanging open, was Sister on the ground, and Little Heiny tangled up in the dress of Sister's habit and struggling to get out of it.

"Heiny," Sister said. "Stop. You'll pull my dress off."

It was like the world stopped. Heiny went dead still.

Sister got them untangled.

Heiny jumped to his feet and howled, "I'm going to hell!"

"Now, now, Heiny," Sister said. "It was an accident. You're not going to hell."

"I was under your dress!"

Heiny cried. Snot ran out of his nose.

Sister hugged him and assured him he was not going to hell. If anyone committed a sin, "It was me," she said. She held Heiny by the arms. "You did not commit a sin. You are not going to hell."

The front of Sister's chest was wet with tears and shiny with snot and brown from dust.

The end of recess bell rang.

Sister said, "Go back to the classroom. I have to change. I will be there as soon as I can. Be very quiet. Understand?"

I understood.

Sister Superior!

I spun around. Sister Superior was not there on the sidewalk at the end of the school. *Phew! She didn't see Little Heiny commit a mortal sin.*

But, it turned out, Sister Superior had seen it and heard what went on after. She took Little Heiny to the rectory and made him go to confession right away. Sister Daniels didn't come back to teach us. Ever. Sister Superior sent her away and even got her booted out of being a nun.

The only nice nun I ever knew. Actually, I had two aunt nuns. One of them was nice.

Losing Sister Mary Daniels stunk to high heaven, though. And it didn't seem fair. Little Heiny had committed the mortal sin by getting under Sister's dress.

What happened was when Little Heiny saw Sister cut to the far side of Large Louie, he hustled to cut her off. He came shooting out from behind Large Louie and ran smack into Sister's legs. She went down, and they rolled, and he wound up under there.

Walking home that night, he reported to Jimmie Joe and me that she wore black stockings that went all the way up.

Clarence Fenstermacher, an eighth-grader, heard us, and said, "Yeah. Nuns wear stockings but they don't wear underwear."

Jimmie Joe said, "You don't know what you're talking about."

"I do know. They wear nunderwear."

Clarence thought it was the funniest thing.

Sister Mary Daniels was gone. Not one stinking thing about that was funny.

When Sister went down, according to Jimmie Joe, she fell hard and didn't fumble. There was a lot to admire about Sister Mary Daniel.

And even more to miss. For me, she'd become Necessary Nun.

3

A big thing happened the summer before sixth grade. We moved into our own house.

Building our new house took all of fifth grade. Once the foundation was poured, the outside walls and roof were done, Pop did a lot of the inside work himself. When he had the kitchen, front room, and two bedrooms done, we moved in. He still had to finish the upstairs. After he put in a full day at the grain elevator, he laid the wood floors, hung sheetrock, taped the seams, and mudded over the tape. I asked him if I could help.

"You really want to help," he said with a couple of flooring nails between his lips.

"Yeah, Pop, yeah!"

"Then don't help."

Mama said, "Now, Eddie, don't feel bad. Pop only has so many hours to work on the house, and he doesn't have time to teach you how to drive a flooring nail."

"Okay," I said and went outside. Living on that end of town, I could always find somebody to play with.

In the new house, Lennie and I shared a bed, the same as in the old place. Our almost two-year-old brother Bobbie had a crib in Mom and Pop's room, the same as in the old house. The new thing we had was half an in-house. We still had to go to the outhouse for that business, but we had a sink and bathtub in the little room next to our bedroom. You could run warm water into the tub from a faucet right on the wall. No more lugging in heavy buckets of water from the well and Mama heating it on the stove and then dumping it in the washtub so we could take a bath in the kitchen. We had a room for that now, just like the rich Grossmans had. And like the Grossman's bathroom, ours had a door on it, too. Pop was going to put a toilet in, but that had to wait while he finished the attic. He didn't say why he was finishing the attic.

Then Ronnie got born. That was a big thing, too. Bobbie got our room. Lennie and I got booted into the attic. The new kid made my life harder, too. With him around, Mama needed help, and I had to give it. Lennie didn't. If he did a chore, Mama had to do it over. Or I did.

All of that summer, I worked mornings for Mama. Doing girl work. In the afternoons, Mama let me be a boy. I wouldn't have minded working mornings if I could have done boy work. You know, like chopping down a tree or something.

Six days a week, Mama was the boss of mornings. God was the boss of Sunday morning.

I used to grumble when Mama set me to sweeping and mopping and dusting and washing and drying dishes. I really grumbled at changing Bobby's wet diapers. I thought that was the worst job. Then she told me I had to do a dirty one.

"If you puke," she said, "you'll have to clean that up, too."

I hated being a girl in the morning. Especially living on that end of town where all the other boys lived. Often, they played in our neighbor Jimmie Joe Meinerschlagen's side yard. It sure sounded like they were having fun. One morning, I opened the bathroom window and hollered, "Hey!" They stopped yammering and looked at me.

"You want to have some real fun," I said, "come in and I'll let you help me with this really fun job I'm doing."

Sam Waterman was a year older than me. He had an older sister who was in high school. He also had a baby brother. Sam said to the others, "You smell that? Bleach. He's dealing with a dirty diaper," and to me, "You ain't gonna Tom Sawyer us, Eddie Walsh."

Their jabbering cranked up again.

Rats.

Who's Tom Sawyer?

Nobody in town or on the farms around had that name. In the meantime, there was the diaper, and poopy diaper bucket and the first bucket of bleach water for rinsing and the second for soaking—and being boss of my stomach. It wanted to puke, but I gritted my teeth and my stomach.

In the afternoon, I was a boy again. And not just a boy, I was Boss of Afternoons. Being boss of all day would have been better, but as soon as I started being boss of afternoons, I forgot about being boss of morning baby poop.

After lunch, when us town boys gathered and started figuring out what we were going to do, ideas came winging in like a baseball game where there was one batter and five pitchers. Baseball, fishing, gigging frogs, swim. I'd listen a minute and say, "Fishing."

"Where?" someone would say. "Up the creek?"

"No. Down," from another.

"Up the creek," I'd say, and no one ever argued my decision.

Being the boss of afternoons made up for being a girl in the mornings. Mostly.

If Mama hadn't made me eat lunch, I'd have skipped it and joined the boys outside that much sooner. But lunch didn't take long, even with Mama harping at me.

"Slow down. Chew your food. Don't drink your milk with a mouthful of food. Ach! Half chewed bread floating on the top!"

When I got outside, the afternoon of Tom-Sawyer morning, I asked who that guy was.

Sam Waterman wasn't there, but the Grossman kid knew. He had books. Real books, not just comics. Tom Sawyer was in one of them.

"Show us," I said.

I didn't call Simon Grossman by his first name because he didn't do much with us ruffians. That's what his mother called us. She wouldn't let him swim or fish. Simon might drown or get a disease from the creek or get his eye jerked out on a fishhook. Simon didn't play football, and baseball not much. He was almost as bad at baseball as Large Louie. Grounders rolled between his legs and he missed fly balls. At least the fly balls didn't bounce off his forehead, but he couldn't hit worth a hoot. And most times, after he muffed a grounder or struck out, he'd quit and go home.

Anyway, the Grossman kid led us to his back porch. There were eight of us. We had to take our shoes off before we could go in. We trooped in through the kitchen and upstairs to his bedroom. His bedroom made my mouth hang open. It was as big as half our attic. Our attic was one big open space, but Lennie and I didn't use much of it. We had a bed, a table and chair, and a chest of drawers. Simon had those, too, plus a goldfish in a bowl and a hamster in a cage. Books filled the shelves of a giant bookcase. And his stuff looked fancy.

"Your mouth's hanging open," Jimmie Joe said and giggled.

"You giggle like a girl," I said.

"Yeah, but I don't work like a girl all morning."

My face got hot and I shut up.

Simon pulled a book from a shelf, flipped through some pages, and read us the part where Tom Sawyer bamboozled other kids into painting a fence for him. When he finished reading, he looked at me. I don't know what he expected me to say.

The whole thing hadn't taken much time at all. We still had the whole afternoon.

"Swimmin'," I said.

"Yeah!" from everyone. Not Simon. He stayed there sitting on his bed with the book in his lap as we sock-footed it down the stairs and put our shoes back on and got our bikes and pedaled like crazy through town, across the bridge over Verruckt Frau Creek, to where the road crossed the railroad tracks.

We dumped our bikes in the ditch beside the

road and walked down the embankment next to the tracks to get to our swimming hole.

Many years earlier, a train had derailed and dumped a half dozen concrete pillars on the side of the creek bank. A perfect spot for a swimming hole. You could get out of the water on those pillars and not have to stick muddy feet in your socks.

That day I decided we'd have a who-can-swim-the-farthest-underwater contest. The water in the creek was, well, you couldn't see through it. It was pretty much the color of one of Bobbie's diapers after Mama fed him Gerber's strained spinach. The water didn't taste bad, though.

I won the contest like I usually did. The other guys seemed to be happy if they came in second. On my winning run, I could have gone farther except I ran into the jagged rusty remnant of the railcar that had carried the pillars. I got a cut on my chest. It bled a little. It didn't hurt much, not like getting punched in the mouth by Large Louie.

Afterwards, as we dressed, we talked about the wreck that flung that car the length of a football field. It would have been so cool to have seen that train wreck.

"Soooooooooo cool!" Jimmie Joe agreed.

When I got home, Mama screeched. The

right side of my tee-shirt was bloody. She wanted to know what happened.

"Ach! You did this to yourself swimming in *Verrucht Frau* creek!"

Mama packed up Bobbie and Ronnie, hustled Lennie and me ahead of her, and stuffed us all into the Plymouth, and she drove us to the doctor. Where I got a couple of shots and some stitches.

The doctor said, "They should change the name from Crazy Woman Creek to Crazy Boy Creek."

But let me tell you, I got the neatest scar next to the little round brown thing on the right side of my chest. Jimmie Joe measured it with a ruler. Four and one-fourth inches long. If I hadn't already been the boss of summer afternoons, that scar would have made me it for sure.

The attic in the summer was hotter than blazes. We slept on top of the bedding in nothing but tighties and still sweated the sheets sopping wet. Fall was getting close, though, and it got half ways pleasant in the attic.

In winter, it was cold as all get out. We wore flannel jammies and socks to bed and had ten blankets and quilts over us and let nothing but our noses stick out from under the covers. Lennie said we were like Tarzan in the summer, wearing nothing but leather underpants, and in the winter, we were Eskimos. We sure appreciated fall.

Bobbie had a little potty seat in the in-house. So, I didn't have so many of his dirty diapers to deal with, but little Ronnie made sure the poop kept coming.

Pop put the toilet in the in-house. That was cool. No more flashlight trips to the outhouse, but the biggest deal with that was it was so much easier dealing with dirty diapers.

But school was starting, and I could stop being a girl in the mornings. Stop with the dusting, sweeping, mopping, washing dishes, hanging clothes on the line, and cleaning the in-house. And stop with the diapers.

That's what I thought.

B

The first day of school started badly. Sister Superior didn't seat us in alphabetical order. She plonked me in Alice Ashe's seat, the first one in the sixth-grade row. I, Eddie Walsh, did not feel special to get the desk closest to Sister. The first day of class last year came to mind. I'd gotten a no-recess-for-a-week punishment for dropping my bat. On an accident. From Sister S. SS. Like a snake hiss.

Eddie Walsh, do not smile! Do not say a word. Do not ask a question. Sit on your hands so one of them doesn't shoot up. Become the Invisible Man, well, Boy.

"Young men and young women of sixth grade," SS began.

I thought this was strange. Why didn't she say, "Boys and girls?"

"By the time you enter *My* classroom, you are expected to have learned how to behave responsibly. Unfortunately, last year, your discipline declined instead of improving."

That wasn't how I looked at it. SS booted Sister Mary Daniels, not only out of our school, but out of the convent as well. That's what Alice Ashe said happened. Then SS brought Sister House Nun in to teach us. Most of us, and I'm talking boys *and* girls, had really, really liked Sister Daniels, and we took it out on Sister House Nun. Sister House Nun lasted two days before she left. Again, according to Alice, Sister House Nun had a nervous breakdown and returned to the convent. Which made Sister Superior even madder at us, because she had to teach two classrooms instead of one. Even Sister Everest, the first and second-grade teacher, was mad at us. Besides teaching, she had to take over Sister House Nun's job.

SS stood on the edge of the raised platform with her hands up opposite sleeves, and she went on about the importance of discipline. She looked big and sort of like a talking statue. Only her lips moved. And her eyes. It made me squirm when those eyes lit on me.

"Last year," SS said, "*You* gave Sister Bartholomew ..."

Sister House Nun. I always forgot she had a regular nun name.

"... a nervous breakdown. She is still receiving psychiatric treatment."

I pulled my dictionary from my bookbag. Sister Mary Daniels had given it to me so I wouldn't stick my hand up every time I heard a word I didn't understand.

"It means she's in the loony bin." Seated behind me, Jimmie Joe Meinerschlagen whispered.

"Silence!" Sister Superior stomped down next to me, whipped a ruler out of her sleeve, and smacked it down hard on the edge of Jimmie Joe's desk. The ruler broke in half and the broke half flew up and hit me behind the head, and I said, "Ow."

I thought SS had been as mad as she could get, but she had a higher gear to shift into.

Sister stood Jimmie Joe in one front corner of the room and parked me in the other.

For the sixth grade, the most important thing for us to learn was discipline. Discipline was the pathway to heaven. Discipline was the pathway to learning and to the blessings God has placed on earth for us.

Sister went on about discipline, and she whacked the top of her desk—since Jimmie Joe broke her ruler, she confiscated his—to emphasize a point now and then. It also seemed like a promise of what was going to happen to our knuckles. The way she acted and sounded, I wouldn't have been surprised to see her whack a girl's knuckles.

It was a relief when it was time to march to church for Mass. Sister kept Jimmie Joe and me next to her. Large Louie was right in front of her.

The whole sidewalk from church to school was filled with kids shuffling along. Eighth-grade girls walked beside the lower grades and hissed at them if they spoke.

Last year, when we filed to church, I went along with the stream of kids; I don't know, happy; I guess. But after Sister Daniels left, I went back to dragging my feet.

Once Mama asked me, "Why do the heels of *your* shoes wear out so fast. Lennie's don't."

"I don't know," I said, which was the best answer to most questions. Except I wondered if it would work this year with Sister Superior.

There was another surprise after Mass. SS moved Large Louie to the first seat in the seventh-grade row.

"This year, Louis." SS pointed Knuckle Whacker at him. "You will learn enough to graduate from first grade, or you will not be allowed to return to school next year."

Now Louie was a hard kid to teach. I can tell you that from when I tried to teach him how to play baseball in third grade. Batting for instance.

"You gotta keep your eyes open when you swing at a pitch," I told him.

So, he kept his eyes open and flung the bat clear out to center field. It was like he could remember one thing but not two. Keep your eyes open AND hold the bat tight.

Sister Superior had her work cut out for her. Which I thought might be a good thing. She'd be paying so much attention to Large Louie, she wouldn't have time to worry about me.

"And you, Eddie Walsh!"

Uh oh.

"The first half of last year, your grades went from the eighties to nineties."

"That's because Sister Daniels was the best teacher I ever had," I told her.

Sister flew at me like a hawk after a baby rabbit. "Give me your hand."

"You." *Whack.*

I grimaced and gritted my teeth.

"Will never mention." *Whack.* "That woman's name." *Whack.* "Again." *Whack.*

I tried real hard to not let her know her ruler hurt me, but I could feel my lips twitching around some. My eyes wanted to cry, but I wouldn't let them.

Sister stepped back. So she could glare at me better, I thought. I didn't know why she hated Sister Daniels, but she surely did. And that made me, mad and I glared right back.

SS whacked the front of my desk, and like before, the ruler broke and the broke part flew up, bounced off the ceiling, and then onto Sister's head before clattering onto the floor.

I went from mad to scared as all get out.

Everybody else must have been scared too. It got real quiet. I didn't breathe cause it would make noise.

Sister stood still, too. Only her eyes roved over the classes. She made me think of a cat watching several mice, and just waiting for the first one to move. I wasn't going to move. If one of them did, maybe Sister would stop picking on me.

Finally, SS stepped up onto the platform and went to the blackboard.

With her back turned, I breathed. I was sure glad we'd had all those swim-underwater contests in Verrukt Frau Creek in the summers.

Sister wrote assignments for all three of her classes; then she said, "Eddie Walsh, come with me."

Sister Superior marched me to the rectory and inside the parlor. There was a phone on a little table next to a big chair. Sister sat and called Mama.

"Your Eddie needs disciplining. He sassed me. Lennie behaves himself. Eddie needs to be like him. Mrs. Walsh, unless you teach your boy to respect my authority as a teacher, I will not have him in my classroom. I am sending him home. Straighten him out and you can send him back to school tomorrow. With a note. Do you understand what I require?"

Sister hung up and glared at me. "Go home."

I just stared at her. Nobody in my five years in school had ever been sent home. Unless they were sick. Not even Large Louie.

"Close your mouth, Eddie Walsh. And go home!"

Outside, I trudged down the sidewalk toward the bike rack, and I wondered, *How the heck did it happen? How did Lennie get to be the good Walsh kid and me the bad?*

What I should have wondered about was how would I handle a bad day turning into a really bad day.

C

As I went home, I pushed my bike instead of riding it. I wasn't in any kind of hurry to get there.

Some of the boys I played with told of the thing they dreaded most, which was their mamas saying, "Just you wait till your father gets home."

Mama never said that. When there was punishment handed out, there wasn't any waiting.

As best as I could remember, I hadn't been spanked since last year. When we still lived in the old house, but after Sister Superior called Mama, a spanking was sure as the sun rising over St. Louis every morning.

What happened last year, Lennie and I had gone into the chicken house and gathered up an armload of eggs. Lennie got on one side of the chicken yard, me on the other, and we took turns throwing eggs at each other. Lennie couldn't throw as hard as me, and I dodged his cackle-berries easily. But I had nailed him three times and was about to get him again when Mama walked out the back door.

She cut loose with the loudest Eddie-Lennie screech ever and hollered for us to get out of the chicken pen and wait by the cistern until she got finished. Finished with her visit to the outhouse. Of course, she didn't holler that.

Rats! I still had two eggs left.

We waited on the grass, me clean, Lennie dripping yolk and white's slime from his shirt and pants onto his tennis shoes.

Mama came stomping down the brick walk and passed us to get to the washstand. She always put clean water in the basin. This time she didn't, just used the old. But she used soap.

She dried her hands and looked at Lennie and said, "Ach!" and told Lennie to take off his shoes and clothes. So, Lennie stood there in socks and tighties. In the backyard! Where people might see.

Apparently, Mama wasn't worried about what people would think. I was pretty sure Mama thought our behavior was egregious. I hadn't had an opportunity to use that word since I learned about the N-word in first grade. Sometimes I learned a new word, but then forgot it and had to look it up again. Egregious, however, stuck in my brain like a cocklebur to a pants leg.

Anyway, Mama administered a six-smack to Lennie. Spankings on tighties sounded different from ones on blue jeans. Lennie, as usual, didn't let out a peep.

"Go in the kitchen and wait for me. You need a bath," Mama told Lennie.

Then she looked at me. "You're the oldest. You should keep your younger brother from getting into trouble, not lead him into it. Bend over."

I did and put my hands on my knees. Mama whapped away at my butt. I counted. The way the whaps came, the sting from one hadn't totally gone away before the next whap landed. Always before, I was crying by whap number three. But that day, I got through three and all the way to six, and I hadn't cried. I stood up and Mama said, "We are not done, yet. Bend over."

So I did, and she went back to whapping.

I was glad I wasn't Jimmie Joe Meisenheimer. His mama used a ping-pong paddle to spank him.

By whap number ten, the stinging from back there was getting close to egregious bad, but I hadn't started crying, and I was determined to tough it out. How many whaps could she give me?

An even dozen, actually.

"Okay," she said. "Your brother needs a bath. Bring in two buckets of water."

I stood up and rubbed my butt and sort of snickered or giggled. Mama couldn't hurt me with a spanking. This was a major turning point. Mama couldn't hurt me with a spanking.

Her face clouded over. "Eddie Walsh! Turn right around. Drop your pants and bend over."

I did, and with the first smack, I started crying. I didn't even count them, but when she finished, I had snot running out my nose and into my mouth and I was crying like nobody's business.

"Pull your pants up and blow your nose. Use your handkerchief."

She always said, "Use your handkerchief," even though it had been a couple of years ago when she caught me teaching Lennie how to pinch your nostrils together just a little and huffing air out your nose and blowing buggers and snot onto the ground.

I pulled up my pants, dug out the handkerchief, and as I honked into it, I saw Mrs. Hemsath's poodle, Dolly, looking up at me with its stupid pink tongue hanging out and wagging its stupid butt.

Dolly was old and died a couple of weeks later. I've always figured that dumb dog died happy after seeing me get a pants-down spanking in the backyard.

I was thinking about all these things as I walked my bike home, out in the road a bit, not right on the edge. I kind of hoped I'd get run over and hurt sort of bad, so maybe Mama wouldn't want to spank me.

I didn't get run over, but I got hollered at, and a couple of times, which if I said those words in Mama's hearing, would get my mouth washed out with soap. To this day, as I'm pushing eighty, I hear a cuss word, and my tongue vividly remembers the taste of lye soap from when I repeated a four-letter word, one a lot worse than ain't, I'd heard Tommie Elginfritz say when I was in third grade.

Oh, I was going to get spanked, but I wondered about whether or not I *should*. Sister said I'd sassed her. All I said was Sister Daniels was a good teacher. I thought she was. Didn't my grades show she was? Heck, she even got Large Louie a little interested in learning.

Oh, I was going to get spanked all right. But, *It wasn't FAIR!*

At home, l leaned my bike against the side of the garage and went into the house.

There was Mama, waiting on me. While I'd dawdled and dragged my feet and even took baby steps for a while, all I'd done was give her more time to get mad.

"It's all over town," she said. "You sassed

Sister Superior. Everyone thinks I'm the worst mother in St. Ambrose!"

Our phone was on a stupid party line. Shoot! When I was in first grade and sent Mama to hell, it got all over town in a day. Now, thanks to the stupid phone, things got all over town like greased lightning.

"Turn around," she said. "Drop your pants and bend over."

I thought I was ready for the first one, but it smarted sharp and stinging, and I let out an, "Uh."

I gritted my teeth and found that notion I'd had: *It isn't fair,* and I hung onto it.

Smack. Not fair! Smack. Not fair! Smack. Not fair! SMACK!!

It was the hardest smack so far, and she said, "Oh!"

Turned out she'd broken a bone in her hand.

D

Mama made me ride my bike to the Farmer's Co-op Elevator where Pop worked. She wasn't about to call there. Pop worked a block away from the main office in a really tall building next to the railroad tracks and without a phone.

"Someone from the office would have to stop what they're doing to go down and get Pop," she said.

The Walshes did not like to put people out. Also, I was pretty sure Mama didn't want to give the party-line busybodies anything else to talk about that day.

So, Pop took Mama to the doctor in St. Charles. They were gone for three hours. I babysat my two youngest brothers. While they were gone, one-year-old Ronnie had two dirty diapers and three-year-old Bobbie did number two in his potty chair. How was it possible two little kids could produce so much poop?

Hurry up and get home. I thought that had been pretty close to a prayer.

Well, they did get home, but that prayer was not answered because I was not done with baby poop, not by a long shot. Mama walked in the door with a cast on her right hand. I sure hoped that spanking that got interrupted didn't need to be finished with a concrete glove on her spanking hand.

Pop came in behind her and got right up close to me and bent over and spoke in my face. "Whatever your mama needs doin', you do it." It was all said in that I-don't-like-to-say-a-thing-twice tone of voice. Then he went back to work. I was already there. Besides baby poop, there was dinner to prepare, so the babies could make more poop.

Mama took me down to the basement and had me dig a roast out of the freezer. She thought we should fix something we could eat off of for a spell. I had to put that out in the sun to thaw. Then she had me pick peas and hull them, pull carrots, clean, and slice them. I liked peas and carrots, but they tasted a lot better when I didn't have to do all the work cooking them. The same with the pot roast.

While I cooked supper, Mama fussed at me continuously. She was like Sister Superior with only one student to pick on.

"Check on the roast. Open the oven door.

Now use the hot pads and slide the rack out of the oven. Ach. Careful you don't burn yourself. It won't do to have two of us crippled up."

So, I lifted the lid off the heavy black iron pot so Mama could see and smell what was happening in there.

"Good. Now put the lid back on and slide the rack back in. Ach. Be careful. Do things slowly. You get in a rush and you will ruin the dinner and burn yourself."

I had no trouble understanding ruining dinner would be the biggest sin.

The whole afternoon was cooking and diapers, except for dusting the furniture in the living room. Once I got the roast in the oven, my at-home Sister Superior set me to doing that.

"Ach. You're always in such a hurry. Slow down. You can't dust by giving everything a lick and a promise. Wipe down every inch of the end table. Every inch, *verstehe?*"

I *verstehed* that all right. What I hadn't *verstehed* was how much work it was to be a mama. I thought man-work was hard and woman-work was easy. By supper time, I would have traded two full days of man-work to get out of an hour of woman-work. But who could I trade with?

And, of course, cleaning up after was more work than fixing supper. Did Lennie the plate-dropper have to help? He did not. He lit out and played until dark.

Finally, the dishes were stacked in the cabinet and the silverware in the drawer, and I thought I was done. I wasn't. Mama sat me at the very clean table and had me write her letter to Sister Superior.

Mama said, "Write 'Dear Sister Superior'."

"That's called the salutation."

"Don't be a smarty pants. Just write what I tell you. Now write, 'I am sorry for my son's bad behavior'."

I said, "I think 'egregious behavior' would say it better."

"Ach! Just write what I tell you."

Sometimes Mama didn't like to say a thing twice either.

After we had the letter in an envelope and the envelope in my bookbag, we, Mama and me, got the little poopers to bed. Then, I thought, I'm done for the day, but Mama told me Pop wanted to talk to me. He was in the living room reading the paper. I expected him to look up and say, "Don't sass Sister Superior," and go back to reading. Instead, he folded the *Post-Dispatch* and put it aside.

"Boy, learning everything you can from a teacher is almighty important. Whether you like the teacher or not doesn't amount to a hill of beans. You got good grades in the first half of last year. You best get good grades from now on."

Four sentences. Most times he spoke one. "Go to the outhouse." Sometimes two. "You come home bleeding, you vex your momma. Do not vex your momma."

Pop didn't talk to me much, but the things he said, they stuck. Kind of like that word egregious.

E

"Get up."

Pop's voice came to me like I was at the bottom of a well full of sleep.

"Get up, I said."

My eyes popped open to see Ruprecht hovering over me. My heart started hammering. Then, in the dim from my night light, I saw it was Pop, and he was getting ready to say it a third time.

I flung back the quilt and swung my legs over the side. Lennie moaned and pulled the covers back around him. Pop went downstairs. I hustled into my clothes and followed.

Pop went into the in-house, which is where I wanted to go, but Mama had me wash my hands at the kitchen sink. She told me how to make coffee and how to fry bacon. Pop came out and took his chair at the table. I poured him a cup of coffee. Then Mama said I could use the in-house.

When I finished there, Mama stood beside me and told me how to fry eggs and potatoes in the bacon grease. She put toast in the toaster with her left hand, then she sat at the table and I waited on Pop and her. I had to butter her toast. When they both had plates in front of them, I got to sit down.

Since I'd made the coffee, I decided I deserved some, too. Without asking, I poured myself a cup. Pop put milk in his. Besides milk, Mama dumped a spoonful of sugar in hers. I watched them drink their light brown stuff: then I looked at the nasty black stuff in my cup. Black is how Uncle Ed used to drink his. I decided the more you put into your coffee, the bigger sissy you were. I needed to be as tough as Pop in something, because so far, that morning was the most girl morning I'd ever had, and it wasn't even started for Lennie the Loafer yet. I would drink my coffee black. I lifted my cup and sniffed it. Sure smelled good. I sipped. *Huh.* Not bad. It didn't taste quite as good as it smelled, but it wasn't bad. And it made me as tough as Pop in this one little way. I couldn't think I was tougher. Even in the one little way. And I thought I wasn't a total girl. I was a boy, even if it was just in that one little way.

Pop left for work. Lennie the Loafer came down for breakfast and the Little Poopers woke up. Mama put cereal on the table for Lennie, and I helped Big Little Pooper do his business on his potty chair. Then I dumped it and flushed his doings away. When I was a boy, I appreciated the in-house a little bit. When I was a girl, I appreciated it a big bit. After helping him get up on the step stool and wash and dry his hands, he went to eat cereal in his highchair, which Lennie helped Bobbie into. *Big Whoop! Lennie the Loafer did something useful.*

Meanwhile, I was taking care of yowling his head off Little Little Pooper. By the time I was finished with him, Lennie had left for school. Mama took Ronnie into the bedroom and closed the door and he finally quit caterwauling.

It was probably a sin to think about this, but I tried to imagine Mama dealing with Little Squirmer with one hand in a concrete glove. I mean she had to undo her dress, drag out her built-in baby bottle, and get Little-Mr.-Frantic convinced that what he was yowling about was right there in his mouth if he'd just stop yowling for one second. Which he did. Finally.

After I finished washing and drying the dishes, I could leave for school. I pedaled like crazy, leaned my bike against the side of Grossman's steeple, and hustled inside and into the pew behind Sister Superior. She spun around and grabbed my arm and pulled me into her pew just before the bell jangled and servers and the priest came out from the sacristy and kicked off Mass.

After church is when I found out sixth grade kicked school into a whole new gear.

Grades one to five had been like in low gear on Simon Grossman's ten-speed bike. Sixth took us directly from first to tenth gear. As hard as peddling was when you shifted like that, that's how hard school was.

Simon sold rides for a penny. I asked Mama for one right after I dealt with a dirty diaper.

"Ach! Money does not grow on trees." But then she put her hands on her hips and said a littler *ach* than the first one. "You're a big help. You're a good boy."

I almost said *ach*. Finally, I was a good boy again. It took six years and rinsing a million dirty diapers to get back to where I began. Plus, I earned a penny. Which I spent riding Simon's bike. Which was really neat in first and second gears. Then, when I shifted into third, my stupid pant's leg got caught in the chain. I'd been so excited about riding that bike, I forget about rolling up my blue jeans on the chain side.

When we got the chain back on the sprocket, I told Simon my ride wasn't over.

"Yes, it is over, Eddie Walsh, and you will never ride it again."

Which made me determined to buy my own bike. If I earned one penny every six years, I wondered how long it would take to be able to buy my own. I didn't know how much it cost. It could be ten dollars. So one penny every six years, I'd be six hundred when I had a dollar saved up. And six thousand at bike-buying time. Which was going to be a problem. Those guys back when the Bible began, some of them lived to be hundreds of years old, but I didn't think any of them made it to a thousand. Much less six thousand.

I never got to tenth gear on Simon's bike, but Jimmie Joe Meinerschlagen did. He spent two pennies one day, and on his second ride, he tried going from first to tenth gear directly. He wanted to spend more time going really fast, but it turned out it was so hard to pedal in tenth before he built up some speed, he never did get going really fast.

Thanks to Jimmie Joe, I knew how hard sixth grade was compared to fifth.

What made it hard was the new subjects we had: History, Civics, Algebra. Algebra, where you added, subtracted, multiplied, and divided letters instead of numbers. Whoever heard of such a fool thing? On top of that, all the books were bigger and heavier than fifth-grade books. Pop had told me I best get good grades from now on. *Poop!*

To make matters even worse, Little Heiny Stiert, a grade behind me, gave me a nickname:

Eddie Iron Butt. Then when he found out I changed diapers in the morning before school, rode my bike home during the morning go-to-the-toilet recess to change another diaper, and had to skip noon recess all together to help Mama with the Little Poopers, he changed the name to Eddie-that-didee-ain't-whitey. My hands being red from being in bleach water all the time didn't help, either. Near the end of the first week, Heiny told Large Louie that all the girls in the whole school wanted to marry me. I'd take care of the house and the diapers, and they'd get a job.

Large Louie liked to tell that and say, "That's funny!"

It was a heck of a first week. After all the diapers and other girl work in the evenings, I had little time to study, but I stayed up an hour later than usual to get the homework done. I also figured out how to get some work out of Lennie. I had him help with the dishes, and told him if he dropped a dish, I'd tell Heiny Stiert that he, Lennie, was now the diaper changer in the Walsh house. My clumsy klutz brother became a half-ways decent girl. Mama even left the after-supper clean-up to us, and she went into the living room and sat with Pop.

On Sunday, a miracle happened.

Pop drove us all to St. Charles to visit Uncle John and Aunt Beatrice. We had an early supper with them. Then we watched "George Burns and Gracie Allen" on their TV. It was cool to see things happen and hear it, like over a radio, even if the screen was way small and the whole thing is a great big box. It was sure a far cry from the Dick Tracy wrist TV I'd read in the funny papers when I was a little kid. When we went home, we brought Lucinda with us. Lucinda was the oldest cousin. She had finished high school and wanted to be a nun. Uncle John said she had to wait a year, get a job and see a bit of how the world worked before she could go to the convent. He wanted her to be sure, really sure. He didn't want her to get in the convent, then decide she didn't like it and quit. Walshes were not quitters.

But Uncle John let her quit her job in a dress shop for two weeks to help Mama.

Which for me was just in time. I had almost forgotten how to be a boy.

Lucinda took over Bobbie's room. He slept on the sofa in the living room.

My cousin also took over diapers. And cooking. And cleaning. And gathering eggs and vegetables.

I liked my cousin Lucinda even more than I liked Sister Mary Daniels. Having her helping Mama, I could play baseball at recess. Of course, in my first recess ball game, I caught all kinds of ribbing from Little Heiny and Large Louie lobbing, "That's funny," at me.

I had Sam Waterman, a seventh-grader pitch for my team. He was good. We got Jimmie Joe's team out: one, two, three.

Jimmie Joe was a good pitcher, too. The first two batters on my team made outs. Then I came up. Little Heiny from his shortstop position hollered, "He's a girl. He can't hit. Strike him out. Girl batter, girl batter, girl batter."

Jimmie Joe's first two pitches were over the inside part of the plate strikes, but I knew how Jimmie Joe thought. Two inside pitches, then he'd fire one outside off the plate, a ball. Sure enough, his next pitch was outside, and I stepped on the plate and swung with *girl-batter* fury and smacked a towering drive to right field. I dropped the bat and started trotting to first as I watched Large Louie. With his mouth hanging open, he followed the ball up to right above him. I hoped he'd fall over backward. That would have been funny. But he turned around and watched the ball until it landed. In the meantime, everyone on Jimmie Joe's team was screaming at him to run after the ball. Once it landed, he lumbered after it, but long before he would have retrieved it, Ollie Weisendinger got the ball as I rounded third, so I cranked it up into a run, and easily beat the throw.

In my next at-bat, I smacked another homer to left this time.

The third time, I faced Jimmie Joe from the batter's box; he fired a beanball at me, and I flopped onto the dirt to duck it. I was mad before about being a girl and being called one. Now I was really mad. As I dusted myself off, I glared at JJ, and he glared right back at me. I considered swinging at his next pitch and letting the bat go sailing right at him, but then I decided another homer would hurt him more. I felt my face smile and saw him get madder. His next pitch nailed me in the back. Stung like blue blazes, but I didn't say, "Ow!"

I said, "Ball two."

"It hit you," Jimmie Joe said. "Take first base."

I stepped back into the batter's box, and said, "It hit me? I didn't feel it. If it hit me, you pitch like a girl. It was a ball. Either throw another pitch or forfeit the game."

He wound up and fired again. And hit me again. Close to the same place. I dropped the bat. Glared at him. Clenched my fists, and I was this close... this close to charging the mound and beating the snot out of him when the end of recess bell rang.

Everybody charged off the field toward school. There were ten minutes for a quick trip to the bathroom and to be in our seats before the second bell. Except for Jimmie Joe and I. We stayed and glared at each other.

I heard a *clap, clap!*

Sister Superior stood on the sidewalk that ran from the rectory to the sacristy of the church. She spun on her heel and charged off toward school.

The bat lay on the ground next to my feet. So did the ball. I picked up the bat and headed for school.

At afternoon go-to-the-bathroom recess, Ollie Weisendinger wanted to see my back. I let him lift my shirt and disclose two close-together, softball-sized purple blobs. It would have been cool if those blobs could have turned into scars, like the one next to my right nipple, but they were enough to make me a boy again.

When the end-of-school bell rang, Sister Superior told Jimmie Joe and me to stay in our seats.

We sat and Sister stood by her desk and waited for the stampede noises to die out. Then she placed a book on both of our desks. *World History.* In sixth grade, we studied *American History.* In seventh and eighth, we did the world.

"I marked some pages off with paper clips," she said. "Read those pages tonight. Then think about the end of your baseball game this afternoon. Think hard. Then write a one-page paper about your conclusions."

Then Sister stepped back and looked from one to the other of us.

I was thinking, *Well, okay. Is that it, Sister? There's Little League practice tonight, and this will be the first one I could go to. I missed all of last week because of the Little Poopers and Mama's broken hand.*

"Jimmie Joe," Sister said. "About the ball game at recess, anything you want to say to Eddie?"

Jimmie Joe squirmed in his seat and cast his eyes from side-to-side. It was like he was in a dark room and Sister's eyes were like a flashlight shining right on him and he couldn't get away from the light.

"I'm sorry I hit you."

"You're sorry once when you hit me twice. What about the first time you hit me?"

"I'm sorry I hit you twice."

Sister said, "Eddie." Like I should be sorry for something also.

We were wasting Little League practice time. "I'm sorry I was going to hit a third home off you."

"Eddie." Sister's tone of voice told me I'd swung at a pitch and missed. But I'd held onto the bat.

"I'm sorry I got so mad at you I could spit."

Sister nodded. "The last part of the paper, I

want you to write down the sins you committed on the playground at recess today. You can go."

We went.

Most of the time going home after school, Jimmie Joe and I raced our one-speeds, but that day, I wasn't interested in beating my neighbor at anything. And he and I were on the same Little League team. So, we rode side-by-side, and I told him about my plan to save up for a ten-speed.

"Only thing is," I said, "I haven't saved even one penny yet. I guess that means it will take me six thousand and one years to save enough."

"I bet I can save enough to buy a ten-speed in five thousand nine hundred-ninety-five years," and Jimmie Joe took off pedaling like crazy.

F

That night after Little League practice, my cousin Lucinda placed the plate of supper she'd saved for me on the table. I said the prayer and started eating.

She had black curly hair and a nice face.

I asked her if she got those curls like Mama did from a permanent.

"No. It just grows this way."

"I bet you're glad. That permanent stuff, my Uncle Ed says… used to say, it smells so bad, even cockroaches run away from it."

"I will be happy when I get to the convent and can wear the novitiate habit and cover these curls up."

My fork stopped halfway to my mouth. I wondered if Sister Daniels had curly hair. I asked my cousin, "Why would you want to cover them up? Those curls look nice."

"Eddie, I care about the appearance of my soul. I do not care about my hair or my looks.

And I do not want the appearance of my body to be an occasion of sin for anyone?"

"Occasion of sin means temptation right, and you mean tempting boys?"

"Yes, boys, but girls too. Girls might envy the curls."

"Or your nice face."

Lucinda's nice face always looked kind of cool and kind of warm at the same time, and the little smile she wore, it was like she knew some things nobody else did, and those secret things made her happy. Sort of like a picture I'd seen of the *Mona Lisa*. But now my cousin's smile turned all the way into a Sister Daniels smile.

"God made a beautiful world, and He gave it to us to live in. But, He expected something from us. Do you remember the most important lesson from catechism?"

"I should love The Lord My God with all my heart and all my soul."

"That's right, Eddie."

She put her hand on my arm, and the funniest thing happened to me. It was like she pushed the lever down on the front of the in-house toilet and something warm and wonderful inside me spilled from the top of me all the way down to my toes.

She had brown eyes that were soft and warm

and deep, and for a moment, I thought I was falling into them.

"Sometimes, Eddie, all of us human beings forget that most important lesson, and we let our heart and soul love the things of this world more than we love God. Perhaps that happened to you during your ballgame at recess today."

"Did Lennie tell on me?"

"No. Mrs. Meinerschlagen called your mama and apologized for Jimmie Joe hitting you on purpose, not once but twice."

"That's what Jimmie Joe said before practice. 'I'm sorry for hitting you not once but twice.'"

"What did you say to that?"

"I said I was sorry for hitting three home runs off him. He said, 'You only hit two.' I said I expected you to hit me a third time. After you did, I was going to pick up the ball, toss it up, and smack the third one. 'I was going to and you woulda,' he said."

At practice, Mr. Meinerschlagen—he's our manager—made us shake hands. Since I was the boss of baby poop the first week of practice, all the positions were taken except catcher. So, I was catcher, and Jimmie Joe was the pitcher. We couldn't be mad at each other.

So we weren't.

I told all that to Lucinda.

She said, *"Hmmm!"* And, "You got mad at

Jimmie Joe but then said you were sorry. What about not getting mad in the first place?"

"I wasn't just mad at Jimmie Joe. I was mad at everybody. They teased me about dirty diapers, and they teased me about being a girl." I looked at her and hoped I hadn't hurt her feelings. "I mean, I gotta' think it's neat being a girl if you are one. But I'm a boy. And I never even thought about it until they started teasing me."

"You weren't mad at Jimmie Joe, you were mad at everybody?"

"Jimmie Joe *was* everybody, and sure as shooting, I was mad at him."

That big smile of Lucinda's pushed Mona Lisa aside. "Eddie, it was a blessing for me to come and help your mama."

"And me," I said. "You help me more than you help Mama."

She had her hands together on her lap, and she looked down at them for a moment.

"Can I tell you something, Eddie?"

"You have been telling me stuff."

"So, I have. Thank you for speaking with me as you have. I learned some things about, not only you but myself as well. It will help me be a better teacher after I become a nun. Here's what I learned. I was so sure you had allowed your love for baseball to put your love for God in second place, but that's not the issue at all.

You got mad because the other boys called you a sissy. The lesson for me is, if I am trying to help someone, I have to be careful of my preconceived notions and latching onto the first indication of what the real issue is. That could keep me from discovering the real source of the problem. Do you understand what I'm saying?"

"Sure. It's like Dick Tracy. When he finds a clue, he has to be careful it's a real clue and not one made up by the bad guy to put the blame on a good guy."

"That's not an example I would have used, but it indicates understanding, and that is another lesson for me if I am to become a good teacher. But, I'd like to talk about what the most important lesson for you in all this is. Okay?"

"Sure."

"When the boys called you a sissy, you got mad. Are you a sissy?"

My face got hot. *I was not a sissy! I was the boss of summer afternoons. I had a four and a fourth-inch scar next to my right nipple.*

"Eddie, when people call you a name, it doesn't make you be what they called you."

"So I should say, 'Sticks and stones can break my bones, but words can never hurt me?'"

"The thing is, their words hurt us because we let them. But, the boys calling you a sissy did not make you one. So, there was no reason to get mad at them. And you should not say 'sticks and stones' to them. Don't say anything. Ignore them and they will tire of trying to pester you."

I imagined Little Heiny Stiert calling me a sissy, and Large Louie saying, "That's funny!" but I didn't let it get to me. "Sissy" rolled off me like water off a duck's back. And I just put on a Cousin Lucinda smile.

It would drive Little Heiny crazy. Of course, Large Louie wouldn't have a clue. I hoped Little Heiny would insult me tomorrow so I could ignore him. I almost prayed it would happen.

Lucinda gave me dessert, and she got up to wash my dinner plate and silverware.

"Lucinda,"—I almost called her Sister Lucinda— "will you help me with Algebra when we're done with the dishes? Please?"

Which she did, and the way she did it made sense.

I couldn't understand why anyone would write $A + B = C$ when what you wanted to know was what was $1 + 2$? Why would anyone take such a simple problem and make it hard?

Lucinda said it was meant to serve as a simple, easy-to-understand example, that letters could represent numbers. "Shortly," she said, "you will come to the formula $A^2 + B^2 = C^2$. It applies to the sides of a right triangle. That formula is a rule, and it's always true. "

She drew some right triangles on my pad of paper with a ruler and measured the sides.

Then we used the "A squared" formula, and Holy Cow, it worked!

"You're a heck of a good teacher, Lucinda, and I bet you'll be a nice nun, too. Like Sister Daniels was a good teacher and nice."

"I know about Sister Daniels. She is no longer a nun. She was too worldly."

"Because she smiled instead of wearing a crabby prune face all the time?"

Lucinda sat back in her chair and frowned. For a moment, I thought I hurt her feelings, but that little smile of hers crawled out of her mouth, and she said, "It was wrong of me to judge Sister Daniels. Now, is there anything else you need help with?"

I didn't. I had some American History to read and the assignment from Sister Superior. But that was just reading stories. Ever since Mama taught me to read comics, I liked to read stories.

After seeing all the books Simon Grossman had in his room, I asked him if I could borrow one.

He said. "No. I'll get it back with pages stuck together with dried boogers. If I get it back at all."

Which didn't surprise me that much. All the rest of us kids traded comic books. "I'll give you three of mine for three of yours." But Simon never traded.

Jimmie Joe said Simon got nothing but new comics, and after he read them, he'd rather throw them away than give them to someone else. But I had one more thing to try. The next time I was at Simon's house, his mother was there, and I asked again about borrowing a book.

The look Simon gave me if looks could kill, I'd have been doornail dead. But Mrs. Grossman told Simon he had to let me borrow any book I wanted. That's where I discovered Tarzan. In a set of Simon's books.

Now history wasn't Tarzan by a long shot, but it was still a big book of stories. So, I read the assignment and then answered the list of questions Sister Superior had given us. Now Jimmie Joe and some of the guys took the list of questions and skimmed the reading to find the answers to the questions, but I didn't like to treat a story that way.

And that made me feel like Eddie, the good Walsh boy.

Then I read the World History pages Sister Superior made Jimmie Joe and me read. It was about gladiators in Rome. In Rome, the people went to a coliseum which was like Sportsman's Park in St. Louis, where the Cardinals and the Browns played baseball. Only they didn't go there to see a ball game. They saw people fight with swords and kill each other.

Why did Sister Superior want Jimmie Joe and me to read that? I wasn't trying to kill Jimmie Joe, and he wasn't trying to kill me. I wished I could talk to Lucinda about it all, but downstairs was quiet. I did my reading with a desk lamp on the small table Pop put up there for me to do schoolwork on. Behind me, Lennie slept. I sat there in the light and tried to come up with something to put on the paper that looked back at me like Little Heiny Stiert saying, "Nyah, nyah, nyah! You can't think of a thing to write." Of course, Large Louie appeared and stuck his two words in me like a fishhook.

I managed to get Large and Little out of my head and my cousin in there. My pencil found some words to write.

> The other boys teased me about being a

I almost wrote "girl." Sister Superior might have been a girl once, so I chose another word.

> sissy. I got mad at them and decided to get even by hitting home runs off Jimmie Joe. I didn't have a way to get even with any of the others, but I could get even with Jimmie Joe because he was the pitcher.

I was wrong to get mad. Being called a sissy didn't make me one until I got mad.

I was wronger

Thanks, God, for pencils with erasers. At least some of my mistakes can be made to go away.

I was wrong to take it out on Jimmie Joe. He hadn't called me a sissy. The sin I committed was I did not love my neighbor as myself. I was so mad, I didn't love him at all.

G

The next morning, I woke early expecting to hear Pop's boots clomping up the stairs, but then I remembered Lucinda was here. She would fix breakfast. No need for Pop's clodhoppers to clomp. No need for me to get up yet. I rolled over and thought I'd drop off again, but my eyes didn't want to stay shut. What my eyes wanted to do was for me to get up, go down, and fix breakfast for Lucinda. Well, Pop, too, but Lucinda being with us let me be a boy again. Walshes didn't like to be beholden to people. If I did something nice for my cousin, I wouldn't be holding so much owing to her. That's how Pop talked about being beholden.

Downstairs, the door to the in-house was closed and the one to Lucinda's room was open. I got the coffee and bacon going.

Lucinda entered the kitchen. "Eddie, what are you doing up so early? And you were awake until midnight last night."

The way Pop got heat into the attic, he cut a hole in the floor of the upstairs into Lucinda's bedroom. So, heat from her room came up and light from mine went down.

"Oh. Did the light keep you awake?" That would add to my owing her.

"No. I was saying my prayers and writing in my diary."

"You stayed up late to write in your diary?"

"And say my prayers, but yes. I wanted to write down the details of the talk we had last night. It meant a lot to me. Our discussion. I didn't want to forget any part of it."

She didn't want me to fry eggs for her. It sounded like she thought she was beholden to me. She only wanted cereal. When she told me that, she put her hand on my arm, and that flushing-warm-stuff-inside-me thing happened again.

The night before when I talked with my cousin was the first time I really talked with a girl. I spoke with Mama many times, but she wasn't a girl. She was Mama.

Talking with a girl was sure different from talking with Jimmie Joe Meinerschlagen.

Three baskets sat on the front of Sister Superior's desk, one each for the homework of sixth, seventh, and eighth graders. As soon as I dumped in my homework, Sister snatched it up. She went right to the gladiator paper.

Uh, oh. I remembered sticking words about Sister Mary Daniels in the paper, though I hadn't named her. Now, I wished I'd left her out of what I wrote.

I took my seat and looked up to find Sister staring at me like she didn't recognize me, like maybe I'd talked Lennie into taking my place or something.

Then she smacked her desk with her ruler. "Young ladies and young men, it is time for Mass. Get your hearts and souls ready to visit Jesus in His house. Eddie Walsh, lead the way."

I led over, taking Alice Ashe's job. I couldn't seem to get out of doing girl work. After Mass, Linda Zigmund led us back, and we all filed into the classroom and took our seats in an orderly manner, which pleased Sister Superior. I could tell because she didn't ruler smack her desk or a knuckle.

As soon as we got settled though, Sister told me to gather my things from my desk and to stand in front of her desk. So I did.

"Now," Sister said. "Linda Zigmund and Eddie Walsh stay where you are. The rest of sixth-grade move one desk forward."

Mumbles and commotion started, but not moving forward yet. I stood there facing my classmates, and I would have put a *shhh-ing* finger to my lips, but I had both hands full of books. Sister smacked her desk right behind me. It made me jump, and I dropped my Sister Daniels dictionary.

We're in for it now, my knuckles told me.

The room had gotten real quiet. I turned around and said I was sorry to Sister; then I picked up my book, and I waited for a sure-as-shooting visit from Knuckle Whapper. Boy, were me and my knuckles surprised. Pleasantly.

Sister got us seated—with little commotion and no mumbling—the way she wanted. Jimmie Joe in front, then Alice A. and alphabetic order to me, Eddie W. in front of Linda Z. It felt good to be back where I belonged. Jimmie Joe, and Alice A., I felt sorry for them. A little.

Sister set the three classes to work. Then she asked Large Louie for his homework.

"I forgot to do it."

Which brought silence back for another visit to our classroom. All of us, even Linda Z. behind me, I was sure, watched to see Knuckle Whapper visit Large Louie, but, again, Knuckle Whapper was only Desk Whapper all morning.

Whap, whap!

"Get back to work. All of you."

We did, all of us.

At bathroom recess, Sister asked me to stay

behind a minute. Which squeezed a silent *uh, oh* out of me.

As the others filed out, Sister said, "Your Algebra homework was done very well. All last week, you helped your mother. That didn't leave much time for studying. I understand a cousin of yours is staying with you now to help run the house."

"My cousin Lucinda, Sister. She wants to be a nun. And a teacher. She'll be a good nun and a good teacher. She helped me with Algebra."

"Did your cousin do the homework for you?"

"No, Sister. She explained it to me, and I did the homework."

"You like your cousin, don't you?"

"She's nice."

"All five years you've been at Holy Martyrs School, your grades have been mediocre. Except for the first part of last year. And now your homework from last night. If you like your teacher, you apply yourself. With a teacher you don't like, you don't care if you get good grades or not. Is that right?"

"Uh." I shifted weight from one foot to the other. Neither one seemed to want to hold me up. "That's how I was, Sister, but Pop talked to me. He said I should work hard to learn as much as I can from all my teachers, whether or not I like them."

"You don't like me, but now you're going to study hard, anyway. Is that right?"

Sister stood up on the platform at the front of the room with her hands up her sleeves, looking down at me. Besides hands, Knuckle Whapper was probably up to her sleeve, too. I didn't want to answer that question. I didn't want to answer any more of her questions at all. The more she asked, the more I answered, the more trouble I was in.

The bell rang. End of morning bathroom recess.

"Sister!"

"You can go to the bathroom. Eddie, when you come back, knock on the door before you enter."

"Yes, Sister," and I tore out of there.

If that bell hadn't rung, I was going to tell Sister I *used to not like her.* As I headed down the hallway with everybody else coming the other way, I understood that my answer would have only brought up another question: "And now you do like me?" To stay out of trouble with an answer to that one, I'd have had to lie. And I was sure I would have.

As far as Sister Superior was concerned, me being Eddie, the good Walsh boy didn't amount to a hill of beans.

That afternoon, during sixth-grade Civics Class, Sister told us about the executive, legislative and judicial branches of our government. The founding fathers had established this form because it provided a system of checks and balances within the three branches.

"For instance, if we only had the executive branch… what's another name for the executive branch?"

Alice Ashe's hand, like it always did, shot up, and I raised mine.

"Eddie," Sister said.

"The presidency."

"That's right. Now, Alice, Eddie said the presidency, why didn't he say, 'the president?'"

"Because the president has a staff of advisors and assistants. The term presidency includes all of them as well."

"Jimmie Joe," Sister said. "Give me one example of how the system of checks and balances works."

In his front seat, Jimmie Joe sat up straight. He looked to his left at Large Louie. *As if he'd know the answer.*

Behind me, Linda Zigmund fidgeted and kind of whimpered like she had to visit the bathroom. She was in the last seat and kind of small, and when she wanted to answer a question, she waved her arm and bounced around on her seat.

"Linda," Sister said.

Linda hopped to her feet. "The legislative branch enacts laws. The presidency enforces the laws, but the judicial branch can say that the legislative branch enacted an unconstitutional law, or that the presidency didn't enforce the law properly."

That had been in the reading assignment for last night.

"The judicial branch represents a check and balance on the power of the other two branches. What checks the power of the judicial branch?" Sister asked, "Elmer."

Elmer Elginfritz stood. "The president nominates the names of people he thinks should be judges, but the congress can approve or disapprove them."

That had been in the reading assignment.

Elmer didn't sit down. "I know a place right here in school where we don't have checks and balances and we ought to."

That sure wasn't in the reading assignment, and it sure got quiet.

Sister Superior glared at Elmer, pulled Knuckle Whapper out of her sleeve, and stepped down from the platform and toward the aisle between sixth and seventh-grade desks.

"What do you mean, Elmer?"

I got really worried for Elmer.

"Eddie Walsh is a dictator on the playground."

I got more worried but had none left over for Elmer.

Sister fired questions, and Elmer's answers got more and more *stuttery*.

Finally, Sister said, "So, Mr. Elginfritz, the crux of the matter is Eddie Walsh and Jimmie Joe Meinerschlagen pick the teams for noontime baseball every day. You think that's unfair, and you'd like to pick the teams once in a while. Here's how we will address this issue. Sixth-grade boys will vote on whether Elmer picks the teams for the ball game today, or if Eddie and Jimmie Joe continue to do so."

"Sister." Sam Waterman, a seventh-grader. had his hand up.

"Yes?"

"Sister, the noon ball game affects the boys in all three grades. We should all get to vote."

"A good point." Sister turned to me. "Eddie, Elmer says you pick the teams all the time, and it's not fair. What do you have to say for yourself?"

"Sister." It was Sam again, and he wanted to speak for leaving the team picking a business to stay the same. "Eddie and Jimmie Joe are the two best players on the ball field. They know better than the rest of us just how good each of us is. They pick evenly matched teams. We have good games because of them. They do a good job. We should let them continue to pick the teams."

We voted by raising our hands. Elmer voted for himself. Nobody else did.

"Hands down," Sister said. "The vote was overwhelmingly to keep things as they are, but it was not wrong of Elmer to question why Eddie and Jimmie Joe always pick the teams. It was a good idea to raise the question. In raising it, we all had to dig for the answer, and by doing so, we better understand why things should continue as they are. Do you see that, Elmer?"

"It's just not fair!"

I thought sure Sister would storm down to Elmer's desk and Knuckle Whapper would make an appearance, but SS stayed at the front of the room. Even more surprising, she smiled.

Sister said, "This was a good and practical demonstration of the democratic process where we vote for how we will conduct our affairs. In the end, not everyone will be happy with the outcome, but we have to have a way to proceed. So, the majority rules. Eddie and Jimmie Joe will continue to pick the teams."

Sister returned to her desk and announced that all three grades were going to do a project together. "In November, we are going to vote in our own school rendition of the election of our next president."

In two weeks, the sixth grade would present

to the three classes a summary of the good features of candidate Dwight Eisenhower. The seventh grade would present a summary of the same man's faults and weaknesses. Two weeks after that, Adlai Stephenson would be subjected to the same plus and minus assessment. The eighth grade would be split in half and help the sixth and seventh graders. The most important word there, Sister said, "Is **help.** You are not to do the work, only **help** get it done. Clear?"

A "verstehe" would have worked pretty good there.

I'd gotten bummed when I thought Sister would let Elmer pick the baseball teams. I knew how he'd do it. He'd put Jimmie Joe and me on his team along with a couple more of the good players. We'd have slaughtered the leftovers. Where was the challenge, the fun in that? Then the vote saved me. I got ebullient. I found that word in Sister Daniel's dictionary once and hadn't had the chance to use it before. So, I was ebullient but had just enough sense to keep my mouth shut.

Feeling good was good, but if you let yourself feel **too** good, it always led to trouble. It was one of the things I'd learned from my first spanking.

Then I got worried Sister would let Elmer be the boss of our team for the election stuff. But she picked Linda.

Back to the election, one thing I remember

about Sister's process of listing the goods and bads of each candidate, I thought the bads of each man were hard and factual. The goods, I thought, were squishy. Like those things might be there today, but if you looked tomorrow, the thing you thought was good was either gone altogether, or it turned out to be another bad.

As far as I could tell, pretty much everybody in the three grades felt the same way. When we voted, we were not voting for the best candidate. We voted for the least bad.

Some twenty years ago a book came out: *All I Really Need to Know I Learned in Kindergarten.* Where I grew up in St. Ambrose, Missouri, we didn't have kindergarten. Even if we had, I'd tell you, even though I'm pushing eighty, I'm a long way from knowing everything I need to know. But if you want to discuss what you need to know about how to vote in a presidential election, I'm the guy to talk to, and everything I will tell you, I learned in sixth grade.

Mama got the big cast cut off her hand and a smaller one put on. The doctor told her to wear a rubber glove over it, and she could return to doing reasonable housework.

Cousin Lucinda left. Which was a bummer. Not just because I had more work to do again. But because I liked talking with her. She helped me see and understand things better. It was like being outside and looking at the chickens in the pen, and I'd only see half of them. Then I'd talk to Lucinda, and I'd see all the cluckers, and not only see them but recognize them, and know which were layers and which were bound for Sunday dinner.

Still, it had been a pure blessing to have Lucinda there for those weeks, but, after she left, I wound up being sort of glad that it was Mama and me running the place again.

Winter came. Pop had insulated and sheetrock-ed the walls and the slanted ceiling.

Lennie and I concluded the insulation didn't keep the cold from getting in. It let the cold in, then it wouldn't let it get out again. We slept with ten blankets over us with only our noses sticking out. I had read a book of Jack London stories, and a couple of them worried me. When I got up in the mornings, I went to the in-house and checked my nose for signs of frostbite. Then I did my business.

I moved my schoolwork table over next to the hole Pop had cut into the floor and through the ceiling into the Little Poopers' room. Still, I wore a coat and cap and one glove. I turned pages with the ungloved hand, then stuck it in the coat pocket. But it was quiet enough up there.

If I tried to do my homework at the kitchen table, after I'd done the dishes, of course, the Little Poopers would come in from the front room, where they had been playing while Pop read the newspaper. It was like they knew they weren't annoying Pop, but they knew they could bother the crap out of me.

At Christmas that year, Santa brought us a TV. Which occupied the Poopers so I could study at the kitchen table like a regular American kid instead of in the attic like a Jack London Alaskan gold miner who was going to freeze to death five minutes after the story ended.

That winter, Lennie and I thought we'd

never feel warm again. Eventually, spring came, and with it, the spring thaw. Lennie and I appreciated that phrase a lot more than any stupid frozen over river ever did. The other thing that came with spring was baseball.

We had not only school recess but Little League as well. In Little League, we played teams of other ten, eleven, and twelve-year-olds from other towns around. A couple of those teams, we slaughtered. I liked the squeaker games better, the ones where the final score was three to two. Most of the time, we won the squeakers.

One we lost was my fault. The team was from St. Charles, and they had Negro players. Two of them, Aurelius and Douglas, were pitcher and catcher, and clearly, the best players.

It was the bottom of the seventh, the final inning, and we were leading two to one. Douglas was up first. He stroked a liner to center, a single. The next batter grounded out to first, and Douglas took second. Then he stole third on an outside pitch I had trouble with. I didn't even get off a throw. Aurelius came up to bat and smacked a scorching grounder to our shortstop, Little Heiny. Little Heiny gobbled it up as the runner on third started for home. I tore off my mask and received the throw in plenty of time. Douglas was charging down the line at me. I hunkered over and held the ball tight in my mitt with my right hand.

You are one dead duck, Douglas. That's what I thought. I was also thinking after I tagged out Douglas; I had to keep his brother from taking second.

Right before Douglas plowed full tilt into me, I reached out the mitt with the ball in it to tag him out, and he chopped his right hand down on my mitt and smacked me on the jaw with his left elbow. The next thing I knew, I was lying on my back and the baseball diamond lights were looking down at me.

Somebody was hollering, "Get the ball, Eddie. Get the ball!"

I thought, *What ball?*

I saw Jimmie Joe run past me, pick up the ball, and run back into the field with his arm cocked to throw.

The umpire called time out.

Mr. Meinerschlagen leaned over me and asked if I was okay.

My jaw hurt. "Did we lose?"

From beside me, Douglas stuck out a hand. I took it and he hauled me to my feet. "Not yet, you didn't," he said, grinned, and walked back to his dugout.

Looking at Douglas's face close up surprised me. I thought he looked a lot like Sam Waterman. Except for the skin color. Which didn't seem quite so noticeable up close. And Sam's eyes were not so dark brown. Sam was smart, and his face and eyes looked like he was. Douglas's face and eyes looked like he was, too.

Mr. Meinerschlagen had Jimmie Joe toss me a couple of balls and I threw them back. I didn't throw them back accurately, and Jimmie Joe had to move sideways to catch my off-target throws. Mr. M. pulled me from the game.

Final score: three to two. We had the two.

I thought I was a good catcher going into that game with the St. Charles team. After, I was a better one. Never again did a guy coming home knock the ball out of my mitt, and never again did a runner, no matter how big, hurt me. A big guy would plow into me, and I would hang onto the ball first and foremost, then I would tumble over backward, hop to my feet, and either throw the ball to get an advancing runner, or I'd help the big guy to his feet. I'd learned to move aside just a bit before a collision, and generally instead of smacking me head-on, I'd catch the guy to one side or the other. Generally, that unbalanced him, and he sprawled on the dirt next to home plate. And he was out.

The next summer when we played that same St. Charles team, Douglas was not there. His family had moved away. I was disappointed. I had hoped I could run into him at home just once, and I also hoped he'd try to knock the ball out of my hands again. I wouldn't try to hurt him, and I'd try to keep him from hurting me, but if I could, I'd knock the ball out of his mitt, and he darned sure wouldn't knock it out of mine.

It took some years to figure out the lessons from playing the St. Charles team. One is that if you desperately want a second chance at something, the opportunity to face that same challenge is a low probability of occurrence.

The second thing is, a game is a game. Winning is more fun than losing, but when winning becomes so important it isn't fun anymore, it is no longer a game. I learned that from Sister Daniels, my cousin Lucinda, Sister Superior, and a coliseum full of Roman gladiators.

The third thing, when I looked into Douglas's face and saw a resemblance to Sam Waterman, I didn't see a Negro. I saw Douglas. I saw a person. To that point in my life, I hadn't encountered many Negroes. I didn't need the fingers of both hands to count them up. There was the man Mama peeked out the front door at when I was five. There was Mr. Wilson who worked as a janitor in grade school while I was in first and second grades, and there were four or five others we saw at a place in St. Louis one time when I rode with Pop in the Farmer's Co-op Elevator truck to pick up sacks of seed. I didn't know I was doing it at the time, but when I saw those Negros, say it was five of them, loading sacks of seed onto trucks, I put them in a box in my head that had "Negro" on the label. I didn't look to see if they were smart or dumb, or scary or friendly. They just went into the box as if that was all that mattered to know about them.

When I met Douglas, he looked like Sam Waterman, a white kid I knew, and because of that, I could see that Douglas was smart, too. I could see he was a person. But he had to look like a white person I knew for me to see the person in Douglas.

I figure Douglas was the eighth Negro I'd met in my whole life. Well, if I count Ruprecht, that'd make him ninth. Even though Ruprecht was my Uncle Homer, one of the louts. Most of the time, I count him as negro, with a small "N."

I remember Ruprecht because he scared the crap out of me. Pee, actually.

I remember Douglas because he was the first Negro I saw a person in. But I had to see something of a white man in him first before I could recognize the person. The way I looked at it evolved. There's a difference between people and persons. It took a while to get where I considered people to have skin and the skin to have color. Persons are spirits. They don't have skin, and the skin they don't have... doesn't have a color to it.

I

Another thing happened that spring when I was in sixth grade. Jimmie Joe and I decided we were going to see if we could help Large Louie graduate from first grade. There were five boys in my class, and Jimmie Joe proposed that we all take turns giving up noon recess once a week to tutor Large Louie. I would have made the proposal to the guys, but Elmer Elginfritz considered me to be a dictator, and we didn't want him to vote against the idea. Even so, he voted against the idea.

Sam Waterman heard what we were doing and offered to take Elginfritz's day. Alice Ashe heard, too, and she offered to draw up lesson plans to get Louie graduated on the last day before the summer break. Not only that, Alice spent noon recess in the classroom every day with Louie and us once-a-week boy teachers.

One day after recess, when neither of us had stupid study, Jimmie Joe said we should just let

Alice teach him. "She's a better teacher than any of the rest of us."

"Heck no," I said. "It was our idea."

"I don't care. I'm quitting."

The next day, at the start of recess, they all quit. Even Sam Waterman.

"Well, I'm not," I said.

"We don't need them." Alice wasn't looking at me. She looked into me. "We'll get Louie to graduate."

That "we" Alice used worried me some. Actually, it scared me for a little while, but there was lunch to eat and Louie's lessons to get to before the end of recess bell.

For the rest of the school year, I forwent—I looked in my Sister Daniels dictionary thinking the past tense of the verb forgo would be forgo-ed, but it wasn't listed, even though I thought it made more sense than forwent—anyway, I forgo-ed noon-recess baseball. I still ran home for lunch.

Alice suggested I bring lunch. Then we could discuss Louie's lessons as we ate. The next day I brought my lunch, but there was nothing to talk about. Alice's lesson plans had it all laid out. The day after that, I ran home for lunch again. Then Alice re-proposed that I bring my lunch and the three of us would eat together and get right to studying while we ate. That seemed like a good idea. Until we tried it.

Louie was on his third baloney sandwich. Through the first two sandwiches, Alice drilled him on adding numbers. Numbers that would add up to ten or less. Alice gave him the addition problem: "What's seven plus two?"

Louie would stop chewing as he tried to figure out the answer, and his mouth would drop open. There was like two handfuls of half-chewed baloney and bread and Velveeta looking out at us. Alice grimaced and shivered and looked away.

"Louie, chew with your mouth closed," she said.

Louie did as instructed. He swallowed and raised his third sandwich to take a bite. Alice grabbed his hand and forgo-ed it, getting to his mouth.

"Answer the question, Louie," she said.

"What question?"

"What is seven plus two?"

Alice had been drilling him with the addition problems in order. What's 1 + 1? 1 + 2? All the way up to 1 + 9? Then she started on the two pluses and had gotten up to 2 + 7?

Louie had a funny look on his face. I couldn't tell if he had a tummy ache, had to go to the bathroom, or maybe a bug had crawled into his ear. He was looking around like he was trapped and wanted to find a way out. That's when he puked.

Alice was sitting facing him, and she got it right in her lap. She screamed and tore out of the classroom, and I could hear her scream run down the hall, descend the steps to the basement, and into the bathroom. Everybody was out on the playgrounds, so the school was quiet. Except for Alice. After her screams stopped, she cried.

Louie was spic and span clean. Not a spot on him. He did have a chunk of baloney stuck to his bottom lip.

There was a big puddle of vomit on the floor by Alice's desk. And puke footprints leading to the door. She stepped in the puddle before tearing out of there.

"Louie," I said. "Go out to the playground."

"I get to have recess today?"

"Yes."

"Can I get a drink of water first?"

"Get a drink of water first. But don't step in the puke."

Louie nodded and left.

In the rear of our cloakroom, there was a small closet with cleanup stuff. A bucket, mop, brooms, dust rags, and rags to wash the blackboards.

The Little Poopers puked sometimes. I knew how to clean up puke. And it wasn't the first time I cleaned up puke at school.

One winter when Lennie was in third and I

was in fifth grade, Lennie got sick during Mass. In winter, we attended Mass in the chapel at the end of the school building. It was only big enough to handle one classroom full of kids, and it was our turn. During the service, I heard that "urk, urk" sound that only meant one thing. All of us turned around to see Lennie holding his hand over his mouth and running for the door. He jerked it open, and as soon as his feet hit the landing at the top of the long flight of concrete steps leading to ground level., he barked his toenails up. Actually, it was scrambled eggs. He'd eaten a lot of them.

He was my brother, so I had to clean up the mess. It was cold out, fortunately, and his puke froze. So, I chipped it off with a broom handle. Let me tell you, that's the way to clean up puke. Freeze it; then chip it away. Of course, God doesn't always oblige with the right kind of weather when puke happens.

It wasn't almost zero in the classroom, so cleaning up Louie's mess had to be done the messy way. As I cleaned it up with my stomach lurching to contribute to the puddle, I told myself to be grateful Louie didn't wear a diaper. No matter the stinky mess you're in, there's always something to be grateful for.

Alice didn't come to class that afternoon. The next day she told me she was quitting on Louie.

"Well, I'm not," I told her.

That noon, we had a new plan. Louie and I started studying immediately after the noon recess began. We stopped at ten minutes before the end-of-recess bell and ate lunch.

The day after that, Alice stayed with Louie and me and resumed her role as teacher. When we quit for lunch, we left Louie in his front seat, and Alice took Linda Zigmund's desk and she put me in the last one of the seventh-grade row. I ate. Alice nibbled and talked. She told me about her mother and father, about her mother giving her a corner of the garden to grow flowers.

Why would you grow something in a garden you can't eat? I don't remember what all else she talked about, but she reminded me of our old house when the women would come and quilt with Mama, and how they talked as they sewed. There was never a pause after one talker talked. It was like the next one couldn't wait to jump in. And Alice talked as much as six women all by herself.

Fortunately, it only lasted ten minutes, not all blinking afternoon.

On the last day of school, a half-hour before the start-of-recess bell, Sister Superior announced she was going to test Louis to see if he would graduate from first grade. I figured Sister didn't want to ask Louie hard questions with his belly full of baloney.

She asked Louie arithmetic questions. Addition and subtraction with none of the numbers bigger than ten. He knew the answers. Then he had to read a book. He moved his finger along the lines of print, and we heard him tell us about Dick and Jane, and we saw spot run. Sister had him write some things, like "My name is Louis," and a few other things. His printing stayed within the lines on the first-grader print-your-letters paper.

Sister announced Louis graduated from first grade and that we should all give him a round of applause. Which we did. Louie grinned. Sister raised her hand, and we shut the heck up. Then she said Alice had done a great job developing lesson plans to get Louis through first grade. She was a good teacher, and we should applaud her. We did. Alice cast her eyes down. *Miss Modesty.*

"And Eddie Walsh," Sister said. "Teaching Louis what he needed to know to graduate was his idea."

I raised my hand. It was Jimmie Joe's idea as much as mine. I wanted to tell Sister that, but she glared at me and hissed at me, and my hand came down.

"And Eddie, once he got the program started, he stuck with it. Determination to see a good project through to a happy conclusion is almost an eighth virtue of the Holy Spirit. A round of applause for Eddie."

The start-of-recess bell rang.

Alice stayed in her seat and clapped. Jimmie Joe wasted no time clapping. He was up and out the door like a flash. The rest of us scholars jammed the aisles between the desks and shoved to jam into the press of bodies, trying to squeeze through a door that was wide enough for coming to school but not wide enough to get out of class and into recess.

As I walked past her, Alice asked me if I brought my lunch.

"No. I'm running home and getting back for baseball."

Alice was disappointed, I could tell, but over what? We got Louie through her lesson plans. Louie graduated. What's she disappointed about?

On the baseball field, I was happy to play again. And I did not hit a home run off Jimmie Joe. I was feeling too virtuous to do that to him.

From third grade to sixth grade, I'd gotten pretty good at playing baseball. The other thing I was really good at was being the boss of summer. In the afternoon, anyway.

The summer after the sixth grade was the same old deal. Mama was the boss of summer mornings. The Little Poopers still pooped. That was what they were really good at. And, even though Mama's hand wasn't broken anymore, I still had to be a girl in pants until noontime. No sense bellyaching about it. It was a thing that had to be. Which was how I looked at it: Monday and Tuesday of the first week of summer.

On Wednesday, Mama told me three other ladies were coming for coffee and cake. When we had company, Mama was always on her feet and only sat down when everyone at the table had everything they needed.

"Today, Mama," I said, "you sit with the

ladies from the git-go. I'll serve all of you, but you have to show me how."

So, Mama sat and, with the coffeepot filled with only water, she talked me through pouring and not spilling, taking someone's plate and not dropping the fork and serving them another piece of coffee cake.

Being a girl wasn't too hard. You had to be careful and not be a clumsy klutz. It was sort of like *Thou shalt be careful,* and *Thou shalt not be a clumsy klutz.* With Mama coaching me as Mister Meinerschlagen did on the Little League ball field, I got the hang of it.

The ladies showed up at ten. Mama sat with them. And I served.

Mrs. Meinerschlagen's mouth dropped open when I poured the first cup of coffee. And, at the end of the morning, the ladies were all talking about what a fine job I'd done. Mrs. M. was to host next week's coffee, and she hoped Jimmie Joe could do half as good a job as I'd done.

The ladies went home at eleven. They wanted to say goodbye to me, so I left the mop in the bucket in the hallway and stood beside Mama as they left. Each of them gave me a nickel.

Mama said I'd done a really good job and gave me a nickel too.

Holy smokes! I had twenty-five cents. Maybe it wouldn't take me till I was six thousand years old to save enough for a ten-speed bike.

Mama gave me a jelly jar for my bike money, and she set it next to her egg money dish. Whenever I saw that dish, my heinie remembered its first spanking. But that heinie memory quickly gave way to a dream of sitting on the seat of a ten-speed and pedaling and going really, really fast.

After lunch, I went over to Jimmie Joe's front yard. That's where we always met and figured out what we'd do that afternoon. The guys would toss their ideas out, and then they'd ask me, and I'd decide, as boss of afternoons, which of the ideas we'd do. Only that day went differently.

Jimmie Joe was mad at me. His mother told him he was going to serve the ladies at coffee next Wednesday, and that he was going to have to practice hard to do half as good a job as Eddie Walsh had done.

"And not only that, I'm going to have to wear an apron when I serve the ladies." Jimmie Joe was madder at me than he'd been when he hit me twice with hard pitches that day at recess baseball.

Jimmie Joe stuck out his chin and glared at me. "Eddie's too much of a girl to be the boss of boy afternoons. I'm the boss of afternoons now. And we're gigging frogs."

"Now you just hold your horses, Jimmie Joe Meinerschlagen," Elmer Elginfritz piped up.

"Eddie always lets us think up things to do. After he listens to all the ideas, he picks the best one for that day. I don't want to gig frogs."

The others started tossing in "How about we," and "What if we," and pretty soon, everything we could possibly do had been said.

Elmer said, "So, Eddie, what're we gonna' do?"

Jimmie Joe looked like he could have bitten a nail in half.

I thought about saying "Gig frogs," but if we gigged a mess of them, we'd be hours cleaning and skinning them. Fried frog tasted good, but skinning the slimy green croakers was a lot of work. And just then, I didn't want to do anything that was only going to make more work.

"Swimming," I said.

Jimmie Joe stomped away and into his house.

The rest of us went swimming.

Next Wednesday, Mrs. Meinerschlagen hosted ladies' coffee. Jimmie Joe was her coffee server boy. She made him wear a white apron with a frilly ruffle around the whole bottom part. I know because at ten after ten, Jimmie Joe stomped out of his house and sat on the swing his dad tied to a branch of the big Elm in their backyard. I was cleaning the in-house with the window open. He crossed his arms over the top of that apron and glared at the strip of bare dirt under the swing where his feet had worn away the grass.

Ten after ten. His mother must have fired him from his coffee server job. Jimmie Joe was already mad at me for getting him into that job. Now he was mad because he got fired from it. He'd probably blame me for that, too.

I let him be mad all by himself and went back to my job. It took more than an apron to make a girl out of a boy. The more I thought about it, the surer I was. Being a girl was like baseball. To be good at either took practice.

I sure had practice at being a girl. It started that August after I turned six and stole Mama's egg money. The rest of that month, I worked right alongside Mama all day, every day. Doing girl work. Inside and outside the house girl work. Like in the garden. There we pulled carrots and picked beans and peas. Boy garden work, spading up the whole garden and planting the seeds and digging up taters—it still seemed like Zeke's name for them was the right name—I always asked Pop if I could help, and he always gave me the, "You wanna' help?" Then the "Don't help," bits.

When I did girl work for Mama, she didn't

mind letting me try something and then showing me how to do it the right way. Pop, he didn't like to say a thing twice. He didn't like doing a job twice even more.

I finished up the in-house and looked out the window. Jimmie Joe was gone, but his apron lay draped across the swing seat. He was probably with the guys doing summer morning boy stuff.

Mama had time to show me how to be a girl, but Pop didn't have time to show me how to be a boy. That's what I thought that summer after sixth grade. Boy, was I wrong. But I'll tell that later.

Doing girl work, Mama and I talked to each other a lot. Or, like when she was with the coffee ladies next door. Doing girl-work, when I wasn't talking, I was thinking. Doing boy stuff didn't involve thinking.

Just then, Lennie came to tell me Ronnie had a dirty diaper.

Since she was going to be gone, Mama made Lennie stay home and help me watch the Little Poopers. That's all he did. Watch them. Still, it enabled me to get some of my girl work done. But could he change a dirty diaper? He could not without puking and making more mess for me to clean up. Lennie wasn't any better at being a girl than Jimmie Joe.

I got Ronnie's poop cleaned from all places poop can get in and onto and the diaper taken care of; then I plopped the baby into the cage, also called a playpen. I went back to work. Lennie went back to watching Bobbie and Ronnie.

Mama came home from the coffee about five past eleven with news. Next week, Mrs. Elginfritz was hosting Wednesday coffee, and she wanted to hire me to be the server. She'd pay me a quarter, Mama said. The other coffee ladies wanted to hire me, too.

Whoa. A quarter a week. I could picture the coins stacking up in the jelly jar. I could see myself buying a ten-speed and I wasn't six thousand years old. I wasn't even six hundred. The summer after the sixth grade was turning into something really sweet.

K

That summer, I stopped grumbling about girl mornings. Being a boy in the afternoons had a whole day's worth of fun in it. I sure enjoyed that summer after sixth grade. All the way to August.

That's when Simon Grossman had a birthday party in his basement and invited the whole sixth and seventh-grade classes. All eighteen of us. Nineteen counting the Birthday Boy.

I'd never been in Simon's basement. To his bedroom, yes. Then we entered through the back and into the kitchen and up the stairs. The evening of the party, we got to enter his house through the front door. I remembered my mouth hanging open when I saw Simon's bedroom for the first time. My mouth did the same thing after entering the front door.

There was a living room off to the left of the hallway you stepped into, and it was filled with furniture that looked too pretty to sit on.

The sofa and chairs in our front room weren't worth looking at, just to sit on. To the right, a separate room just for two sofas and a TV, and the screen on the TV was twice as big as the one on ours. Another room served as an office with two big desks in it. One each for Mr. and Mrs. Grossman. The hallway took us past the dining room to the kitchen with the stairs up to the bedrooms on one side, and down-stairs on the other.

Going down the steps, my jaw dropped again. The basement was like ours, one big open space. Our basement, however, had a furnace and a pile of coal in one corner and a bench Pop had built for Mama's laundry tubs with a new clothes wringer contraption bolted to it so she didn't have to grit her teeth and wring out Pop's bib overalls by hand, and one corner was filled with shelves of food Mama had canned.

Grossman's basement had a kitchen in one corner. Littler than the one upstairs. A fridge, a small counter with two stools in front of it, and behind the counter another kitchen sink. Another TV, with another giant screen, sat in another corner with two more sofas in front of it. The remaining corner held a ping-pong table. Plus, the walls of their basement weren't concrete. They looked like the walls in our house, all sheetrock and painted. And above it all, the basement had a regular ceiling, not like our basement where you could look up and see the joists and floorboards atop those. Quite a place, Simon's basement.

Mrs. Grossman had put a big bowl on that little counter. That was for us to put our cards for Simon in. The invitation said "No presents, but cards would be appreciated." Why would someone throw a birthday party and ask people not to bring presents? Wasn't the purpose of a birthday party to get presents?

Well, there were a lot of things about the Grossmans I did not understand.

Mrs. Grossman told us there were sandwiches. Each of us could have one sandwich. Potato chips, we could fill a small paper plate with chips, but no more. She did not want us to get sick. She looked right at me when she said that.

I didn't think it meant she thought I might stuff my face and get sick. She had been to one of the Wednesday morning coffees and seen me serve. She knew how good I was at being a girl. I was pretty sure her look meant if someone did puke, it would be my job to clean up the mess. All evening long, I watched the guys to make sure they weren't snarfing down too many chips.

Mrs. Grossman and her housekeeper, Mrs. Auchs, did the serving. I had never seen Mrs. Auchs up close before. She was tall and skinny as a rail. Her face looked like it had never had a reason to smile. She and her son, Large Louie, lived in a half-fallen-down house on the opposite bank of Verrukt Frau Creek from our first house.

Next to that little counter, there was a door leading to a small narrow room filled with shelves. Mrs. Grossman said they stored Christmas decorations and luggage in there. In there, they'd also hid the biggest birthday cake I'd ever seen. It took Mrs. Auchs and Simon's sister, Darlene, to carry the thing out and put it on that ping-pong table, which it turned out had been a birthday present for Simon.

Simon was thirteen, and I would be in a couple of days. The cake held thirteen candles kind of bunched up in one corner of the big flat cake. The one-to-grow-on candle was in the opposite corner. Those thirteen all bunched together by themselves seemed like it would be bad luck. I thought the bad luck would be aimed at Simon.

Boy, was I wrong.

Darlene lit the candles. Simon blew them out as we sang "Happy Birthday, Dear Simon. Happy birthday to you." Mrs. Auchs cut the cake. Mrs.Grossman put pieces on small paper plates. Darlene passed out the cake to the girls first, then the boys. As we ate, Mrs. Grossman and Mrs. Auchs went upstairs.

When we'd polished off the cake, Darlene

announced we would play a game. Spin the bottle.

What the heck was Spin the Bottle? I'd never heard of a game called that.

Darlene got all of us boys arranged in a big circle. Alice Ashe was the first girl in the middle.

Alphabetic-order Alice Ashe. Who else would go first?

Darlene put an empty Coca-Cola bottle on the floor and gave it a spin. Alice stepped on the bottle with the little end pointed right at me. Boys laughed. Girls giggled. They all looked at me. My stomach thought it might throw up. Before it could, Alice grabbed my hand and pulled me into that little room where the Grossman's kept Christmas decorations and closed the door.

"What're we doing in here?"

"You're supposed to kiss me," Alice said.

"Kiss!"

"Yes." Alice closed her eyes, tilted her head back, licked her lips, and puckered them.

The only thing I could think about was spit. She'd just coated her lips with her spit. I tried to swallow, but I was out of spit. Still, I knew my lips had to be covered with dried spit. No way was I mixing spit with Alice. Or any other girl, and I sure wouldn't kiss a boy. *Yuck!*

Alice, still puckered, opened one eye, and

stared into me. Her pucker disappeared, and she got a look on her face like her dog just got run over.

I had to get out of there, and I did and marched to the TV corner and sat and watched TV, though it wasn't turned on. Behind me, I heard the girls ask Alice how it was. "Fine," she said.

"Fine?" one said. "He looked like you kissed the socks right off him."

"It was good," Alice said. "He's a good kisser."

Behind me, the girls giggled, snickered, and cooed and gabbled. Gabbled. I'd run across that word and found it in Sister Daniel's dictionary. Gabbling, that's what the girls were doing, all right.

"Eddie." It was Darlene Grossman. "Get back in the circle."

I looked up at her and shook my head.

"Are you going to throw up?" She pointed to a door a few feet from the kissing room. "That's a bathroom."

I already knew they had two bathrooms upstairs. And they had another off the hallway leading in from the front door. They had a bathroom in the basement, too. I'd thought our in-house was the lap of luxury.

I didn't want to talk to Darlene. I didn't want to talk to anyone.

I stood up and walked to the stairs and

climbed to the kitchen. Mrs. Grossman and Mrs. Auchs sat at the table with cups of coffee in front of them.

I made my mouth say, "Thank you, Mrs. Grossman. It was a wonderful party, and I had a great time."

"You're welcome, Eddie, but are you leaving already?"

I nodded and left by the back door and got home without puking.

Everybody was in the front room watching our tiny screen TV. I said nothing as I started up the steps.

From the front room, Mama said, "How was the party, Eddie?"

"Fine," I said and kept climbing.

Upstairs, I sat at my rickety-legged table and turned on the desk lamp. The latest book I borrowed from Mrs. Grossman lay there. It wasn't right to say I borrowed it from Simon. If it had been up to him, he wouldn't lend any book to me. But his mother knew I liked to read and there was no library in St. Ambrose, or our grade school, so she told Simon to lend me books any time I asked. It set his teeth grinding every time I brought back a book and asked for another. I didn't like making him mad. He wasn't good at baseball or anything that counted. He didn't go with us in the summer to

Verrukt Frau Creek. He was rich and had a lot of books. Other than that, I felt sorry for him.

I looked at that book. Books always took me places I'd probably never go to. Just then, I wanted to be someplace else. I opened it to the bookmark and stared at the pages, but my eyes wouldn't make words out of the ink. My eyes would not let me go someplace else.

I closed the book, and all that was in my head was a big picture of Alice Ashe and the look of disappointment on her face. Except it wasn't just disappointment. She was hurt, and I had hurt her. I hadn't wanted to hurt her.

But I hadn't wanted to kiss her either. I didn't know they were going to play Spin the Bottle. I'd never heard of that game before, and I'd sure never thought about kissing. Sometimes on TV, a man would kiss a woman. I always wanted the yucky stuff to get over and done with and get on with the interesting part of the story.

Making excuses for myself. That's what I was doing.

Last year, when I was in fifth grade, Pop told me, "Making excuses is the biggest waste of time there is."

To him, a lot of things were the biggest waste of time. He only went to school through fourth grade. Me, being a whole grade smarter than him, I pointed out that only one thing can be the biggest.

He said, "Yesterday one thing can be the biggest problem. Then you get to today and the problem you are facing today becomes the biggest."

I had to think about that one. Fortunately, I had plenty of time to think while doing girl-work for Mama.

Huh. Pop's not as dumb as I thought.

Another thing Pop had told me, "You got a sorry to say, you best get to it quickly. Then get back to work."

After lunch the next day, I pedaled to Alice's house and knocked on the screen door. Mrs. Ashe answered, and I asked if I could speak to Alice, please.

"Have a seat on the porch swing. I'll send her out."

The way Mrs. Ashe looked at me before she went back inside made me wonder if Alice had told what happened in Simon Grossman's kissing room.

Alice came out. I moved to the side, making room for her to sit. She shook her head and just stared at me.

"I'm sorry, Alice."

"I wanted you to be the first," she said and went back inside.

Going home, I walked beside my bike and pushed it.

This was different from when I got mad over being teased about being a girl and I smacked two home runs off Jimmie Joe, and he got mad at me and drilled me twice with fastballs. That evening at Little League practice, Mr. Meinerschlagen made us apologize to each other, and the mads and the reasons for them were wiped away. They never happened. Almost never happened. Actually, they got so little they didn't amount to much.

The look on Alice's face that afternoon showed she was hurt even more than she had when I wouldn't kiss her. And me saying I was sorry didn't make it better for her, it made it worse.

As I walked, I wondered again if Alice had told her mother about Spin the Bottle. I tried to picture myself telling Mama what happened. I could see an image of me yammering my yap to her about kissing, but I could not picture Mama and how she would react. It just didn't feel right to talk about something like that with Mama. I sure didn't want to talk to Pop about it. Jimmie Joe and the others, no way I'd say something like that to them.

I hurt Alice. It seemed like something for

the confessional. Before the first confession in second grade, Father Geist told us he'd been a priest a long time, and that over that time he'd heard every sin imaginable in his confessional, and no sin was too big or too small to confess.

"And after you confess your sins, if you are sincerely sorry for them, you will receive absolution."

The problem with confessing I'd hurt Alice, I'd have to tell she wanted to kiss me. That wasn't my business to tell.

Father Geist was as old as Grandpa Walsh, and he may have heard everything in his confession box, but he would not hear Alice Ashe wanted to kiss me from me. So I would not tell anybody, and the sin of hurting Alice, I'd keep that with me until I appeared before St. Peter. He'd look at that sin and give me a thumbs up or thumbs down, just like the crowd in the coliseum in Rome Sister Superior made me read about.

That left me to figure out what I'd do the next time a girl wanted to kiss me. I was going to have to let her. I sure didn't want to hurt another girl like I did Alice. I was still worried about spit. I decided to carry two handkerchiefs. One for snot and boogers and such. The other to put between our kissing lips, you know, to keep our spit apart.

L

The night of Simon Grossman's birthday party was sort of like confession without a priest and a confessional. In the confessional, at the end of the business, you always said, "I firmly resolve, with the help of Your grace, to sin no more." That night, up in my room, I firmly resolved to not hurt girls like I hurt Alice ever again.

That resolution carried through a week. My birthday was seven days after Simon's. A Sunday that year. We went to church at eight, like always, came home, and ate lunch way early. After that, Mama brought a wrapped-up box from her bedroom and put it in front of me on the table.

"Happy birthday, Eddie," Mama said. Then she put another box in front of Lennie, and said, "It's not your birthday, but this year, you get a present, too."

Lennie started tearing his present open, but

Mama stopped him. "It's Eddie's birthday. He gets to open his present first."

I noticed Pop watching me. Usually at the table, Pop ate. When he wasn't feeding his face, he sat and stared. I didn't know what he stared at, but it didn't seem to be anything in the kitchen. Today he acted differently. Because it was my birthday?

"Open it," Mama said.

I tore the paper off and lifted the lid off the box. *Clothes.* Gray clothes. I wasn't expecting a ping-pong table like Simon got, but clothes wasn't—or weren't? Whatever—a real birthday present.

Mama reached over and lifted the gray shirt out of the box and held it up in front of her.

It was a baseball player uniform shirt and had "St Ambrose" in red letters across the front. She showed me the back, which held "Eddie." There were pants, too, with the legs too short and elastic around the bottom. Also, in the box was a *squooshed* flat baseball cap and red socks. The long kind with no toes or heels.

Mama was smiling at me.

Was she expecting me to wear this uniform to Little League games? *NO WAY!* Nobody on my team or any we played wore a uniform like this. Everybody wore blue jeans and tee shirts.

I looked at Mama just in time to see the smile leave her face like someone ripped it off.

She told Lennie he could open his present. He did, and he had the same uniform inside his box. Lennie was happy. As Mama looked at him, her smile came back.

Pop said, "Use the in-house. Lennie first. Then go upstairs. Put those uniforms on and come back down. Don't dawdle."

By the time I got up to the room, Lennie already had his uniform on. Except he was having trouble with the fly. Buttons. Pants without a zipper down there? Well, I would not help him. Taking care of the Little Poopers was one thing. This was a horse of a different color.

"Help me, Eddie."

"Nuh-uh! Ask Mama."

"But she's a girl."

"No, she isn't. She's Mama."

"You gotta' be a girl to be a mama."

I had my pants on by this time, and the buttons gave me trouble too. I stomped down the stairs and told Mama, "The stupid people who made the stupid uniforms made the buttonholes small and the stupid buttons big."

"Let me see."

I showed her the top button and top buttonhole. That was *ALL* I was going to show *HER*.

"Ach. Take your pants off."

"Here?"

"Yes here. I'll fetch my sewing things and get this fixed in two shakes."

Eunice Fenstermacher walked into the kitchen with Pop right behind her. She was going to babysit the Little Poopers. Eunice smiled.

Pop frowned. "Get your pants on."

"Uh, Pop—"

"Get your pants on, I said."

Mama came back into the kitchen from the bedroom and explained what the problem was.

"Bring your sewing stuff and fix them in the car. We need to get going."

Lennie and I snuck out of the house in broad daylight in our tighties and piled into the back seat, hoping like heck nobody *ELSE* saw us. This was one thing Lennie and I thought the same about. I mean swimming in Verrukt Frau Creek, we were all buck naked. And that was okay for the creek. But sure as shootin', it wasn't okay in town. And a girl seeing us in our tighties, well, that was... was egregious.

Pop drove. Mom sewed. I hoped like heck Pop wouldn't get us in a wreck.

We got on the highway and headed for St. Charles.

"We going to see Uncle John?" I said.

Pop half looked around. He had a funny half a smile on his face. "You'll see."

It didn't take long to drive to Uncle John's

from our house. If Mama only had time to fix one pair of pants, Lennie could wear them. I'd stay in the car and hide on the floor.

Pop took the turnoff for St. Charles, but then he passed the place he always turned to go to Uncle's. We continued through town and crossed the big bridge over the river.

A sign by the bridge said, "Missouri River."

I'd never noticed that sign before, and I hadn't known the river had a name. It was the river that ran by St. Charles. Like Verukt Frau Creek ran by Saint Ambrose. Of course, the number of times I'd been across that bridge, I didn't need all the fingers, on one hand, to count up. Actually, if I counted crossing it to come home again, I needed a second handful of fingers.

I'd already asked Pop where we were going. I didn't like to have to ask a person the same question twice, so, "Where are we going, Mama?"

"You'll see." She didn't turn to answer.

We didn't drive to far-off places often. When we did, Pop always told us where we were headed. Once we went to a place called Eureka. They held some kind of special religious service there Pop wanted to go to. He called it making a pilgrimage. One time we drove through St. Charles but didn't cross the bridge. Instead, we followed alongside the Missouri River and finally came to a place where we pulled onto a ferryboat, and it carried us across a river called the Mighty Mississippi. That day we were going to Calhoun County in Illinois to pick peaches. Pop told us where we were going that day, too.

I was sure we would not pick peaches. Pop still had on his church pants and shirt without the necktie, though. He wasn't dressed for blackberry picking either. That was good. I hated berry picking. Each berry I picked cost me getting stuck by ten thorns. Blackberries tasted good to me until I had to pick them.

All I knew was two places we weren't going to, and I was tired of hearing Mama's and Pop's answer.

Lennie brought a book. A Hardy Boys mystery. It had been one of my Christmas presents a couple of years ago. I wished I'd brought a book. I thought about taking my Christmas present away from him.

From the seat beside him, Lennie picked up another volume of the Hardy Boys and handed it to me. "Happy birthday," he said.

Huh! Happy birthday from Lennie, the rotten Walsh kid. And this book he got for Christmas the same year I got the one he was reading.

I'd already read the book a bunch of times, but reading it again was better than sitting in my stupid whities staring out the stupid window.

I read the first page and couldn't remember what I'd read. Well, there were things to be aggravated about. Not knowing where we were going. Having to wear a stupid baseball uniform and riding around with no pants on. It didn't feel like a birthday. Eunice had seen me in my tighties. She'd probably blab it all over town. It felt like this birthday was headed for the same place that Christmas wound up when Ruprecht came after me with his sack open to stuff me in.

Mama handed Lennie his pants.

He tried to put them on without taking his shoes off first. I guess, he thought with the elastic around the bottom of the pants legs, he could squeeze them through. Maybe he thought he already had his pants off, and he wasn't taking anything else off. Maybe he was just being Lennie.

After Mama ach·ed him, he took his shoes off, put the pants on and the shoes back on, and tied them. Then he set to buttoning up. It went okay, except he couldn't get the bottom button done.

Pop said, "You started buttoning from the top, didn't you? Unbutton and redo them but start from the bottom."

Lennie did and said, "Oh." Like he finally figured out what one plus one equaled.

I looked at Mama. She sewed away up there in the front seat.

There was something about getting lessons on how to button your fly in front of her that didn't feel right. I mean last year, in the old house, Lennie and me took Saturday baths in a washtub in the kitchen in front of Mama. That had been okay. We'd done it that way forever. But this, this was different. Things down there, below the belt, were called privates. Before they hadn't been private, but now they were. As far as I was concerned, tightie whities were private, too.

Mama handed me my pants. I took my shoes off before putting them on. Then I started buttoning them from the bottom. Pop turned around to see if I was doing it right. I was right behind him, so he had to turn some.

Mama screeched, "Paddeeeeee."

The cars in front of us had come to a stop. Pop jammed on the brakes, but we still bumped into the back of the car in front of us.

That wouldn't have happened if the people who made the baseball pants put a zipper in for the fly, not stupid buttons.

The car in front of us pulled off to the side of the road. Pop followed him, and he and that other fellow talked. Actually, the other guy talked. Or cussed, maybe. The other guy was mad. And shorter. But the way he talked up to Pop seemed to little up Pop somehow.

After a bit, the other guy got done spitting words at Pop, stomped up to his car, got in, and, far as I could tell, without looking, he pulled out onto the road. Right next to me there was a horn honk like to scare the liver out of me, and a screeching of brakes, like I heard when I was six and stepped onto Elm Street to get Mama's note.

But there was no wreck.

Mr. Tire-screecher Driver took off after Mr. Little-big-man-mad-as-a-wet-hen Driver. Pop stood there staring at the edge of the road like he did sometimes when he was looking at something nobody else could see. Finally, he got back in the car and we drove on.

To Sportsman Park. The St. Louis Cardinals were playing the Chicago Cubs.

Big whoop!

I didn't like to watch baseball. I liked playing it.

Plus, Lennie and I were wearing the stupid baseball suits. Which, far as I could see, every other kid in the whole big place had on normal clothes.

There were a lot of people in the seats around us and the ones on the far side, I could barely make out if they were grown-ups or kids. I could tell who wore a dress and had long hair and who didn't. In some sections of the Park, there were a lot of kids. In other parts, no kids at all. So, I figured maybe a third of the people there were kids. It would have been easier to figure out if I'd had a pencil to chew on.

"Pop, how many people are here?"

"Thirty thousand."

Thirty thousand! Holy moly!

That was one hundred times the number of people living in the whole town of St. Ambrose. The most important thing though was that meant there were ten thousand kids there, and nine thousand nine hundred and ninety-eight of them wore normal clothes. Only Lennie and I were oddballs. Wearing stupid baseball suits.

Lennie stood in front of his seat so he could see over the guy sitting in front of him. I sat slouched and wished I'd brought the Hardy Boys book.

Pop bought hot dogs for Mama, Lennie, and me. He didn't buy one for himself.

Lennie got ketchup on his dog. Mama and I had mustard. Everybody knows, but Lennie, hotdogs are better with mustard and worse with ketchup.

A little later, Pop bought sodas for Mama, Lennie, and me. He didn't buy one for himself.

What happened next? Lennie had to go to the bathroom.

I was just tall enough to use the trough. Pop had to hold Lennie up after he undid his buttons, of course.

After we washed our hands, we went back to where Mama was sitting. She never went to the bathroom. Like nuns never went.

Pop bought a scorecard, and he had me sit next to him so he could show me how to fill the thing out.

I looked at the roster of Cardinal names. A few of them I recognized from doing my homework at the kitchen table while Pop listened to a ball game on the radio. Stan Musial, Red Schoendiest, and Enos Slaughter. But another guy was Eddie Stanky. Whoa! It would have been cool to have him in my class at school. On the playground, I'd have picked Stinky Stanky first, even ahead of Large Louie.

Finding Stanky was kind of fun. It lasted ten seconds. Then I went back to slouching and moping.

Pop looked at my scorecard. I hadn't been making the marks he'd showed me to make.

"Lennie," Pop said. "You want to learn how to keep score?"

"Yeah, Pop. Yeah."

He was sitting on the other side of Mama, so he and I exchanged places. Pop showed him how to keep score. Things would happen on the ball field, and he'd make a mark and ask Pop if he'd done it right.

"You did it just right."

Inning after inning, the game went on. Not a thing happened to cheer about. A kid about my age sat in front of me. There'd be a crack of the bat, and he'd jump to his feet. He wore a Cardinals tee-shirt. A tee-shirt would have been so much better than the stupid baseball suit. Anyway, after the kid jumped to his feet, he'd stand for a moment and either say a disappointed "Oh," or a relieved "Phew." Then he'd sit and slouch back in his seat again.

I was already slouched.

In the big leagues, baseball games went on for nine innings. Nine! In Little League we played for five or seven innings, depending on how many games had to be got in that night.

There was a big scoreboard in center field. It showed nothing but zeros for seven and a half innings. Good. Only one and a half more and we could go home. But then I remembered. In Little League, if the game was tied at the end of seven innings, we quit playing. In the big leagues, the teams played until somebody eventually won.

Please, God, don't let this stupid game go to stupid extra innings.

A bat cracked hard on a baseball. Everybody around us hopped to their feet and hollered except Mama and me. She slept. I slouched.

When the noise subsided and people sat again, Pop said to Lennie, "Musial hit a double. Put a '2B' in the box there. Okay, the Cardinals are putting in a pinch-runner for him. Let me show you how to put that on the scorecard."

A sacrifice bunt moved the runner to third.

A sacrifice fly scored the run. All scoreboard zeros in the eighth and top of the ninth.

Everybody around us stood up and started filing out. Everybody was happy and excited. The Cardinals won one to nothing. I was happy and excited, too. We could go home now.

Walking out, some woman grabbed Mama's arm and said, "They look so cute."

Cute! Great. A perfect end to a perfect day.

At home, Pop paid Eunice, and she walked home.

Mama closed the bedroom door to nurse Ronnie.

Pop turned the TV on for Lennie and Bobbie, then he said, "Eddie, come with me."

He led me to the backyard picnic table he'd built. In late afternoons, the table got shade from the Meinerschlagen trees.

Pop and I sat across from each other. "Boy, 'member when you sent your mama to hell when you were in first grade? Well, you did it again."

The women at Wednesday coffee had talked about Simon Grossman's birthday party and how special it was. Mama wanted to do something really special for my birthday. After Lennie and I went to bed, she stayed up sewing the baseball uniforms. Last night she didn't get any sleep at all putting the buttons and buttonholes in.

"We both thought you'd like the uniform and seeing a game in person. Lennie appreciated both."

Pop got up and went into the house.

That year, Lennie got his birthday, and he got mine, too. Worse, I sent Mama to hell again.

I sat there and felt rotten. After I disappointed Alice Ashe, I apologized and found out apologies don't always count for much. Sometimes, they maybe even make things worse. Also, disappointing Alice, there didn't seem to be a right way to confess that.

Disappointing Mama, I could figure out a way to say what I'd done to her, and I'd say it at confession on Saturday.

And I gave myself penance. I would quit my job as boss of summer afternoons for the rest of the month and do girl work for mama all day.

M

The day after my birthday, I didn't tell Mama
I'd given penance to myself. I just didn't run
off to join the guys after lunch. I knew the stuff
needed doing, and so I went back to work. Mama
didn't say anything about it either. She knew I
was trying to make up for sending her to hell a
second time. Not many things can make up for
sending another person to hell. Ronnie helped.
He filled his diapers with stuff that made what
I was doing feel like penance all right.

That afternoon I thought about Sister Daniels
and what she'd written on the chalkboard the
day I dropped my bat and Sister Superior gave
me "No recess for a week" penance.

Sister had written *Having fun is not a
sin—Necessarily.* The idea I got was that there
was good no-sin fun and bad-sin fun. To go to
heaven, you just had to steer clear of the bad
sin-fun. If you weren't having fun, you weren't
in danger of committing a sin.

Yesterday hadn't been any kind of fun at all. For me, anyway. Lennie had fun. In fact, the way it worked out, he got two birthdays this year, and I didn't get any. Back to sin and fun.

Mama wanted me to have fun. She wanted me to have a big bunch of it and worked really hard on those uniforms—even now while doing penance; I had to stop myself from thinking: *Stupid uniform.* Pop, too, thought it would be fun for me to see a big-league ball game in person, not just listen to it over the radio. But I'd had no room in my head to think about what they put into making my birthday special. I, special Eddie Walsh, thought I was not having any kind of good time, much less a specially good time. They dressed me up like a little kid, stuck me in the middle of thirty thousand people, where I stood out like a sore thumb. It embarrassed the heck out of me.

I couldn't see any of what Mama and Pop had done trying to make my birthday special. All I could see was other kids snickering at me. I even pictured women saying, "Aren't those St. Ambrose kids cute." Not only would they see we were from St. Ambrose, but they'd see our names on our backs. I even pictured a photo of Lennie and me showing up in Pop's newspaper with words saying, "Cute kids see Cards beat Cubs."

If that had really happened, I'd have had to

run away from home, which would have been tough, because I didn't know how to run away from home.

Anyway, I had plenty of trouble dealing with what had happened, much less also dealing with what might have happened. But that was the trouble with doing girl work. It gave you time to think, and the stuff I thought about—Poop!

On Tuesday afternoon, when I got home from practice, my Uncle Ed was there. The Army had transferred him from Texas to California. He also had leave, so he came home, even though it wasn't what you'd call on the way.

I was happy to see him but not as happy as I used to be, before Ruprecht Christmas.

Uncle was to spend a couple of days with us, and a couple more with the ignorant louts and Aunt Ruth and grandpa before heading west. He got the Little Poopers' room. Ronnie's crib moved back into Mama's and Pop's bedroom. Bobbie fell asleep on their bed. Later, when everybody was ready to go to sleep, Pop would carry him into the front room where he slept on the sofa.

When Uncle Ed visited, Mama *happied* up a couple of notches. Wednesday morning, after Pop left for work, Mama and him—Mama and he stayed at the table and talked and drank coffee. I made a second pot for them in between changing a diaper and washing dishes and putting Bobbie's quilt away.

It was Ladies' Coffee Day at the Elginfritz's. Mama said she wasn't going, but I had to because Mrs. Elginfritz wanted me to help.

Uncle said, "Both of you go to the coffee. Lennie and me will babysit the little ones. But I ain't changing no dirty diaper."

Mama sure liked her brother. She liked him, even more, when he said that, and she could have talk and coffee with the other ladies. I liked him, too. But I was glad no one else was there to hear him speak egregiously.

Ain't. I wanted to ask him, *Where'd you grow up? In a stable?*

But I kept my mouth shut. I'd learned I could think a thing and keep it in my head without my mouth feeling like it just had to say it. Sister Superior taught me that.

Funny. It hadn't occurred to me before, but I was sure Sister Superior must have had a regular nun name, like Sister Mary... Heiny or something. But I never knew it. I thought I'd ask her her real name. After I graduated from eighth grade. Even Sister House Nun had a regular name. The new one, after we gave Sister Bartholomew a breakdown, was Sister Mary

Frumentius. Now, if I had a name like that, I'd rather be called Sister House Nun for sure.

When it was time for the coffee, Mama and I walked up Main Street to Mrs. Elginfritz's house. I'd served for her before and knew what to do, so she sat and talked a gallon of words for each sip of coffee she took.

Most of the time, the ladies didn't seem to know I was there. They talked about other people in town, whose boy dated whose girl and would they get married, whose flower garden was prettiest. That day, Mrs. Elginfritz talked about a year ago, about trying to use some of the girls from town to serve at their coffees, and how the girls didn't want to feel like servants.

"Now, Eddie," Mrs. E. said, "he does a good job, doesn't complain, pours coffee without spilling, and we don't even know he's around."

Boy, did I come close to spilling coffee in Mrs. Fenstermacher's lap. I didn't know they appreciated what I did. I thought they gave me a quarter because they were nice ladies.

Mrs. E. said to Mama, "Loraine, how about I trade you all five of my boys for Eddie?"

Mama said, "I already have one Lennie. What on earth would I do with six of them?"

I sure never heard the ladies laugh so hard at a coffee before.

But here's what stuck in my craw. They, including Mama, had said, in effect, I was worth more than five other boys because I did girl work better than a girl. Getting paid a quarter for serving had been just fine before. Now it wasn't. I would not do it anymore, even if the ladies promised me a ten speed for doing it just one more time.

After pouring another round of coffee, I gathered up the plates and silverware and washed and dried them and put them away. Then I took the coffeepot and set it on the table and left. It was time to get home and fix lunch for Pop. Mama stayed and talked. That was okay. I didn't owe the coffee ladies anything more, but Mama, I owed her penance work.

Penance work. Ever helpful, Ronnie was always happy to help with that. Uncle Ed and Lennie weren't. Uncle was happy to hold the baby once he got *unstunk*.

By the time I had lunch on the table, Pop and Mama walked in.

When we didn't have company, lunch, and supper, too, were eating and not talking affairs. With company, there was plenty of palaver— this was one of those words I came to call a "Sister Daniels Word." Before she gave me the dictionary, I'd encounter palaver or some such word, and I didn't know what it meant. I'd kind of shrug and just keep on reading. After having the dictionary, I looked those words up, and if I found opportunities to use that word now and again, it stuck. I don't mean to say I used those words in talking with the guys. I didn't want to act like a smarty-pants—between Mama and the company. With Uncle Ed there, it was like being back at Wednesday Women's coffee. Mama was chock full of little stories from the coffee ladies about people Uncle knew. After she completed a story, Uncle would grin and say, "I remember the time when—"

Like usual, Pop ate and sipped coffee and stared at stuff nobody else could see. When he was finished eating, he stood up. Uncle stood up, too. "Sit," Pop said, grabbed his cap from atop the fridge, and was out the door.

Uncle sat, and he and Mama started talking again like before. Pop was as gone as he'd been when he'd been there.

Mama sent Lennie to watch over Ronnie play in the sandbox until he got tired enough for a nap. I washed dishes and thought about a wedding a couple of Saturdays past.

I'd served at the Mass. Us... we boys liked to serve at weddings. Afterward, while pictures were being taken and rice was thrown, we servers hung up our cassocks and surplices and hustled down Church Hill and strung a rope across the road leading to town. The wedding party cars always stopped at our rope, and the drivers would give each of us holdup men a dollar. A whole buck! Sometimes a cheap one would give us a half dollar.

But, during the wedding, I'd noticed how the bride and groom had looked at each other. They were as happy with each other as the Coffee Women were with those at their gabfests. I watched Mama and Uncle. They looked as happy with each other as that bride and groom had been.

After our holdup, I walked home with the eighth-grade Elginfritz kid. I asked him if he noticed how happy the bride and groom looked.

"Of course, they're happy," he said. "Tonight, after the dance at the American Legion Hall, they get to do *hanky-panky under the blankey.*"

"What's that?"

He looked at me. "Ask your dad."

Ask Pop? I was pretty sure I never asked him anything. So, I asked Mama. In front of Lennie and the Little Poopers.

"Ach!" she said. "Do not say that... that... hanky thing ever again. Ever again. *Verstehe?*"

A hanky was a snot rag. What's the big deal with that? Don't say it ever again? I verstehe-ed not say it, though.

That night in bed, Lennie asked if wanted to know what hanky-panky was. Mama hadn't told him to never say it again.

"Sure."

"Hanky-panky is when a man and a woman

take off all their clothes and they get in bed and make a baby."

"I thought women had to go to a hospital to get a baby. Mama did."

"You're stupid, Eddie."

"I get nineties on my report card. You get seventies."

"There's other stuff you gotta' know besides school learnin'."

"Well, how did you learn the other stuff?"

"Everybody knows it, Eddie. But stupid you. Bobbie knows, and he's three and a half."

Well, that knocked the stuffing out of me, about like Large Louie smacking me and knocking me clean across a ditch.

Lennie rolled onto his side. I figured it meant he was done talking.

I lay there looking up at the blackness hiding the ceiling and remembered the start of third grade. I thought I knew everything I needed to know, so why did I need to go to third grade? But here I was ready to start seventh grade, and Lennie, two grades behind me, and even our second-youngest brother, knew more than I did.

In the black above me, one thing sort of clotted up, like blood on a blackberry thorn scratch on the back of my hand. Lennie had exaggerated. Bobby didn't know a thing about hanky-panky either.

Then I rolled onto my side and fell asleep.

N

The next day, there was no time for hanky panky. Until after supper.

In the morning, Uncle Ed would go out to the farm and spend a couple of days with Grandpa Schneidermeier. Before he left, he wanted to talk with me.

Mama said, "You and Eddie go out and sit at the picnic table in back. It's shady and the skeeters won't be too bad till the sun goes down. Lennie and me will clean up."

As we walked out, 1 thought, *Great. I can ask Uncle Ed about hanky-panky.*

Pop had built the picnic table so it wouldn't tip over, even if Fatty Arbeiter sat on one side of it all by himself. Fatty worked in the main elevator building on Second Street. Everybody else worked there, too. Pop ran the really tall skyscraper place by the railroad tracks. Fatty might have had a normal name, but I never knew it. He wore bib overalls his wife had to sew extensions onto the straps of. It looked like the straps across his shoulders turned the bib into a big sling to hold Fatty's belly up so it wouldn't drag on the ground or something.

Every once in a while, whilst us… while we guys were talking, Fatty's name would come up. Fatty wasn't tall as Pop. I knew Pop weighed a hundred ninety pounds. The going-into-eighth-grade Elginfritz boy said Fatty weighed over three hundred fifty.

Back to Uncle Ed and me. He sat on one side of the table.

"How much do you weigh, Uncle Ed?"

"One seventy-five."

I told him about Fatty and how Pop made the table so it wouldn't tip, even if Fatty sat on one side by himself.

"Give your dad an axe, a saw, a hammer, and some nails, and he can chop a tree down, turn the tree into lumber, and the lumber into a picnic table so it won't tip over even if Fatty Arbeiter sits on one side by himself and do it while he's home from the elevator for lunch."

"You make Pop sound like Paul Bunyan."

"Folks in town here say he does the work of two men."

"Mr. Grossman told me Pop is the hardest working Irishman in St. Ambrose."

Uncle humphed. "That's one of those things that could be an insult. Some Germans call

Irishmen white,"—and here he used the N-word. "They think an Irishman does only enough work in a day to buy a night's worth of whiskey."

Uncle poured coffee from his cup into his saucer and slurped it up. "Some folks always want somebody to look down on. Snooty English look down on Germans. Some English think *they* beat the Germans in both World Wars. The Germans look down on the Irish. Whites look down on darkies. We are all Americans, no matter where our grand-folks came from."

"Why do you call"—I thought about using *Darky,* but then used the only term I knew was okay— "Negroes the N-word?"

"If I think about what I'm saying, I don't use it. But for half my life, that was the only word for them I knew." Uncle smiled at me. "I know when you were in first grade, you sent your mama to hell to learn the N-word was wrong."

"She told you?"

"In a letter." Uncle drained the coffee from the cup and set it on the saucer.

"What I wanted to talk to you about, Eddie, is hurting your mom. I hurt mine and never told her I was sorry. She died before I got smart enough to know I needed to say that to her." Uncle looked at his hands resting on the table and opened them up as if they wanted to look back at him. "A thing about a boy hurting his mom. Do you know that painting in church of the Blessed Virgin with a little sword stuck in her heart? Well, that's what happens to a mother when her child hurts her. And that little sword never gets pulled until she passes by St. Peter. He pulls it out so she can get into heaven.

"I'm sure it bothers you, that you hurt your mama over the baseball suits. That's why you help her all day instead of only a half-day, and she knows why you're doing it, but you need to say the words to her. 'Mama, I'm sorry I was such a stupid jerk over the uniforms. I don't expect you to forgive me. There is no forgiveness on earth for what I done to you. I just want you to know I am sorry.' You need to do that. Say it to her."

I gotta' tell you, I hadn't expected that from my uncle. For a moment, I thought I might cry. Like a girl.

The end of August was short-sleeve weather. I wasn't expecting to have to kiss any girls, so I had no handkerchief in my pocket. I wiped my nose on the back of my hand.

"One other thing, Eddie. You acted the way you did over the uniform because you worried about what people would think of you. Every day of your life, you will be faced with decisions as to the right and wrong thing to do in a partic'lar situation. Don't let what other people think steer those decisions."

He stood up. I was grateful for how well Pop

had built that table. Otherwise, it'd have tipped and dumped me on my butt.

"Eddie, I'm glad Ruprecht didn't get you in that sack of his. You turned out to be a halfway decent kid."

He took his cup and saucer back inside and left me out there with the blood-sucking skeeters and what he'd said.

I'd thought I'd felt as bad as I could feel over what I'd done to Mama. Uncle made me feel worse. When I was a kid, I used to say *more worser* in such a situation. Just then, *worse* was weak wienie compared to *more worser*. And that's how I felt, more worser.

I thought about going inside and saying, "Sorry," to Mama in front of God and everybody. But If I did that, it would be because Uncle told me to.

Tomorrow. I'll tell her tomorrow.

That way it'd be from Eddie me, not Eddie Uncle.

Until I said the word to Mama, I was not going to feel like a halfway decent kid. The skeeters didn't care. Maybe I even tasted better to them being a rotten kid.

Poop. I forgot to ask about hanky-panky.

The next morning, Uncle Ed left for the farm.

A bit before lunch, I told Mama I was sorry for being a stupid jerk over the baseball uniforms. Mama hugged me.

It was the first time she hugged me when I wasn't bleeding or crying.

The other thing I did was to go into Mama's room and dump my jelly jar of ten-speed bike money into her egg money dish.

On Sunday, Uncle Ed, his two lout brothers, Aunt Ruth, and Grandpa Schneidermeier ate lunch with us after church. On Monday, Uncle Ed headed west for his new duty station, and school cranked up seventh grade for me.

On Tuesday, people started dying.

Uncle Ed died first. On Route 66, near a place called Tucumcari, New Mexico. A trailer truck driver fell asleep at the wheel, crossed the centerline, and plowed head-on into him.

Mama cried her eyes out.

The day after we found out, I told Jimmie Joe about it just before we picked teams for recess baseball.

"Man!" he said. "Think about it. A trailer truck and car smacking into each other. Both going sixty. Your uncle's car would have been a bug splat on the bumper of that truck!"

My head filled with movies of bugs going

Splat against the windshield of Pop's car and leaving a big yellow *splop* of bug guts behind and the dead bug being scraped off and thrown away like dog poop, you scraped off your shoe. I didn't like to think of my Uncle Ed that way, but that's what my mind couldn't stop doing after Jimmie Joe said what he did.

"Hey, Eddie. You pick first," Jimmie Joe said.

So, I picked somebody.

"For crap sake, Eddie! You always pick Large Louie first."

"Large Louie," I said.

"You already picked somebody."

So he picked somebody, then reminded me it was my turn, and I picked somebody, not Large Louie.

Jimmie was totally disgusted with me. He told Norm Siling, an eighth-grader, to be the other captain.

It was okay with me. I walked away from the ball field and went into the church. I sat in a pew all the way in back, the one Pop and Lennie and me always sat in on Christmas Eve.

It was the first time I went to church all on my own idea. I just didn't know where else to go.

I had the church to myself. Of course, God was there. The sanctuary lamp was lit. I hoped He wouldn't mind if I was there without a nun or a parent to fuss at me if I did something wrong.

Silence usually meant there was nothing to

hear, and it was never something to see or smell or feel. But that day, I felt it. Not quite seeing it, not quite feeling it. But sort of feeling it.

It was like going to the city swimming pool in St. Charles. That pool was filled with water you could see through! I liked to sit on the bottom and hold my breath as long as I could and just look around. It was quiet down there. Like now. I could hear the kids on their playgrounds making all kinds of noises, but their noises, even though I could hear them, did not disturb the silence inside the church.

And that silence filled the whole church. I even imagined it filling the inside of Mr. Grossman's steeple all the way to the top.

The end of recess bell rang, but I stayed there in the blessed silence.

Sometime later, the main door into church opened behind me. I just stared straight ahead. Until Sister Superior asked me to scoot into the pew and make room for her.

I scooted and looked at her as she sat next to me.

"Your mouth's hanging open, Eddie." Her face looked like she'd put on a kindly face mask for Halloween.

"Your namesake uncle died, which, of course, was bad enough. What really bothers you, though, is the horrible manner in which he died. Is that right?"

Well yeah! When Uncle Ed came home, Mama lit up like a Christmas tree.

I always felt like he did us the biggest favor coming to visit, and I was grateful he spent time with us. Like he was a movie star or something, or Satchel Paige, the baseball player Pop admired most. There was the Ruprecht thing, but, heck, I'd ripped my pants.

I nodded to Sister. She was right. Although Uncle Ed winding up as a bug splat on the front of a honking big trailer truck was a much more worser way to think about it than the *Horrible manner in which he died.*

Sister sat there, quietly, beside me for a moment. Then she said, "Eddie, some people die peacefully in their sleep. Others die in accidents, or from a disease, or in a tornado. And these kinds of deaths are horrible to think about. But look up there, above the altar. See the crucified Jesus?"

"Uh, Sister," I whispered. "Is it okay to talk in church?"

Holy crap! Sister Superior smiled at me. I mean, it wasn't a Sister Mary Daniel smile, but it was a smile all right.

"In this case, it is. And most appropriate. You are carrying a terrible grief in your heart, and Jesus, Our Savior, wants to help you bear the burden. And when you look at a crucifix, you see He suffered a cruel and horrible death.

But that was why He was born, to suffer that death and redeem our souls, so we could live forever with Him in heaven."

In my head, I saw Sister Daniel next to me saying the same words.

Sister Superior made the sign of the cross, genuflected in the aisle, and left.

I wasn't sure what I should do.

Go back to class, Eddie.

The voice in my head sounded like Sister Daniel.

I made the sign of the cross. In the aisle, I genuflected twice. I'd forgotten to do that coming in. Us Walshes didn't like to be beholden to anyone. I figured I best not be beholden to God any more than I already was.

When I got home from school that afternoon, I carefully closed the screen door. You never knew when a Little Pooper might be taking a nap and sleeping Poopers was a blessing not to be carelessly thrown away.

Our house had a front, a back, and a side door. We almost always used the side door. Never the front and rarely the back. So, I entered the side door. Inside there was a flat area.

From there you could turn left, climb three steps and enter the kitchen or go straight ahead and down to the basement. Above was the underside of the stairs leading up to the attic. I stood there on the landing listening to the sound of crying. But it wasn't a Pooper.

In the kitchen, I found Mama leaning against the fridge, her forehead braced on her arms, and sobbing. She wasn't making much noise. Seeing her, hearing her hurt my heart.

"Mama, what's wrong?"

She acted like she didn't hear me. I put my hand on her shoulder and asked again. Still no response. Just the weeping.

I got down on a knee and looked up at her and said my question again.

She slapped me, hard. I stood up, and she leaned back against the fridge and went back to her crying.

I checked on the Poopers. They were asleep. Quietly, I climbed the stairs up to the attic and sat at my table desk and rubbed my cheek where she'd slapped me. It hurt more than a bare heinie spanking.

I thought about Uncle Ed telling me a boy could stick a tiny sword in his mama's heart.

Well, Uncle Ed, mamas can stick a pocketknife-sized sword in their sons' hearts, too.

I picked up my current book from the Simon Grossman lending library and became someone else living somewhere else.

A couple of chapters later, Lennie hollered

up through the grate in the ceiling of Bobbie's room. "Supper."

"Not hungry," I hollered back.

Which was a lie. My stomach told me it was a stupid lie, but I went back to *Adventures of Huckleberry Finn*. I read a chapter but had no idea what I read. My ears and nose were busy keeping track of what was going on in the kitchen.

When the sounds from down indicated they were done eating, I went down to do the dishes. I figured that'd get back at Mama for slapping me.

At the foot of the stairs, I saw Lennie in the in-house watching Bobbie poop on his potty chair. The door to Mama's bedroom was closed, so she was taking care of Ronnie. The clink of silverware came from the kitchen.

Who was washing dishes?

I stepped around the corner and knock me over with a feather!

Holy crap! Pop! At the sink washing dishes!

I didn't know he knew how to do girl work.

"I'll wash 'em, Pop."

"Dry."

I grabbed Mama's last flour sack dishtowel. When I started drying dishes, flour sack towels were all we had. But now, the others had all gone into the rag bag. Mostly now, we had store-bought dish towels

Pop washed and rinsed. I dried and put away.

Pop handed me a handful of silverware. "Your mama is sorry she slapped you."

She didn't seem sorry right after she smacked me. She went right back to crying against the fridge like she had fourteen or fifteen of those little swords all stuck in her heart.

I wondered if that was why people got married. If you did something wrong, the person you were married to could apologize for you. It would have been nice to be married when I apologized to Mama for the baseball suits.

I put the silverware in the drawer, and Pop handed me more.

"When you found your mama crying, she'd just found out Uncle Ed would not be buried in our church cemetery. He chose to be put in an army one. She thought Uncle Ed loved his army family more than he loved her."

It had been easy to see Mama sure loved Uncle Ed. And if she thought he didn't love her back, that would hurt. For myself, I liked Uncle Ed a lot. I wasn't quite sure what the difference was between liking and loving. I just knew there was a difference. It might have been that girls loved and boys liked. If Uncle Ed was still here, I could ask—

But I'd never be able to ask him anything

again. That's when I knew that death was a real thing.

Oh, I'd served in lots of funeral Masses. Sometimes I'd see women crying after the service. And sometimes, in our old house, we'd dress up in Sunday clothes and walk down the sidewalk to the Grossman Funeral Parlor, where someone Mama and Pop knew was laid out. People cried at those things, too. Sometimes. But other times people talked with each other like they were at a picnic. When you walked into the funeral parlor, you could tell right away if it was going to be a crying one or a picnic one by how it sounded. The crying ones: There was a dose of that quiet you felt in church when no one else was there but you. And Him.

I should have known when Mama cried the first time for Uncle Ed. When someone who you liked died, you got a stab from one of those heart-swords. But I had to see Mama cry for her brother twice and she had to slap me and I had to see Pop wash the dishes before I got it.

Sometimes, I, Eddie Walsh, felt stupid.

Like in third grade. I thought I knew everything I needed to know, so I shouldn't have to go to school anymore. I started serving at Mass too. After I served at a couple of weddings, and the rice throwing was going on, us servers would run down the hill and string a rope across the road and "hold up" the wedding cars. They paid us money to let them go.

After I served at a funeral the first time, I said, "Aren't we going to hold up the funeral cars?"

Maury Nadelmann, an eighth-grader, stopped hanging up his surplice and looked at me. "You are so dumb, Eddie Walsh. I ought to knock the snot out of you for even thinking such a stupid thing."

There was a lesson in what Maury said, and I should have learned it. You shouldn't think stupid things, but if you do, keep your stupid mouth shut and no one will know you're stupid. If I had learned that lesson, I wouldn't have laughed at Large Louie when he was right behind me and he wound up punching me in the snot locker.

The other thing, when I walked in on Mama crying at the fridge, I thought she was feeling bad and I wanted to make her feel better. But when somebody you love dies, you feel bad and you don't want to feel better.

O

A couple of weeks later, Grandpa Schneidermieir died. I served at the funeral Mass.

Most of the Schneidermeier family took pews on the left side of church. Mama, with Pop and the Poopers, sat in the front row. During the service, a few sobs got away from some of the ladies. Mama was one of them. She had a handkerchief in her hand and used it. I wondered how one dainty little hanky could hold so many tears and so much snot.

From up on the altar, it was funny seeing Pop and Mama in front of church. Usually, they sat halfway to all the way to the back. Mama cried and blew her nose. Pop might have been a statue if you didn't see him stand up, kneel, and sit.

The Schneidermeier family pretty much filled up the left side of church. Mama was one of nine kids. One of them, Father Maury, celebrated the Mass and Father Geist co-celebrated.

After the Mass, we altar boys, me with a crucifix on a pole and Lennie and the others with candles on a stick, led Father, the pallbearers with the coffin, and the rest of the congregation down the center aisle of the church, out the front door, and down the steps.

At a funeral, the steps were the tricky part. Based on how pallbearers acted, caskets must have weighed a ton, even without somebody like Fatty Arbeiter inside. I always wondered if the pallbearers would drop their load trying to go down those steps. But three of my uncles and three cousins held on and carried Grampa through the cemetery gate to the grave. Grandpa would be right next to Grandma. She died when I was little.

Following the graveside prayers, the Fathers and us altar boys went to the sacristy. The Fathers devested. We servers de-surpliced and de-cassocked. Then we hustled over to the school basement where the Ladies Sodality ladies served lunch, and we knew for a group the size of the Schneidermeier family, they'd run out of food pretty quick. We got there just in time to scrape the serving pans clean.

After lunch, the Schneidermeier family drove out to Grampa's farm. The Walshes always came to big doings at the farm, too.

Us kids, whether we were Schneidermeiers or Walshes, loved the farm. As soon as our fathers parked the car on the grass opposite the barn, we'd pile out and go running off and play in the woods or by the pond, throwing rocks at frogs or climb into the hayloft. There were always gazillions of things to do. And our parents let us run wild. Sometimes one of us would get hurt a little, but unless there was blood, nobody went crying back to the house where the grownups sat drinking coffee or beer and talking. Of course, Pop didn't talk, but everybody else did. Well, Pop's oldest brother, my Uncle Sylvester, didn't talk either.

When I came in from running around wildly to get something to eat, I saw the two of them, Pop and Uncle Sylvester, sitting with the men in a circle of chairs, and all of them talking except the two of them. Both sat staring off at a place that was someplace else.

I also saw Mama leaned against the side of the house crying. It made me feel bad, and I wished I could cheer her up, but I wasn't going to get my face slapped again. And I was hungry.

In the kitchen, as one of my aunts dished food onto a plate for me, I saw two of my my-age girl cousins with Ronnie and Bobbie. They carried the Little Poopers around like living dolls. Most of the younger girls ran wild with us boys. Grampa called us... used to call us wild-busted-off-the-reservation Injuns. Around sixth and seventh grade, the girls didn't want to be Injuns anymore.

When us kids were played out, the women were cried out, and one of the men said, "Gotta' go to work come mornin'," we all piled into cars and went home. And even though I was a seventh-grader, I fell asleep in the back seat like a little kid before Pop drove us down the driveway hill.

In October, Grandpa Walsh died.

I didn't see anybody cry for him. Mama, I figured, was still all cried out over Uncle Ed and Grampa Schneidermeier. Uncle John didn't cry. Pop wouldn't. Their oldest brother, Sylvester, didn't. Pop's two sisters, Sister Constance and Molly, stayed dry-eyed, though Sister's usual pleasant little half a smile was gone, and at the funeral, Molly held a hanky in her hand but didn't use it.

I didn't cry. Grampa Walsh acted like he didn't want anything to do with me or any of his grandkids. Which was fine with me. We didn't visit them on the farm other than when there was butchering or crops to harvest.

When I was in fourth grade, Grampa Walsh sold his farm and moved to St. Charles and lived next to Uncle John. We saw him and Sylvester and Molly when we visited Uncle John.

When the farm was sold, I asked Pop why Grampa did that.

Pop said, "Boys ask lotsa' questions. Not alla' them need to be answered."

So, when Uncle Ed was home for Christmas that year, I asked him why Grampa Walsh sold his farm.

Uncle said, "The way it works on a farm around here, a farmer has a passel of kids. The oldest boy, if he doesn't become a priest, inherits the farm. The youngest girl doesn't get married until there's no need for her to cook and clean house. For some of them, it gets too late for them to find a husband. Like your Aunt Molly. And my sister Ruth."

Uriel, one of cousin Lucinda's brothers, said, "Uncle Sylvester isn't good for much of anything. He isn't all the way smart, but he's pretty far all the way dumb. He's an old maid man."

I wondered if that made Molly an old maid woman.

Anyway, back to Uncle Ed. "The boys, if you weren't going to inherit the farm, you got booted out and told to find a job. Sylvester was the oldest. Your Grandpa Walsh, the way I heard, when your Uncle John and then your Pop, too, turned sixteen, told them, 'You fed long enough at the family trough. Find yourself a job.' Your

Uncle John told me he packed all his clothes in two flour sacks and walked to the highway and hitched a ride to St. Charles. When it was your pop's turn, he walked to St. Ambrose."

Uncle Ed and I were sitting at the kitchen table in our apartment we rented from Mr. Schwartz in the house next to Verrukt Frau Creek. Uncle Ed sipped from his highball. When he came to town, Mama always bought a bottle of whiskey so Ed could have a highball.

"The way it worked in our family," Uncle said, "James was the oldest of my brothers. The owner of the farm next to ours got gored by a bull and died a year after he got married. James married that widow a year after that. So Homer was the next oldest, and so he would inherit the farm. Course, Homer, and Fred were a year apart, but more like twins than some actual ones I knew. So, the name on the deed doesn't matter that much. The Ignorant Louts will own it together when Dad dies."

He sipped highball. "On the Walsh farm, and this is what I heard my brothers say, I was little when this happened, but when your Uncle John and your pop got invited to leave the farm, pretty much everyone knew Sylvester wasn't smart enough to run a place like that. Everyone but your Grandpa Walsh, that is. So, he booted the younger boys. Finally, when Grandpa Walsh got too old to run the farm himself, he finally sees Sylvester can't handle it. Nothing for it but to sell the place. I think your Uncle John was mighty miffed to get shoved off the farm because it was clear Sylvester couldn't handle it. If he'd left the place to John, it would still be in the Walsh family. Owning property is important to some.

"Your Uncle John has done right well for himself in St. Charles. It started out kind of rough for him. He spent some time sleeping on benches in the park and begging for food, but he kept after it and got a job before winter set in. He always said he was grateful to his dad for not booting him off the farm right at his sixteenth birthday because his birthday is in December. He also said, 'That's the only thing I'm grateful to the man for.'"

So, after Grandpa Walsh was buried, there was no Walsh family farm to go to for the post-funeral get-together. We got together at Uncle John's place in St. Charles. Compared to the Grampa Schneidermeier gathering, we didn't need a farm to hold the get-together for Grampa Walsh. Still, there seemed to be something important missing. At the Schneidermeier farm, we kids played till we couldn't play anymore; the women cried till they were plumb out of tears, and men talked themselves out. At Uncle John's house, the gathering for Grandpa Walsh felt like everybody wanted to get it over with and get home and listen to the radio.

As a seventh-grader, all this made little sense to me. I couldn't understand it, and it didn't seem important that it should. Years later it made sense, and every once in a while, I remember to be grateful I have always been better at remembering stuff than making sense of it.

The gatherings at the Schneidermeier farm always happened on the first Sunday of the month. The first Sunday in November came and went with no gathering at the farm. Before the grandpas died, we always went to the farm on the first Sunday and we visited Uncle John in St. Charles on the third Sunday. After Christmas, we began visiting Uncle John on first and third Sundays.

I missed those farm Sundays. I missed Grampa Schneidermeier. He seemed to like his grandkids, as opposed to Grampa Walsh. To him, we were a botheration.

Anyway, on farm Sundays, we kids ran around like wild Injuns, like I said. When we got hungrier than interested in having fun, we went back to the farmhouse to eat. We went in twos and threes or fours, while the rest of the kids kept on whooping and hollering and tearing from one thing to another.

When we came in to eat, Grampa always got up from the circle of men talkers and went into the kitchen and sat with us and asked us questions. It was fun to talk about myself. If Grampa hadn't been there, I know I'd have snarfed down my food like a hog at the slop trough and hustled back to being an Injun.

Like I said, I missed farm Sundays and Grampa, but at Christmas, Pop gave me his shotgun and a .22 rifle. He taught me to shoot on the Schneidermeier farm, but we didn't eat a big meal like before. Aunt Ruth always fixed lunch for Pop and me. She was always disappointed Mama didn't come with us.

Pop showed me how to shoot both guns, sort of like he taught me to swim. He expected me to pick up shooting straight without wasting a bunch of bullets. He also told me about sitting quiet and patient under a hickory tree waiting on a squirrel. When he saw I could knock a tree rat out of the top of the hickory, he didn't come with me anymore.

He showed me how to skin and gut rabbits and squirrels. Once. And frogs. He taught me how to clean those too. Rabbits were easy. They shucked their skin almost as easy as me pulling a sock off. Squirrels you had to pull on their fur a bit. Frogs were really hard to skin. You had to use pliers to make them let go of their green clothes.

I liked to eat fried frog legs but didn't like all the work to skin a mess of them. A squirrel was good eating, and not too much work. Rabbits would have been good eating if I could have learned to hit them in the front with the shotgun blast, but I could not get the hang of leading a running bunny properly. I either shot the ground in front of my target or hit it smack in the butt, ruining those big bunny hind legs.

I did a lot of hunting that winter. The shotgun Pop gave me was an old ten-gauge double barrel. Grossman's hardware store didn't carry ten-gauge shells. They carried twelve-gauge ammo. The problem with the twelve-gauge, though, was it was a wee bit too small for the ten-gauge chamber. When I fired, the brass end of the shotgun shell expanded and stuck in the gun. I had to carry a stick with me to ram the jammed shell out so I could reload.

Mama let me hunt every other Saturday. Usually, I went with Jimmie Joe. His dad bought him a pump-action sixteen gauge. Jimmie Joe shot rabbits in the head. His dead rabbits were better to eat than mine. But I used the rifle on squirrels. He used his shotgun, so his tree rats wound up with the carcass full of shot, just like my rabbit butts did.

Any rate, that first year hunting, it felt really good to be a boy every other Saturday instead of a girl, every stinking one of them.

In the Spring, baseball cranked up again. Which was cool. But hunting season ended, and I went back to being a girl on Saturdays. Every stinking one of them.

P

Uncle Sylvester died in April. There weren't many people in the church for his funeral.

The first week in May, Uncle John put the house next to his up for sale. It had been Grandpa Walsh's house, then Uncle Sylvester's until he died. Aunt Molly didn't want to live there and moved to an old folks' home.

"Your Aunt Molly wanted to go into an old folks' home?" Jimmie Joe asked.

"Yep. We visited her, and she said, 'Finally, after seventy years cooking and cleaning up after men, here, the folks take care of me.'"

Jimmie Joe told me his Grandpa Meinerschlagen fought hard against going into a home. But he got so he needed someone with him all day every day, and his family decided he had to go in whether he wanted to or not.

"Three days after he was put in, he woke up dead," Jimmie Joe said.

Me, I figured if I was still doing girl work

when I was eighty years old, I might want to go into an old folks' home myself.

No ball game could make a day as good as the last day of classes before summer.

Seventh grade let out on Friday afternoon at three-thirty. Not one minute sooner. The nuns just had to keep us under their thumbs right up to the last second. And those last minutes, we, at least us boys, scootched around on our desk seats like we had ants in our pants.

Finally, the blessed bell jangled and unholy pandemonium cut loose. Yesterday, like every other day of the school year, we stayed in our seats until sister said, "Dismissed." But not that day. That day we dismissed ourselves and no force on earth could stop us. We pushed and shoved and laughed and pinched each other and jumbled down the steep steps to the sidewalk like a landslide.

And all the while we sang, "No more classes, no more books, no more teachers' dirty looks." Over and over we hollered it as we flooded past the church, past the cemetery and the nuns' house, and down the long flight of steps to Hickory Street leading us across the highway to town. I thought we'd continue to sing all the way home, but at the foot of the hill, when the nuns couldn't hear us anymore, the song faded away.

No matter. School was out for the summer, and good as I was at baseball and football, there was one thing I was even better at: being Boss of Summer Afternoons.

I went to bed that night thinking about what we'd do the next day. Well, I thought about the next afternoon. Not the dirty morning with its dirty floors, dirty furniture, dirty clothes, dirty toilet, dirty *diapers!* I decided what we'd do. We'd go fishing, catch a mess of catfish and carp—hopefully more cats than boney-as-all-get-out carp—and Mama would fry them up for us. A fish fry to celebrate the first day of *No more classes, no more books, etcetera.*

It did bug me having to waste half a day helping Mama when I could have been playing with the other town boys all day. That stunk like the outhouse in August. But Mama was the boss of mornings.

Saturday morning, I was dreaming about the fish fry when Pop shook me awake.

"Get up, get dressed, come down, and eat."

"It's Saturday, Pop. School's out for the summer."

"Get up, get dressed, come down, and eat. I don't like to have to say a thing twice."

I got downstairs at five-thirty. Breakfast got

itself eaten a lot slower than lunch would have if I were going out to play after.

At five-forty-five, Pop said, "It's time to go."

"I'm not done eating yet."

"You're done."

He gave me that *I-don't-like-to-have-to-say-a-thing-twice* look.

Outside, I put my bike in the trunk of the car like he told me. Pop drove me out to this farm next to the parish picnic grounds and parked next to the sidewalk leading to the back porch of the farmhouse.

The farmer was waiting for us. He was shorter than Pop, younger, too.

Pop said, "You're working for Mr. Neidlinger. Do what he says."

Pop took my bike out of the trunk, leaned it against the fence around the backyard, got in the car, and drove away.

"Come with me." The farmer led me to his milk barn. Inside, there was a room with a big tank and pipes and tubing running into it. But he wanted me in the next room and opened a door; and stink, like from a dead skunk and a maggoty dead dog piled on top of a bunch of dirty diapers, punched me in the gut. I didn't know whether to puke or try to breathe.

Mr. Neidlinger laughed. "You'll get used to it."

Yeah. Right after my nose dies and falls off.

I breathed. Through my nose. I wasn't letting that smell into my mouth.

Tolerable. I'd looked that word up in Sister Daniel's dictionary, but I never really understood it until that morning. But tolerable didn't necessarily mean I'd ever get used to the stink. I didn't puke, though.

The room had two stalls for the cows and a pit between them for the farmer to operate the business end of the milking machine. The business end was four rubber-lined aluminum cylinders to plug onto a cow's teats. With the S on the end, teats was a five-letter word, so it was okay to call those danglies from the udder that word. That other word, with the I in it and the S on the end, was a four-letter word, and that made it nasty.

I asked Mr. Neidlinger how the milking worked. He explained. I never knew that's how milk got into our refrigerator. I sure never imagined anything like that. Nor did I imagine that while the cow was being milked, it stood there and ate. And pooped. I mean, there was a good six or eight inches of runny cow poop on the floor of the stall.

"Now this is the only part of the operation you need to understand. Use the scoop shovel. Get as much of it out as you can with that. Then use the hose and spray the place down good. An inspector comes around to check and make sure I have a clean operation. So, keep that in mind. I'm going to eat breakfast. We'll see how you did when I get done. Oh. Put these boots on. They'll be big on you, so, be careful you don't trip or you'll plop in the flops."

Great! Instead of the boss of summer afternoons, I was the boss of morning cow poop.

So, I worked for Mr. Neidlinger for two weeks. We did a lot of different things. One of them I liked. Driving his tractors. He had two of them. One was a red Farmall like Lennie and I played with in the sandbox when we were kids. The other was a green John Deere. Mr. Neidlinger called it Poppin' Johnny. I thought it made more of a *put-put* sound, but I wasn't going to mention that. The other thing that wasn't mentioned was pay. So, I asked Mr. N.

"Your father said I didn't have to pay you. Didn't he tell you?"

Huh. There were some things Pop didn't like to say even once.

We baled the first cutting of alfalfa that day, and I rode my bike home in the dark. My bike had a headlight that attracted bugs more than it illuminated the road. I pedaled with my lips pressed tight together.

At home, Pop was reading the paper in the living room. I asked him if he told Mr. Neidlinger he didn't have to pay me.

"A boy needs to learn how to work. He don't need no practice getting paid."

He went back to his paper.

That night I lay in bed thinking. I had wanted to help Pop build the house, but he didn't have time to teach me to work. So, he gave me to Mr. Neidlinger for free. On the plus side, it was man work, not girl work. Though dealing with one dirty diaper was sure easier than dealing with what Mr. Neidlinger's whole herd of cows produced. Tomorrow was Sunday. I tried to make up a song, like *No more classes, no more books—*. All I got was the last line, *No poop to scoop today.*

I knew that milking cows was a twice a day, seven days a week deal, and Mr. Neidlinger would be up Sunday morning. And he'd have to scoop his own cow poop.

Then I wondered if Pop was going to wake me at five-thirty and make me ride my bike out there to scoop poop and come back in time to go to church. Wondering about that kept me awake for a while.

It turned out I didn't have to worry, but the little bit of sleep I got caused me to fall asleep during the sermon. Which caused Pop to shake me, and he gave me his *Don't-make-me-shake-you-twice* look.

The Neidlingers had five boys. The youngest was four months old, the oldest younger than

Lennie. I ate lunch with their family every day I worked. Mrs. Neidlinger never sat down. She served her husband and me and the children. When we went back to work, I presumed she ate, then.

After working there a month, Mister N. and I went to lunch on a Monday. There was a girl in the kitchen. Gladys was eighteen. She'd graduated from high school and needed to earn money for college that fall. Mr. N. hired her to help Mrs. N. the rest of the summer.

That afternoon, I asked Mr. Neidlinger, "So, you're paying Gladys to do girl work? Shoot. Why didn't you say you needed girl work done? I clean, I do dishes, I do diapers. I can't cook, but I can do the other girl work. And I'll do it cheaper than Gladys."

He started paying me two dollars a day, and I stayed the boss of cow poop.

Also that summer, my sister got born. Pop sure liked Laura. Each evening, he'd put aside his paper to hold her a spell. I never saw him hold Bobbie and Ronnie, and that made me wonder if he ever held Lennie and me. I didn't ask Mama, and I sure would not ask Pop. I pictured him saying "Nope." I could not picture him saying "Yep."

We graduated from eighth grade on Friday. For the ceremony in the big hall on the second floor with the stage on one end, I had to wear a white shirt and a necktie. The evening before, Pop tied it around my neck. Then he untied it, told me to pay attention to how he did it and knotted it again.

Necktie tying, he could do twice. Actually, he had to show me four times. I couldn't remember how hard it was to learn how to tie a shoe, but this was harder.

"Tomorrow night, you knot it yourself." Then he gave me the *Don't-make-me-have-to-say-it-twice* look. "And," he said, "from now on, you wear a tie to church of a Sunday like I do."

"Does Lennie have to wear one too?"

Pop got a look on his face I'd never seen before. It was sort of like his he's-not-saying-a-thing-twice face, but instead of being hard and cold, this one wasn't all hard and all cold.

"No. Because he's not as growed up as you." He put his hand on my shoulder. "Mr. Neidlinger says you work hard. That farm work put some muscle on you. Come fall, you'll be going to high school. You're going to learn stuff I never did. Maybe you'll learn enough to do clean jobs, like in a grocery store. But, whatever you do, whether you use the muscles in your arms and shoulders or those inside your noggin, always remember to make those muscles sweat for the man you're workin' for."

"If you work hard, do you get paid more?"

"If a man gives you a job, you worry about are you sweating enough. He'll worry about how much to pay you."

Pop picked up the paper, which said, *Don't bother me no more.*

I wanted to ask one more question. *If working hard doesn't earn more money, why not just do like Lennie?*

Since I started with Mr. Neidlinger, Lennie the Loafer—that's what I called him—had to help Mama. Mama called him Better-than-no-help-at-all-but-not-by-much. I heard her say that at one of her Tuesday Night Rosary Ladies meetings.

Lennie did wet diapers, but not the dirties. Faced with one, he'd go "Urk, urk," and he made it look like his stomach lurched so strongly it made his shoulders move.

"Ach! Go outside and puke in the yard," Mama would tell him.

I knew Lennie had Tom Sawyer-ed Mama, but I didn't say anything. I had tried to Tom Sawyer people a couple of times, but it never got me out of anything. It was one thing Lennie was better at than me.

But it sure deepened the puzzle I was trying to work out. Why had Pop talked to me the way he did?

I had always been able to talk to Mama. About most things. I remembered when Lennie went through his *why* phase. No matter what someone said, he'd say, "Why?" One day, Mama, Lennie, and I were in the kitchen. I sat on the windowsill and practiced letters and numbers, and Lennie asked her questions. She'd answer, and he'd say, "Why?" Even dumb as I was at five, I could see Lennie only asked the question so she'd answer, and he could ask his stupid word. Over and over. I expected her to "Ach!" him and put a stop to the game, but she didn't.

It took me a moment to figure out how to ask my own question without using Lennie's stupid word. "How come you let Lennie get away with asking that word over and over and over? It makes my ears hurt."

"It's a phase all boys and girls go through growing up."

"Me too?"

"Yes, and you were just as persistent as Lennie."

"Did you go through it?"

"Yes. One time when I was a bit older than you, one of my cousins was giving the 'whys' to my mother. I asked my mama the same question you asked. My papa answered it.

"He told me all children went through that phase, just like I said. Then Papa told me each of my brothers and sisters was a better why‑er than the one before. And me, being the second youngest, I was the best why‑er of all. Until Ruth got *why* old."

It was hard to think Mama was ever as dumb as Lennie, and even harder to imagine I was. I had another thought.

"Did Pop *why* everything, too?"

Mama looked at me and shook her head. "Your pop had it tough growing up."

"Why?" from Lennie.

"Ach," Mama said. "You boys go play in the sandbox."

So it was Lennie's fault I didn't get an answer to my question, and a few others until I was twenty‑six. Why had Pop spoken with me the way he had at my graduation from eighth grade? Why hadn't Pop why‑ed the heck out of things like other boys and girls did?

Another thing happened after I graduated from eighth. That spring, Mrs. Neidlinger had another baby, and Gladys came back to help during the summer. Now, I won't say I didn't notice Gladys the previous year. Of course, I noticed her. She cooked and served food. But that summer after eighth, I noticed she was a girl. Not just *a* girl. Gladys was beautiful. Light glistened off her golden hair, pulled back into a ponytail. And her chest stuck out some.

For the life of me, I cannot remember what her face looked like.

But she was beautiful.

4

High school was way different. It was way, way different from grade school.

First off, St. Peter High School was six miles away in St. Charles. Even I, Eddie Walsh, was not going to run home for lunch and back all that way. So, I took a baloney sandwich in a paper bag.

To get there, I rode with Ollie Weisendinger in his older brother's car. Ollie was a senior at St. Peter, and his older brother worked in a place close to St. Louis. To ride with him, I had to be at the Weisendinger house on Second Street by quarter till seven. He drove right by my house, but he wouldn't stop to pick me up there. I asked.

"You wanna ride with me in my car, you be here, at my house, and in my car by sixteen minutes before seven. I walk out the door at quarter till and we leave as soon as my butt hits the driver's seat."

Except for how many words he used, he sounded like Pop. The other thing was Mama said I should give him two bits every day I rode with him. It bought a gallon of gas, she said, and, "We Walshes don't like to be beholden to no one."

The other thing about high school: no recess. We did get an hour off at noon. For lunch. But how long does it take to eat a baloney sandwich? I could snarf one down in a minute, but city people needed an hour. And in the cafeteria, there was a lot of talking going on and not much eating. Even the boys talked. I expected it of girls, but the city boys jabbered away, too, like an Elm tree full of chippies next to a wheat field being combined.

Linda Zigmund and Alice Ashe were the only kids from my grade-school class at St. Peter. Their mothers took turns driving them to and picking them up from school every day. Mama said Linda's pop said, "We can afford the high school and the gas to get there and back, but my wife shopping in St. Charles every other day all the while school is in session is going to put us in the poorhouse."

Mrs. Zigmund told that story on herself at Wednesday coffee, and Mama repeated it at our supper table. When he ate, Pop always sat a little hunched over and staring at his plate, like if he didn't watch his food carefully, some of it would get away. He looked up and said, "That'd do it."

That was Mama and Pop yucking it up over a joke.

Anyway, Alice and Linda seemed to fit right in with the St. Charles girls. And with the boys, too. They were always in the middle of a multiple-table giggle and gabfest. I watched them a little and got a lot of homework done.

Most days, a passel of kids would troop down the hill to Ochsner's Pharmacy and Confectionery for malts. I wouldn't have gone even if somebody invited me. Ever since I stole Mama's egg money for one when I was a kid, I didn't like those things. Too sweet. Besides, just thinking about a malt made my butt remember my first spanking. Back then, before I became Iron Butt Eddie Walsh, spankings hurt.

Another thing hurt in my freshman year. Tryouts for the school baseball team.

The school used a ball field at Blanchette Park, probably two miles from St. Peter. Some juniors and seniors had cars, and they gave rides to those of us who didn't.

I thought sure I'd make the team. But I had gone from being the tallest boy in my grade-school class to the shortest one trying out for the team. I was a fast runner, but not the fastest. I could play any position on the field, except pitcher. What I couldn't do was hit a curveball.

"Eddie," the coach said. "Work on hitting a curve and try out again next year."

I, Eddie Walsh, the best baseball player in grade school—after Sister Daniels, of course—couldn't even make the team in high school.

I had to get from Blanchette Park to the corner of Kingshighway and Clay so I could hitchhike home. Near as I could figure, it was about a mile, but it was as long as that walk I took at the start of sixth grade when I pushed my bike home to get my spanking that broke Mama's hand. The longest walks are not measured in how many miles long they are. The longest walks are the ones where you don't want to get where you're going, but you have to go there anyway.

When I got home, I found Bobbie and Ronnie, now five and four, playing in the yard. They said, "Hi, Eddie," like they were one kid. I didn't answer, just passed them by, and passed by the steps to the house. Next to the garage, I lifted the lid off the garbage can, deposited my ball glove, and said goodbye to it.

I stood there holding the lid to the garbage can. After the coach told me to try again next year, I felt sort of numb inside. Not making the team hurt, but it was like that other mind I had kept the hurt outside of me and wouldn't let it in. The other mind seemed to get tired, and the hurt was shouldering its way in.

The glove doesn't deserve to be in there. You do, though.

I wished I could get that other mind out of my head and put it in the garbage.

"Wishing for something you ain't never gonna' git, that's the biggest waste of time there is." Pop told me that once.

I put the lid on the can of garbage and the ball glove and entered the house.

Mama had supper in the oven. Every other day, supper smelled good. That day, I wished I could tell my nose to not smell it—that almost stopped me in my tracks. I was pretty sure I'd thought up a split infinitive, which we'd just heard about in English that day, and which I, at best, halfway understood.

Anyway, back to that day. I knew noses didn't listen from dealing with the Little Poopers and Mr. Neidlinger's milk cows.

Mama sat at the table reading the paper. Once she got supper in the oven, she had a few minutes to read the paper. She looked up. "How was school?"

"Fine."

I didn't slow down but took the stairs to the attic. I had a book I'd checked out of the school library and sat at my table-desk and opened it. It had been a long time since I borrowed a book from Simon Grossman. He started high school a year before me, and I hadn't seen him anywhere during his freshman year but at church. So, I was pretty hungry for a book and plunged right into it.

It was pleasant outside, and I had opened the window facing the Meinerschlagen's house. Tires crunched on gravel. I looked up. Jimmie Joe's mom stopped their car in the drive. Jimmie Joe piled out of the shotgun seat and Sam Waterman bailed out of the rear.

"Thanks, Mrs. Meinerschlagen. My mom will pick us up tomorrow."

"You're welcome, Sam, and congratulations again on making the team."

Making the team?

Did Jimmie Joe and Sam make the St. Charles High baseball team?

"Got time to play a little catch?" Jimmie Joe said. "I want to work on my curveball."

"Gotta' get home. How about Eddie?" Sam looked up at my window. "Hey, Eddie, you up there?"

I didn't answer, being busy with trying to get a hold of the notion they made the team in the really big public high school and I couldn't make it in my little Catholic school. The notion was harder to understand than a word I never heard before. For new words, I had Sister Daniel's dictionary. This was different.

"Come on, Eddie." Sam again. "Answer me. I know you're up there. You got your light on."

Poop!

The other thing, something good had happened for them, and I should have said, "Thanks, God, for blessing Jimmie J. and Sam." But the only words that would form up in the box of rocks between my ears was, "What the heck, God? I've always been a better ballplayer than everybody except Sister Daniels. What happened?"

Why won't my mind do what I want it to? Why?

I wished I had Cousin Lucinda to talk to about this, but she was in the convent and happy to be there. *Thank you, God, for blessing Cousin* Lucinda *with happiness.* At least my stupid mind agreed to pray that prayer.

"I gotta' get home," Sam said. "Go knock on the Walshes' door. Eddie'll catch for you."

I dug a sigh out of my toenails, huffed it out, and stood by the window. "I'll catch for you, Jimmie Joe. I got to get my glove first."

Down the attic steps, out the side door, to the side of the garage, pick my glove off the top of the garbage; then I could play catch.

Boy! Was I surprised when I got to the Meinerschlagen's front yard. I hadn't seen much of my neighbor since eighth grade let out. All summer I worked nine hours, or longer, six days a week for Mr. Neidlinger. It was eight p.m., or later, by the time I got home. At the start of summer, Jimmie Joe and I were about the same height. Now he was quite a bit taller. And heavier. He looked as big as Large Louie. Well, not really, but big.

We threw the ball back and forth as he warmed up. Then he took a rubber home plate from his front porch and placed it on the grass in front of me.

"A couple of fastballs first." Jimmie Joe growled. His voice had grown up some too.

He threw hard. If I didn't catch his pitches in the web of my glove, my hand hurt like blue blazes.

"Here comes a curve," he said.

Holy Crap! I didn't know a baseball could do such things. That ball was coming right for me, a little high, but in the strike zone and aimed at the middle of the plate. I put my glove up, and the stupid ball dove and cut to my right and I missed catching it by a country mile.

Jimmie Joe grinned. "I told you a curveball was coming."

The ball went all the way into our yard, and I ran to get it. His next two pitches I had to chase after also, but then I got the hang of it, mostly. I didn't catch all his curves, but I got my glove on them and kept the ball in front of me.

No wonder I couldn't hit that kind of pitch. I couldn't even catch them most of the time.

"The catcher on our team is a senior," Jimmie Joe said. "He's really good."

That stung.

"I was getting the hang of the curve this summer, during Little League. But you were busy being a farmer."

That stung, too.

We always said farm boys did not make good ballplayers. They didn't have time to practice. I used to be a good ballplayer. Not anymore. Not since Pop gave me to Mr. Neidlinger, and he turned me into a farmer.

Jimmie Joe said, "Did you try out for your high school team?"

Then he gave the hand signal for another curve, wound up and threw. This pitch I caught. It started out off the plate inside, then curved and caught the corner of the plate. If I'd been the hitter, I'd have backed out of the batter's box. Jimmie Joe was good. I tossed the ball back to him from my catcher's crouch. I didn't want to answer his question. I hoped he'd just let it go.

Jimmie Joe stood in his front yard staring at me squatting behind his portable home plate. He frowned. "You didn't make it?"

This was one of those questions I didn't like. To answer properly, I'd have to say, *Yes, I did not make it.* A stupid way to say a thing. But also, one of those questions it'd be better if it wasn't asked in the first place. Bad enough I didn't make the team but having to admit it out loud, in front of God and everybody. Well, it was just Jimmie Joe and me playing catch, but it'd be all over town before bedtime.

I stood up from my crouch. "Yes. I did not make it."

I walked away and went back to the trash barrel and lifted the lid. This time I'd throw the glove away for good.

"What're you doing?"

When Pop's voice surprised me, it was as if he grabbed my heart like it was a chicken neck about to be wrung. He stood on the bottom of the three steps leading up to the side door of our house.

"Bring me that glove," he said, and went inside.

Mama was in the kitchen at the stove.

Pop said to her, "Supper kin wait. Find out what's eating at Eddie."

Mama turned off the burners under the mashed potatoes and the string beans. Lennie sat at his place and Ronnie and Bobbie at theirs, and all three stared at me as if I'd stolen their dinner instead of delaying it a tiny-teeny bit. Laura sat in her infant seat atop the table.

Mama led me into the front room. We sat on the sofa.

From the kitchen, I heard five-year-old

Bobby say he was hungry. Pop told him supper had to wait.

"Why?" Bobby the why-er. I felt like he'd grown up and out of Little-pooper-dom, and I'd grown down into Little-can't-make-the-team Guy.

Mama asked what was wrong. I told her. She walked out to the kitchen and told Pop. I stayed on the sofa. Mama talking to Pop about me. It felt like she was talking about Lennie.

"Eddie," Pop said, "wash up and come to supper."

I did, and we ate. After dessert, Mama took Laura and the three boys to the front room. Pop and I stayed at the table, me across from him.

"Boy. I am not spending money to send you to a Catholic high school to play baseball. I am sending you there to learn two kinds of things. First, I expect you to learn what you need to get a job so you can have a better life than your mama and me were able to put together. The second, and this is most important, at Catholic high school, you have God in your life every day. When you graduate, it will be up to you to keep Him in your life every day."

He slurped his milky coffee.

"I knowed plenty of men who were raised Catholic, but when they got out on their own, they let God get away from them and they never got Him back. Do not let that happen to you. Hear?"

Pop glared at me. He expected an answer.

"I hear you, Pop."

"Nuther thing. You want to quit baseball because you can't hit a curve. If baseball is important to you, you can figure out a way to get on top of a curveball. If you decide to quit, make sure it's for some other reason."

Again, he expected an answer.

"Yes, Pop."

He went to read his paper. I washed the dishes. Lennie came to dry them. And break a plate. And drop a whole handful of silverware so I had to wash them again. My younger brother would never be the girl I was. I also noticed he had gotten to be as tall as me.

At least I'm still taller than Bobbie the why-er.

No consolation came with that thought.

After Lennie was done breaking dishes and dropping silverware, I went up to do my homework. Doing homework, I wasn't short anymore.

ii

St. Ambrose consisted of Main Street and Second Street, with Elm, Maple, and Oak Street connecting them. At the west end of town, another street ran between Grossman's Hardware Store and the levee along Verrukt Frau Creek. It headed south, crossed the highway, and climbed Church Hill, and was called Church Street. None of the streets had signs with their names on them. Everybody could remember the names of six streets, even Large Louie.

Anyway, the St. Charles public high school sent a bus for the St. Ambrose kids. The bus parked on the corner of Main and Maple in front of the American Legion. The kids all congregated on the sidewalk in front of the Legion until it was time to board.

When I walked to the Weisendinger house to catch my ride, I walked down Main on the side opposite the Legion. The bus kids never noticed me. The morning after I found out I was short, I saw Little Heiny Stiert—an eighth-grader now—standing beside some of the St. Charles High students and talking up a storm. He wasn't little Little Heiny anymore. He was big Little Heiny.

Poop! Everybody's growing taller but me. And Large Louie.

Of course, Large Louie was born large. That's what folks said.

I turned the corner onto Maple, turned my back on big Little Heiny. I hoped it would cure me of being short like homework had last night.

Poop! Double poop!!

In grade school, our classes were rammed down our throats. In high school, we got to pick one. I thought about picking Home Ec. Only girls took it, but I wanted to see if I was a better girl than the girls. Before pick-your-optional-class day, I remembered Big Dumb Louie and Our Little Heiny. That's who they were to the rest of us, while I, Eddie Walsh, was—had been—the Boss of Summer Afternoons and the best ballplayer, after Sister Daniels of course. Those were cool things to be. If it turned out I was a better girl than the girls, I'd be known as Girl-boy. Girl-boy seemed like it was real close to being a Big Dumb Louie or an Our Little Heiny.

One of the options was Latin. Of course, I knew how to say Latin stuff. If it was written on a card like it was for us, altar boys. The nuns taught us how to pronounce the words on the card, but they never told us what they meant. Until thinking about what optional class to pick, it was okay to not understand the words. The prayers we read off the cards were only used at the altar during Mass. As servers, we put on cassocks and surplices, covering our regular clothes, and we became altar boys, and we helped the vestment-ed priest as he celebrated the Mass. It dawned on me: I was an altar boy and at the altar with the priest, and I didn't know what the crap I was saying to God. That didn't seem okay anymore.

Anyhow, that's how I decided to take Latin as my optional class. Our teacher was Sister Scholastica, which seemed like as good a name for a teacher nun as Large Louie was for him.

Sister told us that to learn any new language, we had to open our minds to the way people who speak other languages think. There isn't a way to make a word-for-word translation from English to Latin, or to many other languages.

She said, "People have created words that combine a noun with a definite or indefinite article, for instance. In some languages, the verb comes at the end of a sentence, not between the subject and the object. To master a new language, you have to master not only the words but the thought process used to create the language."

That sounded hard.

Great! Now you tell me this. Two days after, I threw my baseball glove away for good.

Walshes were not quitters, but I'd quit baseball. So, I selected Latin because, besides the talking to God thing, I needed a new baseball, something to take its place. Except I never expected it to be as hard as hitting a curve. I thought about it, but I couldn't quit Latin. Quitting one thing was bad enough. If I quit two things in one week, well, that would make me Eddie the Quitter.

That Saturday, in the box, I told Father Geist about quitting baseball and wanting to quit Latin.

Father said, "Eddie, life is full of curveballs. It isn't full of easy."

My mid-semester report card smiled an A in Latin at me, and I smiled at the other As on it.

The day after report cards came out, in our afternoon Latin class, Sister gave us a quiz to see how much of the first-semester material we had forgotten. She read the questions to us, and we were to write the answers on a blank piece of paper. Then we were to grade the paper of the person across the aisle from us.

I graded Samantha's paper. Sister read the answers. Samantha had everything right but the answer to question seven. *Zing.* I marked it wrong, and after answer ten, handed the paper back to her. Another St. Charles girl, Teresa Yount, sat in front of Samantha. Samantha handed her paper up to Teresa. Teresa looked at the paper and stuck her hand up.

"Sister," Teresa said, "would you repeat the answer to question number seven, please?"

Sister said it.

"Eddie marked number seven wrong on Samantha's paper, but she got it right," Teresa said.

"Underline that question, Teresa, and everybody pass your papers to the front."

The papers went forward. Samantha turned and scowled at me. So did Teresa. The looks on their faces reminded me of Alice Ashe when I went to her house to apologize for not kissing her. Apologizing to Alice made the situation worse. I'd disappointed her, and my "Sorry" made her live that disappointment all over again. I was trying to decide what to do about my mistake with Samantha's paper. I'd just decided on saying "Sorry" in Latin, but before

I could get the words organized in my head, Samantha got words organized in hers.

"You did that on purpose!" she hissed.

I hadn't done it on purpose. I knew I'd answered all the questions correctly, and I was thinking about going to church and understanding the Latin prayers, finally, and thinking: *God, all those years I prayed all those prayers to You, and I didn't know what the heck I was saying.*

And I wondered if I should figure out how many times I'd been to Mass since third grade and started serving. Should I say all those prayers over again, understanding what I said now? Daily Mass during grade school. Probably two hundred Masses a year. Six years. I owed God one thousand two hundred prayers. It was like putting Mama's egg money back in the glass bowl. That's what I'd been thinking when the St. Charles girls turned me into Latin Louse Eddie.

Poop. Just when I thought I had a handle on high school.

The next day at lunch, a St. Charles guy named Roger Rottermick sat down next to me. I knew who he was because he was the other straight-A student in our class, but he'd never talked to me before.

Roger was my height, skinny, and wore his hair in a perfectly flat flattop. He turned his eyes on me. They were dark brown and bored into me like Sister Superior's used to.

"The girls are saying you graded Samantha's paper wrong on purpose. She's the only freshman in Latin to get an A on her report card besides you. The girls say you want to be the only one getting an A at the end of the year."

I frowned at Brown Eyes. Then I took a bite out of my baloney sandwich.

"You got nothing to say for yourself?"

"The girls—" I almost said *St. Charles girls,* but Alice Ashe was in Latin class also, and she sure as shootin' wouldn't stick up for me. "—will say what they want to say. What I say won't change what they think. I'm a dumb hick from St. Ambrose."

"Did you do it on purpose?"

"I did not. See, Roger. Want to know something, ask a question. You just sat down and threw an accusation in my face. What I did was make a mistake. I should have been paying attention to what Sister Scholastica was saying, but I was thinking about something else. It wasn't on purpose."

Roger put his hand on my shoulder. "You know, Eddie Walsh, for a farm hick from St. Ambrose, you just might be a sort of close to an almost half-ways decent guy."

"That, Roger Rottermick, is the nicest insult anyone has ever given me."

He grinned, stood, and walked away.

After that, Roger always brought his lunch bag to where I was sitting, and we ate together.

At Christmas, I got the two things I'd asked for: Brylcreem and Clearasil. I knew about those things because I'd seen them on Uncle John's TV.

Santa also brought us a TV. Of course, it was Pop who bought it. From Holland Hesse.

What happened was Mr. Meinerschlagen built a new building for his grocery store across Maple Street from the American Legion Post. The post office, which had occupied one corner of the old grocery store, now had its own concrete block building and parking lot behind Meinerschlagens.

One thing was funny. The sign on the front of the old store said "Groceries," but inside the dark building, Jimmie's dad had crammed all kinds of stuff in there to sell. Mama bought my clothes and shoes from the "grocery" store. The sign on the new store said, "Meinerschlagens." All the new store sold was groceries. Inside the lighting was bright, the linoleum floors gleamed, the aisles of canned and packaged goods were straight and orderly. There was room for shopping carts to move around the place. In the old store, shoppers used plastic baskets to cart their things to the one cash register. The new store had four cash registers. Checkout counters, they called them.

Jimmie Joe's dad sold his old building to Mr. Hesse. Holland was the only guy I ever heard about who was named for a country except for that Vespucci guy.

Anyway, Holland set up a TV sales and repair business in the building that still sported the "Groceries" sign. That's where Pop, as Santa's agent, bought our TV. At a grocery store.

The TV was just like the one Uncle John had for two or three years. A big wooden box with a little screen looking out of it. On that little screen on Uncle John's TV is where I saw the ads for Clearasil and Brylcreem.

I'm not sure I would have noticed my pimples if it hadn't been for those ads. And I sure wouldn't have thought of putting grease in my hair, even though a little dab would do me.

After Christmas, the last thing I did in the in-house every morning was to Brylcreem and comb my hair and to smear Clearasil on the pimples on my cheek and chin, and while doing so, I said, "Thank You, God, for keeping pimples off my nose." My nose wasn't a potato nose like Pop's. It was more like Mama's, an upside-down V-shaped thing, but it wasn't short. The last thing I wanted was a pimple on the end of it like I was Rudolph.

Before leaving the in-house, I checked the mirror above the sink. Not too much Clearasil on the red booboos, which is what Bobbie called them. Hair slicked and combed. I looked like the guys in the Brylcreem commercials. Pretty snazzy.

I hope that's not a sin of pride, God.

Going back to school after Christmas break, life was good. Except for one thing. With Brylcreem on my hair, I didn't want to wear a cap and mess up my duck-butt. I was really glad Ollie Weisendinger's brother dropped us off right in front of St. Peter church, which was right next to the high school. Otherwise, my ears would have frozen off. I had a cap in my bookbag for hitchhiking home after school.

On Valentine's Day, St. Peter High School was going to have a Sadie Hawkins dance. One thing was sure. No St. Charles girl would ask me to the thing. Besides not knowing how to dance, I worried over whether there'd be spin the bottle, or other ways for kissing to happen.

I asked Roger.

"Ways for kissing to happen? You were born a boy. Girls are born girls. Those are the only two things required for kissing to happen. Well, maybe you have to like the girl and be on a date."

"Anyway, it won't be a problem. Nobody'll ask *me* to the Sadie Hawkins dance."

"Don't be so sure. The girls really dig your wavy hair and your duck butt, Eddie. They talk about which of your butts is the cutest."

Hot flashed over my face, and I got a little miffed at him. I liked Roger, and here he was poking fun at the hick farm boy.

Before I could say anything more, a girl left a girl-table and headed for ours. I lowered my head and voice, "Sarah Esterhausen's coming over.".

"Do you mind if I sit down, Eddie?"

I'd thought she was coming to see Roger, maybe ask him to the dance. Sarah was way cute. Short black hair. Dark brown eyes that did a funny thing to my stomach when she looked at me. Her complexion was summer suntan. The other girls all looked pale compared to her. She was from Orchard Farm, a town even smaller than St. Ambrose.

"Eddie," Roger said, "your mouth is hanging open. Why don't you use it to say, 'Sure, Sarah. Sit down.'" He got up and walked away.

"Sure, Sarah. Sit down."

She smiled like I said something funny, and she sat, tucking her skirt under her smooth as could be. I admired how girls did that, managed dresses and skirts like it was no effort at all. Us altar boys were such klutzes in our cassocks, ankle-length black dresses, really. All we had to do in them was to stand, kneel, and sit. Standing was the only thing we did smoothly. After kneeling, we scootched around with our weight on one knee while we pulled one side of the dress loose, then shifted weight to the other side. I never thought about hiking up the cassock before kneeling to keep from trapping some of it until after I knelt on it. Standing up from kneeling, you had to be careful the back of your dress didn't hook onto the heels of your shoes or you could rip the stupid thing. Then the church ladies would have to mend it.

At any rate, I admired how Sarah handled her skirt. I admired how she handled being a girl. And as she sat across the table from me, I could no longer think of myself as being a heck of a good girl. Sarah was a G I R L girl, and I was no kind of one, and all the diapers, dishes, and dirty floors to mop in the whole wide world would not make me one.

And that was just fine.

But I was worried. How the heck was I going to know what to say to her without Roger there to tell me?

"I'm Sarah Esterhausen, Eddie. My father has a farm near Orchard Farm."

Well, I knew who she was, but I was surprised she knew my name. I was pretty sure she expected me to say something. But this was way different from sitting next to a girl in class.

She smiled. "What does your father do?"

"He works at the grain elevator in St. Ambrose."

"Do you have brothers and sisters?"

"Three brothers. Lennie and the Little Poopers." Her eyebrows raised. "Uh, Bobbie and Ronnie."

The look on her face and in her eyes changed. I got the feeling she knew stuff about me I didn't know.

"You're the oldest, and you have to help your mother with the little ones. I'm the oldest, too. One younger sister. I help my father with farming more than I help Mother in the house. I drive a tractor, milk the cows, fork manure into the spreader."

Sarah smiled. "Your mouth is hanging open again, Eddie. You probably think that's boy work, driving a tractor and those kinds of things."

They certainly were boy work.

"My father says, 'On a farm, there's no such thing as boy work and girl work. There's just work.'"

I pictured Pop saying such a thing. Only he wouldn't have used so many words.

"Uh, Eddie."

The tone of her voice jerked me from being half there to all there. I'd read about small talk. I understood that's what Sarah had been doing, small-talking me. Her new tone of voice said she'd shifted gears, like on a ten-speed. She had shifted into big-talk gear. I sat up straight.

"Will you go to the Sadie Hawkins Valentine's Day sock hop with me?"

Knock me over with a feather! Of all the things she might possibly have said to me, that was the impossiblest. Now, the right way to say that was *That was impossible.* Once a thing was *Impossible,* that was it. Ball game over. The nature of impossibility brooked no categorization of degrees of impossibility. Sister Hildegard told us that about words like impossible, so I was thinking about impossibility and almost ready to think about answering her when I saw a frown wrinkle her forehead. She'd been looking sunshine at me, and now she was all clouded over.

I thought about saying, *Do you like my duck butt?* but my mouth got smart enough to not say that just in time. What it said was, "Yes."

Sunshine again.

iii

If my next report card depended on how well I paid attention in my afternoon classes, it was going to be all Fs.

Girls like my duck butt!

Sarah Esterhausen asked me to the sock hop!

I felt like I had climbed up to the top of Mr. Grossman's steeple on Holy Martyrs Church in St. Ambrose and I could see all the way to St. Louis. Heck, I could see all the way to Kansas City!

But then it was like the tiles on the steeple came loose and I tumbled down and splatted onto the concrete sidewalk in front of the steps leading to the big double doors.

I, Eddie Walsh, had a problem—a big problem. My feet didn't know how to dance!

Cousin Lucinda had gone to the convent. Maybe she wouldn't have taught me to dance. She had two sisters, though.

Altogether, Uncle John and Aunt Beatrice

had eight kids. The five boys were all named after archangels. Gabriel, my oldest cousin, not the archangel, was in the seminary.

Which reminded me of the annual trip to the seminary that the grade school sponsored for eighth-grade boys. Leading up to my trip, I started thinking about it. Maybe I should be a priest. Being a priest, I knew I'd have to give up things, some of them important like—I didn't know what to think. Before, I would have stuck baseball there, but since I didn't make the school team, baseball no longer filled me up. It emptied me. So maybe I wouldn't be giving anything up to be a priest.

Anyway, at the seminary, they talked to us about all the school we'd have to complete before we could be ordained. There was high school, regular college, then actual priest school. It sounded like two full doses of college. Lotta school. Now Pop was big on school. He only went through four grades and Mama six. According to him, the more school you could get, the better off you'd be. After high school, I'd have done twelve years. After Seminary, it would be something like twenty. I'd be twenty-six years old and have spent practically my whole life in school. That seemed pretty darned close to forever. But when I thought about it, what did I really know how to do? I knew how to be a girl when Mama needed me to be one; I knew how to scoop cow poop for Mr. Neidlinger; and I knew how to go to school. Maybe it wouldn't be so bad.

The last thing they showed us on the tour was the bowling alley in the basement. A second-year seminarian showed it to us. The way he talked about it, he obviously thought it was the coolest thing. But to me, it was dark and dreary. It just sucked all the feel-good juice right out of me. It was more like a dungeon than a place to have fun.

If I was going to be a priest, I knew there was this celibacy thing, which meant you couldn't be with girls, or get married, and have a houseful of little poopers, which at the time seemed not so bad.

But that was before Sarah Esterhausen asked me to the sock hop. Which took me back to Uncle John's kids.

So after school let out that day, I waited for Uncle John's youngest daughter, Esther, a junior at St. Peter High School. As we walked toward her house and my hitchhiking spot, the corner of Clay Street and Kingshighway, I told her about my problem and asked her to teach me how to dance.

She sighed like I did when Mama had her hand in a cast and it was time to change yet another dirty diaper, but she agreed to do it.

The first lesson lasted half an hour. I lost count of her "Ows!"

She didn't. "Eleven times you stepped on my toes, Eddie Walsh." She sat on the sofa in the living room, took her shoes—flats, she called them—off, and rubbed her abused dancing implements. "You're not even hearing the music."

Well, I concentrated so hard on trying to get my feet to move the way Esther told me, the noise coming out of the box on the coffee table with the crank-up handle and the small record playing on it distracted me. I tuned that crap out.

"You have to listen to the music, Eddie. I do, and not only do I listen to it, I *feel* it. The music drives my feet. I don't know what was driving your feet, but it wasn't the music."

She took the record from the player and placed it in its paper envelope and snapped the lid on the player closed.

"Take my phono home with you. There are three records inside. Listen to them until you hear the count."

"The count?"

"Yes. One of the records will have a 'one, two. One, two' count. Another has, 'one, two, three. One, two, three.' And the other has a 'one, two, three, four. If you want another lesson tomorrow, you're going to have to show me you hear that count. Otherwise, my toes won't dance with you again. Understand?"

Of course, I *versteh*-ed the words she said, but those numbers inside the music? This was way weirder than algebra had been until Lucinda explained it. So I walked the two blocks from Uncle John's house to my hitchhiking corner, toting the portable phono in one hand and my book bag in the other. The last thing Esther told me was that I should consider buying my own phonograph. If I was serious about learning to dance.

Well, of course, I was serious. Sarah Esterhausen asked me to the sock hop! That made her my girlfriend.

But here was another serious thing: Two more paydays from Mr. Neidlinger in the summer and I could buy a ten speed.

Life was sure simpler when I was in grade school.

That night after the dishes, after homework, I cranked up Esther's phono and listened to the record she said was a one-two, one-two song. She said, "You don't hear those numbers being counted, you feel them." As she said that, she swayed side to side a bit and bobbed her head a bit.

When you feel things, hands are there

to do the feeling. They felt the handle of Mr. Neidlinger's poop scoop, the twine of his bales of hay. Or the wire, if he bought hay from a guy who had a wire baler. I hated wire bales. The wire bales were twice as heavy as the twine ones and even through leather gloves, that wire felt like it was slicing my fingers and hands to pieces. And of course, my hands knew the feel of a dirty diaper being rinsed in the toilet. But the stupid hands could not feel the music. But they were smart enough to remove the One-two record and put on "Miss One-two-three."

At first, my hands couldn't feel the numbers in that music either, but I played the record a second time. With my eyes closed, and Holy Crap! I felt it, but not with my hands. I felt it with my whole upper body, from my belly button up to the top of my Brylcreem-ed duck butt. I listened to the other records, and I felt them, too.

I tried to dance with a pretend Esther. I put on One-two-three record, held my arms out to hold my cousin, and my feet started moving around the attic. My feet, they felt the music, too. Around and around Pretend Esther and I spun, and it was like we were angels, and we were dancing on a cloud.

But then I smacked my head into the sloped ceiling. Smacked it good. Not quite as good as

Large Louie smacked me when he broke my nose, but I put a dent in Pop's sheetrock.

I rubbed my head, re·cranked the phono, and re·started One·two·three. I stood there a moment with Pretend Esther in my arms and just listened, just felt that one, that two and that three. Then I opened my eyes, and we danced. I didn't smack my head. Pretend Esther didn't step on my toes, and I didn't step on hers.

Was Real Esther going to be surprised at my after·school dance lesson tomorrow!

Which she was. I only stepped on her feet five times.

"Eddie, you obviously did your homework. You *feel* the music, but you have to understand that others might feel it differently than you do. You have to sense not only the music but how your partner senses it as well."

I almost got mad. How stinking complicated was this stupid dancing business? It was like she let me in on one secret, and I show up for my next lesson only to find out there is another secret thing I need to master. *Poop!*

"Eddie, I'm doing this as a favor to you. If you want to quit, that's fine with me. My toes would rejoice with an *Alleluia* in five·part harmony."

She was right. Teaching me to dance was a big, big favor. And I did, occasionally, step on her toes. But I owed it to my girlfriend Sarah to figure this thing out.

"Sorry."

"Apology accepted. Now then, back to feeling the music. You felt it, but we weren't dancing. We were *rasslin'*."

Boogers! St. Charles kids like to make fun of how we talked in St. Ambrose. I didn't even know I said *rasslin'* until one of them poked fun at me. Now I say wrestling. Esther was doing this out of the goodness of her heart, so I couldn't be mad at her. Actually, I was beholden to her.

"I didn't mean to *wrestle* with you, Esther."

She smiled at my *wrestle*.

"I know, Eddie." She looked into my eyes. "I think you feel the music more deeply than I do. I mean, I feel it, too, but it grips you harder, and you try to drive me to feel it the same way you do. Dancing is something two people do together. It's a shared experience."

"I think wrestling is a shared experience."

Her hands went to her hips. Compression happened to her lips. I thought she would tell me to hit the road, Eddie. But then her hard face softened.

"We have to put together the way you feel the music and the way I feel it, so it can be a shared experience, not your experience you are ramming down my throat. Do you understand?"

"Huh!" I understood. "Esther, you are the best dance teacher I ever had."

"Anybody ever tell you, you are a piece of work, Eddie Walsh?"

Actually, Mr. Zeke had said that same thing to me when I was five. I didn't want to go into that with only seven minutes of dance lesson left. I still had the difference between dancin' and *rasslin'* to work out with no more toe stompin'.

After we started the fifth lesson, Esther said I was a regular Fred Astaire. Well, who the crap was that guy? She explained, then she wanted to know if I wanted to learn how to jitterbug. I asked, "What's that?" and she explained and fetched her brother Archangel Michael, a senior at St. Peters. They demonstrated.

Jumping Jehoshaphat!

First of all, the music just went crazy. And what they were doing, I thought two Jehoshaphats jumping all over the place, arms swinging like crazy, described it pretty well. It looked to me like a girl wouldn't be worried about getting her toes stomped on. She'd be worried about getting her lights punched out by the boy's arms swinging like a demented windmill running away from Don Quixote.

When the music quit, Archangel Michael bowed to Esther, and she curtsied to him.

"See." Michael grinned like an evil spirit

who roamed the world seeking the ruin of souls. "Piece a cake. Nothing to it."

"He's right," Esther said. "Sort of. Just like slow dancing, you have to get the hang of it."

"Yeah, and if you do," Michael piped in, "You'll be the most popular freshman boy at the sock hop."

But, see, I didn't want to be the most popular freshman boy at the sock hop. What I wanted to do was to impress my girlfriend, Sarah.

As it turned out, I sure wasn't the first thing, and I sure didn't do the second thing. And Sarah sure wasn't my girlfriend. Although for the first dance, a slow one, I thought she was. For the first dance, we walked out onto the gym dance floor side by side and faced each other and that toilet flushing thing happened to me. Warmth just dumped out of the top of me and cascaded down to my shoes. The music started and Sarah took my hand and put her other on my shoulder and firmly established the distance between us. I would have been happier to be a little closer, but we danced together well. I didn't step on her toes once.

My hand got a little sweaty. It seemed like a girl's body was acres and acres of places you couldn't touch, but only that one place on her waist, and I could hold her hand. Thinking about all those places I couldn't touch is when my stupid hand started sweating. Some of the couples talked and laughed as they danced. I didn't know what to say to Sarah, and she didn't say anything to me. By that time, my feet found the music and knew what to do without me thinking about it for them. So my stupid brain thought about things that made my hand sweat.

The music stopped. I said, "Maybe they'll play a jitterbug next. I only know a couple of moves. I hope that's okay."

Sarah pushed away from me. I'd forgotten to let her go.

She grabbed my waist-touching hand, told me to follow her, and led me to the side of the gym where some of the girls with no dates sat on folding chairs. We stopped in front of Hilda Westfall.

Hilda stood. She held a hanky in her hands and was twisting it around.

"Eddie," Sarah said, "I'm giving you to Hilda for the rest of the sock hop."

"Giving me to Hilda?"

Sarah smiled. "It's a Sadie Hawkins dance. You're my date. I can do what I want with you. Now you're Hilda's date."

"What?"

Sarah put a smile on her face like it was a mask. "Have fun, Hilda," she said and walked away.

I felt like I'd been hitchhiking home from school, and the guy I caught a ride with lost control on Dead-man's Curve and smacked into the huge oak beside the road. It seemed like I might still be alive, but I wasn't sure. That image of crashing into that tree burned so vividly, it surprised me when it faded, and I wound up in the gym watching Sarah walk towards a cluster of girls. They were all in Sarah's covey of popular ones. According to Roger Rottermick, the coveys formed around three or four popular girls with two or three hangers-on, girls who were homely or dreadfully shy. Hilda was a hanger-on. She was shy. And some of the guys called her homely Hilda.

Sarah had Tom Sawyer-ed me. She was halfway across the gym to rejoin her covey, when anger flared up in me. *Go after that rotten Orchard Farm girl and punch her in the snot locker.* That thought formed. Then cousin Lucinda appeared in my head and reminded me of the "sticks and stones" discussion we'd had when Jimmie Joe and I got mad at each other.

I turned around and found Hilda staring at me. She was scared as a baby mouse looking up at a tomcat playing with his dinner before eating it. Her eyes were big and full of pleading and yearning and devoid of hope.

Cousin Lucinda pulled up the corners of my lips. "Hilda, I guess Sadie Hawkins makes you the boss of our date. Is it okay to ask you to dance?"

For a moment I thought the air all went out of her and she'd collapse, but then she lit up like a just-plugged-in Christmas tree. Hilda, I was sure, was a heck of a lot happier than Alice Ashe would have been if I'd just said the heck with the spit and kissed her.

Hilda was a good dancer. She made my feet feel like they'd been dancing for a hundred years instead of two weeks. Not only the slow ones, but she taught me a bunch of new moves during the jitterbug numbers.

We danced every dance until the DJ called a break. Then we got sodas. She had to pay, she said, because it was the way it was done on Sadie Hawkins Day. We took my 7-Up and her Coke to side-by-side chairs along the gym wall.

"Eddie, are you mad at me? For the way Sarah and I did this."

I looked at my soda and told it, "I was. For seven seconds."

"Seven seconds. You know exactly how long you were mad for? Did you look at the clock?"

There were large clocks mounted high on the walls on both sides of the gym.

I shook my head. "My stomach. It always knows what time it is. It's been that way since I was little."

Her face looked like it had just encountered a new Algebra problem it couldn't solve, when, suddenly, a light went on. And it looked like she was happy to have something to laugh at. "Your stomach tells time. That's funny."

When Large Louie said that, it set my teeth to grinding. But with Hilda, it felt good to be funny. It felt good to be with her. I probably felt better about just being me than I had back in the fall before I found out I didn't make the cut for the baseball team.

She put her hand on my wrist. It was cold from her soda bottle.

"I am so glad you didn't get mad at me. For more than seven seconds. I wanted to ask you myself, but I was afraid you'd say no. If you had, I'd have just died."

Boy, that was all I would have needed. A girl dropping dead and it was my fault.

iv

When I finally got to bed, I didn't sleep at all. There was way too much to think about.

I remembered when I started sixth grade and I thought school kicked into a whole new gear. Boy, talk about shifting into high gear. Sadie Hawkins lifted me off a ten-speed bike and dropped me onto a *motorsickle*... motorcycle, and I'd roared down the highway going a hundred miles an hour.

I lay there on top of my pillow staring up at the slanted ceiling in the dim from the nightlight and tried to catch up to everything that happened to me that Tuesday night.

I rode to the dance with Ollie Weisendinger. He had his parents' car, and he stopped at my house to pick me up on the way to the dance. After I got in, he said, "I wanted to borrow my brother's car. He wasn't going anywhere tonight, but would he let me use it? The stupid, stinkin', stingy shithead."

Whoa! All I did was get in the car, and I already had something to confess on Saturday. Father Geist told me once that hearing somebody else cuss didn't mean I committed a sin. "It depends on what you think after you hear it."

"It makes me think I committed a sin, Father," I replied.

But Ollie settled down after cussing his brother, and the rest of the ride went sinless.

When we walked into the gym, it was crowded and filled with happy noise. All I wanted to do was find my girlfriend. Which I did. We danced the first dance. She gave me to Hilda. I got mad, but then I decided I couldn't hurt Hilda. I'd do something nice for her.

And wound up doing something really nice for myself.

I enjoyed the heck out of being with her, dancing with her, talking with her. Thinking about it, I was pretty sure Hilda had given me the best time of my life.

Of course, caboose·d onto that thought were the things for the confessional come Saturday. Not only the cussing going to the dance. There was the ride home.

Hilda and I rode in the backseat of Ollie's car. He and his date, a girl who attended St. Charles High, sat in the front so close together they were both behind the steering wheel. As we pulled out of the school/church parking lot, Hilda scooted over real close to me, too.

Uh oh. She had kissing on her mind. I scootched my leg forward so I could get my kissing handkerchief out of my pocket. Before I could, Hilda leaned over and smashed her lips against mine.

Huh! I couldn't tell if she left spit behind or not. I could tell I had sort of liked it. That kiss. The other thing about it, Hilda had this little mustache. Fine hair that you could only see if the light was right. During a bathroom break, one of the St. Charles kids in my class told me I should tell him tomorrow how it feels to kiss a girl with a mustache. Well, I would not do that, but it made me wonder. What happened was I hadn't felt the mustache at all. Maybe my lips didn't know what to look for though, so I leaned over and kissed Hilda.

Nope. Couldn't feel the mustache.

I leaned back and Hilda put a serious kiss on me and stayed all pressed against my face. I held my breath. But even the champion underwater swimmer of Verrukt Frau Creek had to come up for air at some point. When I broke us apart, Hilda giggled.

Which made me wonder what I'd done wrong.

She leaned close and whispered, "Breathe through your nose, Silly."

Oh! That worked pretty well. It worked really well. This kissing business was kind of nice, once you figured out you could breathe AND kiss at the same time. When we pulled apart for some mouth-breathing time, I could see Hilda wasn't disappointed in me, not like Alice Ashe had been. I looked at her in the dim light in the back seat, and she looked at me, and that toilet flushing thing happened like had happened with my cousin Lucinda. It was like I had a tankful of something warm and wonderful stored high up in me, and she pushed the flushing handle, and all this feel-good-all-over juice gushed down and through me.

The last kiss Hilda had put on me had been a little ferocious, and a little frantic. The new one she did was all soft and tender, and stuff began to happen inside me that came close to scaring me. This thing I was feeling was becoming the boss of me, and I didn't know what this new boss was going to have me do.

That's when Hilda took my hand, the one that held her hand when we were dancing, and the next thing I knew, that hand was on her breast.

I jerked back from her and jerked my hand away from... from where it had been.

"I... I'm so sorry, Hilda."

That's when the car stopped.

"Hey, in the backseat," Ollie said. "We're

here. Eddie, walk Hilda to the door. I'll wait two minutes. You got in enough kissing for one night."

We got out of the car. Hilda took my hand. We started toward her front door. Lights burned to either side. I hadn't anywhere near said *sorry* enough.

"Hilda."

"Eddie, I wanted your hand there. I put it there."

First, I thought: *Well, that's okay then.*

But then I knew it wasn't okay. And there wasn't time to sort it out there. Not unless I wanted to walk home.

"I had the most wonderful time, Eddie. I'm so glad you didn't get mad at Sarah and me. For more than seven seconds." She smiled at me. For seven seconds or so. Then she kissed me and went inside.

This kiss was sort of cool and dry. The others in the backseat had been wet and sloppy. I stood there on Hilda's front step and realized I hadn't worried about spit since she put the first kiss on me.

"Hey," Ollie whispered loud. "You want a ride home, or not?"

Ollie had some kissing of his own he was anxious to get to. That's what I thought. But when he parked in front of Violet's house, Ollie and she piled out the driver's door and hustled up the walk. I thought he'd kiss her goodnight and we could go home. The two of them didn't stop on the little porch, they went inside. Ollie stayed in there a long time. I wondered if Violet let Ollie put his hands in places they shouldn't go. I wondered if hanky-panky was going on. Was he hanky-pankying her?

Hanky-panky, the way I understood it, was a noun. Was there a verb form of the term? The term wasn't in my Sister Daniels dictionary. I'd looked. Before I decided about the verb form, I fell asleep and woke when Ollie got in the car and started the engine.

"What time is it?"

"One," Ollie said. "You want to get up front or stay back there?"

I moved up to the shotgun seat, and Ollie headed us back to St. Ambrose.

"You and Homely Hilda put on quite a show at the sock hop. Everyone was talking about how well you danced together."

Homely Hilda! I didn't like that *homely* any more than I liked the N-word. But Ollie was giving me a ride. I kept my lips zipped but figured I'd have to tell it to Father Geist in the sin box on Saturday. Ollie had said something I knew to be wrong, but I didn't call him on it. I didn't want him to get mad at me and not let me ride with him and his brother to school anymore.

Thinking about all these things as I lay there on my pillow looking up at the upside-down V-shaped ceiling above me, Lennie beside me sleeping like a log, I recalled Uncle Ed telling me about the N-word, that he considered it wrong to say it, but for a lot of his life, it was the only word he'd known for Negro. Like, *I know it's wrong, but see, I have this excuse, so it's not wrong anymore. See?*

Laying there, I thought the N-word and Ollie's H-word were sort of like cussing. The older I got, the more people around me took to cussing. When I'd been the boss of summer afternoons, none of us cussed. I didn't allow it, and nobody argued about it with me. Now, of course, I wasn't boss of anything. Even baby poop. Nobody would listen to me if I told them to stop cussing. That was my excuse, see?

What the crap was the right thing for me to do? Maybe Father Geist would have the answer come Saturday.

Then my thinking took me back to riding home with Ollie. Halfway home, going around Dead Man's Curve, Ollie said, "You two put on another show in the backseat. Take her out again, and I bet Homely Hilda will let you go all the way."

I got mad at him for using the H-word again.

"Jesus Christ, Eddie, she is homely."

"Stop the car. I'll walk the rest of the way."

"Jesus, Mary, and Joseph and all the rest of the goddamned saints! What the shit is the matter with you? It's three miles to your house."

"Stop the car. I'll walk the rest of the way."

"I'm not stopping the car, you stupid son-of-a-bitch."

"Then stop calling her homely."

"All right. All right." Ollie looked at me. "Jesus Christ. I didn't know you liked her."

"Watch the road and stop your goddamned cussing."

Rats. I didn't know where that cuss word had come from. The way sins were piling up, it was going to take me two Saturdays to confess them all. Plus, I thought I might have made Ollie mad enough to stop the car and push me out.

But he started laughing. Then he said, "Eddie Walsh. You're a real piece of work. Stop your goddamned cussing." He laughed some more.

So, laying in bed, I had that to think about too. Ollie and I were getting madder and madder at each other. Then I cussed like he'd been doing, and we were friends again.

It brought to mind the time a front wheel fell off Mr. Neidlinger's wagon after we'd loaded it with hay bales and dumped half the load. Mr. N. looked at the dipped-down front corner and scattered bales and a couple of them with their twines busted. He put his hands on his hips and said, "Sometimes a thing like this happens, and there ain't nothing for it but a good goddamn."

So I wondered if my goddamn to Ollie had been a good goddamn.

I woke the heck up when my hand, the one that wound up on Hilda's breast, got ripped off. I sat up with my heart hammering and breathing hard and scared as all get out.

It took twelve seconds to figure out it had been a dream. The past summer. Early August. Baling hay with Mr. Neidlinger. The Massey Ferguson guy. Mr. N.'s brother Luther. And me, One-hand Eddie. Almost.

That day, just before my birthday, Mr. Neidlinger bought hay bales from Mr. Haussmann, a neighbor. The neighbor had accepted an offer from a Massey Ferguson field test agent. The Massey Ferguson guy would bale the neighbor's hay for free for the opportunity to test a new model hay baler on an operating farm.

The field test agent wore a Massey Ferguson ball cap and a Massey Ferguson short-sleeved shirt.

"I bet he wears Massey Ferguson underpants," Luther Neidlinger said. He was there to help pick up the bales from Mr. Haussmann's field and get them in Mr. N.'s hayloft.

"Now, Luther," Mr. Neidlinger said, "I asked you to help. You piss off the free baling guy and he pulls outa' here, that'll piss off my neighbor, and the price of hay will go up."

Mr. Monogrammed Underpants acted like he hadn't heard the comment. "Okay, Mr. Neidlinger, you said you want to drag a sled behind the baler, right?"

A sled was a contraption you drug behind a bailer. A guy rode the sled. As the baler, according to Luther, pooped out bales—Great! More poop—Sled Rider grabbed the bales and stacked them on the sled. When the sled was full, Sled Rider grabbed a steel fence post, jammed the post in the ground, and slid the load of bales off. Slick, see? That way the guys loading bales onto wagons only had to stop a couple of times to gather a complete load.

Anyway, I was Mr. Sled Rider. I grabbed the bales, stacked them, and pushed full sled-loads off. My boss and his brother loaded them onto a wagon. The first couple of hours, everything went fine. Then the experimental baler got constipated.

The machine was still running, but no bales came out. Mr. Monogrammed Underpants stopped the tractor and climbed onto the baler and started working on something with a wrench. I got closer to see what he was doing. At the rear of the baler, there was a cover over some sort of belt drive powering the machine. I placed my hands on that belt-drive cover and leaned forward. I didn't notice that the cover didn't have a shield on the front of the belt drive.

The next thing I knew, the belt grabbed the fingers of Mr. Hand-Who-Touched-Hilda's-Breast and ripped it off my arm. And I stood there looking at the stump spurting blood.

That's what happened in the dream.

What happened on that day back in August is the belt grabbed both my hands and tossed me about two yards. Luther came running to me and helped me to my feet.

"Jesus Kid you okay?" Luther didn't pose his question to me with any commas in it. Commas or no commas, I had no idea what the answer was. I'd stuck my fingers in that Massey Ferguson baler and it grabbed me and tossed me aside like I was a doll some girl got tired of playing with.

One thing settled out of the fog in my head. I'd come really close to getting hurt really bad. If that baler had grabbed a whole hand, it could have gotten itself ripped right off my arm. I saw Little Heiny calling me Eddie One-hand Walsh.

Luther helped me to my feet all the while he cussed me for being stupid. "Farm machinery is dangerous stuff. You can't work around it with your head up your ass."

Which cut through the fog in my head. How in Sam Hill could I get my head up there? On second thought, as powerful as that Massey Ferguson baler was, if it wanted my head there, it was sure strong enough to put it there.

Luther checked me over and had me move my arms around a bit. They worked. They were a little sore where they hooked into my shoulders, but that's all.

After Mr. Monogrammed Underpants told me working around farm machinery was dangerous, Mr. Neidlinger told me, then we went back to work.

Luther said I should drive the tractor pulling the wagon and not lift bales for a while, but I told all of them I was okay. "Almost hurt isn't really hurt," I said.

So I got on the sled again, and I stacked the bales again. Despite what I'd said, though, being almost body hurt real bad is being really soul hurt. Still, I got the job done.

That's what really happened in August. That dream told me I ought to thank God I didn't get my hand ripped off, and that I also should thank Him it was Hilda putting my hand where it went and not me putting it there.

I lay back down again and did more looking at the dark hiding the ceiling.

I thought about Hilda, and how much fun she seemed to have. The only thing wrong was she never had a Sister Daniels tell her, "Having fun is not a sin. Necessarily." If she had, she'd never have put my hand... you know, there.

The evening had been fun for me, too. Thinking about it as I looked deep into the dark above me, I thought the evening had been not only fun, but the most fun ever.

But there'd been the sins. The cussing, going and coming home, and once it was even me doing it. I'd gotten mad at Sarah. And then my hand went where it did. Come Saturday, I'd dump those in Father's lap.

I huffed out a big breath of air.

Then the stupid alarm clock went off and set my heart to hammering again.

In the in-house, I was glad I'd let that goddamn slip out. Ollie and I were buddies again when he let me out in front of our house. I could still ride to school with him. Otherwise, I'd have to walk to the highway and hitchhike to school.

Me and the in-the-mirror Eddie wondered if Hilda would sit with me at lunch.

V

None of the morning classes had been in a hurry to get themselves over and done with, but, at last, they did. Hilda always ate lunch in the cafeteria, never went down the hill to the soda shop/drug store. But that day, she wasn't in the cafeteria. I couldn't go to the soda shop because I had no money.

Poop!

I unwrapped my baloney sandwich and took a bite.

Poop! My mouth wondered how good it would have tasted if Hilda had been there.

Roger Rottermick sat next to me. He had two fried drumsticks. That didn't sound any better to me than plain old baloney.

"You know if there'd been a contest for the best couple on the dance floor last night, you and Hilda would have won." He took a bite of chicken.

What he'd said could have been a question,

but it hadn't sounded like one. I didn't feel like answering a question that wasn't one. I took a bite of my gourmet sandwich.

"The other thing, Eddie, I've gone all through grade school with Hilda. She had it rough growing up. Her dad was a carpenter and fell off a ladder. Messed his back up bad and couldn't work for more than a year. Her mother had to get a job as a waitress. Hilda had to sit out second grade to take care of her younger brother and sister."

Holy crap! I bet Hilda knows more about baby poop than I do.

The next year, Roger explained, the St. Peter church ladies took turns caring for the younger Westfall kids. Mr. Westfall was able to go back to work in his boss's cabinetmaking shop. He could only do light work, sanding and staining the wood. He made less money than before but, with his wife's waitressing, they managed to hang onto the house with Hilda doing all the cooking and cleaning.

And I'd thought I was the world champion of girl work. I sure didn't think an actual girl could have done more girl work than I did.

"The Westfall kids would have gone naked if the church ladies hadn't kept them supplied with hand-me-downs."

At first, I thought that had to be an exaggeration. Then I remembered how much sewing Mama had done on Lennie's and my clothes. When we were little, all our clothes were homemade. Except for the tighty-whities of course. And go-to-church stuff had been store-bought.

A part of my mind was hard at work trying to build a picture of Hilda. In tighties. I shook my head and shattered the image like a mirror hit with a hammer. I looked at my sandwich. I'd forgotten about it. Even though my mouth didn't think I was hungry, it took a bite and went to work chewing.

"When we got to sixth grade, guys started calling her Homely Hilda. I think by the time this year started, and she'd heard that homely word a bazillion times, she believed that's what she was and that no boy would ever ask her out or want to dance with her."

"Eddie."

Sarah Esterhausen stood there looking at me. "Do you mind if I sit down?"

I got the feeling even if I said no, she'd have sat, anyway. I shrugged.

She told Roger to *amscray*. He *amscrayed*, and she took his seat.

"Are you going to eat the rest of your sandwich?"

What the crap else did she want to take from me? All I had left was my shirt, pants, and shoes. My mind whipped up a picture of me hitchhiking on the corner of Kingshighway and Clay Streets like that, and me freezing to death and into a sock-footed statue with my thumb sticking out and pointing toward St. Ambrose and wearing nothing but tighties. I wanted to say something clever and snotty. But then I thought I'd had a great time last night, and it wouldn't have happened without Sarah asking me to the sock hop. I handed over the sandwich.

She took it, bit off a boy bite, chewed, and swallowed. "Thanks. I didn't get up in time for breakfast, and I missed lunch."

Out late with your real boyfriend.

Another bite wolfed down. "I heard the last of what Roger told you about Hilda. It's true. She wanted to ask you to the dance but was so afraid you'd say no. If you had, she'd have died. She'd have just died on the spot."

I watched the last of my baloney disappear. Then she looked at my lunch bag. I handed it over. She removed the apple, snarfed off a bite, and handed the empty back. She must have known Walsh kids got a lot of use out of a lunch bag before it was tossed.

"A couple of us," she said with a mouthful, "decided to help her. And that's why I asked you to the dance. I'm almost sorry I tricked you."

You Tom Sawyer-ed me, stole my lunch, and you're almost sorry!

"What you did for Hilda was the biggest

blessing she's had in her whole life. You worked a miracle, Eddie Walsh."

"Eddie," from behind me.

I hoped the bell would ring soon so people would stop sneaking up behind me.

I turned. "Holy crap, Hilda!" That's the way I said it.

Homely was a word that wouldn't come within a mile of her now. Her hair looked nice. Her face was made up. Even her mustache was gone. She was... I don't know. Gorgeous. Not quite like Sarah, but gorgeous aplenty. Sarah and two of her friends had just spent a half-hour in the bathroom with her.

Ho-oh lee crap!

That's how she stopped being Homely Hilda and became HolyCrapHilda for the rest of the school year.

That night, after supper, after the dishes were done, Mama went into the front room with the kids, and Pop came out and sat at the table where I was doing homework. I was sitting in his place and he took Mama's, closest to the stove.

"You want to sit in your chair, Pop?"

He shook his head and stared at me.

My Adam's apple bobbed as I tried to swallow

spit that had all dried up. There was no mystery what Pop was looking at now. This was a Sister Superior stare.

"Boy, this morning, your mama found your pillow all covered with lipstick. You kissed all the lipstick clean off the girl you were with. Did you and the girl keep your clothes on?"

Pop wasn't talking loud, but I had no trouble hearing him. From the front room came the sound of TV laughter. It sounded like it came from far, far away. I wanted to look at something far, far away. Better yet, I wished Pop would look at something far, far away. Like he always did when he sat at the kitchen table. But his eyes had a hold of mine and they would not let go until I answered the question.

I couldn't remember how he'd phrased the question and whether I should answer "Yes," or "No." No question of Sister Superior's was ever as important to put the right answer to as this one.

"Boy!"

"We... uh, we kept out clothes on. All of it."

"Your zipper. Did it get itself pulled down?"

Well, yeah, in the bathroom, but I knew that's not what he was asking.

"No, Pop."

He let out a big breath like he'd just swum underwater in Verrukt Frau Creek and broke my record. His eyes let go of me, and I felt like he'd been holding me above the floor and I just fell back down. I breathed. I'd been holding my breath, too.

"You didn't do IT with her?"

"No, Pop."

"Good, cause that's more important than just committing a sin and having to confess it. You do IT with a girl, likely she'll get pregnant. Then you'll have to marry her, and you'll ruin any chance for having a *good* life. We've spent a lot of money trying to get you a *good* education so you can have a *good* life. Better than your mama and me had. If you finish high school, the job you can get will be much better than any I could do. But you get a girl pregnant, and all that goes out the window. You will ruin your life, the girl's life, and the baby you make, what kind of life would it have starting out like that?

"You don't do IT until you are married. And you don't get married until you can afford to take care of a wife and a family."

I hoped he was done talking.

"One more thing."

Rats!

"The amount of lipstick on your pillow—" His eyes got full of Sister Superior fire again. Like when she talked about discipline.

"That much lipstick indicates you and that girl were close to doing IT. The thing is, a boy and girl can get each other all het up. You might think you won't go all the way, but at a certain point, it's like the heat of it just grabs ahold of the both of you and sweeps you away and no power on earth will keep IT from happening.

"You don't let yourself get even close to doing IT until you are married."

Please, God. Now can we be done talking? At least he didn't mention the sticky mess I'd made in my underpants that morning before I woke.

"One more thing."

Oh, Poop!

———⁓⁓⦿⦿⦿⁓⁓———

The next day Ollie told me he was getting the family car again on Friday. He was taking his girlfriend to see a movie at the Strand Theater in St. Charles. "We can double date. If you can get one."

This wasn't a Sadie Hawkins thing where the girl paid. "What'll it cost? For a movie? With a date?"

He told me what the tickets cost.

Ten-speed bike money was gonna take a hit.

"Plus, a popcorn and soda for the two of you."

I knew Ollie well enough to know that look on his face. He had one more thing up his sleeve. Finally, he got tired of waiting for me to say something. "And ice cream after at St. Charles Dairy."

Holy crap! This date was going to cost me the earnings from two Saturdays of work on Neidlinger's farm.

"What else you gonna spend your money on?"

A dad-burned ten-speed I'd been saving my whole life to get! That's what.

"So, get a date," Ollie said.

I asked Hilda. She smiled and said she'd love to go.

I asked Hilda because I had some things I needed to figure out. Like what Pop talked to me about and what had happened on the way home from the Sadie Hawkins dance. Like, as we rode home from the dance and Hilda and I were smearing spit and lipstick all over each other, I was pretty sure I felt what Pop had talked about. About getting het up and almost getting swept into doing IT.

I sure didn't want to ruin Hilda's life, or a baby's, or my own. On the other hand, that Sadie Hawkins dance was the most fun thing I'd ever done in my whole life. Better than baseball, better than being the boss of summer afternoons, better even than going to school in Sister Daniel's classroom or talking to my cousin Lucinda.

Girls. I thought I knew a lot about them. I thought I was one when Mama made me be one. But I didn't know a blinking thing about them, and I sure wasn't one, no matter what kind of work I did.

Friday night, at 6:30, I knocked on Hilda's front door. It opened. She stepped out and closed it. *Holy crap!*

"You look good," I said.

Man, she looked good, but she frowned. I thought she'd be pleased I said that.

She walked toward Ollie's waiting car. When she reached it, she stopped and waited for me to open the rear door for her. Which I did, then I got in.

Ollie and Violet hi·ed Hilda. Then Violet said, "You look nice, Hilda."

Hilda smiled big, warm, and friendly. I felt like Violet got my smile, and I'd said it first.

On the way to the theater, she sat all the way on her side.

What the crap was going on here? One thing seemed clear already. I would not have to worry about getting all het up. She was acting like Alice Ashe after I apologized to her for not kissing her. Did Hilda expect me to kiss her right there at her front door before we even said hello?

At the theater, Ollie and I bought tickets. We had nothing to talk about, so we didn't talk. Violet and Hilda seemed to have lots to talk about. They gabbled. So far, that was the highpoint of this date. I had an opportunity to use "gabbled." It wound up being the only high point.

At one point, I got wrapped up in the movie playing on what looked like a TV screen big as a house, and I took her hand. After I'd eaten a handful of popcorn. And forgotten to wipe my hand clean with a paper napkin. She took her hand back and wiped me and popcorn grease off it.

This was sure different from the Sadie dance. There, she liked being with me and I liked being with her. In the car afterward, there was spit and lipstick to hoolay the rail. I thought I was going to have to be careful, so there wouldn't be too much of that. Now, I was sure there wouldn't be any.

What the crap happened? Even though I got Tom Sawyer-ed into dancing with Hilda, it turned into the best night of my life. We had a kind of fun I didn't know existed. Tonight, I was not sure if we'd have a new best time ever, but I expected we'd have some kind of fun. But I'd be mindful of Sister Daniel's "Necessarily" and Pop's "It." Here we were, though, not having any fun at all. And it cost me a fortune for the movie and the ice cream after.

A fortune all right. Back to being six thousand years old before I could afford a ten-speed.

When we arrived back at Hilda's house, I started to get out to open the car door for her.

"Don't bother," she said and opened her door, walked up her walk, and went inside. The front porch light blinked off.

At Violet's, Ollie turned off the engine, and they both went inside. I lay down on the backseat. I didn't think I'd sleep with my stomach feeling like I'd eaten rotten popcorn and ice cream made with spoiled milk. But I was wrong about that, too.

I woke up when he opened his driver-side door and invited me up front.

"Violet told me what torqued off Hilda. You wanna' hear it?"

"Yeah."

"After you knocked on the door and Hilda came out, you told her she looked good."

"I did. I thought she'd be pleased to hear that."

"According to what she told Violet in the bathroom, she said you looked surprised that she looked good."

"That's what made her mad?"

"Yeah. And this is my interpretation of what Violet told me. She spent her whole life being Homely Hilda. She just became HolyCrapHilda, and she thought you expected Homely Hilda to walk out her front door. Like you didn't think she could be beautiful."

"I've told her the same thing at lunch at school, every day since Holy Crap Wednesday. This doesn't make sense."

"First off, Eddie," Ollie glanced at me and the glow from the instrument panel lit his features enough for me to see his grin. "We're talking about a girl here. What makes sense to a boy isn't necessarily going to make sense to a girl."

Necessarily.

Hilda and I had had such a good time together Tuesday night. What the crap happened between Tuesday and Friday? And when I ate lunch with HolyCrapHilda, she still acted like she liked me. Even lunch on Friday went that way.

"So, Eddie." A new four-lane highway was going in between St. Ambrose and St. Charles. Ollie negotiated this S-shaped curve connecting the new highway to the old right at Deadman's Curve. "Your next girlfriend, look for one like Violet. She's the absolute best kind of girlfriend."

"Because she's good-looking?"

"Well, that doesn't hurt, but what makes her ideal is her mother is divorced and a nurse who works the night shift."

Hanky-panky! Sure as shooting, Ollie and Violet were doing the hanky-panky under the blanky. I sure hoped Ollie wasn't ruining Violet's life, or the life of that baby they were making, either. He for sure wasn't worried about it.

It. That's what Pop had called hanky-panky. What Pop had said about it, what Lennie had said, and what Ollie said, I was having real trouble putting all that together in a way that made sense.

Ollie dropped me off by the driveway to our house. I stood there and watched his taillights move away and turn right down Oak. I wished I'd had enough guts to ask Ollie about hanky-panky. I for sure would not ask Lennie. Mama said to never say the words ever again. Pop had said all he was ever going to say about *It.*

Thank God the next day was Cow Poop Saturday on Mr. Neidlinger's farm. Cow poop. Finally, something I could understand.

After I climbed into bed, I lay there looking up at the dim light puddled against the ceiling and wondered if I'd get any sleep that night.

Then I thought: Ollie Weisendinger's ideal girlfriend is not necessarily Eddie Walsh's ideal girlfriend.

The next thing I knew the alarm went off.

vi

The high school put on a sock hop every month. Hilda didn't come to any of them. I always danced a slow dance and a fast one with Sarah Esterhausen. She'd Tom Sawyer·ed me, sure, but she'd Tom Sawyer·ed me into the best night of my life. Besides, she wasn't mad at me. Seemed to me most girls were. During a slow dance in April, she told me that Hilda didn't want to come to a dance where everyone remembered her as Homely Hilda.

"Well, she was homely until you helped her gussy herself up."

"What I did was dress up the outside. By dancing with her and talking with her, you helped her dress up her spirit."

"She danced with me and talked with me in a way that dressed up my spirit. Doesn't that count for something? I mean, if it had been me, and I'd been ugly, and I suddenly got handsome, I'd go *Whoopee!* Look at me. I'm handsome!"

We'd been dancing with the music, but I stepped out of it and twirled Sarah like a jitterbug move. Which I did without stepping on her toes. Which reminded me to thank my cousin for being a good dance teacher. After the twirl, I slipped us back into the music.

"Huh." Sarah's eyes grew bigger. "That was smooth, Eddie Walsh. Your cousin Esther is a good dancing teacher."

That knocked me out of the music to a dead stop. "How do you know Esther taught me to dance?"

"The day after Sadie Hawkins, Esther asked me how many times you stepped on my toes. 'None,' I said. Then I told her I didn't dance with you, but once. 'Oh,' she said. 'That explains the *none*.'"

I humphed and caught up with the music and launched us into it again. After two steps, the music ended.

I let go of her.

Before she left the floor, she said, "Hilda. Being homely for all her life, we can't know how much that hurt her."

That night in bed as I lay on my pillow and looked up at the inverted V ceiling, I got the feeling that if Pop hadn't put that ceiling above our bed like he did, everything I learned during the day would get away from me, but that V shape, it held those thoughts in the attic until I got them stashed inside my head.

That night I wondered about hurting Alice Ashe and Hilda getting mad at me for trying to be nice to her. In fact, that had hurt. A bit. The Hilda hurt probably didn't hurt me as much as I hurt Alice; me being a boy and all, and she being a girl. Still, I wondered if those two sins balanced each other out. I hurt a girl. A girl hurt me, and the blackboard is wiped clean with a wet rag. Right?

I thought about Sister Daniels, Cousin Lucinda, and Sister Superior all looking down at me, and I could see they all agreed. One sin cannot erase another. Only Jesus on the cross can erase sins.

Crap! That wasn't the answer I was looking for, but I knew what I had to do.

Alice, I'm sorry I hurt you.

Hilda, I forgive you.

Then wondering stopped and sleep came.

The last sock hop of the year was coming up, and there was one thing worrying the crap out of me. Could I get a date to go to the sock hop with me and have it happen without either of us getting hurt? I wanted to know the answer to that question before I spent another fortune on a movie, popcorn, and ice cream.

At this point of our freshman year, some of the girls were going steady. Most of the steady girls dated older guys with cars. Hilda was steady-dating a guy from across the Missouri River in St. Ann's. I couldn't ask one of the going-steadies, and I wouldn't ask a girl who was taller than me.

Noreen Nash wasn't taller. I asked her. She said she'd love to go to the dance with me. She was, body shape and size-wise, Sarah Esterhausen. The head sitting on her shoulders was her own, though. Her hair was blonde—some of my male classmates called it dirty blonde. I didn't like sticking "dirty" in front of anything to do with a girl. Her hair was a dark shade of blonde. Sarah was beautiful. Noreen... had a nice face and remarkable green eyes, like a pond next to a forest on a no-wind day. In a way, her eyes reminded me of my cousin Lucinda's. The soul looking back out of those eyes was a peaceful soul, both Lucinda's and Noreen's.

The school library had a thesaurus, and I looked up "peaceful". Peaceful was a good word, but it was too ordinary for un-ordinary eyes. Placid. That was a better word.

I remembered Hilda's eyes. The soul looking

out of hers was hungry and close to begging me to not see her as homely.

At the Sadie hop, once Hilda saw I was going to dance with her, she threw herself into the evening like she might never have another. Noreen, on the other hand, well, she was nice, but there was a feeling I had that she was sort of going through the motions. Like going to sock hops was expected of her, and so she attended. If someone asked her to dance, she'd dance, but she seemed just as happy to sit on the side of the hall and listen to the music.

Music. When Noreen talked about music, something stirred the placid surface of her green eyes.

"I like dancing with you, Eddie. Most boys, they memorize steps. And their feet move to what they memorized. Like there isn't even any music playing at all. But the music moves your feet."

It was obvious Noreen liked music a lot and me not a lot. Which kind of bothered me for a moment. But then it was okay. I didn't really want a steady girl. It was way too expensive. I'd never get a ten-speed. By the end of the evening, I had gotten what I was looking for. A normal date. I'd ridden with Ollie again, and when I walked Noreen to her front door, she turned to me and puckered, but kept her eyes open. I pressed my lips to hers, and she jerked back, as if trading a little boy spit for a little lipstick was okay but trading a lot of those things was sure as shooting not okay.

She entered her house, locked the door, and turned off the porch light. I walked back to Ollie's car and wiped my lips with my extra handkerchief, which after the night with Hilda had become Lipstick Hanky instead of Girl-spit Hanky. When I got in the car, the overhead light showed Lipstick Hanky to be pure white.

If I dated Noreen again, I'd only have to bring one handkerchief.

Ollie drove his ideal girlfriend Violet home, and I didn't even wait for him to get there. I fell asleep in the backseat on the way. And, of course, I got a couple of hours of sleep while they were inside her house. Tomorrow was cow poop Saturday, so I was happy to grab what sleep I could.

The next evening, when I got home from Mr. Neidlinger's on my one-speed, what did I find leaning against the side of the garage but a Holy Crap ten-speed. A jolt of feel-good spurted up out of my belly and then fell back. *What if the bike is Lennie's?*

But it wasn't. Mama had spoken with Mrs. Grossman at a Wednesday coffee, and Simon didn't ride his ten-speed anymore. Pop had spoken to Mr. Grossman and bought the bike for ten dollars. I had twelve in my ten-speed money jar.

Boy, did I pile the thank-You-Gods onto my *Now I lay me* prayers that night.

Another thing happened when summer started. Mr. Neidlinger gave me a Holy Crap pay raise. $2.50 a day instead of just two bucks.

During my six-day work week, I always sat at the table with the Neidlinger family for lunch. They never fed me dinner. Even on hay baling days when we always worked until after the sun went down. Then I rode Ten-speed home at a good clip. With my mouth closed. Otherwise. I swallowed bugs. Bugs see a headlight on a bike, they just have to kamikaze it.

Towards the end of June, Ollie Weisendinger told me he and Violet were going to the Fox Theater in St. Louis on a Friday night. Did I want to get a date and double with them?

"But you ask a St. Ambrose or a St. Charles girl. I ain't driving to East Timbuktu to pick her up."

Which was easy enough. The only girl I knew who lived outside of those two towns was Sarah Esterhausen, and she was going steady. I knew Noreen, though.

"Oh, yes, Eddie," Noreen said. "I'd love to go to the Fox."

I thought a "with you" would have fit real nicely after that "Fox."

When we picked Noreen up from her house, I held open the door for her on the passenger side of the car. Before I could close it and walk around, she scooted across the back seat. "Just get in, Eddie," she said.

Okay. Every other time I'd double-dated with Ollie, we had a boy's side and a girl's side of the car. So Noreen was mixing things up a little. *No biggie.*

Riding to the Fox, Violet sat on the shotgun seat, half turned around so she could see Noreen. They talked up a storm. Ollie drove. I sat behind Violet against the side of the car and became Pop. Sort of. It was like I wasn't there. I stared at the back of the front passenger seat and looked for the things that Pop saw that nobody else could.

Ollie had to be there to drive. The girls had to be there because they had to talk. I didn't have to be there, so, just like Pop, I wasn't there.

When we got to the theater, I found out why I had to be there. To buy Noreen a ticket, and popcorn, and a soda. *And holy crap!* If it cost a fortune to take a date to the Strand Theater in St. Charles, it cost three fortunes to go to the Fox. Plus, I paid the ransom to get Ollie's car out of the lot.

But it was a double feature. And one of them was a cowboy movie. So that was cool.

As was the ride home. Violet scrunched up against Ollie. He put his arm around her, and she operated the steering column gearshift lever. She was a heck of a good shifter.

Noreen leaned against her side of the car and went to sleep. That was another way to not be where you were. I went there with her. It was the first time I slept with a girl.

Sometime later, Lennie explained to me that "sleeping with a woman" meant not actually sleeping, but doing other stuff. Doing actual hanky-panky. But back to the Fox Theater date.

When we got to Noreen's house, she woke and scooted over next to me, and said, "Open the door, Eddie. We'll get out on your side."

Just like my first date with her, Noreen and I walked up to her front porch and she turned, and puckered. With her eyes open. I just stood there.

She unpuckered and put her arms on her hips. "Aren't you going to kiss me?"

I grabbed her arms and pulled her to me and laid a bend-your-Bucky-Beavers back on her. I held it for One-potato, Two-potato, Three-potato. Then I let her go and said goodnight and walked back to the car.

As Ollie drove away, I could see out of the corner of my eye, Noreen's front porch light was still lit. I turned and found her standing there looking at us leave. I wished I could see if her eyes were still cool and placid, or was there something warm and glowing in them. But that I'd never know.

vii

The week after the date with Noreen, Mr. Neidlinger's alfalfa was ready to be baled. Mr. N. always drove the mower tractor. After the hay dried, he had me tow the hay rake which rolled the hay into rows for the baler to gobble up. On baling days, I rode the sled behind the baler.

Baling days were late days because you couldn't start early. After mowing, the hay had to lie for a day to dry out some. On baling day, you waited for the sun to burn the dew off the hay before you baled it. When we finished hoisting the last bales into the hayloft, it was dark, even though it was daylight savings time.

Pedaling home, I was sure glad I had a ten-speed. I was tired and hungry enough to eat a boot I wore scooping poop out of the milk barn. Mrs. N. always fed me lunch with her family, but I never ate dinner with them, no matter how late we worked.

The road from Neidlinger's led to the top of Church Hill, skirted the church and school property, then headed down to St. Ambrose. Just before the road started down, I saw two guys standing under the pole light. One was Not-so-little-anymore Heiny Stiert and the other, I thought at first, was Still-large-as-ever Louie.

"Hey, Eddie. Stop. I want to introduce you to my cousin," Heiny said.

The cousin was Axel Fant, "But everybody calls him Big Ax."

"Hi. I'm Eddie Walsh."

"Actually," Heiny said. "You're Little Eddie Walsh."

Uh oh.

We were right next to the football field third through fifth graders used. Sister Superior never let us play football once we entered sixth grade. The boys were too big by then, and, the way we played, we could hurt each other. It was the field where I used to like to trip up Little Heiny and Large Louie.

I would have pushed off and headed for home, but Big Ax stepped in front of me and grabbed the handlebars. He grinned. "This is a nice bike, Little Eddie. Get off. Let me take a look at it."

I did not want to do that. I wanted to get the crap away from these guys.

"Get off, I said." Big Ax didn't look friendly.

He probably didn't like to have to say a thing twice.

I got off, and now Big Ax grinned. It wasn't a friendly grin, though. He looked at the bike as if he admired it. Then he kicked a big boot through the spokes of the front wheel.

"Hey!" I reached a hand to grab his arm when Heiny clobbered me on the side of the face. My head filled with a flash of white light and I wound up sitting on my butt in the ditch beside the road. My bike lay on the road and Big Ax stomped on the rear wheel. I charged out of the ditch to stop him and Heiny clobbered me again. This time he hit me in the mouth. I wound up on my butt again. Big Ax tossed my ten-speed into the ditch close to me.

"It was a real pleasure meeting you, Little Eddie," Big Ax said. Then he and Heiny walked away chatting and laughing, having the time of their lives.

The right side of my face hurt. I didn't know if my face had a left side or not. I felt my mouth. Lips are swollen, but the teeth behind them seemed okay. I didn't think I'd have to go to either the dentist or the doctor, like when Large Louie knocked the snot out of me.

My ten-speed, however. The wheels were bent so badly it wouldn't roll. I was going to have to carry it. So I carried it. Down Church Hill and across the highway to Main Street and from one end of it to the other. It was past ten p.m. Nobody was about. Going by Oscar's Tavern, talking and laughing noises came out. The same at the American Legion Post a block down. Most of the houses were dark, but a few had lights on. I didn't see anyone, though.

At home, I leaned Simon Grossman's bike against the garage and stood there looking at it from the dim streetlamp light. It didn't feel like my bike anymore. Of course, if it had been Simon's, his dad would just get him a new one. Except Simon didn't want it. So it was my bike, and I was going to have to pay to get it fixed.

The other thing I was doing standing there in the dark: putting off going inside the house. When Mama saw me beat up, it would vex her and stick in another of those little heart swords.

"Boy," Pop told me once, "you got a 'pology needs saying, get to sayin' it."

Poop!

Well, this wasn't exactly an apology situation. I mean, what was I to say? "Mama, I'm sorry two big guys knocked the snot out of me and wrecked my bike." Actually, I was sorry, but this sorry was a different kind of sorry than the one you had to apologize for.

I sighed and went in to face the music.

The music was Mama screeching, "Eddie!"

Which brought Pop and Lennie in from the front room. The Little Poopers slept through it.

Mama started firing questions. "Who did this?" "Did you start it?" "How bad are you hurt?"

Pop held his hand up, and Mama shushed. "Sit."

I sat.

"D'juh git supper?"

I shook my head.

"Yuh want some?"

I nodded. Pop looked at Mama, and she pulled a plate from the oven. The snot had been beaten out of my face, not my stomach.

"It'll be dried out," she said. "I expected you an hour ago."

Lennie started walking back toward the front room where the TV played for nobody. Pop told him to stay in the kitchen with us. He sat across me from next to Pop.

I said the before meal prayer, amen-ed, and took a bite. Mama's meatloaf was heaven on earth just then. I remembered my cousin Lucinda told me once, that no matter how bad a day had gone, there were always things to be thankful for. And I found two. Heavenly meatloaf and teeth to eat it with. Thank you, God, those two didn't mash my upper teeth behind the lowers like Big Louie did that time.

I swallowed that first bite and before I could take another, Mama sat on her chair nearest the stove and fired up her questions again.

I answered. Pop held up his hand again, and I took a big bite of mashed potatoes and gravy and string beans all mixed together, chewed, and swallowed it down. Pop reached across the table and took my hands in his.

"You didn't get in a lick, did you?"

"No, Pop."

"Did you kick 'em?"

"No, Pop."

Pop took in a deep breath and huffed it out. "I hoped I wouldn't have to have this talk with you. I hoped the world you are growing up in was not so tough anymore."

Pop looked at me, and it was just like Sister Superior right before she whacked my knuckles.

"Boy, the Bible says to turn the other cheek, but I'm saying if you turn the other cheek, they're going to keep beating the crap out of you. You come against these two again, you don't wait for them to get in the first lick. You start it. Go right at them, and they're bigger, so you kick, bite, scratch, do whatever you have to. 'Specially kick. Kick 'em in the knee or the crotch."

"Paddy!" It wasn't a screech, but Mama was clearly fussing at him.

Pop held up his hand again. She shushed.

I was flummoxed. Pop talking about fighting. Pop talking against the Bible. *Holy crap!*

"Eat, boy."

I ate.

"Think on it," Pop told me, and to Lennie, "Go to bed."

Lennie brushed his teeth and went upstairs.

When I brushed my teeth, boy, was I a sight. I had a big purple bruise around my left eye. I looked like a raccoon with only half a Lone Ranger mask. My lower lip on the left side was big enough for two mouths.

When I got into bed, Lennie was already zonked. I had to think about what Pop said.

The first thing, when I thought about fighting, I thought about fists. Pop said kick. I wondered if Heiny and his cousin thought about fists first. *Huh!* Kicking. Funny. I never thought about Pop being smart.

The next morning, Pop and I left the house at 6:15 a.m. I carried my bike. He pushed my old one speed. We took my busted up one to Elginfritz's Garage. At Elginfritz's, they repaired everything from roller skates to balers and combines and everything in between. That's what folks said. My ten-speed got parked in their dirt lot between a grey and white Studebaker and a combine.

I looked at Pop.

"Nobody's gonna' steal it like it is."

I didn't lock the bike up at home. There were no worries about someone stealing it there. But, for some reason, at the garage, I worried.

"Ain't never had nothing stole from my lot," Mr. Elginfritz told me. He turned. "Gonna' hafta' order them wheels. Gonna' hafta' check the gear shifting gizmo. Don't know how long it'll take."

Pop elbowed me on the arm.

"Uh. Thanks, Mr. Elginfritz," I said.

Pop and I walked out of the lot to Main, where he handed over my one-speed.

"Boy, he said. From now on, every day till you git your bike back, you leave for work ten minutes early and stop by the garage here and see how they're doing with the job. When you come home of a night, if they're still open, stop and see how the job is coming along. Don't be snotty about it. Just ask nice like."

Pop never said *verstehe*. I nodded anyway, and he set off for the elevator and me for the climb up Church Hill. All the way down Main and then up the hill, I thought about kicking instead of fists. But Big Little Heiny and his cousin weren't there, so I got to my poop on time.

After I had cleaned the milk barn, I walked up the hill to see what Mr. N. had for us to do today. His brother Luther was visiting for a week. Luther had been in the Marines for twenty years, and now he had a job as deputy sheriff about an hour's drive from St. Ambrose.

"So," Luther said, "they busted up your bike and beat the **** out of you. Did you get any licks in?"

Luther had used what amounted to the N-word for poop. Poop was an okay word, but **it wasn't. It was profane. Mama and Pop didn't say even poop all that often. I didn't say it as much as I thought it. Pop, in late winter every year, would tell Lennie and me it was time to clean poop out of the chicken house and spread it over the garden before he spaded it, and that we had to spread that chicken poop out thin, "Cause chicken poop is hot. A little is good for stuff to grow. A lot is bad."

"So, is cow poop better than chicken poop for fertilizer?" I said.

"Yep."

Rats. Did that mean he was thinking of getting a cow and building a cow house for it? I sure hoped not.

Now, by that time in my life, I had completed nine years of schooling. I knew some history, how to elect a president, Latin, reading, writing, and all kinds of arithmetic, but the thing in all the world I knew most about was poop.

Anyway, back to Luther. I had shaken my head to his question.

"Nobody ever taught you how to defend yourself, how to fight?"

"No, sir."

"Call me Luther."

"Yes, sir, Mr. Luther."

Mr. Luther was going to teach me how to fight, but first, he seemed intent on teaching me to cuss. That was the thing he seemed to know most about. But once he got enough cussing done, he took me down the hill to in front of the machine shed, where Mrs. Neidlinger and the kids couldn't see us.

He squared us off facing each other, and said, "Now, I'm going to slap you. Try to stop me."

So I got ready. I thought the slap would come right away. It didn't, and I looked down at his right hand when his left slapped me hard. Stung, and made my head fill with light. Just as the light went out, I got a sharp smack on the other cheek, and I was backpedaling and he was coming after me slapping one cheek, then the other. There wasn't a stinking thing I could do to stop him. Finally, he stopped himself.

My cheeks stung from the outside and the inside. I was breathing hard like I had been working hard. All that slapping he'd done to me didn't make him breathe hard.

"Even a girl would fight back," Luther said

and walked back down the hill to our starting point. "Now, slap me. Go ahead. Whenever you're ready."

I was thinking he probably expected me to use my right, so I used my left. He parried it easy-peasy and slapped me with his other hand. A spike of anger fired out of my head and down to my belly. I tried a right, and he parried and slapped me with his other. And my anger cranked up to white-hot.

I started another right-handed slap, and he raised his hand to parry, and I kicked him on the shin. Hard.

"Ow!" And "Jesus, God" started the longest string of cussing and taking the Lord's name in vain I'd ever heard.

He cussed and hopped on one leg while holding where I'd kicked him. I pushed him over and stood over him with my fists clenched and my teeth bared.

Luther went from cussing a blue streak to laughing his head off.

He stopped laughing. "Boy, I'm going to teach you how to fight. One of the things you need to know is if you're going to fight a girl, check and see if she's wearing work boots. If she is, run like hell." Then he started laughing his head off again.

For the week Luther was there, he'd spend an hour every day slapping me silly and trying to teach me to take it without getting mad. "Make the other guy mad," he said, "then it'll be him does something stupid."

His principal lessons—now principal, and the other way to spell it, I still have to look up in Sister Daniel's dictionary—were:

1. Avoid a fight if you can, but sometimes you can't. When you can't, fight to win, and remember, there ain't no rules.
2. If you get into a fight, don't be afraid. You're going to get your butt kicked or the other guy will get his kicked. Letting yourself be afraid will not help you, and, sure as shootin', it will help him.
3. Don't get mad for the same reasons as above.
4. You got other stuff to fight with besides fists. (This one sounded like Pop. A little) Feet for stompin' and kicking. Teeth for biting. Fingernails for scratching. Hands to grab with, like an ear to rip off.
5. Stomp on feet. Kick knees and balls— Now, here, I got a lecture on not only being tough but talking tough, too. Sometimes you can talk your way out of a fight, but not if you sound like

a sissy. "Now you let me alone, you big bully, or I will kick you in your privates." He looked at me and then went on with principle five—Elbows are great nose breakers. Ears—bite or grab them. They are easy to rip off. Stab a finger into eyeballs. Jab a guy in the throat. If a guy goes down, kick hard where it'll hurt the most. "Where will it hurt the most?" he said. "Balls," I said, but I confessed it the next Saturday.

A week after Luther left, I got my ten-speed back. The repair cost twelve bucks. Two dollars more than Pop paid Mr. Grossman for the bike in the first place. That frosted me some. Sure felt good to shift gears going up Church Hill, though.

That day on the farm, Mr. Neidlinger bought five wagonloads of hay bales from a neighbor, Orson Grundmeister. Orson and his wife had twenty-one kids. All girls, except for the second youngest one. Folks said those Funk and Wagnalls people had to write a new definition for a "spoiled rotten kid" because of how Orson treated Orson Jr.

The older Grundmeister girls did boy work as good as I did. The oldest drove the hay baler. A wire baler. I hated wire balers. Twine bales generally weighed sixty pounds or so. But the wires one crammed more than a hundred pounds of hay into one. After hoisting a few, the wire felt like you weren't even wearing leather gloves. Grundmeister didn't pull a sled behind the baler, so the bales were strung out across the field. Mr. Neidlinger's oldest boy, Mikey, drove the tractor. Mr. N. rode the wagon and stacked the bales after I hoisted them up. He stacked them four bales high and getting those bales up to the fourth level, which needed every ounce of strength I had, and Mr. N had to use a bale hook to snag what I lifted and hoist it to the top.

Mr. Grundmeister had his next three oldest daughters load a wagon, too. They drove down the field along the row of hay bales, right next to the row we followed. Before we had the first layer of bales loaded, Mikey and the tractor-driving Grundmeister girl started racing. They couldn't go too fast, or us, bale hoisters would be left behind.

"Hey, Mikey," I hollered. "Slow down."

The bale hoister Grundmeister girl hollered, "Keep going, Nelly." Nelly, the Grundmeister girl tractor driver. Then the two bale-hoister girls grinned at me.

Which frosted me some. Mikey didn't seem to care about me. He just wanted to get to the end of the field before Nelly did. I hoisted a bale up to Mr. N. He hooked it and shrugged. He was probably happy we'd get his five wagons loaded quickly. Part of his deal was he had to pay the Grundmeister girls by the hour.

By the time we got the five wagons loaded and parked next to Mr. N's barn for unloading the next day, I was one pooped puppy. I had just enough left in me to pedal home. I was hungry enough to eat a wire-bound hay bale, but I thought I might just go to bed dirty.

Sure as shooting, though, Mama wouldn't let me do that.

... viii

The road from Neidlinger's farm to the top of Church Hill climbed a gradual slope, not like the steep sucker on the town side. By the time I reached the top, though, I was pretty close to saying the heck with it and sleeping with my bike in the ditch alongside the road.

I rounded the corner, and there they were again.

Heiny Stiert and Axel Fant. One stood in the middle of one lane, the other in the middle of the other. They were like twin statues with their hands on their hips. The streetlamp behind them hid their faces in dark as sin blackness.

My face remembered where Axel hit me the last time. A big bucketful of ice-cold fear filled my chest and belly, and my arms hung like dead looking limbs on a tree in winter. I stopped and hiked my leg off the bike and looked at the two of them.

Rule one. Avoid a fight if you can. Well, I

could have turned around and maybe gotten up enough speed before they could catch me, but I would not do that. Those two poop-heads were not going to make me sleep in Mr. Neidlinger's hayloft.

Rule two. Don't be afraid. And suddenly I wasn't. Holy crap. I wished I'd known this a long time ago. If you don't want to be afraid of a particular situation, just make a rule against it.

Luther should have made a corollary to rule two, I thought. When you're done being afraid, don't get stupid cocky.

The two big guys just stood there, legs spread, arms akimbo. A good word that akimbo. I thanked Sister Daniels again for the dictionary she gave me. Anyway, I could feel Heiny and Axel watching me. I could feel them thinking I was going to turn tail and run. I could feel them thinking they'd catch me before I could get away.

I rolled my bike to the side of the road and placed it gently in the ditch.

They still hadn't moved.

I started slowly toward them, staying to the right edge of the road. Axel was the one in the right lane. He was a couple of inches taller than Heiny. Axel came out of his statue pose and so did Heiny.

"Hey, Eddie," Heiny said. "Bring your bike so we can see what it looks like fixed up and all."

"Yeah, bring your bike."

I started walking two gears faster. Axel moved over toward the side of the road. To be right in front of me. To cut off my escape route. Axel went into a wrestler's crouch and Heiny started running toward me. When he got close, I stopped and as he flew past me he threw a swing which I ducked and kicked him on the side of the knee and he flew howling into the ditch.

Then I started toward Axel again. He came out of his wrestler pose and cocked his right arm with his big fist on the end of it. I hustled right into his wheelhouse and he swung a looping punch, which I stepped inside and kneed him in the crotch so hard it lifted his feet off the ground.

Axel held himself and backed a couple of steps away from me. I checked on Heiny. He was still in the ditch. "Ow, ow, ow. My goddamned leg is busted."

Axel was bent over and saying, "Oh, oh, oh."

I went to Axel and grabbed his right ear and twisted it. He started howling, "Ow, ow, ow."

"Axel, do you know how easy it is to rip an ear off?"

"No."

"Would you like me to show you?"

"NOOOOO!"

"So listen, Axel, you ever come after me

again, I mean ever, I will rip off one of your ears. You understand?"

"Yes." I twisted the ear harder. "I understand. I understand. Jesus God, I understand."

I let go of the ear and stepped back as Axel straightened up a little. That's when I smacked an uppercut to his face and knocked him into the ditch. He'd have a shiner for sure.

Heiny was on the edge of the road, bent over and holding his knee. He tried to walk without putting weight on the hurt knee for more than a second or two.

I walked up to him.

"Don't hurt me anymore."

"Heiny, you ever come after me again, I will mess up your other knee. You'll be in a wheelchair. You got that?"

"Yeah, Eddie. I got it."

I thought about whether he needed a shiner, too, but decided him limping was enough.

Axel climbed out of the ditch. He was still bent over and holding himself with one hand. He went to Heiny and took an arm over his shoulder, and the two of them limped toward Heiny's house.

The rectory was off to my right. I got my bike and pedaled to the sidewalk connecting the priest's house to the church and parked the ten-speed, the good as new ten-speed, against the fence, and went to the porch and rang the doorbell.

Father Geist swung the door open. He stood there a moment, looking at me, taking me in. Then he invited me in, and said, "Confession?"

"Please, Father."

He led me to his office, put on his confession stole, and said, "Go ahead, Eddie."

I told Father the whole story. What Heiny and Axel did to me, the black eye, and how that vexed Mama. How they busted up my ten-dollar bike to the tune of twelve dollars in repairs. How Luther Neidlinger taught me how to fight and use the rules. I told him after I had pretty much disabled Axel and Heiny, and I punched Axel, I enjoyed having that power over him, when a couple of weeks earlier, he had that power over me. And Heiny, I crippled him up some on that one leg. And I considered hurting Heiny more, and I came close to doing so, even though he begged me not to.

"You considered hurting more, but you didn't?"

"That's right, Father."

"Why?"

"I didn't really want to have to fight those guys just to get home and have dinner and go to bed. But I did not want them to hurt me. That vexes Mama. It hurts her more than it does me. And I did not want them busting up my bike again, which I saved up money for six thousand years to buy."

Which sent the confession down a side bunny trail to explain that. Then I told Father I thought the odds were sixty-six and two-thirds percent that Heiny wouldn't want to ever fight me again.

Another bunny trail to explain that. At school, Sister Mary man's-name Francis conducted an optional class during the lunch hour. It was called "Statistics, Combinations, Permutations, and Probabilities. Sister allowed us to eat our baloney sandwiches while we attended her class.

"If she'd made you chose either Statistics… and those other things or baloney…?"

"Baloney, Father."

The corners of his mouth tweaked up a bit.

"Anyway, Father, I decided, knowing Heiny as long as I had, that's what I figured the probability, the odds were.

"You're a piece of work, Eddie Walsh. Anybody ever tell you that?"

"Yes, Father. As best as I can recall, you are the fourth person to say that to me. That's with a statistical certainty of around seventy-five percent."

Father folded his hands and raised his eyes. "God in heaven, hallowed by Thy name. Thank You for this visit from young Eddie Walsh. Now

I can say I truly have heard every possible sin under the sun in confession." He lowered his eyes to mine and unfolded his hands. "And that's with a statistical certainty of ninety-eight-point-five percent. And it'll be true until your next confession."

The rest of the summer slipped away as summers liked to do. When school cranked up again, I, Eddie Walsh, was now a sophomore. No longer a goober freshman new guy from Hicksville, St. Ambrose. As a sophomore, I was sort of human even. Almost somebody. But to really be somebody, you had to have a car. And I didn't even have a driver's license.

And the other thing about that second year of high school, we got a new schoolhouse to go to. Last year we attended St. Peter High School associated with the parish of St. Peter and located next to the church. This new school was called Duchesne (sounds like Do Shayne) High. It was a neat place. All bright with shiny linoleum on the floors, like Meinerschlagen's new store, and lots of windows in the classrooms letting in lots of sunlight. St. Peter High building was a lot like Holy Martyrs Grade School. Old as dirt with stairs creaking and groaning when a whole class trooped up or down at the same time and you wondered if the whole staircase would collapse and dump us in a heap at the bottom like when we played tackle football in fifth grade and Sister Daniel got excommunicated from being a nun.

I confess that notion of the stairs collapsing and dumping twenty students or so in a pile, with two-thirds of them being girls. It was a thing I thought about from time to time. That's the way it was in my Duchesne class. Two-thirds girls. Anyway, like I said, I thought about falling into a pile of girls, and it seemed like it might be fun. As long as I didn't hurt any of them. But then I thought about Sister Daniels' words about having fun not being bad, necessarily. So I confessed to Father Geist in the box one Saturday that I dreamt about falling into a pile of girls.

"In this dream," Father said in his in-the-box whisper, "What do you do after you fall into the pile of... bodies?"

"Well, I help the girls up, Father."

A sound came out of his side of the box, sort of like he was about to cough when a sneeze snuck up on him, and he wound up with a lap full of snot and boogers. I pictured him in the gloom in there, hankying up the mess off his stole and his cassock.

Then it was quiet for a long time. I expected

him to say something, but since he didn't, I said, "Another thing, Father."

He cut me off with, "I forgive you all your sins."

"Even the ones I haven't said yet?"

"Yes. You can go."

"But I didn't say the Act of Contrition yet."

"Go kneel in the front pew and say it."

"Aren't you going to give me a penance?"

"Go kneel in the front pew, and after the Act of Contrition, say one Our Father and one Hail Mary."

He slid the wooden cover over the hole in the wall between his side of the box and mine. From his side of the box, I heard a mumble which ended with a "piece of work."

The first sock hop of the year was coming up. Ollie Weisendinger was a senior that year, but he wasn't bringing Violet to the sock hop. I asked Pop if I could use the car. "I know how to drive. I drive Mr. Neidlinger's car. And his truck. And his tractors. I can even back up a tractor with a wagon behind it."

Pop had stopped reading his paper to look at me.

When my mouth finished talking, he

twitched his head like a fly landed on his nose or something and went back to reading.

So much for that idea.

On the night of the sock hop, I stayed in St. Charles after class and ate supper with Uncle John and his family. Which was a longer walk than from the old school. Esther gave me a ride back to school in time for the dance. There, I danced with several of the girls from my class. And I danced with a couple of freshman girls as well. A couple of them were kind of cute and they were nice.

I did not dance with Teresa Yount and her friend Samantha. Samantha was the girl whose quiz I had marked with an incorrect answer when she'd gotten them all correct. I was pretty sure both girls were still mad at me.

At the end of the evening, I asked Roger Rottermick for a ride to the corner of Kingshighway and Clay Streets so I could hitchhike home. Instead, he, with his girlfriend close beside him, and me in the shotgun seat, drove me all the way to St. Ambrose. After I'd agreed to pay him fifty cents for gas.

Once Ollie Wiesendinger asked me if wanted to do a double date with Violet and him, but I had no one I wanted to spend a fortune on to see two movies at the Fox Theater in St. Louis.

My sophomore year classes were much more interesting. Trig one semester. Geometry the next, and Chemistry and Physics. The History was sort of like, in grade school we saw the tip of the History iceberg. In high school, we saw the underwater nine-tenths of it. I liked going to school during my sophomore year.

In the summer I resumed working six days a week for Mr. Neidlinger. The money in my ten-speed jelly jar started piling up. When I had fifty-three dollars and seventy-five cents saved, Pop took me and the jar to the bank and had me open a savings account. Pop put down two twenties and a ten, and he told me to dump out my jar. The teller took our money, and he gave me a little book with little numbers showing the balance in my account.

The teller smiled at me. "See this column here in your passbook? That's where the interest goes. Your hundred dollars is drawing interest as of this very minute. Your balance will grow without you having to lift a finger."

"It's compound interest, right?" We had a class about that.

"Don't be a smart alec," Pop said.

The teller smiled again. "Paddy, it's refreshing to meet a young man who understands the importance of investing and saving."

I could feel Pop thinking: *The boy don't understand nothin'. He's here cause I made him be here.*

From that point on, half my weekly earnings,

I gave to the bank. In no time at all, my account earned twenty-five cents in interest. Just in time for my sixteenth birthday and my driver's license. Twenty-five cents bought a gallon of gas.

Not that that quarter could be used for such a purpose. "You don't touch that money," Pop said. "Except for something really important. Like getting married."

I hadn't thought about getting married. Now that Pop kicked me into thinking about it, I remembered what he thought about his oldest brother: an old maid bachelor. "Be a priest or get married. Don't be your Uncle Sylvester."

Heck. I didn't even have a girlfriend. BUT. I had a driver's license. With the use of the Plymouth now and then, maybe I could get one. A car and being a junior come fall. I mean, I didn't think I was SOMEBODY. But I was at least somebody.

ix

One of the coolest things about turning sixteen and getting a driver's license: It was the first thing in my entire life Simon Grossman didn't get to do a year ahead of me.

I thought about thinking about that. What I'd done, in fact, was to gloat. "Ha ha, Simon Grossman The Rich Kid, I finally got to do something the same time you did!" And It sure felt good. Until the next stinking thinking happened.

At first, a voice in my head said there isn't a "Thou shalt not" about gloating. But then another voice said, "There is thou shalt not covet."

Voice 1: Wait. Are you saying gloating is coveting?

Voice 2: Think about it.

Well, I knew if there was any real thinking going to get done, it had to be me doing it. Those two jibber-jabberers in my head weren't going to.

Gloating was coveting, but not exactly. To get to the gloating, I had to covet all the stuff Simon Grossman had and got to do that I couldn't. For a long time, sure as shooting, I had coveted. For a bit, I tried to convince myself that coveting and gloating was one sin. Like gloating was the tail on a covet dog. If you love your neighbor as yourself, you don't aim a lot of gloats at him. *Poop!* Two sins to confess instead of one.

You can probably guess what Father Geist said in the box come Saturday when I explained gloating and coveting to him.

So I got my driver's license on my birthday. There were still a couple of weeks before school started, and I wanted to try out this driving a girl on a date thing. Ollie Weisendinger just looked so cool with his girlfriend Violet all pressed against him like a slice of Velveeta against one of baloney that had been in the bottom of book bag with a history and a geometry book on top of the sandwich.

I asked a St. Charles girl from my class named Amelia to go to a movie with me at the Strand Theater. And it turned out to be a... nice date. It sure wasn't Hilda smearing me all over with girl spit and lipstick. Neither was it a Noreen date, she not giving a thing to it or taking anything from it either. On the ride home, after ice cream, Amelia sat smack in the middle of the space between me and the passenger door.

When I thought about it, I was happy she sat where she did. I was happy to find a girl I could talk to and not break out in a sweat trying to dredge up something other than cow poop to talk about. She was a nice girl. I was glad I asked her out.

"Thanks for asking me out, Eddie," she told me on her front porch; then she leaned toward me and kissed me lightly on the lips, stepped back, smiled, and entered her house. She left the porch light on until I got back to the car and started the engine.

I thought about Amelia all the way back to St. Ambrose. I hoped she'd be my friend girl. No way did she want to be my girlfriend. I don't know how I knew that, but I knew it. Maybe though, she might like to be my friend. I sure hoped so, cause I liked her a lot. Like the sister I'd have had if Lennie had been a girl. And that thought lasted in my head for about one and a half seconds. Lennie, a girl! No way. Or maybe a cousin like Lucinda. There was such a thing as kissing cousins, but, of course, I couldn't kiss Lucinda. *She's a nun.* And you just don't go around kissing nuns. Even Sister

Daniels. Kissing her would be a matter for the confessional, sure as shooting.

At any rate, kissing my friend girl had put the perfect cap on a very nice date. I lay in bed thinking about Amelia, about her lips touching mine as light as a butterfly landing on a lily—

When I woke up the next morning, before my eyes opened, I saw Amelia smile at me like she had after our kiss. Then my eyes opened, but I just lay there wondering about how I felt. Always before, when I woke, I got up, used the in-house, and ate breakfast. What else was there to think about when you're awake before the sun comes up? Well, that morning, I thought about Amelia. For eleven seconds. Then I went to use the in-house.

Ollie Weisendinger graduated last year, but I still rode with him and his older brother. Ollie now worked in the Ford plant, too. So, I still walked to Second Street. I still paid a quarter a day.

On the first day of classes, we got in the brother's car, and before the engine started, Ollie said, "I haven't seen the new school building. I bet it's cool. I'm going to have to drive by just to see it one of these days."

He was right. This morning I would go to

a brand-spanking-new Duchesne High School, not old-as-dirt St. Peter. I hadn't seen it either. And it was a ways away from the old place. Last year, his brother dropped Ollie and me right in front of the school. Because it was on his brother's way to the bridge over the Missouri. Now though, he would drop me at the corner of Clay and Kingshighway, and I'd have to hoof it down Kingshighway a piece, then hang a left onto Elm Street. I knew it was about the same distance I used to run home for lunch in grade school. Of course, I couldn't run to high school. If I did, I'd work up a sweat and stink up my pits.

Last year as a freshman, among a few other things, I'd learned about—besides Brylcreem and Clearasil—deodorant. I'd learned those things from the TV, not school, but the guys, and in some ways the girls, taught me how important those three things were, and that sweating could cause the Brylcreem to run down in a greasy mess onto the collar of my shirt, cause my Clearasil to wash off and let my pimples run wild, and it could cause deodorant fade out. So, once the Weisendingers dropped me off, I knew I'd walk, not run.

I thought about all this before we passed my house on the way out of town. When we passed it, I committed what I called the Weisendinger sin. I pictured myself, Eddie Walsh, standing there at the end of the driveway, and Ollie's older brother driving up and stopping and Ollie piling out and moving the shotgun seat forward, and I saw me, with my book bag in one hand and a quarter in the other, climb in the rear and Ollie flop the seat back and get back in and close the door, and then we'd drive off. The whole thing would have taken ten seconds! But it didn't happen that way, so I looked at the back of the driver's head and thought: *You stink-bomb, snot-wad Weisendinger! Ten seconds! It would only take ten seconds!* Pretty much an egregious three exclamation point sin.

The next thing I thought: *You Stupid, Eddie Walsh, you gotta confess that come Saturday.*

Last year I came to call that my Weisendinger sin, and, in the box, I'd say, "I committed the Weisendinger sin five times this week."

After I'd done that two weeks in a row, Father whispered from his side of the box, "Eddie, you commit this sin every day. Can't you get a handle on this? At the end of each confession, you resolve to sin no more. Try this. After getting in the car each morning, start saying Our Fathers and Hail Marys and don't let up until you are on the highway and headed for St. Charles."

The next week, I did that, but each blinking day, I'd start out saying the prayers, and Ollie's brother would start driving us down Second, and he'd turn right onto Oak and pass the elevator where Pop worked, and then he'd turn left onto Main, and there would be our house. On the right. And in my mind, I'd see me standing at the foot of our driveway, and I'd see the car stop and pick me up and the whole thing taking just ten stupid seconds! And my mind would push Our Fathers and Hail Marys right out of my head, and I'd, in real life, glare at the back of Snot-wad's head and commit the Weisendinger sin.

At the next confession, Father whispered, "Did you really pray like I told you to?"

"Yes, Father," I whispered back. "I really pray. But, what happens is, we start driving, and I start cranking out the prayers, but then we turn the corner, and there's our house, and in my mind, I see me standing there, at the foot of the drive, and I see the car stop and me climb in and all of it takes only ten seconds. That makes me mad at Ollie's brother. What it is, Father, my mind has a mind of its own."

It got heavily quiet in Father's middle of the box. After a while, I wondered if he'd fallen asleep in there, but then he said, "Anything else?"

Heck, yes, there was other stuff, so I told all those other sins through that screen you couldn't see through and onto Father's lap. He told me it was time for the Act of Contrition, which I said, and then he gave me a handful of Our Fathers and another handful of Hail Marys for penance and slid the sliding door shut on my side. I heard the door on the other side slide open. Time for Eddie to get the heck out of there. That other mind of mine had enough ways of committing sins without getting ideas from other sinners.

Thinking about it now, that was the last time Father ever said anything other than the standard stuff in the confessional. And of course, all this happened last year.

When we got on the highway, Ollie said, "Man. I wish I could have gone one year to Duchesne. A brand-new building and I heard the Chemistry lab has all kinds of neat stuff in it."

Then he went on to bad mouth the old St. Peter building for a while. Then he started talking about the French nun they named the new school for. "Rose Philippine Duchesne. I mean, Rose is okay and Duchesne is her last name. But what's with Philippine? I mean, isn't it weird enough nuns take man names? Why would one take the name of some islands on the other side of the world?"

As Ollie jabbered, I was thinking about not committing the Weisendinger sin. Had my mind's mind finally gotten over me having to leave the house ten minutes early to save Ollie's brother those ten seconds?

Maybe there was a lesson here. Maybe if you commit a sin often enough, you get tired of committing it. And that just stops the old sin dead in its tracks. I was pretty sure Father Geist would not think that was a good path to follow to holiness.

Ollie's brother stopped the car. We'd arrived at the corner. I got out, crossed the street, and walked down the sidewalk next to Lindenwood College. Lindenwood College for Women, actually. Looking over the low rock wall into the campus, it occurred that I hadn't thought about going to college. I knew Pop expected me to find a job after high school like Ollie Weisendinger did, but walking by Lindenwood got me thinking. College costs a lot more money than a Catholic high school. I knew that much. Still. I wondered if Lindenwood knew how good I was at being a girl, would they let me in?

College. Pop only went to school through the fourth grade, and he wanted his kids to have it better than he and Mama did. Would he want me to go to college?

I knew Simon Grossman's older sister went to college. Gladys, who worked for Mr. Neidlinger's wife, was in college now. She had to work to save money for it. I had no idea how much it costs to go to college. Heck, I didn't even know what it cost to go to high school. When it was time to pay tuition, I carried a sealed envelope in my bookbag and turned it in at the school office.

Oops. I'd slowed down as I passed Lindenwood. It was time to pick up the pace. Walshes didn't like to be late.

Kingshighway was a busy street. Up ahead of me, a number of cars made a left turn. Elm, I wondered? Some of the cars passing were jammed full of kids my age. Some of those jammed-full cars made that left turn. I knew the public high school sat on Kingshighway several blocks down. Jimmie Joe went there.

Two blocks past Lindenwood, I came to Elm. Elm had sidewalks on both sides of the street. In St. Ambrose, we had a sidewalk on one side of Main, and there was one on one side of Second as well. Big cities sure had a lot of sidewalks. As soon as I had that thought, the walk on my side of the street quit, and I had to cross.

I came to the top of a hill, and Elm dropped away below me. Up ahead I could see a steady stream of cars turning right into a big parking lot. The building behind the lot had to be Duchesne. And it was.

Duchesne was named after a French nun like Ollie'd said, who came to America in the early 1800s. She established schools to teach kids on what was, in those days, the edge of civilization. And that French nun's last name.

It looks like it should be pronounced "Do Chez Knee," but it's actually "Do Shane," you know, like the greatest cowboy book ever.

At any rate, Sister Duchesne set up schools and taught Indians and other heathens and savages, "like teenage boys." That's how Sister Superior at St. Peter High School described the patroness and namesake of our new school at the end of last year.

At the corner of the school property, I stopped and just looked at this long one-story structure, taking up a considerable *splop* of land. My grade school building, and the high school one last year both looked like they were scrunched onto a tight spot with no room to spare, and both were two stories. This looked like there was room to spare to double the school in size and still have some property left for the important stuff. A long time ago, I'd have said, like for a ball diamond.

The Duchesne parking lot was full of cars, and other cars lined past the front door and dropped kids off. Along one edge of the parking lot, and next to a moving line of cars, a sidewalk led up to where a steady stream of kids flowed inside. Arrayed along that walk, three clumps of kids huddled. They seemed to be talking about something a lot more important than a new school building.

I approached the first clump of kids and

Roger Rottermick broke out of the group and stopped me. His forehead was crinkled up by a frown. He said, "Eddie, Holy Crap Hilda got herself knocked up and dropped out of school."

That's what I learned the first day of school my sophomore year. It's all I learned that day.

X

New school. New books. New teachers. Well, a handful of those came from the old school. And there were a lot more of us. Last year, my class held thirty-seven students. This year, seventy-five. In all of Duchesne, there were over two hundred of us. The population of St. Ambrose wasn't much more than that. "277," the population sign said.

That stuff kind of registered with me, but my head was full of knocked-up Hilda, and that Sadie Hawkins sock hop. Sarah Esterhausen had told me I had changed her from Homely to Holy Crap Hilda at that dance. Well, Holy Crap was my name for her, but the meaning of what Sarah said was the meat of it. Homely Hilda would never have gotten herself knocked up. That's what that other mind in my mind told me. I changed her into Holy Crap. It was my fault she got knocked up.

Roger Rottermick had walked with me to our

first-period classroom, homeroom. He told me Hilda had been going steady with another guy named Eddie from St. Ann's across the river. The Missouri River. St. Ann's Eddie was a year older than us. He'd dropped out of school and had a job. And a car.

"I wonder if he'll marry her."

Roger stopped and looked at me. "No. The guy's family moved to Columbia, and he went with them."

"And left Hilda a Hester Prynne."

Roger wanted to know who she was.

"The main character in *The Scarlet Letter.*"

We'd entered the school by this time and turned down this long corridor. The walls on both sides were nothing but lockers and doors into classrooms.

"The scarlet letter is A for adultery, right?"

"Yes."

"So, Hester lived through hell on earth. That sums it up."

"Close enough."

"Poor Hilda." Roger shook his head. "Her life is going to be—her life is hell on earth. How did it turn out for Hester... Pin?"

I didn't want to get into the nobility of her character, or redemption in the end, or the fact she suffered punishment more for the sin of the male partner to their hanky-panky than her own. "Pryne. Pretty much like you said, hell on earth."

The morning passed in a blur of bells and walking to class and Hilda at home, or somewhere, suffering hell on earth. At lunch, I wanted to talk to Sarah Esterhausen, but she was at a table full of girls and they were all kind of huddled together and whispering up a storm. I didn't even try to get her attention. Instead, I walked to the chapel and just sat there in the quiet. I should have been thinking about heaven, but I was thinking about hell and me putting Hilda there. And Hilda's seemed a lot worse—more worser—than the one I put Mama in in first grade. Putting Hilda there tore a big hole in my stomach. If I'd eaten my baloney sandwich, I'd have puked.

I sat in the chapel until the bell rang.

The afternoon, not one little bit different from the morning, passed in a blur. The bells chopped it into chunks of blur. When the final bell rang, I recognized it as such because all the kids I followed walked out of the building.

Oh. Time to go home.

Walk to the corner of Kingshighway and Clay. Stuck out my thumb. A flatbed truck stopped and I climbed up into the cab.

"Where you goin', Kid?"

"St. Ambrose, Sir."

"Goin' right through there. I'll drop you on the highway. That okay?"

"That'll be great, Sir. And thank you."

Mr. Truck Driver started us moving, shifting gears, and asking me questions. I answered with "Yeps," "Nopes," and "Uh huhs." I didn't want to talk to him, but I had to answer something, or he might have stopped and shoved me out.

Who I wanted to talk to was Father Geist.

When we got to St. Ambrose, I asked the driver to let me out at the second St. Ambrose street crossing the highway, the one town folks called Maple and leading to the long flight of concrete steps climbing Church Hill to the sidewalk running between the cemetery and the nun's house.

After the topping the hill and passing the church, I went to the rectory and rang the bell. The housekeeper answered, and I asked if I could see Father.

"Wait here." She closed the door in my face. Pop would have been her kind of housekeeper.

Pretty quick the door opened again, and she led me to Father's study. I went in.

"Close the door."

I did.

"Yes, Eddie?"

So, I told him about Hilda getting knocked up and that it was my fault.

"You had sexual intercourse with her?"

I knew what that was. It was hanky-panky. "No, Father."

"Well then, how is it your fault?"

"Until Sadie Hawkins dance last year, Hilda was shy. Everybody called her Homely Hilda. At least the guys did. Some of the girls thought they could gussy Hilda up so she wouldn't be homely anymore, and one girl, Sarah, tricked me into dancing with her at that Sadie Hawkins thing."

"This is the girl who took your hand and put it on her breast?"

"Yes. Uh, Father, do you remember the sins of all 277 of us in St. Ambrose?"

"No, Eddie. Only yours."

"Oh."

"Eddie, I'm teasing you."

"Oh."

Father had more questions. Almost as many as Mr. Truck Driver had, but I answered Father's.

Finally, he said, "Eddie, you did not get Hilda pregnant. It's not your fault. What you and that girl—Sarah was it—did for her was a nice thing. Hilda's life wasn't happy, and you made it happy for her. A good thing. Once she got happy, though, Hilda made choices that led directly to her sin and out-of-wedlock pregnancy. Unless she was raped, of course."

Father looked at me like his last sentence

had been interrogative, but I hadn't heard a question mark. I answered anyway. "Nobody'd said anything about rape."

Boy. This getting knocked up business was complicated, and there sure were a lot of different ways to talk about it.

"So, Eddie. The only thing you did to Hilda was a nice thing. You told me before she helped you have the best day of your life. I am absolutely certain she would say the same thing about that Sadie Hawkins dance. To that point, it was the best day of her life. And that can be nothing except a good thing."

Father took off his confession stole. "I don't need this thing to absolve you of a sin you did not commit. You did not sin, but you have been punishing yourself for having committed one. Stop giving yourself punishment, but I want you to say ten Our Fathers and ten Hail Marys. Not in atonement for sins, but for Hilda. She may suffer the rest of her life for her sin, and the child that is born of this sin. Father, God, who art in heaven, please take this little one to your bosom, and shield him, or her, from the consequences of her mother's transgression."

The housekeeper ushered me out like she was glad to get rid of me. On the front porch of the rectory, I set my book bag down and dug out my baloney sandwich. It was flat as a communion wafer. But, man, did it taste good.

And it was gone before I passed the front doors of the church.

I went inside and knelt in the back most pew and said those ten Ours and the ten Hails for Hilda and her baby. Then I went home with half my heart filled with light, happy stuff, and the other half filled with heavy sorrow for the life Hilda would have that would be so much worse than the one she had when she was just homely.

The only sidewalk on our end of Main Street was on the other side of the street from where our house sat. When I got to the Grossman house, I stopped; then I went up and rang the bell. Simon opened the door, and I asked him if I could borrow *The Scarlet Letter.*

With his hand on the doorknob, Simon looked right at me for a few seconds. Then he closed the door. The answer could have been no. It could also have been yes, so I waited. After enough seconds passed for him to go to his room and get the book and return, the door opened again. He had the book in his hand. Beyond him, I saw Large Louie's mom carry two bowls, with steam lifting from them, into their dining room.

"Don't mess up any pages. Especially no boogers sticking them together." Simon held out the book. "We just sat down to dinner." He closed the door.

That night after Mama put dinner on our

table, and we ate it, and Lennie and I cleaned up, I went upstairs and read the last part of Simon's book. Mr. Hawthorne created Hester Prynne. Her character hadn't been a real person, but I was sure there was a real spirit of Esther about in the spirit world. She was a good spirit, not an evil one, roaming about the world seeking the ruin of souls. Like the line in the prayer to St. Michael, the archangel.

I closed the book and said a prayer for Hilda. I prayed to God and to all holy angels and saints and all the good spirits to help not only Hilda but her baby as well, *and if it be Your will Father God Who art in heaven, squeeze some of the hell out Hilda's life and out of the life her baby will have. Amen.*

I almost lifted my shirt to see if I had the letter I, for innocent, branded on my chest, but I didn't. After I crawled into bed next to Lennie, I said a final prayer for Father Geist who absolved me of a sin I didn't commit so I could feel innocent.

Then I slept like I sure the heck was.

XI

The second day of second year of high school and I was two weeks behind in my schoolwork. That's what it felt like. Turned out there'd been homework assignments in each class—except homeroom, of course. To pass that class, all you had to do was to find it. Roger Rottermick led me to it yesterday. Today I found it on my own. The classrooms were numbered, in order, and the number of my homeroom was printed on the schedule they'd mailed to our house before school started.

Heck, even Large Louie would have been able to find his homeroom. Even before Alice Ashe and I helped him graduate from first grade.

Alice. She was assigned to my homeroom, too. Yesterday, before I found out about Hilda, I wondered if Alice would ease up on me a bit. All freshman year, every time we wound up in the same place, I'd get this look from her. Her face would frown up, and it made me think that might have been how Superman looked when he cranked up his X-ray vision. Only Alice didn't want to see through me with her look. She wanted to turn me into a pillar of salt. Yesterday I'd been too concerned over getting Hilda knocked up to pay attention to her.

When I opened the door to homeroom, out of the twenty-four kids already seated at their desks, my eyes went to Alice, and her eyes went to me. I looked away. Her turn-me-to-salt stare had lost none of its power. It had gotten stronger. I looked away, and as I slunk toward my seat, I felt like I'd looked away just in time.

As I took my seat, I wondered what would have happened if she had turned me to salt. Would they have scooped me up and put me in a sack and delivered me to Mama with a, "Here's what's left of your Eddie, Mrs. Walsh. Enough salt to last a hundred years. At least he was worth something."

The bell, the blessed bell, jangled the start of the first period and obliterated Sodom and Gomorrah and the fire and brimstone thunderstorm knocking the *bejeebers* out of the twin cities.

Sister Scholastica was our homeroom teacher, and I was sure glad when my mind decided to listen to her.

At the start of the second period, and third,

and fourth, I found out how behind I was. All my teachers had assigned homework yesterday, and all of them wanted to use what we were supposed to turn in to assess where we were in the mastery of the basics of those courses. Since I hadn't done any homework, I got detention from each teacher.

Detention, also called Stupid Study, required us to stay an hour after the dismissal bell, and if we needed extra help on any subject, help would be available during the hour. If we didn't need to be cured of stupidity, if it was a matter of discipline, just buckle down and get the homework done, well Stupid Study gave us the opportunity to get a head start on what we should do at home.

I was sure coming up in the world. Eddie Walsh, wrecker of girls' lives and three hours of detention by noontime. However, a good thing happened at noontime on the second day of school. Father Godfry—he was called Moderator of Duchesne High, which meant he was boss of Sister Superior. Which, in my mind, turned her into Sister Sort-of Superior.

After my morning, though, Mass was what I needed. And I knelt on the hard floor even though Father said we could sit during normal kneel times since we had no pews with kneelers in the school chapel.

Maybe it was the kneeling, maybe it was the

Mass itself, maybe it was that I offered the Mass and all the prayers I prayed for Hilda and her baby, for Alice Ashe, and for Mama and all those little swords I stuck in her heart. Whatever it was, at the last Amen, I felt a little bit innocent again, like I'd felt right up until Alice tried to turn me into salt.

That afternoon, in each of the three classes, I got three more hours of detention. Serving my sentence would carry me into next week. But the day wasn't over. After detention, I was told to stop by Sister Sort-of Superior's office.

She was about as short and skinny as Sister Everest, my first and second-grade teacher, had been, and she was as hard and tough-looking as grade school Sister Superior.

I knocked on the office door and was told to, "Come in," which I did.

"I'm Eddie Walsh, Sister—" Whoa. I'd almost tacked on that *Sort-of.*

"Mr. Walsh. Take this home with you." She handed me an envelope, sealed. "Give it to your parents. I require a reply from them, signed by both, and you are to deliver it to me before the first bell tomorrow."

I took the envelope and stood there. I half expected a *verstehe?* What I got though was an Alice Ashe glare. I spun around and was halfway out the door before I stopped and lobbed a "Yes, Sister," over my shoulder.

As I hustled along Elm and then Kingshighway toward Hitchhiking Corner, that voice in my head yammered at me. *Way to go, Special Eddie Walsh. You're special good at wrecking girl's lives. And at getting detention. And at falling behind with your homework.*

I walked faster, trying to get away from the voice, which is probably worth an extra stupid study. Walking faster will not get you away from something inside you. *Duh!*

I stepped into the kitchen and stopped. Mama was reading the paper, at her place at the table, with her back to the stove. She looked up. "How was school?"

My nose figured out supper was cooking. I wasn't worried about that. I worried after Mama read the letter, she might spank me, and my stupid iron butt might break her hand again. All the way home, I'd been thinking about that. If Mama broke her hand again, this time with three little kids in the house, she'd need more help than the last time. Lucinda was in the convent. She couldn't come. Maybe cousin Esther. But would Pop even ask Uncle John? That would sure make us beholden.

Six miles' worth of thinking about it brought

up no answers, but it sure piled a heap of worry on me.

I took in a deep breath, huffed it out, walked up to Mama, and handed her Sister Superior's letter. Mama folded the paper and put it on the highchair tray next to her as the table was already set for supper. I knew what was coming next. "Turn around. Drop your pants. Bend over." It was like I was anxious to hear her say that so I could get to doing it.

She opened the envelope, took out the letter, started reading, and frowned.

Here it comes.

"Ach." Then she folded the letter up, stuck it back in the envelope, and went back to her paper.

Crap. This could not be good. I remembered the first spanking I ever got. Mama gave it and every other one I ever received. I wondered if this meant I was going to receive my first Pop spanking. That would definitely not be good. If that were to happen, it would be a while. Fall was busy at the elevator. Harvest time. Which gave me plenty of tick-tocks to heap up more worry. Riding home with a stake bed truck driver, I wondered if I got a Pop spanking, would he break my butt? If that happened, I couldn't imagine what kind of cast they'd put on me. I'd sure have to drop out of school.

Eddie Walsh, how the crap do you get yourself

in so much trouble all the time? There, I said to that stupid other voice in my head, *answer that for me, Mr. Smarty-pants.*

Of course, Mr. Smarty-pants, when you wanted him to say something, he was silent. Heck, he wasn't even up there.

It was nine-thirty that night before Pop hollered, "Eddie."

I left my homework on the table in the attic and hustled. Whatever was to come, it would only be worse the longer I made Pop wait to give it.

He sat at my spot at the kitchen table, opposite Mama's seat with her back to the stove. A dirty plate—and I only knew it was dirty because the silverware lay on the plate— occupied Pop's spot. After he ate all the meat, potatoes, and vegetables, he used a piece of bread and wiped his plate clean. His plate, when he finished eating and plate-wiping, looked as clean as it did before Mama put supper on it.

I looked up from Pop's plate and found him glaring at me.

"Read this." He handed me a sheet of paper. Sister Superior's letter.

It said I hadn't done the homework for any

of my six classes. This was no way to start the year. Last year I had gotten good grades. It said:

> If your son does not correct this egregious behavior instantly, he will make extra work for his teachers. They should be focusing their attention on the students not blessed with Eddie's intellectual gifts. Talk to your son. Make sure by tomorrow he is ready to start school with the rest of the seventy-four young men and young women in his class. After you speak with Eddie, I want both of you, Mr. and Mrs. Walsh, to sign the letter and have Eddie return it to me.

I finished reading and looked up. Pop stuck out his hand, and I gave the letter back to him. He placed it on the table, took up a pen, and started printing across the bottom of the sheet. Pop didn't do longhand.

"Mama," Pop said loud enough to ride over the TV.

She entered the kitchen carrying Laura. Pop got out of the chair and told her to sign the letter. Mama handed the baby to Pop. She sat and signed, and Pop told her to give me the letter and that I was to give it to Sister Superior first thing tomorrow morning.

Pop had printed: "The boy been spoken to."

"Boy," Pop said, "Don't you never bring a letter like this home—"

He stopped and frowned for a moment, and then he unfrowned. "Boy, don't you never give Sister cause to write such a letter about you ever agin."

Pop started toward the front room carrying the baby.

Mama looked up at me. "Something was bothering you yesterday, Eddie. What was it?"

"Don't make no never mind what it was," Pop told the both of us.

I was sure glad I didn't have to answer Mama. I'd felt guilty over getting Hilda knocked up. Father Geist told me Hilda's pregnancy wasn't my fault, that I was innocent. Talking to Pop, I felt guilty all over again. I sure didn't want to tell Mama that I had innocently gotten a girl knocked up.

Upstairs, I got back into homework like my life depended on it.

Next Saturday when I arrived at Mr. Neidlinger's, he and his oldest boy, Elmer, waited for me by the fence around the backyard. He told me I was going to have Elmer, his oldest boy, follow me around.

"Show him the ropes. Time for the boy to earn his keep, and I won't need to pay him two and a half bucks a day." He looked me in the eye. "I won't be needing you after today."

My working for him had begun on one heck of an abrupt Saturday morning. Why would I expect getting canned by him to be any different?

Elmer glared at me like it was my fault he had to go to work. I turned and started walking toward the milk barn.

"Go with him," Mr. Neidlinger said.

"No!"

"Eddie."

I stopped and turned around.

"Take him with you," Mr. Neidlinger said. "Even if you have to drag him."

He had his son by the arm. Elmer must have tried to run away.

I walked back up the hill.

Elmer was twelve. The same age I was when Pop gave me to Mr. N. The kid was skinny as a pitchfork handle, blond hair with a bowl-on-his-head haircut, and the meanest looking face I'd ever seen on a kid.

"Do what Eddie says."

I grabbed Elmer's arm. Mr. N. let go of the

other, turned, and walked back toward the house.

Elmer tried to kick me, but I jerked him off balance, and he would have fallen if I hadn't held him up. Then we headed for the milk barn, too fast for him to work a kick. I dragged the kid through the room with the milk storage tank and into the compartment with the stalls and the pit for the milker.

"Take that scoop shovel and start shoveling the poop toward the far door."

Elmer crossed his arms over his chest and glared at me.

I crossed my arms and leaned against the door to the tank room. "This is my last day working for your dad. I don't care if we spend the whole blinking thing, right here, just staring at each other. He doesn't expect me to do any work. He expects me to tell you how to do it, and he expects you to do it."

I started cleaning dirt from under the fingernails of one hand with the nail of a finger on the other hand. My nails were pretty clean. But I had to do something. I hated just standing there and not doing a blinking thing. I wished I'd brought a book.

I cleaned all ten clean nails. What the heck was I going to do next? Pick my nose and fling boogers at the rotten kid?

"Enough wasting time. Elmer. Pick up the scoop and do what I said."

More crossed arms and glare. Plus, a little smirk. He'd gotten a rise out of me.

A lightning bolt of mad flashed across my mind, and I rushed at the kid. He dropped his arms and fear supplanted his smirk. I grabbed his arm and thought: Supplanted. That was a good word, and I was glad I had the chance to use it. Elmer was good for something. But good words or bad, it was time for a little motivation.

I dragged the rotten kid down into the pit between the stalls, then I sat on the bottom step and threw Elmer across my lap and I spanked him. With the first whap, he yowled like the Little Poopers used to yowl when they got diaper rash and were sitting in a load of what gave them the rash. I kept whapping on his blue-jeaned butt until my hand started hurting.

I stood him up and he put both hands on his backside and had his head tilted up a bit and his eyes closed and hollering like to hurt my ears. Snot ran out of his nose and into his mouth.

Like a statue of a kid with an air-raid siren wailing out of his open mouth. I knew what an air-raid siren sounded like because of a war movie, one of a double-feature I'd seen at the Strand Theater on a double date with Ollie Weisendinger. Afterward, after we'd dropped off my date and after waiting for Ollie and Violet to get done saying goodnight to each other, and we were driving home, Ollie told me that when the theater put on a double feature, they played one boy movie and one girl movie. So, the war movie was the boy one.

Anyway, Elmer wailed on and on. The noise he was making, I wouldn't have been surprised to see Mr. Neidlinger come busting in to see what the crap I was doing to his kid. Or Mrs. N. At lunch, several times, I'd seen how she coddled her precious Elmer, and him acting rotten as an egg forgotten in the back of the fridge, and you cracked it into the bowl for scrambled eggs; then you had to throw the whole mess away.

Just then I remembered when I was five, and on Christmas Eve I'd ripped the inseam of my jeans from crotch to bottom. When Mama didn't spank me, Uncle Ed told her she spoiled me rotten. So, I looked at rotten Elmer yowling his head off and I saw, not Elmer, and not special Eddie Walsh, but rotten Eddie Walsh. Me and Elmer, two rotten eggs from the same store-egg carton.

Well, I'd had enough of us, two rotten kids, all packed into one skinny one. I grabbed Elmer's arms and hollered, "Hey!" Which impressed Little Air-raid Siren not one little bit. But, "HEY!" shut him up.

We were standing in the pit between the

stalls. "Elmer, enough. Get up there and scoop that poop toward the far door like I told you."

Elmer wasn't afraid. He looked at me like Heiny Stiert, and his cousin looked at me before they wrecked my ten-speed.

"Get up there, or I'll spank you again, and I'll keep spanking until you get the work done. Verstehe?"

My mouth must have been mad, too, to let that *Verstehe?* blurt out.

Elmer climbed the steps and took up the scoop as I turned and headed to open the far door. When he got the poop in front of the door, I'd bring the Poop Barrow, the wheelbarrow we used to haul the manure to Poop Mountain, a pile of it away from the milk barn and saved to use as fertilizer come spring.

I'd taken one step toward the far end of the milk barn when it hit me. A big scoop of runny cow poop hit the side of my head. I had one eye squinched shut. Elmer had this evil little what-are-you-gonna-do-about-it smirk on his face.

I bounded up the steps, grabbed him by the arm, dragged him right back down in the pit, pulled his pants and tighties down, and wailed the daylights out of his little white buttocks. More air-raid siren. "HEY!" I hollered right in his face.

He shut up.

"You don't do what I tell, you, it's gonna get worse each time."

What was worse than a bare heinie spanking? I had no idea, but the rotten kid didn't know either, and I hoped all he saw was how mad I was.

I dragged him up to the stall again and stayed behind him. He got the poop scooped, and the stall hosed down and shovel and poop barrow rinsed out as good as I would have. Then I grabbed clean Elmer by the arm and pulled him along up to the back porch of his house, and I banged on the door.

Mr. N. answered it. His mouth dropped open as he took in the upper half of me covered in half-dried cow manure.

"Mr. Neidlinger, after some persuading, he," I hooked my thumb at his kid, "got the milk barn cleaned up. The next thing I was going to do was to drop bales of straw out of the hayloft and spread them around the barn. I use a pitchfork for that. No way am I going to put a pitchfork into the hands of this kid. You're going to have to teach him how to work, because I quit."

"Sh—!"

I'll tell you, he didn't say shoot.

"I'll get your day's wages," he said.

"No, Mr. Neidlinger. I didn't work a full day. You don't owe me anything. And actually, I was beholden to you. Pop told you you didn't have to pay me. After I bellyached to you about paying Gladys and not me, you paid me. Like I said, I *was* beholden. As of right now, we're even. I learned a lot from you, Mr. N. Thanks. And please thank Mrs. N. for, must have been, three hundred lunches, she fed me." Though, truth be told, Gladys probably fixed sixty of them. Still, I didn't want to water down the thank you for mathematical purity.

All pooped on Eddie Walsh rode his ten-speed home.

Walshes weren't quitters. Pop had said that.

Well, Pop, now one of us is, and you're just going to have to live with it.

xii

The weather was nice-part-of-fall nice. Still warm enough, even riding a ten-speed with the left side of me wet from hosing as much poop off me as I could get. Of course, I still had poop packed into the ear on that side where I'd tried to finger it out but had fingered it tight in instead. That eye watered also. Other kids got red-eye and pink-eye. Eddie Walsh got poop eye.

I pedaled down the Neidlinger drive, with the parish picnic grounds on one side and my erstwhile employer's pasture on the other with his cows snarfing up the yummy grass, and onto Horstmueller Road, leading up the gentle slope to the top of Church Hill.

I pedaled my bike like a John Deere tractor, not a Farmall. The Deere went "putt, putt, putt." The Farmall purred. The difference, according to Mr. N., was the number of cylinders in the two machines. The Deere only had two cylinders. When it went "putt" that was the tractor pumping out a stroke of power. It completed one stroke, and one putt, completely. Then it putt-ed out the second one. The Farmall, however, had six or was it eight cylinders, and each cylinder emitted its own putt, but the power strokes were packed so close together, the putt-putts got their Ts knocked off and lower case Rs stuck on. So, it purred. Like that, see? That's what Mr. N. told me. Made sense, sort of.

The way I pedaled, I did most of the power stroking with my right leg. The left just got that right pedal up to the top again so the right leg would do all the work. I could have called the left my Lennie-leg. But with my ear full of cow-poop, I wasn't feeling jocular.

Pumping toward Church Hill, with each right leg downstroke, I got madder and madder at that little snotwad Elmer. Spanking him twice wasn't near enough punishment for that rotten kid. I wanted to punch him like Large Louie punched me that time and broke my nose and almost knocked out my front tooth.

Whoa there, Eddie.

That other voice in my head sometimes seemed to push me to do bad things. Other times it seemed to want to *stop* me from doing bad things. I wished it would make up its stupid mind.

I topped Church Hill and Horstmueller Road, turned a sharp left and became Church

Street. The rectory was there to my right. I thought about stopping and asking Father to hear my confession. He could have come out onto the porch of the rectory and held his nose while I confessed. Then I thought about his housekeeper. She'd probably chase me away with a broom. So I kept pedaling, coasted down Church Hill, crossed the highway, and turned down Main Street.

When I passed Meinerschlagens, I saw a sign in the window saying, "Stock Boy Wanted."

Clean work.

Of course, a fellow couldn't go in and ask for a clean-work job all covered in cow poop.

At home, I was sure glad Pop rigged up a shower in the basement with a plastic curtain around the showerhead above the drain in the floor. Mama was glad, too. She didn't let me come into the kitchen, but told me, "You keep that stink out of my kitchen get in that shower straight away."

With Laura on her hip and Bobbie and Ronnie tagging after her, Mama brought me a towel and clean clothes. Once I dressed again, I went upstairs, and she used a Q-Tip and this little squeeze bulb suction thing to clean the cow poop out of my ear. The squeeze bulb suction thing she used to suck boogers out of Laura's nose. After she de-pooped me, she put the squeeze bulb in a bowl and poured hot water into it. I hoped Laura never found out what other work her booger bulb had been put to.

All cleaned up and with drops in my poop-eye, I biked back up Main to Meinerschlagens and asked about the stock boy job.

"Sure, Eddie, the job's yours if you want it. I talked with Mr. Neidlinger at the last parish picnic. He says you're a good worker."

"Thanks, Mr. M. When would you like me to start?"

"Right now, if you can."

"Yes, Sir. I sure can."

"You want to know how much the pay is?"

"I know you'll pay me whatever you think is fair. Can somebody show what to do?"

"Sure. Jimmie Joe's in the warehouse at the back of the store. He'll show you how the delivery truck drivers stack the boxes they bring and how the items are put on the shelves. Jimmie Joe goes home for lunch at noon. Why don't you go at eleven thirty and be back by noon? Can you do that?

"Whatever you want, Sir."

Jimmie Joe showed me around the warehouse. Stacks of boxes, a walk-in freezer, a walk-in meat cooler, and another for fresh fruit and vegetables. And an employee restroom.

Restroom. That's what people liked to call an in-house. But in-house was stuck in my head.

After the warehouse tour, Jimmie Joe led

me up and down the aisles in the store and showed me where the cans and bottles and bags of groceries were shelved. He also showed me how to stamp prices on the items, and how to change those prices when we opened a new box. When a new box came in, the price of each can of green beans, say, would change a penny or two, and we would wipe the old price off the top of a can with alcohol and stamp the new price on. Otherwise, the customer would pick the cheapest price items and penny-more cans would just sit there. I knew Mama would do that when she picked up groceries. By eleven, I was stocking cans while Jimmie Joe did bags of flour.

At eleven-thirty, I pedaled home and was stuffing lunch down when Pop came in.

"What you doing home?" he said.

Mama told him.

"Elmer Neidlinger flung cow poop on you, and that's why you quit?"

"He did fling poop on me, but the next job we were going to do was fork straw around the cow barn. I wasn't going to put a pitchfork in that rotten kid's hands. If he tried to stick me, and I expected him to, I'd have had to hurt him to stop him. That's why I quit."

Pop said, "Huh."

Mama said, "He's already got a new job stocking shelves at Meinerschlagens."

"Huh." Pop looked at me. "What's this job pay?"

"Mr. Meinerschlagen asked me if I wanted to know. I told him I knew he'd pay me what he thought was fair."

After huh-ing again, Pop set to shoveling in his lunch.

At three minutes before noon, I got back to the store. Jimmie Joe left, and I set to stocking shelves. On my own. Doing a clean job. And not getting anything but a "Huh" from Pop over quitting.

Pop's sayings had seemed like *Thou shalt nots* chiseled into stone, but apparently, there were exceptions, like, *thou shalt not quit, unless you have to work with an evil pitchfork-wielding demon.*

The real *Thou shalts,* however, were a different matter. It was really hard to stick a proper *except for* onto them. That's why I asked Mr. M. if I could take off an hour for confession. I'd come awful close to wanting to kill that snotwad Elmer. Not in those words did I want to kill him, but I wanted to grab him around his chicken neck and squeeze till his evil eyes bulged and his tongue hung out. Had I done that, I sure could have killed the little creep.

When I confessed that to Father Geist, he said my penance was to find a kinder, more gentle way to think of the object of my homicidal intention. "He is, after all, a child of God. Just as you and I are."

That was the hardest penance I ever came out of the box with.

Back at work, I found out my pay was, HOLY CRAP, fifty cents an hour! That first day, I worked six hours. Three bucks for six hours. At Mr. Neidlinger's I never worked less than nine hours, and the longest day I put in was sixteen during hay baling one time with rain forecasted for the next day. And no matter how many hours I worked, I got two-and-a-half bucks.

I was inclined to say, "Thank You, God, for Rotten Elmer making me quit," but not inclined enough to actually say it.

xiii

The rest of sophomore year was all studying and working in Meinerschagens. I did two hours every evening after I got home from school, and all-day Saturdays stocking shelves, bagging groceries for women who'd just unstocked my shelves and smashing cardboard boxes the groceries came in and burning them in a barrel behind the new post office. But boy, was I raking in the dough.

Pop noticed that too. He opened an account for me in the bank that sat across the street from our old house. I got paid on Saturday and the money went in my money jar, which I still called the Ten-speed Jar. On Monday, before I started work, I rode my bike to the bank and handed my money to the teller. He took the dough and wrote the amount I gave him in this tiny book that went with the savings account, and he added up the total I had saved, and also added any interest, which had accrued. My bank money didn't just sit there waiting to be spent, like the bills and coins in my Ten-speed Jar, or Mama's Egg-money Dish. It earned its own money.

Boy, was I raking in the dough.

In early June, Ollie Weisendinger asked me if I'd like to get a date and double with him and Violet. But I had no one I was interested in spending any money on. Much less a trip to the Fox Theater in St. Louis. Which cost a fortune compared to the Strand in St. Charles. I turned him down.

"Violet can line up a date for you," Ollie said.

"Thanks for asking, but no," I told him.

He asked again a couple of weeks later. After I turned him down a second time, he didn't ask me to double date again. Fine with me.

When school let out for the summer, I worked at Meinerschlagen's from when they opened, at eight in the morning until they closed, eight in the evening, with a half-hour off for lunch and supper.

In early August, one Saturday when he gave me my weekly earnings, Mr. Meinerschlagen said that I hadn't taken any time off from work since I started working for him, and if I wanted some time, you know, to go on a date, or take in a ball game in St. Louis, just say so. I had no one to date, and I sure didn't want to spend money to see other guys play baseball. So I just thanked him and got to work.

On my birthday, Jimmie Joe told me he and I were taking off at five that day, and we were going to celebrate me turning seventeen with some other guys.

"Uh, Jimmie Joe, I really—"

"I already told my Dad. He said to have a good time and to tell you Happy Birthday. Pick you up at six-fifteen."

Crap!

Taking off at five meant losing out on a buck fifty. For what? Celebrate turning seventeen. What was there to celebrate? Sixteen. Now there was a birthday to whoop it up over. Driver's license, man. Mama baked my favorite, an angel-food birthday cake for dessert that night.

Do you want to guess what Lennie's favorite cake Is?

And why did it seem like I was the only one who didn't have a say in whether we were going to celebrate stupid seventeen in the first place?

Ollie Weisendinger drove. He had his own car now, a used one he'd bought from Elginfritz's garage. With money, he borrowed from the bank. Every two weeks, he paid the bank back part of the money he'd borrowed, plus the interest. Interest worked that way, too. And that kind of interest Pop did not like at all.

We were on the highway headed for St.

Charles and Ollie was talking about his car, and Jimmie Joe, riding shotgun, and Sam Waterman, in the back seat with me were all jabbering questions. Their questions dripped with *Man! Wish I had a car.* Ollie's answers dripped, too, with: *Eat your heart out, little boys.* Jimmie J. and Sam didn't seem offended by the tone, and they yammered on about the car and taking care of it. The way they talked, changing the oil, giving it a tune-up—whatever that was—and putting air in the tires was more fun than driving it.

While they jabbered, I was thinking about a bank loan. Pop didn't like to borrow money. That was the reason he didn't build our house until he'd saved enough to pay for the whole thing at once.

Interest. Interesting. I learned about it in a freshman math class, but at the time, I'd just thought it was fancy arithmetic. A new way to mess with numbers as homework. I couldn't remember how the nun—we had only nun teachers at St. Peter High School, but three male teachers at Duchesne—talked about the subject. It took Pop making me open my passbook savings account to understand that what I'd learned in that class had some application to things that went on in my life. Things I ought to know when I finished going to school.

Finished going to school. There was another thing to think about. That was probably going to happen someday. And not only someday, but someday soon. Like in two years. Like ripping through seventh and eighth grades soon.

I sat in my corner of the backseat thinking about interest and finishing school when something Jimmie Joe said cut through the mud in my head.

"Beer!"

I said, "You got beer?"

"Yeah," Ollie said. "In the trunk. My older brother got it for me. I'm driving so I can only have two."

Beer.

Pop didn't drink beer, or the highballs Mama used to make for Uncle Ed when he used to visit. My Uncle John, though, sometimes drank a bottle of beer while we watched TV in his front room. You weren't supposed to drink beer until you were twenty-one. An old man like Ollie's older brother. If I drank beer at age seventeen, was I going to have to confess that?

I hadn't asked where we were going. I hadn't wanted to come along, wherever that was. It was like a date with boys. I didn't even want to think that thought, but once again, would my Other Mind listen?

We were driving down this hill on the edge of St. Charles, and Ollie turned us into the drive-in movie place. Plenty of times I'd driven by it. Sometimes after dark and a movie was playing on the humongous screen, I tried to imagine that screen fitting into a TV box. Such a box would be as big as three Umpire State Buildings—when I first heard the name of that building, I thought the nun said *Umpire* State Building, and now, even though I knew its proper name, my Other Mind had it stashed away as Umpire State—side-by-side.

Ollie stopped by the booth where a guy took money before he'd let us in. Jimmie Joe and Sam paid. Ollie drove, so he didn't have to pay, and neither did Birthday Boy.

Why would anyone want to come to a drive-in to watch a movie? No popcorn or soda here. That's what I was thinking as Ollie drove us toward the back of the big parking lot, even though there were plenty of open spaces close to the screen.

When I asked Ollie why he didn't park closer, he said, "The screen's so big, you can see it from a mile away."

"From a mile away, the screen would be a postage stamp."

"Eddie, you're a klutz," Jimmie Joe piped in.

Great! Not only was I short and couldn't play baseball, now I was a klutz, too. *Happy birthday, Eddie Walsh.*

Sam said, "Eddie, we don't want a whole

bunch of people seeing us get a beer out of the trunk."

Poop! Confession for sure.

I thought about walking or running home. Six miles. I walked that far rabbit hunting. During most of the grade school, I ran a mile home, snarfed lunch, and ran the mile back to school again and got there before the bring-your-lunch guys finished eating.

I thought about it, but then I thought about what Jimmie Joe would call me if I got out of the car and walked home. So I stayed.

Well, there was popcorn. I went with Jimmie J. and Sam to buy two tubs of it from the concession stand, which was in a low flat roofed building in the center of the parking lot, side-to-side-wise, and about a third of the way back from the screen, length-of-the-lot wise.

"What about sodas?" I said.

"You're such a klutz," Jimmie Joe reminded me, in case I'd forgotten.

As we left the concession stand, Sam whispered, "We got beer."

I liked popcorn and soda together. I wondered how beer and popcorn would go together. Other Mind did not anticipate a favorable comparison. Neither did Other Mind anticipate what we'd find back at the car.

Ollie and Violet sat together. In the backseat of his car. Strange. It was Ollie's car. Why wasn't he behind the wheel where he belonged? And who was the girl sitting in the shotgun seat?

Shotgun got out of the car as we approached. "Who's the birthday boy?" Her face took on some kind of look. A smile, maybe. Other Mind thought she looked like grade-school Sister Superior must have looked on her first day in the convent before she had her first Introduction to Knuckle Whacking Class. She was my height, had her brown hair in a ponytail, wore Bermuda shorts with a white blouse tucked in—that blouse reminded me of Mrs. Neidlinger's Gladys—and white Keds with no socks. I wondered if her feet would stink if she took them off.

I knew I should answer her question, but my mouth was so dry of spit, I wasn't sure any sound would come out if I tried to say even just, "Me."

Jimmie J. and Sam both hooked a thumb at me.

"Come along, Eddie." Shotgun's face lit up a real smile and she grabbed my hand. "I'm Eve."

I didn't think of arguing with her any more than I would have argued with Pop.

Eve led my sweaty hand along the same row that Ollie parked in a couple of cars closer to the fence on the side, away from the entrance, to a station wagon, where she let go of my hand and wiped hers on her shorts. She told me to get in. Into the driver's seat. Two other girls were there, one on each of the back seats. As I got in, Jimmie J. crawled in behind and farther into the last seat. Sam got into the second seat and *squooshed* himself against Second-seat Girl, behind the shotgun seat. Jimmie J. and Backseat Girl sat in the middle of the car. Eve got in and *squooshed* up against me, just like Violet used to ride with Ollie.

I got it. We were arranged so all of us could see the movie.

Sam handed me a bottle of beer. I took it. The back-seaters all had bottles in their hands. They all raised them, and Sam said, "To Birthday Boy." They drank. I saw Sam's Adam's apple bob a couple of times.

"Don't you want one?" I said to Eve.

She took my bottle, took a swig from it, and handed it back. "I'm driving. I'll just have a couple of sips of yours."

I took the bottle from her and looked at it and saw the girl spit on it. Well, not quite see it, but how could it not be there.

"What?" Eve said. "You think I have cooties?"

She grabbed my chin, turned my head, and planted a kiss on me that, if the window had been up, I'd have bumped my head against it. That kiss lasted long enough that I had to remember to breathe through my nose.

Eve pulled back and said, "There. Now you have cooties, too."

The couples in the back seats thought that was the funniest thing. Which made me as hot as an August afternoon in the sun rather than an evening with the sun just down. My upper lip grew a sweat mustache, and I hoped I hadn't suffered deodorant fade-out.

"Drink your beer," Eve said. "Beer kills cooties."

More yucks from the rear.

The movie started. Eve pulled a speaker box from the pole next to the car and rolled her window up a bit and hanged the speaker there. Then she scooted back next to me. Close. Her shoulder pressed against mine. Her bare arm touched my bare arm. I liked the way her smooth, bare skin felt. Her leg was against mine, too. And she wore shorts. I thought her bare leg would have felt good, too, except I had pants on.

I took a big slug of beer.

Yuck!

Eve snickered, took the bottle from me, and sipped. "Ah, ambrosia."

Ambrosia was food that made the Greek gods immortal. It also meant something that tasted good.

People did not live forever, and beer did not taste good.

Eve grabbed my chin again. And kissed me again. This time it wasn't banging-your-head-against-the-window if it was up, but still firm. Softer though, so I could feel her lips cushiony against mine. Until *Her* tongue got pushed into *My* mouth.

Surprised the heck out of me. For a moment. Then I kind of liked it. Then I really liked it and grabbed Eve's shoulder and pulled her closer, but she pushed me away and laughed.

"I thought maybe you didn't like girls. That you liked boys instead."

Both back seat girls giggled.

"Have another beer, Romeo." Sam handed a bottle over the seat back.

"I'm not done with this one yet."

"Well, drink up, Birthday Boy," Eve said. "It's your party."

My eyes popped open. I thought I was going to puke. Eve wouldn't like it if I puked in her station wagon. But I wasn't in her car. I was in bed, looking right at the clock. With the nightlight, I could see it was five.

Morning? Of course, morning, stupid. It's not dark out at five p.m.

Puke!

I had to get to the outhouse, quick. I threw the covers back. No time to pull on pants or put on shoes, so I barefooted it the length of the attic and down the stairs and outside.

Where's the outhouse?

Oh yeah. We had an in-house. No time to make it back inside. I made it between the garage and chicken house. There I puked. What came up tasted like I'd eaten a soup bowl full of match heads. My stomach sure seemed determined to get rid of every one of those bits of sulfur from the bottom of hell. I felt like I threw up everything I'd ever eaten, but I still couldn't quit. Now I was puking up stuff I hadn't eaten yet. My stomach felt like I was tearing it to pieces. I got to the point where I felt like with the next lurch, my puke muscles would rip my whole stomach out onto the top of the puddle I'd made, but then it stopped. I stood there with a hand on the back of the garage and the other on the chicken house. I was dead tired, like I'd been hefting wire-bound bales of hay onto Mr. Neidlinger's wagon all day.

For all that puking, no part of me felt better. A god-awful taste filled my empty mouth. My head hurt something fierce, but it wasn't a headache. It was a mind-ache, and I had two of them and both felt like rusty, dull saws were hacking them to pieces.

Holy Mary, Mother of God, pray for THIS *sinner, now and at the hour of his death. Amen.*

And now wouldn't be a bad time for that death to happen.

But it didn't.

Inside the kitchen, Mama was at the stove. The god-awful smell of bacon went right to my stomach, but then those puke muscles must have remembered there was nothing in there anymore.

Pop walked into the kitchen from the hallway. His eyes scanned me down, then back up again.

I stood there in my tighties and a tee-shirt, in front of him and Mama. The front of my tighties felt cold. Had I peed my pants?

"Boy," Pop said. "Go to the basement and take a shower. I'll bring you clean clothes."

I did, and when I turned the water off and reached through the plastic curtain, Pop handed me a towel.

I took the towel and looked away from him as if not seeing him kept him from seeing me.

"Look at me, Boy."

I looked.

"Dry off."

I dried and pulled on clean underpants.

"It wasn't your idea to drink, was it?"

I thought about shaking my head, but it might have hurt more. "No. Pop."

"Don't you never, ever drink again because it's someone else's idea. Hear?"

"Yes, Pop."

He picked up my dirty underwear and looked at the tighties. Sometime before I woke up, I'd made a sticky mess in them.

I thought he was going to fuss at me about that, but he didn't.

"Get dressed, come up, and you eat bacon and the potatoes your Mama's fryin'. Hear?"

"I'll puke again."

"Eat the bacon and potatoes." It was like his eyes punched his words into my head.

After I got dressed and climbed the stairs and sat at my place, Pop put a bucket beside me. Surprised the heck out of me when I didn't need it. The bacon, the potatoes stayed down, and then so did the toast and the two fried eggs. On my fourth cup of coffee, it occurred to me that I felt pretty good. Dying no longer seemed like such a good idea. My mind-aches had been cured as well.

But with the aches gone, worry rushed in, into both minds.

What the crap had I done last night?

I couldn't remember how many beers I'd drunk. And that girl, Eve, what had I done with her? There'd been kissing. Tongue kissing. I frowned as bits of memory staggered from the fog. As we kissed, without tongues, my left hand tried to grab Eve's right breast. She pushed the hand away but kept right on kissing me.

Was that it? I couldn't remember.

Holy Mary, Mother of God—

Pop got up to go to work.

"Pop," I said. "Can I use the car to go to seven o'clock Mass?"

I could have taken my ten-speed and not said anything about church, but I was too tuckered to pedal up Church Hill.

"You got your head on straight?"

"Yeah, Pop."

He nodded, then he went to work.

xiv

I got to church fifteen minutes ahead of Mass kickoff time. It was just me and four old ladies scattered about the church as if we all wanted to be as far away from each other as possible. One of the women was Large Louie's mom. I sat in the last pew on the right side of the church, the one I'd sat in the day Sister Superior talked to me about Uncle Ed dying.

Louie's mom sat in the second last pew on the other side of the central aisle. I hardly ever saw her around town. She looked old and skinny. And like she felt as bad as I had before the puking started. I wondered if she was sick. You know, sick-sick. Not beer sick. I hoped she was okay. I looked away from her and at the big crucifix above the altar. I had my own problems to deal with.

One of my minds remembered words saying, *if your hand is an occasion of sin, cut it off. If your eye is an occasion of sin, pluck it out.*

I remembered more and more from the night before. My eyes were safe from needing to be plucked out. My hands, though, were in big trouble. Eve and Sam Watermann kept handing beers to me. My right hand kept taking them and lifting the bottles for me to drink from. Then there was what the left had done. It kept trying to grab Eve's right breast. At first, she kept pushing that hand away, but when I finally stopped trying to grab her, she took my hand, just like Hilda had done, and put it where it wanted to be. Only then that left hand tried to reach inside her blouse. Eve stopped that hand again, and said, "Next time, Eddie."

That left hand, by all rights, should get chopped off, but so should the right for taking all those bottles of beer and getting me drunk. And then I remembered my tongue. Eve had licked spit from inside my mouth, but then my tongue licked spit from inside hers. And I had liked that.

Thinking about tongue kissing and breast touching, I felt myself stir, you know, down there.

And here I was in front of God, in His house, and having these thoughts. My minds, they'd have to get chopped out too.

The bell jangled and the altar boy and Father Geist paraded to the altar from the sacristy, and the old women and old feeling Eddie Walsh rose to their feet.

During the service, I tried to listen to the altar boy recite the prayers from the laminated card, but his voice was just a mumble to me in the back.

After Mass, I asked Father to hear my confession. He told me to go to the confessional and that he'd be there shortly.

"Father, I feel like I'm trying to hide from God in that box. Like in there He can't see me, and then when I confess, and you give me absolution, He won't ever know I had a hand in nailing him to the cross. This morning I need for Him to see me."

"All right, Eddie. I can sit in my chair and you can sit in a server chair beside the altar. But there will be some women in the pews. They always stay after Mass to say a rosary or two. Or three."

"Father, I want God to see me confess. If those women see me, why should that worry me next to God seeing me?"

So, we sat as Father suggested. I confessed. I spilled my guts. It all came out, what all my offending body parts had done. I even mentioned the mess I'd made in my tighties.

Uh oh. I hadn't thought about having to chop that thing off.

Then I told Father about eye plucking and

hand and tongue and mind chopping—and chopping the other thing too.

When I was done, Father said, "Adam and Eve were created and set down in Paradise. They had one commandment. Thou shalt not eat the apples from the tree in the center of The Garden. One commandment, and in the face of temptation, they caved in to the suggestion from the snake.

"Life for us now is a lot more complicated. We have ten commandments to observe, seven deadly sins to avoid, and a host of lesser, venial offenses to stay away from, but all these sins carry their own *forbidden fruit* allure. The fact that we should avoid them makes them attractive to us. And that's why we have confession and sacraments."

Father pointed to the huge crucifix above the altar. I knew that's what he pointed at, but I didn't want to turn around and face Him. I wanted Him to see me, but I didn't really want to face Him.

"He died to forgive every sin every man and every woman on earth ever did and ever will commit." He leaned forward and placed his hand on my shoulder. "Mine, as well as yours."

"Priests commit sins, too?"

He sat back and smiled. "You had me worried, Eddie. In every confession of yours, I've heard, you always give me something to smile about. I wasn't sure there was a smile in this one."

"Father. I see nothing to smile about here. I am really worried. The older I get, the worse the sins I commit. What the crap am I going to do before my next birthday?"

The smile jumped off his face. He sucked in a big breath and huffed it out. "As to chopping things off. I know you read a lot. In high school, I'm sure your English teachers have mentioned literary devices like similes and exaggeration. *If your eye is an occasion of sin to you, pluck it out.* See? That is a literary device. It is meant to convey to you the seriousness of sin. But rather than actually plucking out an eye or chopping off that left hand of yours, for doing what it did, chop off the decision to touch things best left untouched. Do you understand?"

I nodded, but there was another thing. "I was drinking beer, Father, and it was like my mind wasn't inside me anymore. It was outside watching what the crap I was going to do next."

"Beer. I remember when I made my *too-much beer* confession."

I wanted to say, *Hey, wait for the heck of a minute here, Father. This is my confession.* My tongue must have been worried about getting chopped off because it didn't say it.

Then Father looked me square in the eye. "Was it your idea to drink beer?"

I shook my head.

"So it was other boys you were with who led you into drinking too much. Don't let other people lead you into drinking too much, ever, Eddie."

"Did my pop talk to you about this?"

"Eddie, how would your father have talked to me? By phone? I'm not sure he knows how to use one. If he said something similar to you, it's because he and I, and now you, got introduced to beer the same way. Others led us to beer, and we had no clue what beer could do to us.

"Here's a rule I came up with for myself. I never drink more than two beers, two glasses of wine, two of any kind of drink. And If I drink one or two drinks, it is my idea to do so, not anyone else's."

"I'm never drinking beer again, Father."

"When I was your age, I told myself that too. But a couple of years later, I had a couple of beers one night, just before I entered the seminary. But I felt what the alcohol was doing to me, and I stopped drinking right there. For that night. And, later, I came up with my two-drink rule."

The church bell bonged. Once. That meant half hour. Eight-thirty. I had to be at work in half an hour.

"Eddie. Turn around and tell Jesus you're sorry for having offended Him with your sins."

I turned and told Him.

"Promise Him you will try to avoid sin in the future and ask Him to help you live up to that promise."

I waited for something else from Father, but nothing came. I turned around again.

"Go in peace, Eddie. Your sins are forgiven."

"What about a penance?"

"You decide what penance to do."

"This was the strangest confession, Father."

"Eddie, I say that to myself after every one of your confessions."

Father got up, genuflected, and walked into the sacristy. A few seconds later, I heard the sacristy door click shut.

You decide what penance to do.

As far as I could recall, the biggest penance Father Geist ever handed out to me was ten Our Fathers and ten Hail Marys. What my hands and tongue, and that other body part, had done was bigger than a ten-of-each penance could pay for.

I stood and genuflected and left the altar through the gap in the communion rail, and at the center of the church, I entered a pew and knelt. I'd say a rosary. I didn't have the beads with me, but I had fingers. My fingers acting like rosary beads might help make up for what those guys on my left hand had done.

I further confess. I ripped around my finger

rosary like I was on my ten-speed, in high gear, going down Church Hill and pedaling to make the wind whistle ripping past my ears.

I had to get to work by Nine.

After racing through a rosary, hustling from the church to the parking lot, and tearing from the lot to the turn onto Church Street, I heard Pop: *You got your head on straight?*

Crap!

Even a guy with only one mind would have figured out my head was NOT on straight.

What in blue blazes is the matter with you, Eddie Walsh?

If you're going to talk to yourself, it helps to have two minds.

I had just confessed my sins of last night. I had just completed my penance, but now I was in such a hurry to get to work, I wasn't paying attention to how I was driving. I could have run over a kid, or a dog, or an opossum—

Beeeeeeep!

One of the Little Old Daily Mass Ladies' car was practically touching my rear bumper.

I checked both ways and pulled out onto the street and headed for town. One of my minds watched for kids and dogs and opossums. The other was thinking about that confession. It differed from any other I'd ever made. Always before, I left the box feeling like Father G. had helped me reach an understanding with God. I admitted what I'd done wrong. I agreed I was going to try like heck to not do that again. I felt like God and me. We were buddies again, and we hadn't been when I went in the box.

This time, though, I'd confessed up there on the altar. In front of God, so He could see I meant it when I said I was sorry, but I did not feel like we, Him and me, were buddies again. Father said I was forgiven, but I didn't feel like I was.

I'd gotten drunk, and even if I'd had three minds, neither one of them would have been able to keep Left Hand from going where it wanted to go, or Mr. Tongue from—

Without running over any of God's creatures, I parked the car in the garage and hustled up to the grocery store. The one where they sold groceries, not TVs. I was a minute late.

The first order of business every day, check the shelves along each aisle to see which items needing restocking most and get to restocking. Which I did.

Boxes of cans and bottles and bags came in all the time and were stacked in the warehouse part of the store. The prices of the items were always changed by a penny or, sometimes, several. Mr. M. wrote the new per/can price on the cartons with a marker pen. Then we, stock boys, would take all the old cans of soup, for instance, off the shelf and wipe out the old price and mark them with the new price. Then we'd mark the new cans and load them onto the shelves, leaving room for the old cans to get selected first by shoppers.

If we were opening a case of cans of Campbell's Chicken Noodle Soup, say, we use a box cutter. In a case of bags of flour, we ripped the tops of the boxes apart. It was too easy to slice open a bag of flour with the knife if you didn't control your slice through the cardboard precisely. "That," Mr. Meinerschlagen liked to say, "is expecting too much from a teenage boy, given what occupies most of what he's got for a brain."

So, I set to it. As I worked, it was sort of like when I drove home from church. One of my minds was on the task at hand. The other was occupied with the night before.

Why didn't I see what was happening to me before I got drunk? Why did I drink so much beer when I didn't like the stuff? And with Eve—*Crap! I didn't even know her last name*—breast grabbing and tongue kissing. Why didn't I even see that as wrong? And why didn't I want to stop with those two things? Why didn't I even think about getting Hilda knocked up?

Lotta questions. Not one stinking answer.

I got called to man a cash register. Maurine, who graduated from St. Charles High last year, normally manned one of the checkout lines, called in sick. I took her place and started ringing up Mrs. Elginfritz's groceries. When I was finished, she handed me twenties to cover her bill, and I started counting out her change. The bill was $37.15.

I said, "$37.15," handed her three quarters, and said, "and seventy-five makes $38, one makes thirty-nine, and one more makes forty."

Mrs. E. just stood there with her hand holding the money I gave her. "You owe me another dime, Eddie."

I looked at the cash register receipt. I looked at her hand.

Crap!

Eddie Walsh, a straight-A student, couldn't add.

Mr. M. was coming back inside the store from helping a lady get her groceries in her car, and he heard Mrs. Elginfritz.

I gave her the dime, closed the cash register drawer, and started bagging up her groceries.

"Eddie," Mrs. Elginfritz said, "You put cans on top of the bananas."

Mr. Meinerschlagen stepped in then and told me to go to the office in the back and ask his wife to take over the checkout aisle. I was to wait for him in the office.

When he got back there, he said, "What's with you this morning, Eddie? You never make mistakes. But you counted out the wrong change, and you didn't mark the Campbell's Chicken Noodle soup the right price. What's the matter with you?"

I looked into his mad eyes and made mine not look away. "I got drunk last night."

Mr. M. frowned. "You were with Jimmie Joe."

"Yes, sir. I was."

He turned like he was going to walk away, but then he faced me again. "I want you to check the items you put on the shelves this morning. Check them to see if you screwed up the prices on anything else besides the soup. You got your head on straight enough to do that?"

I said I did, and when I checked, the soup was the only item I'd screwed up. Then I got back to regular work, and both my minds paid attention to it.

At lunchtime, I was at the kitchen table eating when Pop walked in.

Pop looked at me and said, "Outside. Picnic table."

I put my fork on my plate and followed him out. We sat across from each other.

"First thing. Was you with a girl last night?"

"Yeah, Pop."

"Did you... go all the way with her?"

"No, Pop."

"But you wanted to?"

I nodded.

"You confessed?"

Another nod.

"Beer. Men been drinking for a long time. Noah got drunk. But that don't make it right for the rest of us to get that way."

"I know, Pop. Now."

"Beer or whiskey don't get you right away. Its evil is sneaky. You get the notion you're drinking water. Next thing, it's got control of you, and you ain't got control of nothing."

I knew that too. Now. Then it hit me like Large Louie's fist when he knocked across the ditch.

"Did you ever get drunk?"

He nodded. "Once. I got so drunk and puked so hard some of it came out of my nose."

Boy. This was a day for extraordinary confessions.

"Lead us not into temptation," Pop said, "is a good part of that prayer, but it don't work worth a hoot when you're drunk."

Pop stared into my eyes and I could feel his eye fingers probing around on my soul. "Boy, that enough talking about gettin' drunk and pukin' for you? Cause I'm hungry."

When I got back to work and entered the warehouse, Jimmie Joe was there.

He scowled at me and charged at me and open-handed smacked me on the chest. "You told my dad we had beer last night. I'm grounded for the rest of the summer."

He was going to hit me again. I slapped his hand aside, grabbed him by the throat, stepped a leg behind his, and grabbed his arm to keep him from falling onto the concrete floor.

"Jimmie Joe, you best back off. You come at me again, you're going to wind up badly hurt. Up to you. You want to keep coming at me, fine. What's it going to be?'

He tried to pull my hand away from his throat, and I pushed but held onto his arm so he swung around to land on his side. He put down his right arm to break his fall. I let him go and stepped back.

"You little piece of shit." He charged at me and swung a looping roundhouse, which I ducked and slapped him so hard on the side of his face, it spun him around. After squaring up and glaring hell and damnation at me, he charged again. This time I slapped his punch aside and slapped him on the other cheek. He staggered back. I rushed at him and kneed him between his legs.

I left him moaning on the floor in front of stacks of boxes and went to find Mr.

Meinerschlagen. He was behind the meat counter. I told him I had to quit. He wanted to know why. Mr. Meinerschlagen, the why-er.

"Because Jimmie Joe doesn't want me here?" I said.

"Over the beer?"

I nodded, and he told me to follow him to the warehouse.

We found Jimmie Joe on his feet, bent over a bit, holding himself with both hands and moaning.

"Son." Jimmie Joe looked up at his father. "This store can get along without you. It cannot get along without Eddie. He's made two mistakes in the whole time he's worked here. Those were both today, and he's already made good on them. You, on the other hand, you make two mistakes every day you work. I never know when you're going to honor us with your presence, and I cannot count on you to work till closing time. If one of you is quitting, it's you. But before you decide to quit, if you are not working here, I will not give you an allowance. And I will also make sure your mother doesn't slip you any money. So, what's it going to be?"

"I won't quit."

"Good. Now look at Eddie and shake his hand."

We shook because Jimmie Joe's father was standing right there. But there was something that got ripped away from the friends we used to be.

That evening, about an hour before closing time, Ollie Weisendinger came to the store. He invited me to go to the drive-in with him and Violet next week. Eve would meet us there in her car. No other girls were coming. Then he handed me a packet. It was a rubber. I didn't take it.

"Ollie, thanks for the invitation, but no thanks. And, I won't go on any more double dates with you."

"Fine. You can get a new ride to high school too, then."

He spun on his heel and walked out the door.

I hoped the day would end before I totally ran out of friends.

XV

J unior year was not getting off to a good start. Ollie did not want me to ride with him anymore. More worser than that—sorry, gentle reader, but this is just not a plain old *worse* situation—during the summer, the highway department completed a new four-lane highway between Sts. Ambrose and Charles, AND along with that, finished work on a brand new four-lane bridge across the Missouri. So I had to hitchhike TO school as well as back home again in the evening. Furthermore, the new highway skirted the edge of St. Charles. The new bridge meant people heading to St. Louis no longer had to drive through St. Charles to get to the old bridge. A ride I hooked on my thumb would not go out of his way to drive into town if he wasn't already going there. Which meant I'd be dropped off way the crap far away from Duchesne. Miles farther to walk. So, you see, definitely a case for more worser. Sometimes the English language just lets you down when it comes time to express the gravity of a particular situation.

But then, the Saturday evening before the first day of classes on Monday, More Worser Monday turned into More Better Monday. The phone rang while I was washing supper dishes. Lennie's hands were dry, so he answered the phone.

"It's for you," Lennie said. "It's a girl."

As I dried my hands, he acted like he would drop the phone in the dishwater. I snatched it and said hello. Lennie was watching with a smirk smeared all over his face.

Well, knock me clear to Wednesday! It was Alice Ashe! She offered to give me a ride to AND from school! Every day! And she'd pick me up right from our driveway!

From her tone of voice, I could tell giving me a ride was not her idea. I wondered if Mama talked to her mother.

Anyway, that summer, Alice Ashe had gotten her own car. A Ford convertible. A new one. Most people I heard about getting cars bought used ones. Not Simon Grossman and his sister, of course. They both got new ones.

So, thank you, God. And Alice, even though the ride she offered was as begrudged as the handshake Jimmie Joe gave me in the warehouse of his dad's grocery store.

On Monday, Alice picked me up, not at my

driveway, but at the end of the Meinerschlagen's. Alice's younger sister, Adele, and Jimmie Joe's sister, Madeline, were both freshmen at Duchesne.

Shortly after my first trip to the drive-in, I'd heard Mama tell Pop, "Mrs. Meinerschlagen said they are sending Madeline to Duchesne. Jimmie Joe went to eight years of Catholic grade school, and after just two years of public high school, he's turned into a pagan."

I could have told Mama that beer can wipe out not only eight years of Catholic school, but the ten I'd been through, as well. I was glad I didn't have to confess to Mama. If I did, it would stick one of those Uncle-Ed heart-swords in her. At least I didn't have to worry about sticking a sword into Father Geist's heart. As soon as I had that thought, my other mind said that maybe I did stab Father's heart.

One sin can sure hurt a heck of a lot of people.

On the first day of classes, Adele rode shotgun. Madeline and I shared the back seat. All the way to school, the two freshman girls, blabbered, chattered, gabbled, twittered, and sometimes both of them spoke at once as if both had such important stuff to say there was no time to listen to the other one.

Tuesday morning, Alice had the two girls sit in the back seat, and I rode shotgun. She had the radio turned on, and she drove with her eyes locked onto the road, and a look on her face that flat out told my tongue to shut the crap up.

Junior year classes, though, were all interesting as all get out. From Physics to Phys Ed. I liked English Lit. maybe the best. Sister Mary Hildegard. There was a book of saints in the library. Sister Hildegard was categorized as a *literary saint*. St. Thomas Aquinas was in that bucket of literary saints. Which made our teacher's namesake *somebody*. This goes to show you, you can be somebody even if no one has ever heard of you.

Junior/senior prom was scheduled for mid-October. Which meant nothing to me. I had no interest in asking any girl to go to that shindig with me. And it wasn't a Sadie Hawkins thing, so no girl was going to ask me.

At the end of September, at lunch one day, Roger Rottermick sat down next to me, unwrapped a sandwich, chomped off a bite, chewed it some, and swallowed.

"If you asked Sarah Esterhausen to go to the prom with you, she'd go."

He said it like it was a sure thing. Not just a theorem that as far as anyone could tell, was gospel truth, but it just couldn't be proven to an absolute certainty. But the way he said it, it was a law of Physics certain.

Which gave me pause. When Sarah asked me to the Sadie Hawkins Valentine's Dance two years ago, she Tom Sawyer·ed me into a date with Hilda. Which, truth be told, turned out to be a good thing. For both me and Hilda. Right until she got knocked up.

Anyway, fool me once, your bad. Fool me twice, ain't nobody's fault but my own stupid self.

That afternoon, after a change·classes·now bell, I passed Sarah going the opposite direction in the hallway. She smiled, big and warm. Which gave further pause to my pause. Nope. Not going to bite.

The next day during first period homeroom, Roger said, "D'ja ask her?"

"No."

"She snookered you into dancing with Hilda at the freshman dance. You're worried she's going to do it again. You don't have to worry. Ask her."

Well, I hadn't had a date since mortal·sins·to·hoolay·the·rail·at·the·drive·in night, and I'd always liked Sarah. What the heck? I'd ask her at lunch.

However, in English Lit. class, we discussed *The Short Happy Life of Francis Macomber.* We'd read the story for homework. When Sister discussed it, she suggested that it might have been possible Mrs. Macomber shot her husband on purpose.

Whoa.

Which gave me a new pause. Lunch came and went with no asking.

But, the next day at lunch, Sarah asked me to take her to the prom. She said she owed me a real Sadie Hawkins invite since the last one hadn't been one hundred percent real. The way she looked at me when she asked, the way it felt when she put her hand on mine, it just didn't matter if she was fooling me twice and that it was nobody's fault but my own stupid self.

I put my hand on top of her hand atop my hand. "Sarah, I'd like to ask you. Will you, Sarah Esterhausen, go to the prom with me?"

Her eyes lit up with so much light that a lot of it spilled out and illuminated her whole face. Bone and muscle softening energy coursed through her hands and mine and turned my whole body into a Jell-O sculpture. And that was before she said yes.

Prom was a three-day affair. Thursday afternoon, after classes ended, the juniors and seniors decorated the gym. Sarah normally rode to and from school with a young woman neighbor who worked in a bank in St. Charles, but Pop let me take the car that day so I could give my prom date a ride home after we finished with the gym.

Driving her home, she sat close against me. Almost Ollie/Violet close. It was nice. After parking behind her house, we got some kissing done. I kept my lips pressed tight together.

"Loosen up, Eddie." She kissed me. "Relax."

She kissed me again. Then I kissed her. We kind of came up for air and kissed again. No tongues or inside the mouth spit exchanging stuff. But kissing. And it was like my first kiss. The ones with Hilda, or any of the other girls, especially the ones with Eve. Those kisses could not unhappen themselves, but they did not count. Sarah-kissing, that counted.

Driving home that night, I'm not sure how the car got home because I was above the car. At least as far above it as from home plate to first base. I, Eddie Walsh, flew home like an angel. Thanks-be-to-God, the car knew enough to follow me.

Friday night, we had a prom sock hop. For the seniors and juniors only, unless you were invited by an upperclassman.

Driving to the Esterhausen farm, I felt like I was on the first real date ever. There were those other things, but they were like baseball practice, not a real game. When I picked her up, her father gave me the business. It was you best behave yourself with my daughter business conveyed in a without-words way. Then, we drove to the sock hop, with her close, and us talking and, at least me, wallowing in the joy of being with her. With my GIRLFRIEND, not my friend girl. Boy. Were those two things different?

I had thought the Sadie Hawkins dance was the best day of my life. I now had a new one of those. Sarah Esterhausen was the center of my universe, and my little planet orbited around her and basked in the warmth and glory of her sunlight.

Saturday, the grand finale, the formal dance, which required a suit from Thro's in St. Charles, which cost a significant chunk of change, but the money it cost was the biggest never mind ever created.

On the way to pick up Sarah, and wondering what she'd be wearing as I drove through St. Charles, I got stuck behind this slow-poke driver. Five miles BELOW the speed limit. Aaaargh!

Would Mr. Slowpoke turn off and get out of my way? He would not? All the way through town, he stayed right in front of me, going to the same place I was. And was there an opportunity to pass him? There was not.

Finally, we hit Highway 94, a two *laner* with light traffic. I whip out into the passing lane and floor it. The old Plymouth might have said, "What the crap is going on here?" but if it did, I didn't pay attention. I wanted to get to Sarah's.

I whipped around Mr. Slowpoke and pulled back into my lane. I just had time for a burst of elation to blossom, when flashing lights filled my rearview mirror and dumped my stomach out between my legs to plop on the floor next to the pedals.

Oh, poop.

A Speed Limit 30 sign flashed by. I was going fifty-five. *Double poop!*

I pulled over. The highway patrolman gave me a lecture and a ticket. Which made me fifteen minutes late. But once I saw Sarah, in a very fancy dress, and wearing lipstick that practically begged me to kiss it off her—but not in front of her father.

At the dance, when we moved around the floor, I did not know a girl could make me feel like I felt. It was as if our bodies were specifically created to move so perfectly together. We danced until she admitted her new shoes hurt her feet.

I offered to kiss them better. "Silly." She swatted me on the shoulder.

Well, I wasn't being silly. She did let me rub her feet as we sat at a table next to the dancefloor. The dancing, the fancy dinner with her across the table instead of next to me so I could continue to look at her, the ride home with her Ollie/Violet close, and the kissing in the drive beside her house, all were just heaven on earth. Until the pole light blinked off and on, off and on, off and on.

We unclinched.

"I have to go in, Eddie."

"I know." Boy, did it hurt my heart for my tongue to say those words.

"I had the most wonderful night of my life."

"I had the most wonderful night of my life too, Sarah."

"Silly." She reached up and touched my cheek.

It was as if my bones all came disconnected from each other and they fell in a pile, kept bagged up by my skin. While I was reassembling, she got out of the car.

"I would have opened the door for you."

"I know."

Then I had to hustle to hold her hand as we climbed the steps to her front porch. I anticipated that last, sweet, that *Parting is such sweet sorrow* kiss. Which, in the thinking of it, I knew there would not be one stinking snot-wad thing sweet about the last kiss of the night with my Sarah.

But at least I'd have that.

We got to the top of the steps when I noticed the front door was open. Through the screen door, a hulking shadow glowered out at me. I couldn't see the glower, but I felt it. I also didn't need to see him to know it was pole-light-flicking Papa Bear.

Sigh.

Sarah turned, faced me, and took both my hands in hers. "Thanks for asking me to Prom."

I raised one of her hands—I should remember which one, but I don't—and kissed it. A Papa Bear growl rumbled out through the screen.

I shook my head. "Thank you, and just to be clear. I'm thankfuller."

It was way too dark to see, but I am sure Papa Bear rolled his eyes. I felt him do it.

I let go of her. She went inside. I turned and walked down the steps. Every step I took, it was as if I had a fishhook in my heart, and every step tugged the line a little harder. I got in the car and just sat there. Thoughts of Sarah, Sarah Esterhausen, slow danced from one of my minds into the other one.

Like we were in our house, which was a grand two-story, with the second floor finished like Simon Grossman's house, rather than a slightly gussied up attic.

Like we'd been married that morning. "Do you take Sarah for your lawful wedded—"

"I do." Father Geist was saying the ritual words so dad-burned slowly, I just knew he did that on purpose. But the service concluded. They threw rice, and we rode down Church Hill and the driver paid the hold-up altar boys the ransom, and we'd had a reception on the second floor of the American Legion Post, and now that was over, only we were not finished dancing with each other, and so, in our new house, we danced from one ground-floor room into another and another and another.

The pole light flicked off and on, off and on, and off.

Poop!

Tomorrow I'd call Sarah and tell her that when we got married, we weren't inviting her father to the wedding.

But wait, one of the minds said, *the father of the bride pays for the wedding.*

Just shut up, I told that mind. And both of them laughed at me.

I started the engine and pulled out onto the road and headed for home. The Esterhausen pole light flicked back on again.

All the way home, I kept the speedometer exactly on the speed limit MPH. I was sure that Highway Patrolman was out there, invisible in the dark, waiting to nail me with a second ticket. We weren't inviting that guy to our wedding either.

As I drove, one of my minds rebuilt Sarah, and prom night, rebuilt the dream I'd been dreaming until the stupid pole light sent me home, and by the time I turned off the highway and onto Main Street in St. Ambrose, Sarah was scootched snug against me. I was feeling her and I could smell her perfume.

Just before I turned into our driveway, I smelled something like burning rubber, and the engine started knocking something fierce. Like it was trying to bang itself to pieces. Next to the house, I stopped and shut the engine off. From the light of the streetlight, I could see smoke billowing out from under the hood of the Plymouth.

Pop came out of the house, one strap of his bib-overalls flapping loose. As he lifted the hood, I got out and walked up next to him. He was shining a flashlight on the dipstick.

"You run the car out of oil," Pop said. His voice liked to scare me to death.

I stood there, waiting for him to—I didn't know what. Maybe hit me and smack me clean into next week.

On the best night of my life, I had encountered three moral avenging angels: the Highway Patrolman, Mr. Esterhausen, and now Pop. And each one more fearsome than the one before.

Pop stood there with the hood up and his flashlight shining on the dry dipstick. He radiated hot mad, like Mr. Neidlinger's electric heater he used in his milk barn in the winter. And Pop didn't even know about the ticket yet.

Holy Mary, Mother of God, pray for... this *sinner, now, at the hour of his death. Amen.*

XVI

To get to church Sunday morning, Mama called her ignorant lout brothers. Homer drove the ignorant lout car in from the farm. Pop drove him back to the farm and then back home again. Then we drove to church. The ten o'clock Mass, not the eight, the one Pop preferred.

I thought I'd felt guilt before, but that Sunday morning, it was as if Pop filled one of Mama's—Mama had a regular washing machine now, but the scrub tubs were still in the basement—scrub tubs, filled it full of guilt juice evil spirits made from cow poop, puke, and dead skunks and dumped it over me. The guilt stink on me rose all the way to high heaven and made the angels, the saints, and all the good people who made it up there, wrinkle their nose. I had so much guilt, I couldn't begin to contain it all. My guilt was so strong, it screwed up heaven.

The worst thing was, for a sin, a person

could go to confession. "Forgive me, Father. I have sinned." You'd tell the sin. Father would absolve you and give you five Our Fathers and five Hail Marys as penance, and that would be it. Shiny-heinie clean soul.

But what could I say to Father Geist?

"Forgive me, Father, I've been stupid." Sins can be forgiven. Stupidity, there's no forgiveness for it.

On Sunday, meals got jumbled around. We had supper at noon. After eating, Pop took Lennie and me outside where he lifted the hood on the Plymouth that I'd killed last night, and he explained things like dipsticks, air and oil filters, points, and plugs. After stupid study for me and education for Lennie, Pop had me steer the car while he and Lennie pushed us down Main Street to Elginfritz's garage. People came out onto their front porches to see how guilty and stupid I was.

That night, as Pop and the other kids watched TV, I asked Mama why Pop hadn't gotten mad at me.

"He expected Mr. Neidlinger to teach you about caring for machinery, but now he knows he should have taught you himself."

Wait one cotton-picking minute!

That sounded like Pop felt guilty. How could that be? Pop knew everything. He could do everything. I'd seen him run that skyscraper elevator building all by himself. Unload the grain from farmers' wagons and trucks, run the machinery that lifted the grain to storage bins in the tall structure, then unload the elevator storage bins into railcars. All by himself. Heck, he practically built the house we lived in. Pop didn't make mistakes. There was the time he rear-ended a guy on the way to the ballgame when I was busy being a poop-head over the uniforms Mama made. That was my fault. Pop wasn't stupid. He didn't even commit sins. Though he went to confession, anyway. I never thought of it in this way before, but he was Pop the Perfect.

The next morning I found out who I was.

Before Alice arrived to pick up me and Jimmie Joe's sister, she told me Jimmie Joe said I had a new name.

"Dipstick Eddie. What does that mean?"

Madeline was a nice girl, not-a-mean-bone-in-her-body nice. Jimmie Joe, however, was getting me back for the little fight we'd had in the warehouse of his dad's store. I could picture him with an evil he-who-laughs-last-laughs-best grin on his face as he pictured his sister telling me my new name.

The day didn't even try to get better. At a class change, I walked past my locker. "Dipstick Eddie" had been marked onto the door. At lunch, Sarah told me her dad didn't want us to see each other for a while. We were getting way too serious about each other.

"Sorry," she said and left to join a girl table.

Living with being a sinner was easier than living with being Dipstick Eddie. Or being No-Girl-friend Eddie.

Two weeks later, Pop and I appeared before a judge.

The judge put on reading glasses, read from a paper, and looked up with a sixth-grade-Sister-Superior look all over his face. "The highway patrolman says he followed you all the way through St. Charles. You were right on the bumper of a car in front of you. You rolled through two stop signs instead of coming to a complete stop, and as soon as you hit the edge of town, while still in a thirty mile per hour zone, you whipped out into the passing lane and reached a speed of over fifty."

The judge's glasses had slipped down to near the end of his nose. He took them off. "That pretty much it?"

"Yes, sir."

"Where were you going in such an all-fired hurry?"

"It was our prom night. I was anxious to pick up my girlfriend and get to the dance. Sir."

"You like this girl?"

"Yes, sir."

"Does she like you?"

"She did, sir. Pop took my driver's license from me, and now she has a new boyfriend."

The judge wiped his hand across his mouth. I still caught a glimpse of the smile he tried to cover. When he took the hand away, his judgely scowl was back in place. He said to Pop, "How long you figure to hold his license?"

"If he's lucky, he could get it back at Christmas."

"Hmm. Two months. I was going to suspend it for one." He flicked his Sister Superior eyes back to me. "I'm going to fine you twenty dollars. Do you have it?"

I did. I had taken a hundred from my savings account to pay Mr. Elginfritz for messing up Pop's car, but Mr. E. wouldn't take my money. Pop had told him not to take it.

The judge spoke to Pop again. "You think your boy learned anything from this, Mr. Walsh?"

"He ain't done learning by a long shot, Your Honor."

The judge winced. "May God have mercy on your soul, Young Mr. Walsh."

I paid the fine at the cashier, and Pop drove me to school to finish out the day there. Then

I rode home with Alice Ashe. She was always happy to see me.

Just before Christmas, mid-year report cards came out. I got As in math and Physics, but Cs in the other courses. The only part of my world that made sense to me was where numbers ruled. Numbers were clear. Three was three, not almost three, or sort of three. And every day it was three. Not like Sarah was my girlfriend one day, but not the next.

Pop wanted to know why my grades slipped so much. I could think that stuff about threes, but how the heck could I talk to him about it? But I had to tell him something.

"I don't know for sure, Pop. But in math and science, those things seem important. The other classes, they don't seem important."

"All them classes. You got good grades in all of them before. Get good grades in all of them again."

I said I would, but English and History could not become important just because Pop said so. One thing became important, though. Getting my own car. If I got a car, Dipstick Eddie Walsh would be somebody again. Maybe I wouldn't even be stupid anymore.

A couple of days later, I talked to Pop about buying a car.

He looked away from his paper.

"You got enough money to buy a car. You don't have enough for insurance and repairs."

He went back to his reading.

"I could get a loan from the bank, so it wouldn't take all my money to buy it. That way I'd have money left to pay for those other things. Besides, I can do a lot of work myself now. Now that you taught me how."

"Walshes don't borrow." This without looking up.

"You're just old-fashioned."

I stomped out of the front room and up the attic steps and read in my Physics book. It was February, but I was sure I could have taken the final exam and A-ed the crap out of it.

The next morning, after Pop left for work, Mama told me I'd hurt Pop's feelings. I had no idea Pop had feelings.

"Well," I said, "he should have let me buy a car."

"You buying a car would have been a big mistake, Eddie. Pop couldn't let you do something, that in the long run, would have been bad for you."

I ate my cereal and went to school half-mad but all convinced Pop really was old-fashioned. And I stayed Dipstick Eddie.

At the end of the month, mid-semester report cards came out. Sister Hildegard gave me an F in English. I went to see her.

Sister Hildegard's face reminded me of Sister Daniels. What Sister Daniels might have looked like if Sister Superior hadn't kicked her out of the nun business for getting tackled by Little Heiny.

When I walked into her classroom, she looked up from papers she was grading atop her nun desk.

"Sister, you gave me an F."

"Yes, I did, Eddie."

"I should have gotten a C."

"No, Eddie. You should have gotten an A."

Then she went back to grading papers.

I just stood there like I was stupid. Or something.

Sister kept grading papers with her red pen like I wasn't there. Or something.

After some time, my feet decided to get us the heck out of there.

That time of year, I got home from the grocery store after Pop got home from the elevator. As soon as I walked in the door, Mama told me Pop wanted to talk to me. He was behind his paper in the front room. He folded the paper onto his lap.

"Give me your driver's license."

I did. He went back to his paper. I ate supper.

Even Dipstick Eddie Walsh knew it wasn't a good idea to buy a car if you didn't have a license.

Not having a license didn't matter much. I'd had two dates after getting the stupid license back from Pop at Christmas. Both had been with sophomore girls. Both were nice. Both were not Sarah Esterhausen in any way, and I was pretty sure they didn't want to go out with me again any more than I wanted another date with them. I knew it was my own stupid fault. I wanted them to be Sarah, but they couldn't be.

Finally, the end of the worst school year of my life snail-slimed its way to... what? Some kind of end. Report cards came out on the last day of junior year. I got all As except for one stinking, snot-wadding B. In stupid English.

I went to see Sister Hildegard again.

"Eddie," she said. "There are four half-semester grading periods. You got three As and one F. I could have given you a B or a C. If you want me to change your grade, I'd be happy to."

Stupid Eddie Walsh wasn't that stupid. A B in the hand was worth a heck of a lot more than a C in the bush. Or something.

For the ride home that afternoon, Alice had put the top down. Alice's sister didn't want her hair blown around, so she took the shotgun seat. Madeline Meinerschlagen sat behind Alice. Which left me behind Miss Shotgun.

The two erstwhile freshmen—now erstwhile was one of those words I'd run across and it just begged to be used before I could forget it and have to look it up again, and of course, the freshmen were not really fresh *men*, they were, or had been fresh girls, so *freshman was* one of those words in the English language that seems to have stuck around only because the word maker-uppers got tired of having to create so many words to cover each unique situation, and once the word got in the dictionary, yeah verily, a girl became a man—were jibber-jabbering like they were in a contest to see who could say the most words before we got back to St. Ambrose and a lot rode on winning.

Alice turned on the radio. Her sister turned it off. Sour Puss Alice rolled her eyes and started the engine and headed us toward the parking lot exit onto Elm Street.

Elm Street. That was the only thing Sts. Ambrose and Charles had in common. They both had a street by that name. Of course, our Elm was about a third of a city block long.

I glanced at Sour Puss. When she was with others in our class, she was bright and cheery. One of the gang and happy to be so. But let old I-wanted-you-to-be-the-first Eddie Walsh walk into view, and I was like a dark cloud that slid in front of the sun, making her face dark and cold. All because back then, I was not prepared for the arrival of girl spit into my life. By the end of junior year, though, four years later, I must have exchanged a bucket of spit with girls.

Sorry, Sour Puss.

But sorry would do me as much good as it did Adam. I mean, I've always been convinced that he must have said, "Wait, God, I'm sorry." But too late for sorry. The archangel—was it Michael or Gabriel? Probably Michael. Gabriel would have busy blowing his horn—was jabbing him on his bare-naked butt with his flaming sword and herding him toward the gate into, or in his case, out of Paradise.

Then God put enmity between Eve and the serpent. I had put enmity between Alice and myself, and our enmity seemed of the eternal kind. I'd begun wondering if St. Peter would make Alice forgive me before he'd let her into heaven. I'd also wondered if he'd let me in if Alice did not forgive me.

I wondered again about being a priest. I mean, my reason for not wanting to be one was the bowling alley in the basement of the seminary depressed me. *Really, Eddie Walsh! That's your reason for not wanting to be a priest?*

Pop had told me I should either get married and raise a family or be a priest. "Don't be an old maid bachelor like your Uncle Sylvester."

And Father Geist was a guy I looked up to. If I could be like him, I could help people like… well like me, Eddie Walsh the sinner, get to heaven. I knew some things about sin. I knew some things about what it took to avoid them.

After Sarah, finding a girl I enjoyed being on a date with hadn't worked out all year. When Sarah's father told her to not see me anymore, she'd just like, "Sure, Dad. Great idea. Wish I'd thought about it myself."

Poop and double poop.

Or maybe I would just be a new Uncle Sylvester. At least I wouldn't tie myself to a girl for life. When we'd worked together to graduate Large Louie from first grade, I'd admired and liked Alice Ashe. Now she was Vindictive Alice. Homely Hilda. I transformed, or helped transform her, into Holy Crap Hilda, and as soon as she transformed, she didn't need me anymore, and she dumped me for a boyfriend with a car. Sarah Esterhausen. She'd stuck a fishhook in my heart and ripped out a hunk of heart meat.

Be a priest, Eddie Walsh.

Was that You, God?

Or one of my stupid voices?

We were driving along Elm, just before the street started climbing the hill when I noticed a girl walking. Blue pleated skirt and a white blouse, so a Duchesne girl. She had books in one arm and a sweater in the other. The way that pleated blue skirt moved, or swished maybe, as she strode along. *Nice.* She marched along at a good clip. I never expected city girls to be walkers. They rode in cars, even if the trip was only a block. That's what I thought.

Vindictive Alice tooted her horn as we passed Walking City Girl. She turned, smiled, and waved. I knew, at least one of my minds knew, she had smiled and waved to Alice, but the other mind registered it as her waving to me. And smiling at me.

Teresa Yount. A classmate. I intended to raise my hand and wave to her, but the hand went over my heart. I'd developed, not pain, but something. I mean, most of the time, you don't know you have a heart. When there's fishhook in it, you know. Well, seeing Teresa, and her bright smile, the sun kissing her brown hair and leaving a golden barrette behind to mark the kissed spot. I knew I had a heart. I also had a lump in my throat.

I swallowed it. "Alice, how about giving Teresa a ride?"

She kept her eyes straight ahead. "Your dollar a week doesn't give you the right to tell me who can ride in my car."

A lightning bolt of white-hot anger shot through my head. I was fed up with Vindictive Alice.

"Stop the car. Stop and let me out."

She didn't slow down.

"Stop or I'll jump out."

I stood up.

Alice put the brakes on, and I almost tumbled over the seat. I'd have wound up upside down in Miss Shotgun's lap. That would have impressed Teresa.

xvii

That night after work at the grocery store, after dinner, I went up to the attic. School had let out for the year, so no homework. But I had something I needed to do. Talk to Teresa, but I didn't know her phone number.

Well, write her a letter then.

But I didn't know her address either.

Oh, for Pete's sake. Write her a stupid letter!

Dear Teresa,

I wrote about riding away from school, seeing her walking beside the road, and Cupid shooting his arrow at me, and that I felt it hit my heart. But not exactly my heart. It hit my gizzard. Until the Cupid's arrow struck me, I didn't know I had a gizzard. But I must have one. Cause after the arrow hit, I got a lump in my throat. That must have been because the arrow dislodged a gizzard stone, and that caused the lump in my throat.

Shoot!

I didn't know if she had a boyfriend or not. That was the most important thing to know, and I hadn't even asked her. We'd walked along Elm to Kingshighway. That's where I turned right to get to my old hitchhiking corner. She kept going straight. She smiled when she said goodbye. As we walked, we talked. About what I couldn't remember. I remembered I did not ask if she had a boyfriend. What the heck did all the rest of that crap matter? Do you have a boyfriend, Teresa? It would have been so simple to ask, but I'd been too stupid.

Stupid, stupid, stupid, stupid, stupid!

I sat back in my chair, immersed in the puddle of light from the desk lamp. It made me feel like that puddle of light cocooned me away from the rest of the world, and in a way, there was just me, seeking a resolution to the most important question in the universe. And from my cocoon, I felt my soul reach out a soul hand across six miles to St. Charles. Reaching to touch Teresa, just to get some reassurance.

But then I knew I needed more than some undefined reassurance that I'd made up myself. I needed to know if she had a boyfriend.

I leaned forward and read what I'd written.

Holy Mary, Mother of God—

If Teresa read that, she'd puke.

Enduring. I had some experience with that. When Sarah Esterhausen couldn't see me anymore, I'd had to endure having a big chunk of my heart ripped out. I'd endured that. I put together a plan for this.

Behind the butcher counter in Mr. Meinerschlagen's store, he had two phones. One was tied to the St. Charles County phone system, the other to the city of St. Charles. That way he avoided a long-distance charge when he had to call into the city. After the store closed tomorrow, I could use the St. Charles phone book to find her number, and then I could call her. And I wouldn't just blurt, "Do you have a boyfriend?" No, I'd ask her to go to a movie with me.

Smooth-talking Eddie Walsh had a plan. I got undressed and climbed into bed and didn't even wake when Lennie came up.

The next day was the longest day of my life, but eventually, store closing time happened, and I made the call. As I listened to it ring on the Yount end, I thought: Saturday night. Even if she doesn't have a boyfriend, she might be out with her friend from freshman year Latin class. I waited for someone to answer with a twenty-pound gizzard stone sitting in the pit of my stomach.

"Yount residence."

It sounded like a young girl. Teresa's sister maybe, though I didn't know if she had one of those any more than I knew about a boyfriend.

"Hello?" The young girl asked.

"Uh, this is Eddie Walsh. Is Teresa home by any chance?"

"Teresa!" Young Girl Voice hollered.

She's home. Thank You, God.

"Hello."

I blurted my question.

"Yes. I'd like to go to a movie with you on Wednesday evening, Eddie."

How sweet the sound that saved me from turning into a wretch.

After that, Teresa and I dated once a week. A funny thing happened to the calendar. Weeks started being only one day long, date day, or evening. One day weeks sure flew by in a hurry.

Teresa came to my house for dinner on my birthday. That's when Mama told her about losing half the babies she had. Heck of a night, that was. I couldn't help feeling like I was, once and for all, no longer Mama's special Eddie, but Teresa became her special Teresa.

We pulled up in front of her house, and I stopped before the big Elm in their front yard blocked the view of the Plymouth from the

Yount's front window. Mrs. Yount had told me on our second date, that if I wanted to continue to see Teresa, I could not park behind that Elm when I brought her daughter home.

So, I stopped the car in the appropriate spot and turned off the engine. Teresa said, "Don't be mad at your mother. There are things women can talk to each other about, but it's hard to talk to a man about. Unless you're married, of course."

It was like a miracle happened. First, "Don't be mad at your mother." I wasn't *mad* at her, but it hurt that I had to find out I had dead brothers and sisters from Teresa and not Mama herself. But, after Teresa said that, I wasn't mad or hurt. Furthermore, the sin of petty jealously I'd committed was absolved by Teresa, as effectively and thoroughly as any sin I'd ever dumped in Father Geist's lap.

Second. "Women can talk to each other." Teresa wasn't a girl. She was a woman. I probably should have figured that out myself, but, being stupid as often and thoroughly as I was, I'd needed her help to see it. I had this niggling feeling that although she was now a woman, it didn't mean I was as much a man as she was a woman.

Third. "Unless you're married, of course." That was a signpost stuck in the ground of our future, not my future and/or her future, but *ours.*

I scootched around on the seat and pulled her to me and kissed her, softly, tenderly, and with restraint, even though urges built, and parts of my body were feeling compulsions to do things she would not like. And neither would her mother looking out the window. I'd felt those maternal eyes on me, and in mid-kiss I opened mine to see her staring. I broke the kiss.

"Your mother's watching."

"It's a free country." Teresa kissed me, and when she let go of my lips, I said, "I love you, Teresa Yount."

"And I love you, Eddie Walsh!"

It was the first time we'd said those words to each other, and on the far side of saying them, those words rearranged and reorganized the atoms and molecules making up Eddie Walsh into a new entity. Heck, maybe even a man entity. An un-stupid man.

I reached for her, to kiss her again, with ardor this time I was thinking.

Teresa put her hand on my chest. "I should go in, or Mother will start flicking the porch light off and on.

My stupid mouth almost mentioned the Esterhausen pole lamp, but I found out what my mouth was going to say just in time to shut the stupid thing up.

We got out of the car, walked to the front

porch, and there we kissed. Softly, tenderly, and with restraint.

We broke apart.

"You make my *wees kneek*, Teresa Yount."

"Silly," she said.

It wasn't silly. I was this close, this close to just melting into a puddle of love and longing right there on her front porch. My lips thought it was time for another kiss, but she put a finger on them. Which meant: That's enough for tonight. Which my lips knew wasn't true at all, but she pulled her arms free of my hands and went inside, closed the screen door, and mouthed, "I love you," then closed the front door.

I just stood there. She'd taken some vital part of me inside with her. And this was different from the fishhook thing. My whole heart? Well, no. If she'd pulled that sucker out of me, I'd be dead. Since I was still alive, near as I could tell, it must have been my gizzard she took. With the broken-off stub of the Cupid's arrow still in it.

I sighed at her closed door, got in the car, and drove home. Sticking to the speed limit precisely. No way did I want a ticket and for Pop to ground me. Again. Probably for the rest of my life this time.

The next morning at seven, I rode my bike to church and entered the cemetery. I found the markers of my three dead brothers and two dead sisters. My brothers had been born in 1937, '38, and '39. I came along in 1941.

Even I could figure out why Mama treated me like was I *special*.

One of my sisters' stones had 1951 across the bottom twice. It didn't say born 1951 and died 1951. It didn't have to. She was Joan. There wasn't a specific date, but I knew when it was. It was the day after Large Louie smashed my face. The day after I vexed Mama.

I'd vexed Mama, and that night she went into labor way early and lost 1951 Joan.

The only good thing that came from that cemetery visit was the discovery that losing those first three brothers had not been my fault, but only because I hadn't been born yet.

All day at work, 1951 Joan slunk around one of my minds. That same mind searched for memories of 1953. That's when my next sister was born and died. Those baseball uniforms Mama made. Were those done in '53? I didn't know for sure, but I thought that had happened in 1952. I hoped that was true.

That night after the store closed, I called Teresa on Mr. Meinerschlagen's St. Charles phone. Boy, did it feel good to talk to that g— woman.

The next couple of weeks of summer, I'm not sure they really happened, except for one thing. Our weekly dates. And our after-date goodnights. Each time it got harder and harder to drive away from her. Each time I did, it hurt more than the time before.

School cranked up again. We ordered our class rings. They arrived, and I gave mine to Teresa without putting it on my own finger even once. Teresa Yount and Eddie Walsh, steadies. A little slice of heaven on earth.

There were dates, movies, sock hops, the prom.

Prom night. Driving to pick her up, two things were preeminent in my brain: Don't get a ticket; don't run the car out of oil. Then, after Teresa's sister opened the door for me, and Teresa walked into her living room, well, I mean, there'd been Holy Crap Hilda three years ago, but Teresa was above a Holy Crap. Just like Cupid-arrow day, the living room lights kissed gold into her brown hair. Hair just above her shoulders and curled up at the end. Her soft brown eyes smiled at me as much as her face did. I was sure she could see on my face that I thought she was beautiful, and it made her happy to see that, and it made me happy to see her happy that—

Then I worried my mouth might be hanging open, and I handed Teresa the corsage and she handed me a boutonniere. Teresa's mother pinned the flowers on her. Her father pinned mine on me. Then he snapped three Polaroid photos of Teresa and me.

Before we walked out the door, Mr. Yount said, "Have fun, kids."

"But," Mrs. Yount tacked on, "not too much fun."

I'd thought last year's prom was the best thing that ever happened to me, right up until the car smelled hot. But this year, prom was one rung on Jacob's ladder below heaven. And, in the end, all that almost heaven time made goodnight time agony. Teresa stepped inside and closed the screen door and stood there looking at me. I pressed my lips to the screen, and Teresa kissed me through it. That kiss saved my heart from just going flat like a popped balloon. And it gave me the strength to drive home. I'm not sure if I got any of Teresa's girl spit through the screen, but I got dust and dried bug guts on my lips. The best dust and dried bug guts I ever had.

Just before Thanksgiving, Pop wanted to talk to me. He put his paper down when I entered the front room.

"Boy."

I wanted to say I was a man now, but swallowed the words so they wouldn't get said.

"You figgered out what you're gonna' do after high school?"

"Well, uh—"

"You best figger something." He went back to his paper.

I knew what some of the guys in my class were going to do. Roger Rottermick was going to college. One of the guys was going to work in his dad's Kroger store. One was going in the army. Two of them had jobs lined up at the Ford plant in St. Louis, where Ollie Weisendinger and his older brother worked. I knew all that, but I did not know where Eddie Walsh was going to work. I knew Eddie Walsh better get it figgered, or steady or not. Once school was out, Teresa would dump me and latch onto someone with a job. She knew what she was going to do, go to nurses' training at a hospital in St. Louis.

At school, we had a male chemistry teacher, and he'd invited us, seniors, to come to talk to him if we had questions about our futures. So, I talked to Mr. Klaus. He told me my grades were excellent, and that I had an excellent chance of winning an ROTC scholarship to college. With the scholarship, the US Army, Navy, or Air Force would pay for college. After graduating, I'd owe the service a four-year obligation.

"Can you get married?" I said.

"Not while you're in college, but after you graduate you can."

Mr. Klaus helped me get an application, fill it out, and submit it.

That evening I told Pop about it.

"College, huh? And the Army or Navy will pay for it? Sounds too good to be true." He went back to his paper.

Teresa was more enthusiastic. If I got the scholarship, I'd go to the University of Missouri. Only a couple of hours' drive away. And we could get married after graduation.

We had a plan. Life was good.

Our weekly dates were joy-filled evenings with gizzard ripping finishes on Teresa's front porch. Leaving her after a date never got easy. Parting was sorrow, but it sure the pooping heck wasn't sweet.

Between the dates and meat counter phone calls, days disintegrated. Every once in a while, I got this sense I was on a train speeding toward this big canyon and I didn't know if there was a bridge across it or not. One of my minds told me there'd be a bridge only if I got that ROTC scholarship.

After high school, Teresa'd go to nurse's training and a future, and I might fall into the pit. And even though Teresa and I had been going together for almost a year, I kept thinking about how I'd felt about Sarah Esterhausen. She went up in smoke. That had hurt. If Teresa went up in smoke, I was sure I'd die. And my future death was a heck of a lot surer deal than Hilda's had been in freshman year.

Holy Crap Hilda, I hope you and your kid are doing okay? Please, God?

Teresa and Roger Rottermick knew what they were going to do after graduation. I didn't know if the rest of my classmates had a plan for the future or not. It was like most of us were lemmings stampeding toward the What-the-crap-do-I-do-now Cliff. My future hung on that ROTC scholarship, which Pop baptized *too good to be true.*

Just before Christmas break, another thing intervened to slow me and my lemming-mates thundering toward the precipice. I was called to the principal's office and asked to carry a letter to my parents.

The letter said my tuition was paid up to date, but the school hadn't received a penny of Lennie's.

Lennie was a sophomore, and he rode to school with the two Dutweiler kids. One was a junior and had a car, the other was in Lennie's class. At the start of the school year, the fall of 1958, the Dutweiler kids and Lennie decided they'd use their tuition money to buy a boat. The Dutweilers had a neighbor with a farm beside the Quiver River. The boys kept the boat there.

After the letter from Sister High School Superior, the boys had to sell the boat. They got back half of what they paid for the thing. The oldest Dutweiler boy was pulled from school. His father got him a job working for a building contractor. The youngest and Lennie got a ride with another junior, Estelle Zimmermann. Of course, I didn't know if there'd been screaming and shouting at the Dutweiler house. I know there wasn't any at ours.

Pop gave Lennie a couple of his pithy zingers, then went back to reading his paper. At first, I thought, what the heck, Pop? Is that all you're going to say to him? But then I noticed something I hadn't seen before. Pop was filled plumb up with anger. I couldn't tell you what I saw or maybe only felt. But Pop was majorly torqued off at Lennie. I got the feeling if he let his mad get loose, he'd have beaten Lennie to a bloody mess of boy meat. Scary, Pop was, and I'd never seen that before. There was the time he came in my bedroom the night after Large Louie punched the snot out of me when Pop told me I was not to vex my mama. That made me scared some, but not as scared as when I saw all that mad bottled up inside him. It made me think I was lucky as all get out when I ran out of oil and the worst that happened was, I became Dipstick Eddie.

From then on, I took Lennie's tuition money to school with me.

Another thing that happened at Duchesne,

lunchtime ran from twelve to one. Mass was celebrated every day, at noon, in the chapel, and Teresa and I attended. The service generally lasted twenty-two or -three minutes. After that, we ate our sack lunch together in the cafeteria together, but this one day, Mrs. Ostmann, who ran the cafeteria, served Mexican food for lunch. Teresa wanted to try the unusual entrée, so I sprung for two lunch tickets. When we got in line, she was in the process of closing the line down. She accused us of making out in a broom closet and forcing her to keep the line open longer than necessary.

If she'd have accused me of something, I'd, most likely, have absorbed it and walked away. But she'd accused Teresa, too. I huffed up and told her we had been at Mass.

Cafeteria Boss-lady knew a lot more about huffing up than I did. She mustered up so much disdain, some of it dripped off her face and onto the trays of Mexican food she'd dished up for us. "I know a bald-faced lie when I hear one," she said.

I didn't mention this before, but I'd been elected to the student council the last two years. It didn't seem important. What the council did, didn't seem important. But then Cafeteria Boss-lady accused Teresa of acting inappropriately with a boy, namely me. And Teresa had been at Mass, not at all doing what she was accused of. Teresa, the finest, the nicest, the most *appropriate* girl in the whole darned school! Oh, this was not right. That woman could not be allowed to get away with this.

I, Eddie Walsh, would not let her. I'd bring this insult, this false, baseless, unjust, despicable, false... egregious accusation up at the student council meeting. And then I'd push and shove and demand that the council do something about it.

xviii

It turned out that a lot of students had been insulted by Mrs. Cafeteria Boss-lady. Doing something to right this wrong took no shoving, no pushing whatsoever. Boycott the Cafeteria sprang to life of its own accord like it created itself. It became our Holy Crusade.

Wendy Accoff, a junior member of the council who worked in the school office two hours a day, told us the school normally sold between one hundred fifty and one hundred sixty cafeteria tickets every day. Holy Crusade week one, the school sold twenty-five. Holy Crusade week two, the school sold zip, none, not one single stinking ticket.

Tickets for the next week were sold on Friday. When we busted out of school that second Friday of Holy Crusade, we, the whole student body, even the people who never bought a cafeteria ticket were elated, ebullient, euphoric. Boy, had we shown that Cafeteria Boss-lady a thing or two.

On Monday, when we came back to school, the class schedule was pushed aside. Father Godfry was called School Moderator. It wasn't ever said that he was the boss of Sister High School Superior, but he and she acted as if he was. Near the start of the school year, at a council meeting, a freshman asked why the priest was called Moderator. Wendy Accoff answered that the archdiocese called the priests assigned to Catholic high schools Moderators because the archbishop intended for the high school priests' main job to be moderating boys' natural inclination toward sinful behavior, whereas girls were naturally good and mostly holy to start with. Let Wendy-the-cut-up intervene, and the council meeting agenda was good for one thing, the trash can.

Anyway, that Monday after two weeks of Holy Crusade, the first order of business was for the members of the student council and the officers elected to represent each class to meet with the Moderator in the staff conference room. There he told us that any grievance we had did not matter. We had rebelled; we had mutinied against the authority of the church. And our behavior was sinful and disrupting our studies. So, before the schedule could resume, we had to squash the mutiny, get the school back to operating normally. Furthermore, we should be aware that our rebellion had cost the school a goodly amount of money. A lot of food had been prepared each week that had to be thrown away. Our parents made substantial financial sacrifices to enable us to attend Catholic high school, and if we didn't have concern for being mutineers, we should be mindful of that. Assembly of the entire student body had been called. And all of us, council members and class presidents would address it and end the rebellion.

"Do any of you have any question as to what is required of you?" Father said.

Well, that flushed righteous indignation right down the toilet.

Roger Rottermick, senior class president, looked at those of us assembled at the table and in chairs against the walls. "No questions, Father."

"Do you need a few minutes to talk among yourselves?"

I looked around the room as Roger had. "No, Father. We had a grievance, but we tried to solve it the wrong way and made the situation something worse than the grievance was in the first place."

"All right then," Father said, "the student body is waiting for you."

We walked into the gym and faced two

hundred and fifty fellow mutineers. Only students had assembled. Not a single teacher, nun, or layperson, nor the Moderator, was there. My Adam's apple bobbed, and my mouth ran out of spit. Fortunately, I spoke last.

When it was my turn, I said what I had about trying to solve our grievance in the wrong way, and added, "Father said cafeteria tickets will go on sale in our homerooms as soon as this assembly is over. I am going to buy tickets for next week. Now it is time to get the school schedule back on track. This assembly is dismissed. Go to your homerooms."

And poof. The Great Cafeteria Strike of 1959 was over. It had been such a thing when it was running full steam. There may have been a dozen goodie-two-shoes, mostly girls, out of two hundred and fifty who did NOT join the strike, but the rest of us did. The goodie-two-shoes always brought their lunches, anyway. The rest of us had been into it: lock, stock, and barrel. Some of the girls, from the baddie-two-shoes gang, brought electric skillets and extension cords. So take that, Mrs. Snotty-pants Cafeteria Boss-lady! The girls cooked lunch right in front of her.

I will admit that after the strike moved into the second week, and we hadn't heard a peep from the administration, I—

I'd read a phrase somewhere: *the silence was*

deafening. Well, I didn't find the silence from the Moderator and the Principal deafening. I found it disquieting.

When it came, it came like lightning out of a calm day, clear blue sky.

"This strike must end," Father said.

And it ended. Just like that.

For the record, going forward, Mrs. Cafeteria Boss-lady no longer needed the "Snotty-pants modifier to her name.

In April—Teresa's birthday month—Sister Hildegard, in our English Composition class, assigned us to write a paper titled Who am I. Like that. With a period at the end, instead of a question mark.

Teresa was also in that class. I told her, "It'd be a lot easier to write who you are."

"I'll write who you are, and you write who I... are."

I almost said, *Who I are. That's funny.*

What was funny was that someone like Large Louie could become so ingrained in you. He popped up all the blinking time.

Hmmm. I think I just got maybe ten words of the thousand Sister wants.

That night after supper, I sat at my homework table in the attic and thought about how Teresa smiled at me when I told her I'd rather write who she is. She'd smiled in that way of hers. The hand of her soul just reached inside my chest and caressed my gizzard with the broken-off stub of the Cupid's arrow sticking out of it. And my knees got weak. And my minds dumped whatever else they'd been working on and filled with just Teresa, and wanting, needing to look at her, to hold her and feel her pressed to me, and to smell her hair. Her girl spit tasted pretty darned fine, too.

I sat there in my bubble of desk-lamp light and let that smile of Teresa's build its own bubble around me. I was in two bubbles in one sense, but in one in another. One bubble was of the physical world, the other of the spiritual. The physical, with its laws of physics, I trusted because I understood it, all right, only a little of it, but enough to trust what I knew of it. The spiritual bubble, I trusted that one because it came from Teresa.

So, I thought about how Teresa made me happy, and I thought about other kinds of happiness I had known. Like baseball happy, when I used to be good at it. Like fifth-grade happy when Sister Daniels showed up and, I discovered nuns could smile. Thinking about those happies, a notion gelled upstairs where my minds resided. Those early happies, like over being the good Walsh, over being one of the best at baseball, I had looked at those like I deserved to be happy over those things. But the Sister Daniels happy, I saw that as a blessing.

For me, happiness changed when I met Sister Daniels. I saw her as a blessing, and where do all blessings come from? Why, from God. So, thank you, Father God, Who art in heaven.

I thought about Hilda, and after Sarah Tom Sawyer-ed me into dancing with her, how I had anger boiling up inside me over being snookered, I saw the look on Hilda's face. She was terrified that I'd walk away from her, and after having hurt Alice Ashe, I could not hurt Hilda, too. I just could not. And then, when I danced with her, Hilda was happy. A happy that held its own happiness to just be able to see her being so happy. But then she got knocked up—

No. I would not go there. *We*, I told my minds, *we're talking happy. Stick to happy.*

And I thought about Sarah Esterhausen. She sure made me happy. For a little while. A very little while. And it sure hurt when—

Not going there.

And it occurred that maybe I had needed Sarah in my life just when she appeared. Maybe I needed to practice at being the kind of happy that she made me so that when Cupid shot me, I was somewhat prepared to handle the kind of happy Teresa made me.

Oh, I knew I had small happies in my life, but the happiness Teresa gave was the highest and holiest kind of happy. Just short of heaven happy.

Teresa made me happy. The place inside me where happiness abided depended on Teresa, the source of high, holy happy.

Teresa made me. Rather, she made that part of me.

And it was like, holy crap, eureka, and run around town with no pants on!

I grabbed a clean sheet of paper and wrote:

The best part of me "_IS_" Teresa Marie Yount. All caps. Italicized. Underlined, and set in quotes.

There. I'd gotten a start on Sister's assignment. Nine words. Only nine hundred ninety-one more to go. *Crap.* I had nine other words I thought of the other night, but I couldn't remember them. We only had a week. *Crap.* I needed to crank out 142.857 words a night. *Crap.* Midnight.

Then the part of me where high holy happy lived reminded me of Teresa Marie Yount. I went to bed and slept... well, happy.

After thinking about that stinking paper all Tuesday, I decided I wasn't all happy. There'd been times when I'd been sad, ashamed, hurt, mad, committed sins. I listed a whole bunch of those times, like when I sent Mama to hell, and stuck little swords into her heart over the baseball uniforms she made for me. I listed Alice Ashe, and others, and I wrote four hundred and twenty words about those other than happy things. And all of those sad and bad and sinful things, and the people I'd bumped into during those times, they were Eddie Walsh just as much as Teresa was. They sure weren't nice parts, much less high holy, but I had to include them in the paper. Sure, as shooting, they were part of me. Without any one of them, I was not the me I was.

Wednesday night, I put more work into the paper for Sister H. Writing that paper shoved homework for my other classes aside. I'd intended to go back to the good things that happened to me as I grew up since the only good thing on that side of the scoreboard was Teresa, and there were good things to list. As I plowed through those, I found good and bad stuff getting jumbled up and some of the things were kind of hard to sort into clear and clean, good or bad. Some of the incidents had aspects of both. But I stuck them into the paper, anyway.

I concluded the Wednesday words with:

> I, Eddie Walsh, am not an angel,
> nor a devil. I am human with

some good to me and some faults.
Big ones.

Sister was big on complete sentences, but I'd read books where the author used incomplete ones. And I liked a lot of those books. Hopefully, she'd give me a D-minus instead of an F.

Altogether I had eight hundred and ninety words, and it was only Wednesday. Actually, it was Thursday by seventeen minutes. And nighty-night-time. My intention was, tomorrow I'd use my remaining one hundred one words writing about Teresa. That one sentence I stuck onto the front in no way did justice to the importance of Teresa in defining Eddie Walsh.

Thursday was the same as the day before. I was anxious to get to the attic and finish the paper. After Mass that day, as we walked toward the cafeteria, Teresa asked if she could read my paper.

"When it's finished. Which will be tonight. I'll let you read it tomorrow."

As usual, we were last through the serving line, and as she served us, Mrs.—formerly Snotty, but now just plain Mrs. Cafeteria Boss-lady—said to me, "Did you pray for me at Mass?"

She'd asked me that the day before. "Yes, ma'am. I did."

"It must be true," she said. "Your pants didn't catch fire."

I looked down. Sure enough, no fire blazing down there. Mrs. Cafeteria Boss-lady and I weren't exactly buddies now, but she'd softened up some. There was that hard, rigid, and maybe bitter, inner core that still shined through in the pants-on-fire remark. She was, I thought, kind of like Eddie Walsh: some good and some bad jumbled together.

That night after work at the grocery store, I was so anxious to get back to writing I almost skipped supper. With the almost forming the inner core of that sentence.

So, in no-pants-on-fire-truth, after supper, I returned to the paper. And writing justice to Teresa into the story. One of the things I'd been thinking about since lunch was the inner core I'd seen of Mrs. Cafeteria Boss-lady.

I concluded the paper with:

> I, Eddie Walsh, am bits and pieces of everyone I ever encountered. And these bits and pieces are stuck into an inner core of me that God created when He gave me life. So, I am thousands of bits and pieces from the many people I've encountered. But none of the other pieces are even close in importance to the one from Teresa. If I lost her, so much of

me would be lost, too. It would be
like being unborn off the face of
the earth. If in heaven, there can
be three persons in one God, here
on earth I can be Eddie Walsh,
and I can be Teresa Yount. I am,
you see, Teresa.

I stabbed that final period onto the paper
after *her* name, and, boy, was I pleased with
myself. Then I counted the words. *Poop! 1132.*

Slashing 132 words was going to have to
wait till tomorrow. I went back to being pleased
with myself and also went to bed.

The next day at lunch, I let Teresa read it.
She did and looked at me. My knees got weak.

"If I didn't already love you, Eddie Walsh, I
would fall in love with you now."

Well, Shazam the crap of Eddie Walsh
and turn him into Captain Marvel, the most
powerful human on earth. Boy, was I pleased
with myself.

That night I went to work on slashing words.
I slashed some but found places where I had to
add some. After three hours of it, I'd gotten it
down to 1022 words, and my minds were both
screaming: *Eddie. For crap sake! Stop already.*

Saturday night, I got it down to 1021.
Tomorrow I'd kill off those excessive snot-
wadding extras.

But on Sunday afternoon, after our supper at noon, I started through the paper and wound up adding eleven words. *Double poop.*

I leaned back in my chair, closed my eyes, and looked to heaven. For twenty-one seconds I stayed like that. Then I opened my eyes, leaned forward, and took up my pen.

> This, Sister, is not part of the paper. It is an addendum to it. So, the word count on the paper is 1021 words.

> Addendum to Who Am I., by Eddie Walsh:

> My story could end with the last line of the paper, but it wouldn't be the complete story. Teresa is most certainly the biggest, the most vital part of me, but if I stop there, I will not have answered your question fully. Because ALL the people I bumped into as I floundered through the life God has blessed me with so far left bits and pieces of themselves stuck to me, and thus, I, Eddie Walsh, am all these people.

Furthermore, Sister, I am you.

And I can feel what you're thinking. You're thinking I want someone else to blame for my faults. Not so. Not so at all.

There are good parts of who I am. Thanks for contributing to those. Thanks too for that F. And there are bad parts. But those are all mine. So, Sister, I am you. But it's okay. I am not your fault.

The story was done. I was done.

I took the portable typewriter I borrowed from Cousin Esther and started clickety-clacking away. I finished typing the paper at nine p.m. and tacked on a cover note.

Sister, I answered your question
as best I could.

I did not stick to the word count,
but if I'd done so, I would not have
fully answered your question.

I, Eddie Walsh, am hoping for
a D-minus on this paper, not
another stinking F.

XIX

The next day, after Mass, in the cafeteria, Teresa asked me, "What's the matter, Eddie? You seem down."

"After turning in our papers to Sister Hildegard this morning, I just felt like handing that paper in cut a big hole out of the middle of me. Like a cartoon character getting shot by a cannon. He winds up with a big clean hole cut right out of his middle."

"Not me. I was so happy to be done with it."

"Well, I hope she doesn't take weeks to get the papers graded. You already read mine, except for the ending I put on it, but I didn't get to read yours."

"When Sister hands them back," she said.

Wednesday morning, we got the papers back. On the front of mine, Sister had written a big red D minus. But after the ending she'd written:

Just kidding. A plus.

Sister Hildegard, the comedian English teacher.

But A plus, D minus didn't matter all that much. Reading Teresa's "Who Am I." mattered. She handed me her paper at lunch but told me to not read it until that night. And I gave her my final paper.

"It'll probably be eight-thirty tonight when I get home from the grocery store. Why don't you read my paper at that time as I read yours?"

When I read hers, two of her disclosures surprised me. One was when she was five years old, she and her family lived in an apartment. A man with a drinking problem lived in another of the apartments. And one day, Teresa discovered the body of this man under a tree in the backyard. He'd cut his throat with a straight razor. The other thing really surprised me. In her paper, she'd written that she was fat and had always been fat.

At lunch on Thursday, I told Teresa I was sorry she'd found the man with his throat cut, but the fat thing flummoxed me.

"At Thanksgiving dinner at your house," I said, "you showed me albums with pictures of you growing up. You certainly were never fat. What I saw in some of those pictures was someone who wasn't happy. I still see those pictures of you, and when I do, it hurts my heart."

Teresa touched my hand.

By the time we got to the cafeteria after Mass, we could always find an empty table. Most of the kids ate and went on to other things before the next class bell rang. Like going out to someone's car and smoking a cigarette.

Cigarettes. Yuck. The one thing that tastes worse than beer. Well, there are other foul-tasting things, but I probably don't need to go into those.

Anyway, Teresa touched my hand, and like so often when she did, though she'd touched my hand a hundred times before, it was as if she touched me for the first time. And now, thanks to my D minus paper, I understood why. Teresa, like me, like all of us, was different from this moment than she had been the moment before. We keep bumping into people and they keep changing us into something a little bit new, and in Teresa's case, a bit more wonderful. It was nice being in love with a... woman who I could fall in love with each and every day I lived.

The go-to-class bell rang.

We both stood.

"I'm glad to see you aren't sad anymore," she said.

"How can I be sad when I'm with you, Teresa Marie Yount.

When I got home from school, Mama said I had a letter from the United States Navy.

The ROTC scholarship!

I tore open the envelope, and tore the letter as well, and folded it open.

I did not receive an appointment.

My knees got weak, and I sat down hard on Pop's chair at the kitchen table.

"You didn't get it?" Mama said.

I shook my head. Inside my head, it was like I was in a car at night and driving down a dark road and these billboards would flash by, and as they passed, the headlights would light them up.

Eddie Walsh is Not Going to College. Teresa Gives Class Ring Back. Eddie Walsh Gets Unborn Off the Earth.

Mama took the letter from my hand.

"Ach. It says you are an alternate."

She handed the letter back, and I read the second paragraph.

Eddie Walsh Gets Reborn Back Onto Earth.

I rode being reborn the rest of the afternoon, and into the evening. Till Pop got home. Mama showed him the letter when he finished his supper. He read it, shook his head, and looked at me across the table from him.

"Too bad," Pop said.

"But I'm an alternate."

"That just means they ain't got the guts to just say it plain. You ain't going to college."

Well, poop. But what did he know? He was old-fashioned. I was reborn that afternoon, and I would not let Pop un-reborn me. On Monday I'd talk to my teacher, Mr. Schwartz, at school. He'd know what being an alternate meant.

The next morning, Saturday, Pop rousted me out of bed.

"Git up. Git dressed. Eat breakfast."

I rubbed a whole bunch of unslept sleep from my eyes and looked up as he walked away and back downstairs.

The other morning that started just like this one, Pop gave me to Mr. Neidlinger as slave labor, or as an indentured servant, maybe.

Who the crap are you going to give me to this time, Pop?

The answer to the question was in St. Charles, at the US Navy recruiter's office.

"Sign the paper," Pop said.

The guy in the sailor suit pointed to a line on the bottom of the paper. Everybody was so stinking helpful. But I did what he said.

Going back home, I saw all those road signs again, except after the Reborn one another appeared: No, He Didn't.

I stared out the windshield at the highway, and it seemed like it could go on forever. Like the world was round, and the highway ran all the way around the globe. Except I knew that view was a delusion. The earth was flat after all, and on the seventh of August, that's the date I'd fly to San Diego and enter boot camp. The highway just ended. I pictured Pop knowing that and him hopping out and rolling into a ditch beside the road. I couldn't hop out, though.

Late that afternoon, Mr. Meinerschlagen let me leave work early. I drove to St. Charles, picked up Teresa, and drove us to Blanchette Park. There we walked. Past baseball and softball games, people playing tennis, past the swimming pool, and all these activities made their own brand of happy noise that I could hear, but sort of not hear. Like the sound got into my ears, but from there couldn't really get all the way into either of my minds. We walked, holding hands, and I told Teresa about not going to college, about going into the navy instead. I told her about the world ending on August seventh.

"Eddie." Teresa squeezed my hand. "God won't give us anything we can't handle. We have to have faith in God, *and* that He won't give us any challenge we can't handle. *And*, Eddie Walsh, we love each other. We need to have faith in that too."

I stopped dead in my tracks. As suddenly as Lot's wife must have stopped. I heard the WE and the US and the other WE. Us and we, the two most important words in the English language. So powerful those words. They *presto-chango-ed* the world from flat to round.

Of course, when I stopped, I jerked Teresa to a stop also.

"What?"

When she looked into my eyes the way she did, she just melted my bones into Jell-O.

"You make my wees Kneak."

"Silly," she said and swatted me on the shoulder.

"Yeah, my knees are weak because I'm hungry. I didn't get lunch. Are you hungry?"

"Hungry!" She swatted my other shoulder.

It turned out WE were hungry.

On August the seventh, my family, and Teresa drove me to the airport. Before we parted, Mama hugged me, Lennie and the Poopers, and my sister said goodbye. Pop gave me a look that contained stuff I never expected to see on his Pop face. Teresa gave me a kiss, a hug, and a birthday present. I could open it on the plane.

The first time I'd flown. I got the window seat and felt lucky until we got up in the air and ran into some turbulence. The way those wings moved up and down! Holy crap. I thought sure they'd break clean off. I hoped like heck that

Teresa's *God won't give us anything we can't handle applied to planes also.*

We got through the turbulence with just as many wings as when we went into it.

Teresa's gift was a box of stationery. And a note.

> I love you, Eddie Walsh. I will
> write to you every day.

Well, poop. I knew what that meant. I loved her more, so I'd have to write her twice a day.

That afternoon, we met our boot camp company commander. It was pretty obvious pretty quickly that I did not want to be his Special Eddie Walsh. I didn't want him to know I was in his company at all. I wanted to be a nameless, faceless, speechless robot wearing navy clothes from hat to shoes, just like everybody else.

God won't give me anything I can't handle.

I had that thought at reveille and again at taps. The one at taps I altered a bit. *Thank You, God, for not giving me anything I couldn't handle... so far.*